GHOST
DANCE

Novels by Mark T. Sullivan

THE PURIFICATION CEREMONY
HARD NEWS
THE FALL LINE

GHOST
DANCE

Mark T. Sullivan

AVON BOOKS ⬦ NEW YORK

AVON BOOKS, INC.
1350 Avenue of the Americas
New York, New York 10019

Copyright © 1999 by Mark T. Sullivan
Interior design by Kellan Peck
ISBN: 0-380-97429-0

For my brother, Matthew,
who has fought with more courage than I could ever imagine.

ACKNOWLEDGMENTS

I am deeply indebted to Linda Chester, my literary agent, wise counsel and friend, and to her ever-energetic associate, Joanna Pulcini. Their constant enthusiasm and support have kept me going through the years.

I am likewise grateful to Ann McKay Thoroman, my editor, and Lou Aronica, my publisher, for their patience and advice while this novel took shape.

Thanks also to my friend Damian Slattery, whose critical reactions and good-natured encouragement have made me a better writer; and to my wife, Betsy, who always gets to read first.

I owe a great deal to the following anthropologists and ethnologists: Father Raymond Bucko; Richard (Fire) Lame Deer and Richard Erdoes, authors of *Lame Deer Seeker of Visions*; William S. Lyon, author of *Black Elk: Then and Now*; William K. Powers, author of *Yuwipi: Vision and Experience in Oglala Ritual*; Joseph Epes Brown, recorder and editor of *The Sacred Pipe, Black Elk's Account of the Seven Rites of the Oglala Sioux*; Renée Sampson Flood, author of *Lost Bird of Wounded Knee*; and Richard E. Jensen, R. Eli Paul and John E. Carter, authors of *Eyewitness at Wounded Knee*. Their works gave me insight into the mind of the shamanic Sioux. Any error in interpretation, however, is mine alone.

I also thank Steve Eddy, Joe Citro and Chris Whelton for sharing their knowledge and research about the nineteenth-century spiritualist activities of the Eddy brothers of Chittenden, Vermont; and thank Bobby Sand for sharing his understanding of the Vermont judicial system.

Communication of the dead is tongued with fire beyond the language of the living.

—T.S. ELIOT

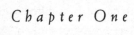

Chapter One

It is the last day of November, 1918. The Green Mountains
rise on either side of the Bluekill River like mute and paralyzed
sentinels, aware of festering intrigues, but powerless to inter-
cede. Sleet pelts the valley floor and the stone-faced buildings
of the town of Lawton. Up on the peak flanks, wet snow falls
and settles on a log cabin in the loft of which a ten-year-old
boy sleeps fitfully under thick wool blankets.

Two hours before dawn the boy stirs at racking, wet coughs
in the room below. His half-lidded eyes take in the dozens of
nailheads showing through the roof planking. The nailheads
have conducted the cold inward and stand out frosted and
luminescent against the dark wood. Were it not for the
coughing, Dylan could imagine himself awakening outside
under the stars in a perfect world where there was no such
thing as dying.

"Dylan. Dylan, wake up, for God's sake!"

The boy rolls over on the straw pallet he uses for a bed.
The woodsmoke is overwhelmed by the stale, sweaty stench

of fever. Lantern light throws twisting shadows on the chinked walls, the hooked rug, the plain pine table his father had crafted the year before leaving for war, and the daybed where his twin sister lies. Anna has not spoken an intelligible sentence in three days and now is but a tiny, gasping face cradled in the puffery of their mother's prize star quilt.

Hettie McColl wrings out a washcloth into a washbasin, folds it and places it carefully on her daughter's flushed brow. "Mama loves you, Anna," she whispers to a girl who cannot hear.

Dylan looks down at his mother and swallows hard. Overnight, Hettie's lovely countenance has ebbed with each defeat in Anna's fight for life; her eyes are sunken and black; her cheeks have retreated around the bones of her face. Her lips have cracked. But it is her expression that crushes the boy, an air of despair defeating the hope that her love alone could conquer this fate.

Dylan thinks of his father, who died the year before during a mustard gas attack in the trenches of France. Instinctively, the boy retreats inward; and he sees the world as if through cold, flowing water.

"Dylan!" Hettie calls again.

"What do you want, Ma?" he asks dully.

"Take the horse and go to town, get the doctor," she orders. "Your sister's in a bad way."

"Ain't no doctors left in Lawton, Ma," he replies. "They all left 'cause they was scared they was gonna get it, too."

Dylan has heard it said that in the past six months, twenty million people around the world have died of the Spanish influenza. More than six hundred thousand in the United States have succumbed, far more than the number of soldiers who have died fighting Huns during the entire war. Lawton is the hardest-hit town in Vermont. Dylan has lost an aunt, his maternal grandmother and two cousins to the spiking fevers, splitting headaches and convulsions. Now his sister is following.

A friend at school said the end comes when the lungs fill with liquids. Anna will drown in her bed. And then his mother will get it and Dylan fears he will be left alone to face the fever himself. The boy wants nothing more than to pull his blankets over his head and hide from the horror that swirls in the room around him.

"Then go get the priest," his mother cries in desperation. "Anna don't have much longer."

The boy has heard stories about the priest and he has a sudden resurgence of faith that Anna will live. He tugs on leather boots, parka, cap and mittens and races out into the night. He bridles his father's chestnut mare. He mounts bareback and kicks her into the storm.

It is nearly dawn by the time Dylan makes it down out of the snow line to town and to the brick rectory next to St. Edward's Catholic Church. The wind has quickened, blowing wet leaves through a freezing rain. Dylan stumbles to the front door of the rectory and pounds until, at last, a light comes on in the front hall and an elderly woman in a flannel robe answers.

"Land's sake, boy, what is it?" she scolds. "It's not even the crack of dawn with you smashing the door and the good father lying upstairs so ill."

"My sister's got the fever," he blurts. "My ma sent me for the priest folks say can stop it."

The woman scowls and shakes a fat finger. "Didn't I just say he's—?"

Before she can finish, Dylan hears a deeper, hoarser version of his sister's slurried cough behind the woman. He sees a tall, exhausted man. The priest puts Dylan in mind of a heron on a spring pond: stooped, gaunt, fish-hungering and yellow-eyed.

3

An oval of damp silver hair fringes a bald head so drawn down of flesh it seems a skull. Dylan takes a step backward from the apparition.

The priest coughs again before extending his palm. "What is it, my son?"

"My sister," he stammers. "Momma said you been helping some folks with the fever and we done lost our Gammy and my auntie Kate already . . . Momma hoped—"

"I'll come," the priest says.

The elderly woman grabs his elbow. "Father D'Angelo, you're sick enough yourself and the weather . . ."

"I am not important," the priest replies thickly. "The girl is. Help me get prepared."

Dylan lets the priest ride the horse. He leads the mare up through the rain and into the snow falling at the altitude of the cabin. Father D'Angelo says little during the hour march and what support he gives the boy is soon drowned out by the ravages of his coughing. Twice Dylan looks back at the priest, who stares off as if into a bottomless valley. Twice the boy shivers and looks away.

His mother waits at the door with a blanket wrapped around her shoulders. Hettie calls out in a voice of strangled disbelief as the priest struggles down off the mare: "It's got her, Father, don't bother hurrying."

"Does she breathe?" the priest asks.

"Barely," Hettie says.

"Then there's hope," the priest says. He comes up the stairs and removes his hat.

Dylan's mother's hand flies to her mouth because his face reminds her of a figure that has visited her at night. Again and again in her dreams, Hettie has found herself on a battlefield of trenches, smoke and mud. The man with D'Angelo's face is a soldier, a deserter who has been captured and returned to the battlefield only to find his unit wiped out. One of the dead men in the trench is Hettie's husband. In her dream, the deserter touches her husband's face and begins to cry. As she watches, the deserter's misery turns to rage and he picks up his gun, leaps the barbed wire atop the trench and charges across no-man's-land toward the enemy, bayonet thrust before him.

If D'Angelo catches Hettie's terrified reaction to his appearance, he does not show it, but pushes past her into the room and toward the kitchen, straightaway to the daybed. He shucks off his black, long coat and kneels by the girl, now wide-eyed and arching in convulsion. The priest draws back the quilt and unbuttons her flannel nightgown from the neck toward her navel. From one pocket he brings forth a small bone and from another a crucifix encrusted with a red jewel where the crossbar meets the spar. He lays the cross, the bone and his hands on the girl's heaving chest, then bows his head in prayer.

Dylan watches it all as if it were winter still and he an observer from within a snow tunnel. Far away he hears his mother sobbing. For the longest time there is just the priest and his sister at the end of a glistening white tube and his mother's muffled weeping.

Suddenly Anna's torso contorts in spasm. She arches. Her eyes roll in her head. Her tongue dances wildly outside her mouth. A moan rattles up from deep within her.

"Oh, God, no!" Hettie cries. She throws her hands over her face and crumples against the doorjamb.

The priest hunches over Anna. His fingers curl and quiver. His jaw moves feverishly, but he speaks not. His shoulders quiver like a wrestler's in a clinch. An icy tongue flickers through Dylan's chest.

Now the priest himself is enveloped in a fit of trembling and sweating. He lets loose with a low-toned wail. Then brackish yellow liquid the consistency of weak oatmeal fountains from Anna's mouth. And when it does, the priest slips one hand under the girl's back and rolls her onto her side so that she will not aspirate the gruel. The convulsions and expulsions continue for several minutes, during which Dylan, frozen out of time and out of place, glimpses a nameless site between two worlds.

As suddenly as it began, Anna's bridging spasm subsides and she settles peacefully back to the daybed. There is a moment of absolute stillness on his sister's part. No breathing. No coughing. No moaning. An isolating silence.

Then, joyously, Anna takes in air, shallow at first, but without labor; and then stronger, deeper and dry. Her eyes flutter and open, float cross-eyed and fearful at the unfamiliar sight of the sallow priest praying over her; and then her head turns toward Dylan and she smiles warmly at knowing him; and then they continue past him toward the door.

"Momma?" Anna whispers.

Hettie lifts her head in wonder. She races past the boy. Father D'Angelo stands unsteadily to let the woman embrace her daughter. The cold white tunnel around Dylan melts. Dylan walks toward the priest, hand extended, wanting to touch him, as if that touch alone can heal the wounds of the past year.

But before he can reach him, Father D'Angelo trips and glances off the kitchen table before landing on his knees. The moist coughing that ensues twists his body until he collapses facedown on the hooked rug.

Dylan and his mother turn the priest over and try to get him sitting up. Father D'Angelo's forehead burns with fever, but his fingers are chill to the touch. His body twitches. Dylan feels the cold reach the priest's wrist and move toward his elbow. There is wretched fear in Father D'Angelo's eyes and the boy knows the priest is dying.

Dylan takes the priest's bony hand. "Don't you fret none," he soothes. "You done saved my sister. You're going to the sweet hereafter."

At that the priest's terror becomes complete. He shakes his head violently, fights for air and croaks out words the boy misses.

"What's that, Father?" Dylan asks, holding his ear right next to the priest's mouth.

D'Angelo struggles against the fluid filling his chest. He manages one last lungful of air, then gasps to Dylan, "Pray for me, boy. I am one of the damned!"

Chapter Two

Shortly before dawn that day, there was a wind shift in direction and intensity from a shrouded breeze out of the southeast to a cruel irregular gale blowing north-northwest. The temperature dove into the mid-thirties. Sleet mixed with graupel snow came slashing across the Green Mountains. The freak meteorological occurrence marked in no small way the beginning of three of the most brutal weeks on record in Vermont.

Lawton Mountain took the brunt of the storm. At the highest altitudes, hail and freezing rain fell, caking the dormant trees with ice. When the gale achieved full force, the trees snapped under their crowns and slumped like so many hundreds of hanged men.

Lower down the mountain, cold rain filled a bouldered brook that in less than five miles plunged three thousand vertical feet to the Lawton valley floor. Other swollen rills disgorged into the brook during its rapid, aerated descent. By the time the channel widened to become the Bluekill River, one of the most famous brook- and brown-trout streams in the eastern

United States, the watercourse raged bronze and whitecapped past sugar maples that edged the mowing fields where Holstein cows browsed on spring's first clover.

The river gnawed at its banks in sight of the under-construction second homes of the flatlander wealthy who were making Lawton their latest weekend getaway enclave; it boiled past Lawton's old millworks that now housed designer outlets and trendy curio shops before sluicing under a red covered bridge and once again charging out through forest and on by a meadow where Patrick Gallagher sat and brooded in his black Ford Explorer.

He let his eyes roll with the river's wild, violent movement, like so many serpents coiling around each other, like the writhing of a woman's body, like a whirlpool sucking him into the unknown. Rivers had always been Gallagher's place of mystery and solace. Rivers are like myths, he believed, capable of carrying us beyond ourselves.

Gallagher's cell phone rang. It rang again. And a third time. And then a fourth before he picked it up.

"Pat? You in Lawton yet?"

"Morning, Jerry," he said dully. "Yes, and I am safe after my all-night drive. Thanks for asking."

Gallagher's best friend and partner, Jerry Matthews, grunted in frustration. "We've got a lot riding on this, bud, but I figured you still knew how to drive."

"I can see the Lawton town sign and its perfect little covered-bridge entrance from here," he replied.

"A covered bridge?" Jerry snapped. "That means there's a river."

"It usually does."

"You are an A-one asshole!" Matthews shouted. "You didn't say anything about a river. You said Vermont. You said a film about this priest D'Angelo, who's up for sainthood. You said nothing about a river."

"The Bluekill just happens to be here, Jerry."

"Bullshit!" he roared. "You've blown three projects in the past year standing in rivers like some catatonic trying to fly-fish his way into the asylum. We have to deliver a documentary in three months, Pat. Three months. You've got to work. You can't fish or our partnership is over. Do you understand? Over."

The sky was cast in shades of slag and ash. The river looked numbingly cold. "Are you going to the wedding tomorrow?" Gallagher asked.

"Ah, Jesus, I've told you a thousand times, get over it, forget about Emily," Jerry groaned. "Molly Francis at the Discovery Channel says they won't be funding us anymore if we don't deliver this film on time. Dick Howard at *Geographic* won't even return my calls. A completed project is what we need. Any project, Pat."

"Are you going?" Gallagher asked again.

"Yes, I'm going," Jerry snapped. "An old friend asks me to her wedding—I go. By the way, I better cut this short. I'm due at the church in Charleston by four. I've got to catch a flight."

Gallagher slumped against the steering wheel. A wisp of fog trailed under the covered bridge and lazed over the rapids. "A church?"

Jerry's voice softened. "Yeah. Ironic, huh?"

"No," he said. "What's ironic is that tomorrow, the same day my ex-wife gets remarried, less than a year after she leaves me, I turn forty."

"Rat-fucker, huh? But hell, shit happens to the best of us. We're born crying, we age disgracefully, we kick the bucket."

"And then what?"

"That's the big mystery," Jerry said. "Go to work, Pat. For both our sakes."

The line clicked. The rain fell in sheets and the river turned a torrent bank to bank, piling on itself in slabs of burned foam. Gallagher put the truck in gear and headed toward the bridge. He hadn't slept in nearly twenty-four hours and was in desperate need of a bed. The floorboards of the Lawton covered bridge rapped, clanked and grumbled under his tires. He caught a flash of movement high in the rafters, slowed and was astonished to see a large barrel owl glaring down. The bird blinked, puffed up its wings, then flared open its ebony beak. It alighted from the beam and dropped like a bomb toward the windshield. The owl extended its talons, curling its tongue and snapping its beak.

Gallagher slammed on the brakes. There was a screech like diamonds cutting glass when the claws struck the windshield.

That disturbing event stayed with him long after he exited the bridge and took a hard left on Main Street, traveling toward Lawton Center. The so-called "south-town" of Lawton is a residential area of almost precision quaintness. All the homes within that twelve-block area are either stone-faced with black shutters or white clapboard with green shutters, many of them finely restored structures from the Federalist era. Every ten yards a wrought-iron gas lamp glows. Every twenty yards there is a wrought-iron park bench next to a planter.

The Norman Rockwell facade continues where Main Street splits around a three-acre village green. A colonial-style rail fence borders the park. The center of the green is dominated by a gazebo painted bright white with forest trim. There are more restored homes on either side of the park, as well as a library, a summer-stock theater and The Lawton House, a luxury inn *Conde Nast Traveler* has called one of the best in New England.

Beyond the green is Lawton's thriving commercial center, where brick sidewalks lead the tourist to art galleries, sundry shops, bookstores and trendy restaurants.

But that day Lawton's streets were almost deserted. The

tourists and the townspeople had been driven inside by the ferocity of the storm. The courageous few men and women who had ventured out into the harsh weather were hunched over, pale-faced and grimacing at the chill, driving rain.

Two miles north, he came to the Otterslide General Store. It is the single hub of activity at the sparsely settled north end of Lawton, a long, gray shake-shingled affair that caters T-shirts and maple syrup to the out-of-state travelers and basic supplies to the locals not up to the trip downtown.

Gallagher pulled into the gravel parking lot, shut off the engine and gave himself a quick look of appraisal in the rear-view mirror. Six feet two inches tall, two hundred and twenty pounds, reasonably fit. Short-cropped coppery hair. Faded freckles. A smirking, high-eyebrowed mug more than a few women had found handsome, aged by wrinkles now and streaks of gray that show plainly at the temples. Sacks of loose skin hung under sunken, bloodshot green eyes twisted into that addled perception soldiers call the thousand-yard stare.

"What's the point, Pat?" he asked himself. "What's the fucking point?"

Gallagher sat there helpless for many minutes, watching the truck's wiper blades lose the fight against the pelt of rain. At last he got up the energy to zip up his oilskin jacket, tug down his Yankees baseball cap and climb out of the truck. His legs tingled with a cold, prickly sensation after the six-hour drive from Manhattan.

After several minutes of standing in the downpour, he had enough feeling return to his extremities so he could walk unsteadily toward the store. The door opened and a middle-aged man and woman dressed in yellow rain slickers stepped out. Their talk abruptly ended when they saw Gallagher. Clear expressions of distrust flitted across their faces.

The door creaked as he entered. Propane lamps hanging from the ceiling dimly lit the store's interior. He realized the storm must have blown out the electrical power. A woman in jeans and a green rain jacket placed a quart of milk and a half-dozen eggs on the counter before a big-bellied man with oily black hair and a scraggly beard. The woman turned, her finger tapping at her lips as if she had forgotten something.

Even in the shadowy light she was stunning—five-ten, trim, with sleepy oval eyes, wide and prominent cheekbones and a riot of auburn hair that cascaded around her shoulders and put Gallagher in mind of the blues diva Bonnie Raitt. She glided away from the counter with the powerful elegance of a trained athlete. She glanced at Gallagher as she entered the bread aisle and for the briefest instant his heart raced. It was a reaction that surprised him. It had been a long, long time since he'd felt much of anything. But in the next instant he shrugged off the sensation as the sort of hormonal blip any mature male might exhibit if he'd been celibate for nearly eighteen months.

"Help ya, sir?" the fat man at the counter asked in the thick, almost Cockney accent of the Vermont hills. His skin was unnaturally waxy. His eyes were slate gray. They shifted from side to side, unwilling to meet Gallagher's.

"I'm new in town," Gallagher began.

"Can see that," the man said, scratching at his beard skeptically.

"I'm looking for a place to stay and fish for a while," he continued. "Are there any cabins to rent locally?"

The man curled his lip as if he'd tasted something rancid, then shook his head. "Nah. Nothing like that in Lawton."

"I have a cabin for rent," came a softy, throaty voice.

Gallagher turned to find the woman appraising him. His heart raced again. Up close, her nose was gracefully upturned, her lips plump and her eyes a deep emerald green. But she had not colored the premature gray in her hair. Nor had she bothered to lay makeup over the emerging lines about her face. She was in her mid-thirties and a wholesome beauty, but there was a veil of melancholy about her demeanor that made her seem older, as if she had seen a lot of the rougher side of life and been on the blunt end of it more often than she deserved.

"Great," Gallagher said, throwing an annoyed look at the storekeeper, who was now scowling at the woman.

"I don't believe it myself," she said. "But a lot of people who've stayed in the cabin say it's haunted. I tell that first thing to anybody who's interested because they'll hear it sooner or later from some idiot in town. Am I right, Bernie?"

The store owner's face reddened and his scowl deepened. "You say so, Andie."

"How close is it to the Bluekill River—the cabin, I mean?" Gallagher asked.

"Fifty yards."

"I'll take it."

She scrunched up one eye in bemusement. "Why don't you follow me and take a look before you go writing any checks, Mr.—?"

"Gallagher. Patrick Gallagher."

She brushed past him and put a loaf of bread on the counter. "I'm Andromeda Nightingale. Most people call me Andie."

"Bernie's a jolly, helpful guy," Gallagher said, nodding back in the direction of the store as Andie Nightingale loaded her groceries in the front seat of a rusty-blue Toyota pickup. The rain had lulled, but the wind had set the rusting metal Coca-Cola sign hanging off the Otterslide General Store to wailing at its braces.

She shrugged. "Vermonters don't take to strangers right off, especially guys like Bernie Chittenden," she said matter-of-factly. "Follow me. The cabin's a couple miles up the River Road."

Gallagher jogged back to the Explorer and started it. She

waved at him out the window, then jerked the pickup into gear. They went east and the paved thoroughfare quickly gave way to a muddy, rutted road. They passed several homes before the road curved south and wound for two miles through a flat of beech and maple. Gallagher figured they were looping around and behind the town. Sure enough, when they emerged from the hardwoods there were farm fields on both sides of the road, and several hundred yards off to the west he could make out the Bluekill River. They passed a tidy white farmhouse and barn on the east side of the road. A quarter acre of soil, a garden, lay freshly turned over in the front yard. The faded lettering on the mailbox read "Nightingale."

But they drove past her driveway a hundred yards before turning right and bouncing down a little two-track road that ran parallel to a hedgerow beside a cut cornfield. Two hundred yards farther on, the field and hedgerow gave way to a glen of electric-white paper birches. Amidst the trees squatted a bizarre-looking cabin.

The right side of the structure had the classic lines of a late-nineteenth-century post-and-beam farmhouse, complete with wraparound porch. But the left side was unnaturally canted; from ten feet off the peak of the slate roof, the wall plunged abruptly to the ground. There were no windows and no doors on that side. The clapboards were warped and weather-grayed.

Andie Nightingale got out of her Land Rover, climbed up on the swayed porch and fumbled with a ring of keys. There were two locks on the door. As she worked on the padlock, Gallagher asked, "You and your husband are farmers?"

"Not married, not a farmer," she said, spinning the combination. The lock whined, then clicked open. "I lease the land out to farmers to cover my taxes. I'm a sergeant with the state police, Bureau of Criminal Investigations. We investigate death in Vermont."

"Really?" he said, looking at her with deeper appreciation. "I make films—documentaries, actually."

She gave him a look of deeper appreciation. "Like a reporter?"

"Something like that."

"I don't like reporters," she said, sliding a skeleton key into the lower lock. The tumblers rolled and the wind gusted and the door blew open. Cobwebs ripped free in the doorjamb. Musty air boiled back and they both coughed and sneezed. In seconds the rank air had dissipated.

Except for a pantry and a mudroom, the entire first floor of the cabin was a kitchen. There was a red-handled pump in the sink, a simple gas stove, a venerable Ashley wood-burning stove and a rough-hewn table with mismatched chairs.

"What you see is what you get," she said. "Bedroom's upstairs. It's a hundred fifty a week."

"I'll take it for a month," Gallagher said, reaching for his checkbook.

"You're going to fish for a month?" she asked, incredulous.

"And research Father D'Angelo for a possible documentary," he said. "You know anything about him?"

Nightingale shrugged. "Just that he supposedly performed miracles here and that the church has begun the process of sainthood. Monsignor Timothy McColl at St. Edward's Church is who you'd want to talk to. He's the expert."

McColl's name was already in Gallagher's notebook. Jerry had called ahead and arranged for him to interview the priest on Monday morning.

After writing her a check, Gallagher noticed two framed etchings on the wall next to the staircase. One was a portrait of a puffy-faced man slumped in a ladder-back chair. He was completely bald and corpulent. He had a pancake nose and the albino's unnatural strain about the eyes. In the second etching, a group of people with their backs turned sat before the mouth of a cave. An Indian stood on a cliff above the cave, hand stretched toward the crowd. A full moon hovered in the sky above the Indian's headdress.

"These are unusual," Gallagher said.

"The albino's name was Caleb Danby," Nightingale replied, as if reciting an often-told story. "He cut this cabin off the side of his brother Joshua's house across town before the turn of the century. The Danby brothers were mediums who made Lawton a center of spiritualism in the 1890s. They held seances during which ghosts were said to have materialized. Then, for reasons no one is quite sure of, the brothers had a falling-out, the seances came to an abrupt halt and Joshua Danby disappeared. Caleb moved the cabin down here by the river. He lived in it for a year before committing suicide by plunging a butcher knife into his heart."

"You're kidding, right?" Gallagher said, rubbing his chest.

"People in my business don't kid about things like that," Nightingale replied coolly. She turned as if to go and he realized he'd soon be alone in the cabin.

"You related to them?" he asked, trying to get her to stay a little longer. "The Danbys, I mean."

She shook that mane of auburn hair. "The last Danby left Lawton a long time ago."

"And the Indian?"

Nightingale hesitated at that and her face took on a pained expression. She looked out the window toward the forest on the far side of the river. "The Indian's a mystery."

Amused by her sudden soberness, Gallagher asked, "So which one haunts the place?"

"Huh? Oh, Caleb, I guess," she replied with a forced flip of her hand. "I've never paid much attention to that old story."

She answered several more questions that he had about the cabin and where in town he might buy groceries and linens. Then she said she was late for her shift and left. Gallagher watched her drive off and realized again that he had been strangely buoyed by Andie Nightingale's presence. She was beautiful. If his reaction was purely hormonal, so be it. He felt better than he had in a long time.

But as Gallagher unloaded his fishing rods, luggage, camera bag and computer, the rise in his spirits drained away. By the time he had his gear all stored inside and had cleaned up the place a bit, he was acutely aware of the silence of the cabin ringing in his ears. Like an addict searching out his next fix, Gallagher looked out the window to the river to provide white noise, to drown out the silence. But the rain was falling hard again. The Bluekill River seethed in full boil, much too dangerous for fishing.

For nearly an hour before total exhaustion forced him upstairs onto the bare mattress under a pile of dusty wool blankets, Gallagher sat in an Adirondack chair on the front porch of the cabin, watching the Bluekill flow and trying his best to avoid an examination of the shards in the midden mound of his shattered life.

Chapter Three

Gallagher slept ten fitful hours, waking shortly after dawn to what sounded like the gentle shake of a gourd rattle and the far-off beat of a leather drum, oddities he managed to dismiss as the vestiges of a fading dream. Outside, the storm still howled. The Lawton radio station announced the worst would be over by midday. To kill time before he could go to the river, Gallagher drove into town, ate breakfast, bought groceries, sheets and towels, then called St. Edward's Church and reconfirmed his interview with Monsignor McColl for Monday morning.

Around noon the rain stilled to a drizzle. Gallagher double-knotted his wading shoes, adjusted the gravel cuff on his waders, then took up the graphite six-weight rod and reel and hustled toward the Bluekill River in an effort to fend off the hot point of a migraine headache that had been threatening all morning. As if the hypnotic pulse of the rushing water could loosen the emotional screws tightening in his head.

*　　*　　*

The river was high and turbulent still, but he did not pause at the water's edge. Gallagher used the spiked wading staff to feel his way out into the surging current. Twice he stumbled, barely managing to keep his balance against the insistent force that pummeled the backs of his knees.

At last Gallagher obtained stable footing on a sandbar and tied on a bright red streamer. The only bleak hope for a strike in the roiled water. Then he played out line and drew the rod back to one o'clock before stiff-arming the tip forward and halting sharply at ten. In the chill mist, the line straightened on the backcast, looped at the braking action, then unfolded neatly and plopped into the cinnamon water against the opposite shore. He stripped line quickly until the crimson streamer reappeared, raised the rod and cast again. The repetitive, flowing movement emptied his mind as a mantra might a Buddhist monk's.

After a half hour with no strikes, Gallagher tied on a yellow marabou, a lure more suited to western rivers, cast it, then watched his fluorescent orange sinking line course rapidly downstream. His thoughts turned sourly to his predicament. He was turning forty alone in a cabin in rural Vermont. His ex-wife, Emily, was remarrying today. It was an exercise in extreme self-pity, but Gallagher did not care, and he was prepared to wallow fully in the feeling as the spool on the reel began to turn, playing out more line on the frothy water.

The fly line snaked and danced hypnotically. It became every fishing line Gallagher had ever cast, a line that arced over his head and splayed itself in the muddy waters of the Ganges River. Six years before.

The ghat, the grand stone staircase that formed the river's bank, was packed with men, women and children waiting to bathe. Goats blatted. A cow lowed in the late-afternoon sun. Six half-cremated corpses lay on the stair at the water's edge,

waiting to be taken to the center of the holy river and released
into eternity.

Gallagher ignored the looks his fishing gear generated, then
waded off the ghat toward the current. He wasn't expecting to
catch a thing. But it had been a long day of travel and he
needed to feel the water around him. After a half hour of
casting and stripping line, he had fallen under the Ganges' spell.

"Orvis comes to Allahabad," a husky woman's voice called.
"I've seen it all now."

Gallagher stopped mending line to glance over his shoulder.
The voice belonged to a big-boned woman with a thick blond
pigtail that jutted out from under a Boston Red Sox baseball
cap. Her freckled face was angular around sparkling blue eyes,
a pert nose and an expression of perpetual bemusement. She
wore round wire-rimmed sunglasses and a red batik skirt she'd
hiked up and tucked in at her hips. Her plain white T-shirt
strained against pendulous breasts. A Leica camera hung around
her neck. A camera bag was slung off her shoulder. She waded
out, looked Gallagher up and down and barked out a laugh.

"Some friends grabbed me in the street up there to tell me
a crazy American was throwing red feathers on an orange string
into the Ganges," she said. "Call me wacko, too, but I just had
to see it."

"Providing merriment for the locals is just part of the job,"
Gallagher quipped.

Before she could reply, a throng of hundreds appeared at
the top of the stone staircase, singing and carrying purple
flowers. Thousands more appeared at the adjoining ghats that
curved away along the bank to the north. Ten by ten, they
cast their flowers into the river, then waded in and started
bathing. Within minutes they were surrounded by a multitude
of people and floating wheels of purple flowers spinning in the
twilight. The woman snapped pictures. Gallagher could not

keep his eyes off her, especially her thighs, which were powerful and tanned a nut brown.

"What's going on?" he asked. "Do they take a bath like this
every day?"

"Once a year they come to wash away their sins," she replied, still shooting. "In the next ten days half a million people
will bathe along this half-mile stretch. Hindu scriptures say the
festival dates back to the origins of the earth when Gods and
demons squabbled over who got holy nectar."

Gallagher watched as hundreds poured water over their
heads. "And the holy nectar does what?"

"A single drop guarantees immortality," she said.

"So we're all here scrubbing up for immortality?"

"I suppose you could put it that way."

"Then I have a chance at immortality?"

She shook her head, grinning wickedly. "I don't think the
waters of eternity penetrate neoprene waders."

"Oh," he said and his face burned. For some reason it
seemed important to him that he impress her, and he was failing miserably.

She snapped another picture. "So who are you? What are
you doing here?"

"Patrick Gallagher. I'm filming a documentary on the spread
of Hinduism, using the construction of the ancient temples to
tell the story."

"Really?" she said, putting her hands on her hips. "I just
published a book of photographs on the temples."

"You're Beckworth?"

Emily Beckworth was legendary for going native in various
cultures around the world, then using her insider status to take
intimate portraits. In the past ten years she'd published award-
winning books on Japanese Zen monks and their monasteries,
aboriginal tribes in Australia's outback, the Yak herdsmen of

Outer Mongolia and the Stone Age peoples of Papua New Guinea.

"I am," she said. She cocked her hips to one side, which triggered a strange buzzing in Gallagher's head.

"You wouldn't be interested in acting as guide and commentator, would you?" he managed to croak.

"Depends on what the pay is."

A flash on the coppery surface of the Bluekill startled Gallagher from the memory.

It is rare, but during big runoffs, lunker brown trout will sometimes leave their carrying positions behind rocks and under banks to flare up to seize grubs, worms and even mice that have been swept into the rivers and churn at the surface. Gallagher cast twenty feet below the flash and stripped line. Instantly there was a surge, then a series of twitches as the hook rattled along the protrusions of a bony mouth. He let the fish chew on it for a count of two, then jerked his wrist back to set the hook. Gallagher's rod bent nearly in two.

Monster! he thought. Bluekill monster brown trout! A fish like this could salvage a fortieth birthday if not erase the memory of an ex-wife!

Gallagher tried to play the fish on the six-weight line, but he felt twelve, fifteen pounds. Maybe more! He would have to wait until the beast tired to have any chance at landing him. The spool gyrated. The line screamed through the ferules. The fish headed straight downstream toward a silver ash tree that had crashed into the river during the previous night's storm.

If the fish swam into the submerged branches, the tippet might snap. Gallagher stumbled forward, trying to close the gap, fingering the line like some voodoo priest preparing for exorcism.

The rod bent again, then suddenly snapped back, and the line lay limp on the water.

"You've got to be shitting me!" Gallagher shouted and slapped the water in disgust. "Damn it!"

You wait a lifetime to hook a fish like that. Gallagher knew it. And the lost opportunity made him want to sit in the shallows and cry. He stood there for a long time just staring at the cupped water surface before sighing and starting to reel in the line. Somehow the fish had shaken the fly free of his jaw, or he'd gotten his teeth into the leader and sawed himself free. Gallagher had brought in perhaps eight feet of the slack when the line tightened again and a great weight rolled toward him, caught the current, then tugged away.

He was still on! But very sluggish. Had he become tangled? Was he swimming in slower and slower circles around a hidden branch as a dog might wind a chain around a tree?

With the wading stick Gallagher eased his way forward, stopping every few yards to reel in the coils until he came to the end of the floating line. The butt section of the tapered leader disappeared under the caramel water just in front of the half-submerged ash.

Gallagher ignored the image of a big brown's razor-sharp teeth, put his hand around the leader and followed it down under the water knot by knot to where it met the tippet. The line was as strained and vibrating as struck piano wire. His fingers found the streamer's hackle, then groped forward, searching gingerly for the hook and the slick flesh of the fish.

Gallagher's fingers brushed what felt like stiff cloth and he startled and jerked back. His heart pounded. He reached down again to feel what lay beyond the hook.

It was stiff cloth.

Gallagher grabbed a handful of the fabric and pulled, feeling that weight roll toward him, catch in the current and jam back into the limbs of the downed ash. He wedged the cork butt of the fly rod tight among the exposed limbs of the tree, then crouched in the chill water. He reached deep, got hold of the cloth with both hands and pulled upward with all his might. The weight came up. It turned over just below the surface, and as if through an opaque, rust-stained shroud, a face appeared.

Chapter Four

Gallagher was screaming even before he was aware he was screaming and he let go of the green fabric. The head and upper body of the corpse slipped back under the water, bumped against him, then disappeared. Gallagher dry-heaved, choked and spun, his only thought to get away from what was in the river. He tried to sprint toward shore, flailing at the surface with his hand and the wading stick.

But the current caught him and dashed him face down in the rapids. Gallagher flipped twice, then surfaced, gasping at the sudden immersion. He stumbled to his feet only to vomit up the brackish water he'd swallowed. The shell-shocked numbness that had surrounded Gallagher for nearly a year had been swept away in an instant. Now every nerve cell in his body fired nauseatingly hot. The white birches around the cabin in the dim woods ashore stood out like frozen flashes of lightning.

Gallagher swallowed at the sobs that threatened to strangle him and struggled toward the birches, unable to shake the crimson vision flooding through his mind. The man had been mutilated. The wounds to his body were frequent, deep and oblong-shaped. Gallagher tripped his way into the shallows and crawled the bank before taking off in a mad sprint across the muddy cut cornfield toward the River Road and Andie Nightingale's house.

The detective was working in her garden, pitching compost with a fork. She wore knee-high green boots, tattered jeans and a tan barn coat. Gallagher staggered out of the field and across the road into her yard, only to fall to his knees short of the garden and gag at the aluminum taste of the adrenaline surging through his mouth.

"Mr. Gallagher!" Nightingale cried.

"Dead," he choked out. "There's a dead man in the river."

Ten minutes later Nightingale spun her beat-up Toyota pickup into the cabin yard. She leaped out, ran through the electric-white birches and jumped off the bank straight into the water. Gallagher halted at the Bluekill's edge, unable to enter.

"Show me!" she demanded.

"No," he said, feeling a twist in his gut.

"You have to," she insisted.

"I . . . I can't."

"I know this is hard," she said, managing a professional's smile of understanding. "But please, just show me where you found the body before it's washed away and I have to bring in a team of divers to search."

Gallagher felt the cramping again, but for some reason Nightingale's sympathetic demeanor bolstered him enough to move woodenly out into the river, once his liquid refuge, now a sinister current. They waded into the swift flow and with each step Gallagher fought to stamp out the wild fire of panic burning in him. They reached the downed ash tree and he pointed to the eddy where the fly line disappeared.

"He's down there."

"You're going to help me, Mr. Gallagher." It was more of a command than a statement. A strange, cutting pressure built behind his eyes, but he nodded. They went hand over hand down the line. Gallagher focused on the gentle curve of her neck as they pulled. This time the body floated quickly.

"Oh, Jesus!" Nightingale whispered in horror.

He wore a green camouflage coat and a matching fleece knapsack. He was nude from the waist down except for a thick wool sock dangling from his left foot. The carnage that had been inflicted on him was like looking at a Rorschach test devised by the darkest of minds, and Gallagher desperately wanted to flee toward shore again.

"Hank Potter," Nightingale said, giving wavering identity to the body shifting in the current. Gallagher's head spun. He feared the river would drag him down and never let him breach again for air.

Over her shoulder came the flashing blue lights of a state trooper vehicle, followed rapidly by another cruiser and then an ambulance. Nightingale had called them before driving back to the cabin. At the sight of the vehicles, her jaw quivered. The first break in her professional composure.

"We're going to bring him in," she said at last.

Two young rawboned troopers realized they were pulling the body ashore and waded out to help. One of the troopers turned completely white when he saw the disfigurement.

By the time they reached the shallows, three more vehicles had pulled into the yard around the fishing cabin. One was a green but otherwise nondescript sedan. The second was a midnight-blue, four-wheel-drive Chevy Suburban with "Lawton Police" emblazoned on the door. A new gray Dodge pickup brought up the rear.

The doors of the Suburban and the green sedan opened simultaneously. Two men got out of the Suburban. The driver wore a gray athletic sweatshirt with a blue "Lawton" printed in an arc across his chest. He tugged on a blue baseball-style cap with gold embroidery that said "Chief" and popped a grape lollipop into his mouth. His sidekick wore a conventional tan police uniform. He was portly, in his late twenties, with a mop-top haircut, a wispy mustache and a sleepy expression. A bleached-white-haired woman in her early fifties sporting a khaki trench coat climbed out of the green sedan. Then the door to the pickup opened and a sharply dressed, pink-faced man with a dramatic silver handlebar mustache exited. He was barking orders into a cell phone. "I don't care what those bankers down in Boston say—it's a legitimate deal and it's going through. Lawton's depending on it. You hear me?"

"Gang's all here," Nightingale mumbled and she ran her fingers awkwardly through her hair.

She turned to Gallagher and gestured toward the cabin. "Wait over there out of the way. I'm going to want to talk with you."

Gallagher shambled to the steps, sat and slumped against one of the support beams that held up the sagging porch roof. The ambulance drivers had already lain a sheet over the body, which now rested on the lime-green grass between two of the birch trees. Talons of chilling ground fog groped through the trees toward the sheet and the body. Gallagher shivered. The shivers turned to chatters. He went into the cabin to get out of the waders and into something dry. He dragged himself upstairs and as he was getting into a pair of flannel-lined khakis and a fleece pullover he felt suddenly seasick, so he opened the double-hung bedroom window to breathe and watch the crowd gathering in the cabin yard outside.

The white-haired woman in the trench coat had led Nightingale away from the others. They stopped right below Gallagher's window, unaware of his eavesdropping.

"Sergeant," the white-haired woman said.

"Lieutenant Bowman," Nightingale replied, smiling stiffly. "I wouldn't have expected you here so soon."

"I was only twenty minutes out and thought you could use a hand," the lieutenant replied. Brigid Bowman wore swaths of makeup that almost concealed acne scars and accentuated a pair of distrusting, pale blue eyes. Her white hair had been razored short at the ears to draw attention to pearl stud earrings and a matching necklace.

Nightingale squeezed her hands into fists. "Or maybe you hustled along because you didn't want me here alone."

"Maybe a little of both, Andie," Bowman replied coolly.

Before Nightingale could respond, the hulking man in the Lawton sweatshirt and the "Chief" baseball cap approached, followed by his sleepy deputy and the nattily dressed chubby fellow with the silver walrus mustache who was snapping shut his cell phone.

The chief's name was Mike Kerris. He was roughly Gallagher's age, but taller, more muscular, with stainless-steel eyes and a shock of thick brown hair. He had one of those pronounced and chiseled jaws that suggests steroid use. He popped the sucker from his mouth. "What do we got?"

Nightingale turned flinty at the question. "Hank Potter. The body's been mutilated."

The pudgy man with the silver mustache waved the cell phone overhead and cried, "Hank Potter! The man's a dentist. He doesn't have an enemy in the— What do you mean, mutilated?"

"Cut up, Mayor, badly," Nightingale said. "Looks like he was hit ten, maybe fifteen times with a heavy, sharp object before he was dumped in the river. Care to see?"

Mayor Bruce Powell's pink skin went as pallid as a trout's belly. He ran his hand across the top of his shellacked sterling-colored hairdo. "There hasn't been a killing in Lawton in twenty years."

"Twenty-eight years, Uncle Bruce," the chief corrected. He had the grape lollipop lodged in the pocket of one cheek like a chipmunk working an acorn.

"Whatever, Mikey," the mayor said. He waved the cell phone at them all. "Listen up: I want this solved and solved fast, you hear me? Lawton doesn't need this kind of adverse publicity. Especially not now while we're in the midst of delicate, delicate negotiations."

Lieutenant Bowman tapped her rubber-bottomed boot in the muddy driveway. "Our bureau has one of the best solving rates in the country, Mayor Powell. As far as publicity is concerned—"

"Mutilated!" Powell shouted incredulously before Bowman could finish. He shook his entire arm at the lieutenant. "You've got to keep that part quiet. Away from the reporters. Damn it, it makes it sound as if there's a madman on the loose in Lawton! I won't have that. Not in my town."

Gallagher watched as the whole lot of them glanced at the sheet, as if they could not believe it was possible. Gallagher had seen the body first. He believed it was possible.

"We'll keep that part of it as low-profile as we can," Lieutenant Bowman promised.

"Lawton's a small place," the deputy with the mop-top haircut offered. "Tough to keep secrets here."

A sardonic smirk passed over Nightingale's face. She looked at the mayor and the chief and said, "And here I'd always considered Lawton a town full of secrets."

The mayor rubbed a finger under his handlebar mustache and glared at Nightingale. The chief licked his lips. The lollipop had turned his tongue purple. His eyelids went drowsy, the way a lizard's do before it strikes at an insect. He turned to Bowman: "Who's gonna be your lead? No offense to Sergeant Nightingale, but we all know, given her past, that she might not be up to the—"

"How dare you!" Nightingale cried.

"That's quite enough, Sergeant!" The lieutenant cut her off. "Sergeant Nightingale will lead for the time being under my close, close supervision. Fair enough, Chief?"

Kerris glanced at his deputy and then at the mayor, who shrugged. The chief's expression turned smarmy. "I'm sure the sergeant and I can figure out a way to work together."

Nightingale said nothing. The light in the birch glade turned suddenly flat as a storm cloud advanced on the river. Rain fell again. An evidence technician drew back the sheet and took pictures of Hank Potter's body. The flashes of brilliant metallic light made the birches look iridescent and shimmery, as if they were part of an old black-and-white photograph printed in silver tones.

"Solve it fast," Powell said. "That's all I want." The mayor waddled off to his truck, his fingers already punching numbers in the cell phone.

Now a green van bounced its way into the clearing and parked. A short, bushy-haired and bushy-eyebrowed man with a big nose and hairy nostrils stepped out. Melvin Allen, the state's assistant medical examiner.

They all walked toward Allen. By the time Gallagher got on hiking boots and went down the stairs and out onto the cabin porch, they were gathered around the body. The medical examiner was tugging at his ear and jerking his head from side to side at the sight of the body. The deputy, whose name was Phil Gavrilis, leaned against one of the birches with his eyes shut. Chief Kerris acted as if he were not a small-town cop, but a hardened New York City homicide detective. He never even blinked.

Nightingale asked, "Can you tell me what he was hit with, Mel, and how long he's been in the river?"

The medical examiner shook off his initial shock at the grisly wounds and knelt next to the body. He cradled Potter's head in latex-gloved hands and tipped it left and then right. He used his fingers to pry at one of the lacerations that showed through the camouflage. Gallagher couldn't watch any longer. He stared up at the sky and imagined himself out on the Taylor Fork River south of Bozeman, casting to cutthroats on a hot July Montana day.

"Can't say for sure until I can get him up on a table under the lights," Allen said at last. "But if I had to make a guess, I'd say some kind of crudely made machete or hatchet. See those little elliptical irregularities in the wound? The blade was hand-filed."

Allen studied the wounds again, then moved his attention lower. "Given the lack of bloating, I'd say he's been in the water no more than eight hours. And, much as I hate to say it, it appears he was raped as well as killed. He lead some kind of secret life?"

"You mean like—" Deputy Gavrilis began.

"Hank Potter?" Chief Kerris cried. "No way. The guy played halfback at UVM."

Allen shrugged. "Whatever. I'll know more once I get him on the table. Autopsy Monday morning. Six-thirty A.M. sharp."

There were groans all around. Allen was known for calling autopsies at the crack of dawn.

"Who found the body?" Bowman asked.

Nightingale pointed toward Gallagher, who had returned to the porch. He waved weakly and all of them came over save the deputy, who heard static on the radio and ran to the Suburban. Gallagher stood up and Kerris gave him a sort of weightroom look that he ignored. They asked several preliminary questions—where Gallagher was from, what he did for a living, why he'd rented the cabin. Gallagher stupidly chanted the highlights of his résumé like an Alzheimer's patient trying to maintain his last handhold on identity—that he had a Ph.D. in anthropology from Cornell, where he had specialized in comparative mythology. He had spent a year teaching under-graduates at Harvard before bugging out of academia to join *The Boston Globe* as a cultural reporter, aspiring to follow in the footsteps of Tom Wolfe. Three years later Gallagher won the Pulitzer Prize for a series of stories that looked at the lives of children caught in the battle zones of religious wars. For the past seven years he had written and produced documentaries for *National Geographic*, PBS and the Discovery Channel. Most of his work focused on the interplay of culture and creed.

"Well, la-di-da," Kerris said when Gallagher had finished. He had a hooded way of looking at you that made you feel as if you could be humiliated in his presence. "What are you doing here? There's no strange religion in Lawton."

"Fishing," Gallagher said sharply. "But I'm also doing re-search on Father D'Angelo—the one who died doing miracles here eighty years ago."

"What about him?" the chief asked, his brows becoming even more hooded.

"D'Angelo's up for sainthood," Gallagher replied. "I'm think-ing about doing a film on the process of Catholic canonization."

At that moment, Kerris' deputy shouted over from the Sub-urban. "Chief, the office just got a call from Paula Potter. She's reported Hank missing. She thinks he's broken a leg out tur-key hunting."

Lieutenant Bowman clicked her ruby-red fingernails. She turned to Nightingale. "Can you handle it?"

"I'll go right up there," Nightingale said, making furtive glances at the rest of them.

"That's not what I asked."

Nightingale's shoulders rose. "I can handle it, Brigid."

Bowman did that clicking thing with her fingernails again. "You'll call me if you find anything up there?"

Nightingale gritted her teeth. "I will."

Kerris tongued his lollipop from one cheek to the other,

obviously enjoying her discomfort. He said, "I'll have my men begin a search of the riverbank this side of town. Maybe we can find the rest of his clothes."

"I'm done?" Gallagher asked.

Nightingale managed a genuine smile that warmed him. "Yes. But don't leave Lawton without telling us. I'll need you to answer some more questions."

"In the meantime?"

"In the meantime, research your film and fish," she said.

Chapter Five

Paula Potter leaned against the doorway to the barn, face into the coarse northwest wind that roared down off the ridge of Lawton Mountain, where winter still ruled and the hardwood trees remained barren of buds. She gaped at a pewter sky tattooed with a stream of purple oval clouds.

Ordinarily, the reedy brunette was talkative, vivacious in gesture, smart and opinionated. Now she rested mute with curled hands jammed into the pockets of the gray wool jacket she wore over a denim dress, knee socks and blue wool clogs. She was blinking and had been blinking for nearly three minutes, ever since Andie Nightingale had told her that her husband's body had been found in the Bluekill.

At last Paula broke the silence. "Lenticular clouds," she said.

"Excuse me?" Nightingale said.

"Those tiny purple clouds are called lenticular," Paula explained. "Hank was a weather freak. Vermont and all the hunting he did, you know? He used to say lenticular clouds came in on turbulence a mile high in the atmosphere. Lenticular clouds are like omens riding before storms. But the storm's already here, isn't it?"

With that, whatever control Paula Potter possessed escaped her. Her jaw stretched wide to the impossibility of her loss and she tried to cover her mouth with her right hand even as she lurched wide-eyed across the uneven barn floor. Nightingale caught the woman and pulled her close. Over Paula's heaving shoulders, she watched the lenticular clouds arcing at the horizon.

Now a red Jeep Cherokee roared into the driveway and halted under the naked limbs of the gnarled elm that dominated the Potters' front yard. An older version of Paula jumped from the driver's seat. Ellen LaVacque hurried, ashen-faced, to her sister.

Ten minutes later Paula said, "I should go inside and tell my boys now."

"It's going to be hard," Ellen said. "They'll think their lives are over."

"I won't let them think that," Paula said resolutely. "He'll always be with us. Won't he?"

The question hung in the air for so long that Nightingale winced. "Paula, I have to ask you some hard questions."

Paula snuffled, but nodded. "I figured you would."

"Did Hank have any enemies?"

"Enemies!" Ellen cried.

"He had no enemies," Paula said firmly. Then she faltered and began to sob. "That I knew of anyway."

Nightingale took a deep breath. "I'm sorry to ask this, but did you have any suspicion he might have led a secret life?"

"No!" Paula cried.

Her sister piped up. "Hank was the hardest-working, truest man I've ever known."

There was silence following her outburst. Paula worked the handkerchief in her hand, then asked meekly, "What kind of secret life?"

"Financial, sexual, emotional, anything you can think of," Nightingale said.

Paula looked at her sister, then shook her head. "When he wasn't working, he was either puttering in the yard, playing with our boys or out hunting and fishing."

The sergeant nodded. "What would Hank's routine have been this morning?"

"He would've followed his plan," Paula said. "He always had a hunt plan, where he'd go and what he'd do first thing in the morning."

"And this morning?"

"With the weather like this, he decided to hunt close to home, up Lawton Mountain on the other side of the river," she said, gesturing vaguely to the west.

"Okay," Nightingale said encouragingly. "Beyond the plan, what would he have done this morning, first thing?"

Paula thought about it, then said, "Up at three-thirty. Dress in long underwear and socks. Eat. Then come straight out here to his hunting locker. Get his clothes, gun, turkey vest, decoys and his pack. If he was going to cross the river, he would have used the footbridge he rebuilt last fall. It's down there in the forest beyond the orchard."

Nightingale looked across the field toward the woods. The glossy black trunks of the hemlocks against the tawny, dead high grass of the orchard looked like India ink that had been spilled across fine stationery. The dormant apple trees in the foreground resembled the jagged metalwork of busted umbrellas a winter's gale had stripped of fabric.

"Go talk to your boys," Nightingale said. "And Paula, I'm so sorry for your loss."

Looking for tracks, Nightingale padded out through the high grass of the apple orchard toward the hemlocks. With every step the river's roar became more deafening. And with every step Lawton Mountain loomed larger above her.

In the shadowy light under the hemlock canopy, Nightingale found a pair of camouflage trousers that matched the jacket Hank Potter was found in. She discovered a pair of high rubber boots tossed in a raspberry patch. She used her flashlight to look for tracks in the soft, wet soil. She found several but the storm had marred their definition.

On the steep bank leading down to the footbridge, she came across shallow troughs in the mud that suggested heels had slipped down the bank. But there were no clear tread marks she could have used to say positively that Potter or his attacker had continued this way before dawn.

The bridge footings were thick, discolored steel set into a granite ledge fifteen feet above the level of the river. New two-inch cables had been tied into the old footings and pulled taut across the thirty-foot chasm. Planks had been hooked to the cables with U bolts. Rope railings ran parallel to the cable.

Nightingale walked out on the bridge above the rushing water. It swayed in the wind and she was forced to grip the ropes for balance. The bridge's movement was greatest at the middle of the span, where she stopped and peered over. Black whirlpools swirled between the ledge walls. Knife-edged rocks slashed the river surface. She was about to turn when she noticed discoloration on the wood planking near the far shore.

Blood. And more blood on the rope railing and splattered there on the exposed rocks below. If the blood matched, Hank Potter had been killed on the bridge that spanned the Bluekill.

Nightingale hurried up the bank, through the hemlock grove and out into the apple orchard, where it was now dusk. She heard a cry. A door slammed. A towheaded boy of about eight raced pell-mell across the yard. He reached a makeshift ladder nailed to a white pine and climbed it toward a tree house. The wind raised water in her eyes and her stomach yawned.

Paula Potter came out of the house looking for the boy and Nightingale went to her. "Paula, I have to ask you and your sons to go to Ellen's house," she said. "I'm going to bring in evidence technicians."

Paula stared blankly. "Did you find something?"

"Enough that I want to bring in help."

"Oh," she said, wringing her hands. "I . . . I was looking for Nathan, my oldest."

Nightingale pointed to the tree house. "He's up there. I'm sorry, but before you go to him, could you let me see the hunting locker you mentioned?"

Paula looked from the tree house to the detective, then nodded uncertainly.

The wind picked up again as they crossed back to the chicken coop, and they bent to it in silence. Inside, Paula went straight to the double-padlocked door. "That's funny," she remarked as she reached toward the locks unhasped in the rings. "Hank would never—"

Nightingale grabbed Paula by the wrist. "Don't touch."

She got out thin latex gloves from her pocketbook, then picked the locks out by their hasps. She flipped on the light and eased the door open.

The locker smelled of cedar and was the size of a large walk-in closet. On the right, hard by the door, were high and low racks of various hunting clothes. Then a built-in, eight-slot, glass-faced gun cabinet filled with three scoped high-powered rifles, a .22 rifle, a synthetic-stocked muzzle-loader with a stainless-steel barrel, a double-barreled shotgun, and two pump-action shotguns, one wood-stocked with a blued barrel, one synthetic-stocked and camouflaged. A single steel cable about a quarter of an inch thick ran the length of the case through the trigger guards of all the guns. Below the glass case were pine drawers and cabinets lined with cedar wood. Beyond the case was a boot rack and pegs on which hung various hunting calls, a set of hip waders and a pair of Gortex chest waders. At the far end of the closet was a low pine cabinet.

"Did he have more than one turkey gun?" Nightingale asked.

"No," Paula said. "Why?"

"Because he never got the gun from the cabinet," she replied.

"Then he met his killer before getting here," Paula said. She began to cry again.

Nightingale held her until she settled down, then asked, "Besides the locks being open, does anything else seem out of place?"

Paula blinked, blew her nose and studied the room. "No, it looks like it always does. Except—"

She gestured toward the pine credenza. "The bottom cabinet door is open. Hank kept his ammunition in there. Locked. He was always preaching gun safety with the boys." She paused, her chin quivering. "Did you hear that? I'm already talking about him in the past tense! Andie . . . I've got to go find my son. He needs me."

"I'm being tough on you," Nightingale soothed. "I apologize again. Go."

When Paula had left, Nightingale went over to the credenza and slid it open. Inside were four heavy-duty, black, padlocked ammunition boxes. On one the lock was loose. She drew that lock from the hinge, eased open the box, which was filled with boxes of shotgun shells, then let her eyes drift toward the inside of the lid.

Taped to the inside of the box was a piece of plain white sketch paper. On it was drawn an intricate illustration of a creature rowing a boat across a river.

The creature had the physical structure of a man, except

that he possessed the nose of a vulture, pointed animal ears and snakes growing on his head instead of hair. His eyes were solid black voids. His mouth was sewn shut with string. The creature and the boat had been etched in precise, delicate black lines. That part of the illustration had the quality of a drawing in an ancient book.

The water below the boat and the creature, however, was rust-red and crudely depicted with the blunt stroke of a child's finger painting. Puzzled, Nightingale tugged at the gold stud in her left ear. Why would Potter put this macabre drawing in an ammunition box? Was he the artist? If there were other drawings here, she'd have to reconsider the psychological dimensions of the dentist and refigure the path of her investigation.

Something about the medium of the drawing bothered her as well. Nightingale reached in and tugged out the box. She set it on top the credenza, then adjusted the overhead light to better examine the illustration. She peered closer at the river.

Her head felt suddenly leaden and pressurized. Icy sweat bubbled to the skin at the nape of her neck and dribbled down her back.

The river had been finger-painted with blood.

Chapter Six

A second violent storm swept in over the Green Mountains just after dark, snapping branches off the birch trees and rattling the blown-glass windows of Gallagher's cabin. The feeble structure creaked and moaned with every gust. Dank brown leaves swirled and settled in the tracks left by the police cruisers, the ambulances and the medical examiner's van that had carried Hank Potter's body from the river.

Over the years Gallagher had taught himself to lock those sorts of horrors away in the mental equivalent of a vault. But the memory of Potter surfacing from the depths of the Bluekill refused entombment. It followed him as he tried to read the pile of research on the Catholic process of canonization his partner, Jerry Matthews, had shoved into his hands before he left Manhattan. The image of Potter goaded Gallagher as he made the bed upstairs and organized his fly box. It taunted him as he tried to cook an official welcome-to-middle-age birthday dinner of store-bought trout.

Why Potter and not me? Gallagher asked himself as the

butter melted in the pan. What matrix of forces had aligned themselves to say that this day was his last while my life goes on? And then Gallagher asked the question he had been avoiding all day—what matrix of forces had caused his wife to leave, for him to be forty and alone?

He went through the motions of preparing and eating the trout, but took no joy in the taste. For want of something to do, he looked at the etchings of the Indian standing above the cave entrance and of the albino medium Caleb Danby slumped in his trance. There was something about his slouching posture that reminded Gallagher of his father.

Seamus Gallagher was born and raised in Brooklyn, the son of an alcoholic stonecutter and devout Catholic who spent his life carving religious statuary for churches across the Northeast. For reasons Gallagher never fully understood, by the time his father was a teenager, he had rejected God and his father's stonecutting trade. Seamus attended City College of New York at night. He got his law degree from Fordham at twenty-seven. By thirty he was a vocal labor attorney and a stalwart of the ACLU and the American Communist Party.

Gallagher's father was a stocky man with a wiry salt-and-pepper beard, a slick bald head and intense eyes that peered out from behind black polymer glasses.

He met Gallagher's mother, Agnes Flanagan, in 1958 at a party for *The Progressive Magazine*. Agnes was one of the staff's best writers, a thin, severe woman with a pinched face who chain-smoked Kents and wrote elegant, acerbic essays attacking the capitalist establishment. In her, Gallagher believed his father found the personification of the mainstays of his life— leftist ideals and booze.

On their first date, they went to Coney Island, flew a kite and got shit-faced on the beach. Gallagher was born some nine months later. "A mistake of too much sun and too much vodka," as his father would describe Gallagher when he was in one of his black moods, which became more frequent the older Gallagher got.

Seamus was rarely home at night, more often at a rally or a meeting of some committee he chaired, followed by a long sojourn at the local pub. He was most vocal as an atheist, and when Gallagher was eight his father was chief litigator and spokesman for a group that successfully sued the New York school system to outlaw prayer in the classroom.

The day after the suit was won, Gallagher was coming down the slide in the school playground when he was surrounded by a group of kids who taunted, "You pinko fuck! You God-hating son of a bitch!"

Gallagher never saw the stone that struck him upside the head.

He woke up with no memory of the three days he had passed in a coma. When Seamus came to see him in the hospital, the first thing Gallagher asked him about was God.

"He doesn't exist, Patrick," Seamus said coldly. He removed his glasses to rub them on his shirtsleeve. As usual, there was the faint odor of liquor on his breath.

"How do you know?" Gallagher asked.

"It's something you feel or you don't," he said. "I don't feel, therefore I don't believe. Neither should you."

"Then what happens after we die?"

"Nothing," my father replied. "It's just the end of it."

"There's nothing else?" Gallagher had demanded. "We don't go somewhere, like heaven?"

"Heaven," he snorted. "We blip out of the darkness. We blip back into the darkness."

Gallagher grew up in a Brooklyn brownstone, a place where there was never quite enough light coming through the windows or glowing from lamps to conquer the dusk in the corners. His fondest memories of his mother were of Agnes hunt-

and-peck typing on her old Smith Corona in her small office off the living room, smoking menthol Kents and sipping from a Bloody Mary.

Agnes was not a very affectionate mother. That is not to say she neglected Gallagher or abused him physically. She did not. But she rarely hugged or kissed him, unless she was drunk. And like most children of alcoholics, Gallagher soon learned the hollowness of liquor-induced emotion.

To her credit, Agnes did instill in Gallagher the great love of books. She taught him to read when he was four—in part, he believed, as a way to keep him occupied while she worked. Be that as it may, books became Gallagher's refuge from the warm and nurturing environment he was raised in.

By the time Gallagher turned fourteen, the bottle had completely consumed his father. There was no single, dramatic incident that precipitated Seamus' decline, just a steady accumulation of setbacks—jail twice during antiwar protests, a string of lost cases, government harassment—that triggered benders that caused more setbacks and so on and so on in a great downward spiral.

One afternoon when Gallagher was fifteen, he happened to board the subway from Manhattan to Brooklyn after a class trip to the Museum of Natural History. It had been one of the best days of his life. The class had heard a talk from one of the curators about masks from the Dogon tribe of Mali in western Africa. The lecturer had spoken about the Dogon belief that both humans and animals have a soul substance called Nyama which returns after death in a mask such as the four-foot carved bird face he held up for all to see. The masks could be used to drive away the souls of the deceased who might harm the living.

Gallagher had left the talk enthralled by the idea that people in primitive cultures all over the world had explanations of why we exist and what happens after we die. It was that day Gallagher decided to study anthropology.

But when he got into the subway car with his classmates and his teacher, Gallagher was shocked to see his father slumped in a stupor in one of the seats. Seamus sang gibberish to the window, then raised a finger to his own reflection and spouted off a line from his closing argument in the school-prayer case. Several of Gallagher's classmates, who did not recognize Seamus, began to snicker and make jokes about the crazy drunk. Seamus' head turned and his eyes focused on them before refocusing on his son. Gallagher turned away from his father, acted as if he did not know who he was and laughed out loud with the other boys.

A week later Gallagher came home from high school to find the front door unlocked. The shades were drawn and the lights were off. The thermometer had been turned down. Seamus liked a cold house.

Agnes had told Gallagher the night before that she'd be spending her deadline day at the magazine offices. He went through the house raising the shades and turning on the lights one by one until he reached the kitchen. It looked like it had when he left early for school—strewn with post-party scud: cigarette-filled ashtrays, half-drunk glasses, empty bottles.

Gallagher cleaned the glasses, emptied the ashtrays and tossed the beer and vodka bottles into the trash. It took him about forty minutes to complete that fond ritual. Then he poured out the remaining vodka so his parents would have to suffer a trip to the corner store. It was his daily act of rebellion.

Finished, Gallagher climbed the stairs to begin studying. As he passed his parents' bedroom he glanced to the left.

Seamus hung by the neck from a rope he'd slung from a heating pipe. He left no note.

*   *   *

There was a public memorial where all the people with whom Seamus had worked on various causes before his downfall showed up and praised him. And raised toasts to him in the pub afterward. The actual burial was just Gallagher and his mother and the casket on a raw April day in a cemetery in Queens.

Two men with shovels waited about a hundred yards away. Gallagher asked his mother if they should say something. She looked down at the pine box.

"I hate you, Shea," she said.

Gallagher understood and hated his father, too, because suicide, to believers in a life beyond, is based on the idea that they are departing this world for something better. Gallagher's old man did not believe. He jumped ship on his wife and son for the void. But Gallagher's hate was tempered and warped by the memory of Seamus' lost expression when he'd laughed at his father in the subway car.

Truck headlights on high beam lashed through the cabin window, startling Gallagher from his memories. He had not allowed himself to think of his father in years and believed he had gotten over Seamus' demise. But for some reason at that moment, Gallagher had the desperate need to talk to Seamus, to explain himself.

Andie Nightingale's rattletrap Toyota pickup pulled in and Gallagher's mood improved considerably. There was something about her that reminded him of a beautiful bird hopping along bravely trying to hide a broken wing from the world.

He opened the door. Her hair sparkled with raindrops. Her cheeks glowed from windburn. She looked nervous, but altogether lovely in a mountain woman sort of way.

He threw her a welcoming smile. "You look like you had as rough a day as mine. Can I offer you some trout? It's store-bought, but it's all I've got."

She gave no immediate response, but brushed by him without even a smile in return. "You're some kind of expert in religion and mythology, right?"

The question deflated Gallagher. "And here I was hoping your visit might be social."

"Are you or aren't you?" she replied sternly.

"I know enough."

"Where were you between three and four o'clock this morning?"

"Tossing and turning in that lumpy bed upstairs," he said, not liking where this was going. "What's this all about, Ms. Nightingale? Or should I be calling you sergeant?"

"Any witnesses to say you were upstairs?"

"I guess I should call you sergeant," he said. "Witnesses? Yes, a trio of mice."

"I'm being serious, Mr. Gallagher."

"So am I. One of the little bastards gnawed a mallard wing I brought up to tie dry flies with. Now, do I need a lawyer?"

"Do you?"

"Don't tell me you think I killed the dentist and then called you in to find him."

"It's crossed my mind," she said.

Gallagher rubbed his fingertips over his temples. "This couldn't get better, could it? Look, Sergeant Nightingale, you've now become part of the worst day of my life—I turned the big four-oh. My ex-wife, my ex-wife! . . . ahh, forget that one . . . and I found a dead man in the river. But the only thing I've killed lately is a cockroach that skittered out from under the sink. Any more questions, I am calling an attorney."

Nightingale studied him for a long time, then her expression softened by several degrees, as if she'd decided to change course in the questioning. "Have you ever come across a myth about a river being blood-red?"

Gallagher screwed up his face, trying to figure where she

was leading with the question, then said, "Doesn't ring any bells offhand. That's all you have—a river that's blood-red? Is the myth Greek, Roman, Sumerian, what?"

"I don't know."

"Can't help you if you don't have more than that."

Nightingale hesitated, then reached inside her raincoat. She came out with a gallon-sized zip-lock evidence bag. She put on latex gloves, then slid out a drawing faceup on the kitchen table under the gaslight.

Gallagher gave the creature, the boat and the river a closer look, then felt himself go weak-kneed. "The red, is it . . . ?"

"Yes."

"From the man I found?"

"I'm assuming so," she said. "We'll run tests."

"The killer left it?"

"I'm assuming that, too."

In the past, getting close to death had nearly always sent Gallagher into a state of paralysis; despite years of studying and filming other religions and culture, he had not found any clear evidence to refute his father's disbelief in God and an afterlife. The finality of death frightened him to his core.

But he sank into the wooden chair to gaze at this artifact of a vicious crime with something approaching awe. The man-creature rowing the boat—with his beak and animal ears, the snakes for hair and the sewn-up mouth—was somehow familiar, but distorted enough that he could not place its significance.

"Why are you so sure this is suggested by myth?"

"Because the killer says so," Nightingale replied, flipping the drawing over. "Don't touch."

Gallagher nodded uncertainly, understanding that she was still studying him. He turned up the gas on the light hanging from the ceiling. The glass in the etching of the Indian on the wall reflected the light so brilliantly that Gallagher had to turn the lamp back down again to see the writing clearly. His mouth ran dry at the words scrawled in the same black ink used to draw the creature rowing the boat:

In the myth, the river's waters are deep and blood-red. I have been the deaf, dumb and blind oarsman to the other side. I have felt your hatred, Lawton, since the day I was born. I have smelled and tasted your treachery. You stole what was ours. You damned me to take the gold coin. You damned me to feel the wooden bow slough against the muddy bank with the black poplars and never know the fields beyond. Lawton, I will be your navigator to hell. But only the oarsman shall return from the other side.

Outside, the wind became a growl. The door blew open and wet leaves billowed inside. Nightingale got her shoulder into the door and shut it while Gallagher read the note over and over. In the year since Emily left, Gallagher had felt clouded, lazy, uninterested. Now his brain felt heated as it considered the words and the pictures. The beak, the boat, the oarsman, the gold coin. He jumped on a connection.

"Charun," Gallagher said in a shocked voice.

Nightingale sat down in the chair opposite him. "Who?"

He spelled the name. "C-H-A-R-U-N. He surfaces in the underworld myths of several ancient societies. The Etruscans believed he was the male demon who escorted the dead to the afterworld.

"Charun had these features," Gallagher said, pointing to the beak, the pointed ears, the blind eyes and the sewn-up mouth. "But he did not row a boat. He carried a hammer or an ax, if I remember. The maritime element does not surface until the Greeks, when he becomes Charon—C-H-A-R-O-N."

"And who's he?" Nightingale asked in obvious puzzlement.

"The ferryman who rows the dead across the river Acheron, the river of sadness," Gallagher said, looking at the note again. "He has to be paid with a gold coin placed on the mouths of the dead. The far shore of the Acheron was supposedly thick with black poplars that the dead had to negotiate alone before they could reach the afterworld."

Nightingale shook her head, trying to absorb it all. He could almost see her thoughts churning: a killer was prowling central Vermont, a madman who saw himself as the embodiment of an ancient death myth. If Gallagher hadn't seen the body of Hank Potter, he could have laughed it off as some over-the-top effort in a Hollywood melodrama. But Gallagher had seen the body.

She grabbed the note and reread it. "Was something stolen from Charun in the myth?" she asked.

"Doesn't sound right. Charun's a minor figure in tales about greater gods," he replied. "I'd think you'd be more interested in who he was writing the letter to."

Gallagher stood up and came around to her side of the table so they both could see the note. Her clothes smelled as if she'd just brushed up against pine boughs.

Nightingale twisted in her seat and leaned away from him. "What do you mean?"

Gallagher pointed at the middle of the note. "He, the killer, is addressing a 'you' in the letter. He says, 'Lawton . . . You stole what was ours. You damned me . . . ' He describes 'your treachery' and 'your hatred.' He says, 'Lawton, I will be your navigator to hell.' "

"So this is revenge on the town for some wrong he believes was done to him."

"That and worse," Gallagher replied. "The note's written in the tone of an oracle, which in mythological terms is both a warning and a promise."

Nightingale stared down at the end of the note. Her shoulders shook with the enormity of it all. "You're saying he's going to kill again, aren't you?"

Chapter Seven

Two hours later Andie Nightingale paced in her kitchen between the table and the alcove that served as her winter greenhouse. On each trip she passed a red enamel woodstove mounted on a brick hearth, two overstuffed leather chairs, a shelf chockablock with cookbooks and gardening guides, as well as a country pine sideboard that she was in the process of refinishing.

On each trip she paused before the phone atop the sideboard and with her finger tapped the coffee cup cradled in her palms. Suddenly, on its own, the phone clanged. She startled and spilled coffee from the mug as she put it down. She reached for the phone with a shaking hand.

"Hello?"

"Andie, honey, is that you?" an elderly female responded. Her voice was as smooth and rich as hot chocolate.

"Yes, Olga," Nightingale said, smiling with relief. "It's me."

Olga Dawson was Nightingale's late mother's best friend, seventy-eight and slowed by three minor strokes in the past eighteen months. Olga lived where she had lived almost her entire life, on a farm at a dead-end spur off the River Road, six and a half miles beyond Nightingale's home.

"Someone's been around the house again," the old woman complained.

Nightingale held the phone in the crook of her neck, walked to the alcove where she kept her plants. She inspected the soil around her tomato seedlings, then began transplanting a fuchsia she'd managed to coax through the winter. "You think someone's there now?"

"A few hours ago, right at last light."

"Could I come tomorrow and see?"

"Oh, that would be so nice, dear," Olga replied. "You'll call ahead so I can have something ready for you?"

"I will," Nightingale promised.

"Maybe it was a bear in the yard, come looking for the new green grass," Olga said. She paused. "Do you remember the time when we went to the bear cave?"

"Now, how could I forget that?" Nightingale replied, laughing. "I was seven and you told me the cave up there on Lawton Mountain was the biggest bear cave in the world."

"Oh, dear, I forget lots of things." Olga sighed. "But some memories still burn bright."

"Of course they do," Nightingale reassured her. "Now, no smoking in bed. See you tomorrow around ten?"

"That would be wonderful. Good night, dear."

Still smiling thoughtfully, Nightingale rested the phone in its cradle. Olga had been crying wolf about seeing a stranger in her yard once a week now for the past five years; it was her way of telling Nightingale she was lonely. Thoughts of tea and Olga's homemade apple pie comforted Nightingale as she built a fire in the woodstove to ward off the chill that had accompanied the building storm. But when the fire crackled, she stood and looked at the phone again, sighed, picked it up and punched in a number.

"Brigid," Nightingale began almost before Lieutenant Bowman had said hello, "I need to stay on this case."

"Why wouldn't you be?" Bowman replied perfunctorily.

The lieutenant came from a longtime Vermont Yankee family from Plymouth and operated in a brusque style that bordered on rudeness. Bowman was not only a smart cop, but an agile and ambitious bureaucrat. At thirty-four, she had been named the first female detective in the history of the Vermont State Police. At forty-six, she had become the first woman lieutenant in the prestigious Bureau of Criminal Investigations. Rumor had it she was in line to become a captain.

Nightingale briefed her on the drawing, the note and Gallagher's explanation of the myth of Charun. After Bowman had her repeat it all twice, there was a protracted silence on the other end of the line. "Why didn't you call me immediately after you found the note and drawing?"

Nightingale twirled the gold stud in her left earlobe and said, "Because I wanted to show you I could use the evidence to move the investigation forward, which I did."

"By not calling in an evidence team and discussing the letter with a likely suspect?" Bowman cried. "Didn't you hear this Gallagher say he was an anthropologist, an expert in myths?"

"Of course," Nightingale retorted. "But I questioned him at length, and my instincts say he's not the one. I agree he's a confused New Yorker, but if that was the sole motivation for this killing, we'd have fifty thousand suspects in Vermont every weekend."

"He's our prime suspect," Bowman insisted.

"I haven't ruled him out," Nightingale allowed. "And I sealed off the Potter house and had his wife and children move to her sister's until after the evidence team is done. They'll be there first thing in the morning."

Silence; then Bowman asked, "How are you feeling?"

"Fine."

"You're sure?"

"Brigid, it's been two years." Nightingale twisted the telephone extension cord into knots.

"I know, but not calling in something like that note—"

"I need you to believe I can handle this . . . like you used to."

There was a third long silence between them; then Bowman said, "We'll take it day by day."

"Thank you, Brigid."

"I want your report on my desk first thing tomorrow," Bowman said. "I want that drawing and that hunting locker gone over for prints and then photographed, and a copy of the whole file sent to the FBI. Clear?"

"Yes."

"The press is swamping us with calls," Bowman informed her. "I hope your Mr. Gallagher doesn't go blabbing about the note. That's how hysteria starts."

"I asked him not to talk with anyone about the note or the body," Nightingale said. "I'd like your permission to keep talking to him. He seems to have insight into the killer's mind."

"Maybe because he's the killer," Bowman said. "I want to be there the next time you talk to Mr. Gallagher."

"Fine," Nightingale promised. "And, Brigid?"

"Yes?"

"Thank you for this chance. I'll see you at the autopsy first thing Monday morning."

Nightingale hung up the phone. She threw her fists up in the air, shook them and did a little victory dance. Almost instantly her elation ebbed. Her palms sweated. Her tongue thickened. Her attention came to rest on the fushcia, which she went back to quickly. She finished repotting the plant, then sat at her computer and tried to write the report, but an edgy energy got the better of her.

Cook dinner, she told herself. She turned on a boom-box CD player to Sade and heard the singer's smoky voice fill the room. Nightingale sang along for a minute before her voice trailed off.

She focused on her breathing as she filled a four-quart pot with water and set it on the six-burner stove. From a drawer next to the stove she got out a two-quart pan and put it on a second burner. She poured spaghetti sauce from a Tupperware container she'd laid out to defrost much earlier in the day, then tugged open a cabinet door above the counter to find some garlic powder for garlic bread, since there were no fresh cloves.

Nightingale moved aside vanilla, soy sauce and Worcestershire sauce, looking for the correct canister. Her hand reached deeper into the cabinet, pulling down colored sprinkles for cakes and a can of baking powder. She halted, transfixed at the sight of a long-forgotten bottle of cooking sherry.

She stood there for almost five minutes, blinking the way Paula Potter had blinked when she had learned of her husband's murder. Her breath came shallow and staccato before she noticed the garlic powder next to the sherry. She grabbed it, slammed shut the cabinet door and spun in her tracks to face the room.

"I'm going to be all right," she said out loud in a wavering voice.

But in the rain-streaked glass of the bay window across the kitchen, she caught her reflection. Nightingale's skin was colorless. Her hands shook with fear.

Chapter Eight

MONDAY, MAY 11, 1998

The rain finally petered after midnight. The wind stilled, the river settled and the sky turned the shattering blue of a freak, late-season Alberta high-pressure system. By 7:30 A.M., the temperature hovered in the high thirties.

But inside the state medical examiner's office in Burlington, Chief Mike Kerris was not grousing about the weather. "I want to know why I wasn't told about this letter thirty-six hours ago."

Lieutenant Bowman, Andie Nightingale and Mel Allen, the state's assistant medical examiner, sat around a simple conference table. Kerris stood. His gray Lawton sweatshirt looked slept in. His stainless-steel eyes were bloodshot and watery. He had guzzled coffee nonstop during the entire autopsy, which had just concluded.

"We wanted to make sure the finger paint was Potter's blood so you didn't get upset without reason," Lieutenant Bowman said. She wore a suit of the palest yellow. "Now we've confirmed it and told you."

Beyond a match of Potter's blood type with that on the

note and the bridge, the state's medical examiner had found little of import during the course of the autopsy.

A careful examination of the wounds about the dentist's head and upper back had given no distinct picture of the type of weapon they were looking for. This much was clear, however: given Potter's height and physical stature, as well as the angle and penetration of the blows, the killer stood over six feet tall and was extremely powerful. He had struck from behind, possibly during or after the rape. Allen felt that despite the dilution of evidence caused by the body's dunking in the river, he had gathered enough seminal fluid for DNA matches should a prime suspect emerge.

At the same time, the evidence technicians had found no strange fingerprints inside Potter's hunting locker, on or in the ammunition cabinet or on the bridge. The blood had been painted on the illustration with a gloved finger. The drawing ink and the sketch paper were of the highest quality, but the sort available in any reputable arts-supply store.

Nightingale had sent her report to the FBI's Behavioral Science Unit at Quantico, Virginia, but the profilers were carrying a heavy caseload already. A psychological description of the killer was at least a week or two away. The only other strong physical evidence the crime technicians had discovered was the faint outline of size-thirteen boot tracks in the dirt under the eaves of Potter's chicken coop.

"Let's not bicker here," Allen said. He had licked his finger and was trying to plaster down a wayward eyebrow bristle. "Focus on the evidence. He's a big man. Big as you, Mike."

"I don't give a damn about his shoes," Kerris grumbled. He slid his sweatshirt up his sinewy forearms before crossing them. "I'm being cut out of the investigation of the most brutal murder in Lawton's history." The chief snapped his fingers and tossed his chin in Nightingale's direction. "Now I get it. You're trying to do this yourself so people forget—"

Bowman cut him off. "That has nothing to do with it, Chief."

"Bullshit," Kerris replied. "And let me tell you something: Mayor Powell's gonna be pissed when he finds out about this drawing. He's in the middle of delicate negotiations and he needs to stay on top of this."

Nightingale snorted. "Mike, it doesn't matter to me whether some developer from New Jersey who's looking to build a hundred-million-dollar hotel on the mountain continues to think Lawton is a perfect Vermont community. It isn't. Never has been. And you'd know better than most, wouldn't you?"

The look Kerris shot Nightingale could have killed.

Chapter Nine

Two hours later Patrick Gallagher refolded the *Rutland Herald* and pushed back his plate at the Miss Lawton Diner, a restored club-car hash joint downtown between the Hard Cider Gifts building and a Ralph Lauren outlet. The booths and the red swivel counter seats were filled with locals: dairy delivery men sat beside lawyers who brushed shoulders with crunchy-granola environmental activists who nodded to country-music singers and bleary-eyed turkey hunters. All of them were either talking in hushed, concerned tones about the murder or reading the coverage in the paper.

The *Herald*'s front page carried a twenty-inch follow-up to Sunday's story and a piece about the ecological ramifications of the proposed massive hotel-and-condominium development to be built at the base of the small ski area up on Lawton Mountain. Gallagher read the latter article until Mayor Powell was quoted spouting a platitude about the development taking Lawton into the twenty-first century.

The follow-up to the Potter killing was much more interesting and he went over it a second time. The story described the state police evidence team descending on the dentist's home and property. The article went on to identify a bridge over the Bluekill as the likely site of the killing but made no mention of the note or the drawing Gallagher had seen two nights before.

Lieutenant Bowman, not Nightingale, had fielded questions about the case. Both she and Chief Kerris had made statements on Sunday about state and local agencies cooperating fully in the investigation. By the second day of the story Gallagher had become an afterthought, referred to as "a vacationing New York City angler who had discovered Potter's body in the Bluekill."

Gallagher had refused to talk with the young reporter who'd called Sunday afternoon. He knew if he leaked the secret of the note, the police would leave him out of the loop. Ever since he'd seen the drawing, he'd been obsessing about the case. The tenor of his questions had shifted from the philosophical to the practical. Had Hank Potter known his killer? From the tone of the note, revenge did seem part of the killer's motivation. Revenge on the dentist? Or revenge on Lawton? Or both?

For Gallagher, thinking about the murder was like finally awakening after a long humid sleep in the hot summer sun. He had always been energized by the exploration of new customs and mores. A murder investigation struck Gallagher as a perfect culture in which to nose around. And, he had to admit, a perfect way to avoid nosing around inside himself.

There was also Andie Nightingale. She had been on his mind as often as the details of the murder probe, a fact that he was trying to cast in a positive light. Since Emily left, Gallagher had had little interest in female companionship of any kind. Several times on Sunday, however, he had tried to call Nightingale, as much to hear her voice as to inquire about the course of the investigation. But there was no answer at her house and the dispatcher at the Bethel Barracks of the Vermont State Police said she was in the field.

Gallagher had considered calling Jerry Matthews to try to convince him that a documentary about the effects of homicide on a small New England town was infinitely more interesting than one on an early-twentieth-century priest and the Catholic rites of sainthood.

But he decided not to push his luck. Gallagher had abandoned work on three projects already in the past year in favor of extended fly-fishing expeditions. Announcing that he was quitting the research on Father D'Angelo would likely send Jerry packing and their partnership into bankruptcy and oblivion.

So Gallagher came up with an alternate plan. He would research both.

Gallagher drained his coffee cup, paid the waitress, then exited the diner onto Lawton's Main Street. As he prepared to enter the crosswalk toward the village green, Chief Mike Kerris' dark blue Chevy Suburban pulled up and blocked his path. Deputy Gavrilis sat in the passenger seat, his straight-cut bangs making it appear as if a bowl had been the template for his haircut. Kerris sucked his lollipop and pressed his sunglasses back up the bridge of his nose as the electric window rolled down.

"Still around, Mr. Gallagher?" Kerris said in a mocking tone. "I figured finding a body in the Bluekill might have spoiled your taste for the local fishing holes."

"I'm not here just to fish," Gallagher said. "Like I said the other day, I'm researching a film on Father D'Angelo."

"That is what you said, isn't it?" Kerris replied. Then he folded his right hand into a gun shape and pointed the barrel at Gallagher. "I saw that note, Pat," Kerris said. "I'm watching you. Everyone who counts in Lawton is watching you."

The tires screeched as he pulled away. Five years before Gallagher spent a great deal of time in Tokyo putting together a film on the intertwining of the martial arts, religion and Japanese culture. Most of his time was spent in an aikido dojo. The sensei there taught a particularly vicious joint-lock technique called *kote gaeshi,* the purpose of which was to bend your attacker's wrist until he either submitted or experienced the spiral snapping of three bones in the lower arm and hand.

Right then Gallagher had the overwhelming desire to perform the move on Chief Kerris.

It was nearly ten o'clock by the time Gallagher crossed the green and walked three blocks east to where Newton Street met Whelton Lane. St. Edward's Catholic Church was a white clapboard affair with a single steeple rising amid hundred-year-old maples whose branches were tinged with the first red buds of spring. The adjoining rectory was stone-faced and in desperate need of repointing. There was a high brick wall around a garden to the rear. Rising above the walls, like a constant shadow on the town, was Lawton Mountain. Up there the trees stood bare and pewter-colored, offering no hope yet that they might soon embrace spring.

He opened the iron gate, mounted the front porch and knocked. Being the pushy type, Gallagher did not wait for a response, but twisted the doorknob and entered immediately. The rectory's interior was all dark wood and rich red Oriental carpets. The walls of the narrow hallway off the foyer were flush with paintings and photographs of the various priests who had served Lawton's Catholic community.

One in particular cried out for attention—an oil portrait of a cranelike priest with a pained expression plastered across his lips. He was bald but for a fringe of white hair around his pate. He stood with his hands clasped around a Bible in a garden containing an ornate birdbath in the center of which were three small stone horses.

Just then a woman poked her head out of a room to Gallagher's right.

"I thought I heard a knock, but I was chitchatting on the phone," bubbled Libby Curtin, the parish secretary. She was in her mid-twenties with a chestnut braid that reached her waist. A simple wooden cross dangled from her neck over a maroon tunic whose neckline was embroidered with daisies. She wore granny-style glasses, baggy, blue drawstring pants and Birkenstock sandals with rag wool socks.

"You're the moviemaker, aren't you?" she said. "You're going to do a film on Father D'Angelo?"

"Something like that."

"The Lord be praised!" she cried, clapping her hands and bending over at the waist, all the while beaming. Then she glanced up at the painting and her voice dropped to a whisper. "Isn't it the pits about Father D'Angelo?"

"The pits?"

She gestured at a hole in the painting the size of a tea bag on the priest's left hip.

"We had a burglar back a couple of months and he knocked the portrait off the hook," she explained in a low, conspiratorial voice that made Gallagher want to smile. "Monsignor McColl went totally ape, let me tell you. A burglar in the rectory! Monsignor McColl has his bouts of irritation, but I've never seen him so ticked."

"I can imagine."

"I'll tell him you're here."

Libby Curtin hurried down the hall toward an imposing set of carved double doors, knocked, then disappeared inside. Gallagher looked up at the painting, half wondering whether D'Angelo's story would be compelling enough to serve as one of the narrative vehicles of an hour-long documentary. The other part of him wondered whether D'Angelo's story would be compelling enough to make him stop thinking about Potter,

Nightingale and a killer who thought of himself as Charun. Gallagher took a notebook from the pocket of his oilskin jacket and grudgingly made a note that with the right lighting, the painting, even damaged, would make a dramatic image on film.

The carved doors opened. Libby Curtin poked her head out and waved him in.

Gallagher sidled through the door into the room and stopped short. Monsignor Timothy McColl dwarfed the heavy oak desk he stood behind. He was a grizzly bear of a man in his late forties, six feet six inches tall, with a broom of mahogany hair, a close-cropped salt-and-pepper beard and a florid bull neck that threatened to pop his clerical collar. He wore his black sleeves rolled to the elbows to reveal the kind of forearms and hands you'd expect of an aging stonemason, not a priest.

Monsignor McColl's massive paw literally swallowed Gallagher's. He squeezed just enough to let Gallagher know that his physical power was real, then released and sank back into his tufted swivel chair. The priest grimaced as he gestured Gallagher toward a Gothic-style seat in front of the desk. He rubbed his belly sourly. "Excuse me a second, will you?" he asked. "My stomach's been acting up lately."

Monsignor McColl went into a small bathroom and shut the door.

Gallagher took a quick inventory of the artifacts in the office for clues to the priest's personality. Behind the desk were several wooden file cabinets and the obligatory crucifix. Off to the right hung three photographs. In one, the monsignor stood emotionless before a whitewashed church amid palm trees surrounded by somber children in white uniforms. In an older, black-and-white photograph, a much younger McColl stood in the snow with a group of equally solemn young boys in front of an aging brick building. One of the boys, a gangly tow-headed kid with a remote expression on his face, strangely reminded Gallagher of himself as a child. In the third photograph, McColl sat atop a mountain peak wearing glacier sunglasses and a backpack laden down with ropes and climbing equipment. Beside the photographs, mounted on wooden pegs were several brightly painted baskets, a bolo knife in a sheath decorated with ornate and brightly colored beadwork, and a necklace made of bleached shells. The office was bathed in soft light from a leaded-glass window overlooking the garden. A hermit thrush splashed in a birdbath at the center of which stood three tiny stone horses. The same birdbath depicted in the damaged painting in the hallway.

"Sorry to make you wait," Monsignor McColl rumbled as he emerged from the bathroom. "So, Mr. Gallagher, are you Catholic or lapsed?"

"Neither," he replied. "I'm an atheist."

The priest's right eyebrow arched. "I thought Mrs. Curtin said you were interested in Father D'Angelo."

"I am."

"Why would an atheist be interested in a priest?"

Gallagher explained his background and gave McColl examples of his other film projects.

"You make films about religion and yet you're not a believer?" Monsignor McColl said.

Gallagher dodged that question by telling him how Jerry Matthews and he had become interested in Father D'Angelo and the process of canonization during a trip to China two years ago, when they had learned about the recent elevation to sainthood of a priest who'd been a missionary there in the 1840s.

"John Gabriel Perboyre," the priest grunted in recognition. "Tortured, hung off a beam and strangled by the emperor's soldiers during a persecution. I spent eight years as a missionary myself. Yucatán Peninsula. All missionaries know about Father Perboyre."

Gallagher nodded, then explained his wish to use Perboyre's story and others to explain the Catholic tradition of sainthood to a lay audience. Jerry had found a brief mention of Father D'Angelo in a Catholic News Service story about canonization. Gallagher had decided to come to Lawton to fly-fish and do the basic research for the film.

Monsignor McColl came up alert when he mentioned he was in Lawton to fly-fish. "Are you the one who found Hank Potter?"

"Yes."

"I'll say his funeral mass Wednesday morning," the priest said. He toyed with his beard and watched Gallagher. "What are the police telling you?"

"Not much," Gallagher lied. "I was just a guy in the wrong place at the wrong time."

The monsignor drummed his fingers on the desktop and stared off at the birdbath in the garden for several moments. He cleared his throat. "As far as a film about Father D'Angelo is concerned, come back in twenty years. Takes a long time to make a saint."

Gallagher shifted in his seat, realizing he was in for a fight. "I don't have twenty years and besides, we are interested in Father D'Angelo precisely because his cause is in the early stages of consideration."

"I'm sure there are others who would better fit your needs," McColl said.

"I get the feeling you don't hold much hope for his cause."

Tiny blue lines popped out along the priest's temples and he gave Gallagher a stiff look. "I've made it my life's work to see that Father D'Angelo becomes a saint and I won't have a damned atheist poking—"

"Whoa, whoa, whoa," Gallagher interrupted. "My personal beliefs or lack of them is beside the point."

"Are they, now?"

"I'm objective and fair when I portray a subject. I can give you references."

McColl made a popping sound with his lips, then shook his head. "It's too early for an outsider to be rooting around, damaging Father's cause."

"Something you know that I shouldn't?"

McColl's already ruddy face turned beet-red. "Absolutely not! It's just that promoting a case for sainthood is a delicate effort. I won't botch it for the sake of yellow journalism."

"Yellow journalism!" Gallagher yelled before realizing the interview was out of control. He took a moment to calm himself, then spoke lower and slower. "Look, Monsignor McColl, as I understand it, politics play a big part in the canonization process. If you're so sure of Father D'Angelo's worthiness, I only see an upside to making his case alongside established saints such as Father Perboyre."

McColl did not reply. He was watching his monstrous hand flex and twist around some unseen object. Gallagher went for broke. "You know, I'm good at this kind of thing. I'll get the story one way or another. I always do. But I'd much rather work with you. You know the man already. You can point me in the right direction."

The priest swiveled in the chair, pressing the pads of his thick fingers together and looking out the garden window. He stayed that way for almost a minute, with his lips flapping, making those gentle popping noises. Gallagher was about to get up to leave when McColl rumbled, "If I get the sense you're not serving Father D'Angelo's cause, I'll withdraw my help. Understand?"

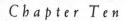

Chapter Ten

At the same time, in an aging yellow farmhouse at the bottom of the south flank of Lawton Mountain, Olga Dawson's little body heaved with sobs.

Nightingale held the old woman tight to her chest. She rubbed the back of her blue cardigan and hushed her as she might a child. Until at last Olga's cries slowed and stopped. Nightingale gazed down at the frightened woman in her arms. Her throat constricted.

Olga Dawson had once been blessed with the ebony eyes, porcelain skin and ruby lips that haunt old black-and-white films. Nightingale's late mother, Grace, always said Olga's face was that of a star's.

Now Olga was seventy-eight and still strong enough to feed a woodstove all winter. But lines like the filigreed branch of the red oak outside her kitchen window etched her mottled skin. Her cheeks twitched, a constant reminder of the strokes she'd suffered the past year and a half.

"I'm sorry, dear," Olga said, sitting up on the couch and

daubing at her eyes with a handkerchief. "I don't know what came over me."

A white Himalayan cat strode into the room. Olga reached absently for it. The cat hissed and arched its back. The old woman jerked backward and scolded. "Tess, you bad, bad girl!"

Nightingale made a clucking noise with her tongue. The cat curled on itself, leaped into her lap and purred contentedly. The onerous stray had shown up at Olga's door two years ago. Tess barely tolerated Olga, but loved Nightingale.

Olga complained: "I wanted to get milk for the little fuss-budget this morning, but I kept coming out of the refrigerator with the juice. I knew what I was doing, but I couldn't get my hands to follow what my brain wanted!"

Her eyes watered. "I'm becoming a burden to you, Andie! It's not right for a young woman to be taking care of an old crone like me. You should be out with a handsome young man."

Nightingale tensed for a moment, then said, "I'm ruined for handsome young men, I'm afraid."

"You can't let the past influence the present," Olga told her.

"It's impossible not to," Nightingale said wistfully before putting the cat down and turning Olga around. She picked up a mother-of-pearl brush and began to work on Olga's long silver hair. "And you're no burden and you're no crone. You're the closest I have to family now. Think of where you were a year ago."

"I was in the hospital a year ago," the old woman said sullenly.

"And look how far you've come. If you continue therapy, you'll only get better."

The old woman pounced on that thread of hope. "Will I?"

"Of course," Nightingale said, finishing the braid.

Olga was silent, then jumped up. "I almost forgot. I baked you a pie."

Over the years, Olga had won a half-dozen blue ribbons

for her pies at the state fair. But Nightingale had a report to write on Hank Potter's early-morning autopsy and the meeting afterward. "Honey, I don't have time."

"Nonsense. You'll have some pie. And some Earl Grey tea." With that the old woman bustled out of the living room toward the kitchen. Nightingale got up and followed her, frowning. Olga was getting worse with every visit, more forgetful, more unsure of herself. Even the oft-told stories of her childhood with Nightingale's mother were beginning to come out twisted. The speech pathologist whom Nightingale took Olga to see once a week said the strokes had caused a mild form of dementia. Nightingale took a chair at the kitchen table and watched the old woman for other signs of deterioration.

Olga deftly cut a slice of apple pie and put it on a plate with a scoop of vanilla ice cream. She placed the plate and a cup of steaming tea in front of Nightingale. After loading another log in the woodstove, she crossed to the kitchen window and peered out past the oak toward the old dairy barn. Daffodil shoots peeked through the sprouting grass along a path that led through towering lavender bushes just showing buds.

"Craziest spring I ever saw, and I've seen a lot of Vermont springs," Olga said. "Do you think the bears have left their dens?"

"Probably a month or more now," Nightingale replied. She was not surprised by the question. The old woman had always been keenly interested in bears.

Olga touched her chin. A simple enough act, but the old woman made it a gesture of confusion. "Indians thought bears were sacred animals," she said. "Did you know that?"

"I think I read that somewhere," Nightingale replied, paying only half attention. She focused on the taste of the pie, puzzled. The crust was vintage Olga, but the old woman had neglected to add nutmeg, cinnamon or sugar.

"Olga, I'm going to arrange for you to see the speech therapist tomorrow morning."

Olga turned and brought her head close to a calendar hanging above the sink. "But my appointment's not till Thursday."

"I know. Still I'd like her to talk to you . . . about the
forgetfulness."

Olga nodded glumly. "If you say so, dear."

Nightingale managed to force down the last of the pie by
smothering it in the ice cream, then announced, "I've got to
go now. You'll be all right?"

"It will take more than a cold snap to do this old bird in!"
Olga responded brightly. But in the next instant her expression
fell. She wrung her hands while Nightingale donned a down
vest and a green rain jacket and reached for her pocketbook.
Olga rushed over and grabbed both her wrists with unexpected
vigor. The tic in the old woman's cheek bulged and relaxed
nonstop. Her hands were surprisingly strong.

"Secrets are hard things to keep," Olga said haltingly and
with great effort. She paused as if trying to decide where that
thought had come from, then added, "Sometimes keeping secrets is the bravest thing we can do."

Olga's focus became unscrewed. "I think bears would keep
their secrets in caves, don't you?"

The light through the kitchen window cast shadows across
the old woman's face.

"You're right," Nightingale said. "A cave is where bears
would hide secrets. But right now, dear, I've got to go back
to work."

Olga's grip grew tighter. "I wanted. . . . I wanted to tell
you something, but I can't. . . . remember . . ."

"It's going to have to wait until tomorrow." Nightingale,
gently pried herself free of Olga's grip. "I'll be here at eleven
to take you to therapy."

The old woman looked as if she might begin crying again,

but kept control. "Come early," she pleaded. "That bear's been around the house again and I know I have something to tell you, something to give you. I'll . . . I'll remember by then."

"I know you will," Nightingale soothed. "I'll call the speech pathologist to reschedule as soon as I get to the office. No smoking in bed, you hear?"

Olga's confused expression turned to a lucid smile. "No, dear, only in my rocker with my ashtray on my lap."

Nightingale pecked her on the cheek and went out the door. The engine to her pickup whined long and hard. The truck had more than one hundred and fifty thousand miles on it. Her mechanic had warned her the starting motor was going, but she hadn't had time to have it fixed. Finally the engine caught and she shifted the vehicle into reverse. As Nightingale passed the door to the kitchen, she slowed and waved at the old woman, who was waving back as if she were a little girl waving to the bears in a circus parade.

Chapter Eleven

The tombstone was a rose marble oblong set flush with the surface of a grass knoll in the far northeast corner of the walled garden behind St. Edward's rectory.

FATHER VICTOR D'ANGELO, MARCH 18, 1859—NOVEMBER 30, 1918
MAY GOD HAVE MERCY ON YOUR SERVANT'S IMMORTAL SOUL

Gallagher broke a sweat just standing there looking at the grave and tried to diffuse his anxiety by making a snide comment: "Not much confidence in sainthood there."

"It's a fairly typical epigraph for the time," Monsignor McColl retorted. "Certainly not something that Rome would take into consideration."

The priest shivered, then zipped his windbreaker up around his bull neck. They walked back toward the rectory down a red clay path bordered by six-foot brick walls and mature spruces.

"What will they take into consideration?" Gallagher asked.

"What I need right now are the high points of Father D'Angelo's story. We can get the details later on camera."

Monsignor McColl stopped in front of a tulip tree, legs spread, hands behind his back as a drill sergeant might stand addressing a recruit. The buds on the tulip tree had been ready to flower before the cold, rainy snap. The lips of the brown cones were split at the tips, showing hangnails of red, suspended between winter and spring.

"Father D'Angelo was born in Calabria, Italy, in 1859, the second son of a master stonecutter and devout Catholic, who immigrated to the United States when Victor was five," Monsignor McColl began. "His father worked in the marble quarries over in Proctor, Vermont. And we know from the little writings left from that period that he urged the boy to pursue a life of God. Victor entered the seminary at age seventeen and was ordained at twenty-four.

"He served parishes in Bellows Falls and Arlington before moving north to Lawton in 1891," the priest went on. "According to letters he sent his parents, the town and the parish suited him. He remained here until his death in 1918. He saw the good and the dark times here."

"Dark times?"

"Lawton was a thriving community when Father D'Angelo arrived," Monsignor McColl replied, moving one shoulder in the direction of town. "There were textile mills along the river. A railroad spur helped the factories move their goods south. There was a thriving farming community outside town, too. But shortly after the turn of the century, Lawton's economy collapsed. The mills shut. The railroad decided the spur wasn't worth the upkeep. It was a pretty squalid place when I grew up here. Of course, that's all changed with the revival Mayor Powell has so masterfully led.

"Anyway, despite the financial setbacks, Father D'Angelo made St. Edward's a vibrant parish," the priest continued in his booming taskmaster's voice. "He organized charities for the poor, built the Catholic school in 1897 and the church itself in 1906. All admirable efforts in and of themselves . . ."

"But not exactly the stuff of saints."

"No," Monsignor McColl agreed. He turned and began to walk down the path toward the rectory again. "But that all changed in 1909. The record shows he became increasingly charismatic in the Christian sense. He spoke in tongues. Which, in all honesty, raised quite a few eyebrows in the bishop's office in Burlington. But he survived two inquiries."

"Inquiries into what?" Gallagher stopped within a few feet of the birdbath, studying the little carved horses.

"Inquiries into his laying on of hands," the priest said. His paw closed around Gallagher's elbow and guided him away, toward the rectory. "Some people thought he was insane. But throughout time, man has not understood that the mystical experience and the crack-up are very close experiences. The man who cracks up is drowning in the water in which the mystic swims."

"He was a faith healer? A Catholic faith healer?" Gallagher asked.

Monsignor McColl nodded. "There are unsubstantiated stories, going back as far as 1908, of Father D'Angelo praying over the dying in silent invocation and having them revive. But it wasn't until the Spanish influenza epidemic of 1917 and 1918 that we find actual witnesses to the miracles. By my reckoning, he saved fourteen."

"You've got eyewitnesses to miracles?" Gallagher said incredulously.

"Seven," the priest said. "One of them was my own father. He saw his sister, Anna, saved."

His face seemed a sunrise at the memory. "Saving my aunt Anna was Father D'Angelo's last act on this earth. He died in my father's arms. That story made me want to be a priest like

Father D'Angelo. Indeed, the more I learn about him, and I've learned quite a lot in the last year or so, the more I become convinced that Father D'Angelo was a conduit of God's supernatural gifts."

"Is that the definition of a saint, that they exhibit supernatural powers?"

"Miracles are evidence of it," Monsignor McColl said. He was looking back in the direction of D'Angelo's gravestone now with a rapturous expression.

"How does one become a saint?" Gallagher asked, already knowing the answer from the information Jerry had dug up, but wanting to hear the priest's explanation.

The priest sketched in broad strokes the steps D'Angelo's cause would take. First Monsignor McColl would have to finish preparing the case file and then forward the materials to the local bishop for approval. After a cursory review in the bishop's office, the case file would be sent to the Vatican, where it would receive meticulous scrutiny from the office of the Devil's Advocate and the Congregation of Saints. Once Rome accepted and approved the documents, D'Angelo would be considered "venerable."

"Beatification follows veneration," Monsignor McColl went on. "To be deemed among the 'blessed,' the Congregation more intensely examines the life, virtues, reputation for holiness, ministry and writings of the person. Proof of a single miracle is required for beatification, usually a physical healing that is scientifically inexplicable, indicating that natural laws have been lifted through the intercession of the person considered for sainthood. To advance the person's cause beyond the blessed to sainthood, a second miracle is usually required, but not necessary.

"The entire process can take a hundred years or more," he concluded.

"And what exactly does sainthood mean to the church?"

Gallagher asked, scribbling as much of this down as he could in a reporter's notebook.

"Upon canonization, the Pope declares, among other things, that the person is in heaven with Jesus. That means the saint can be prayed to and his relics honored."

"Relics?" Gallagher said, scratching at his brow with the butt of the pen. "You mean like bones?"

"Yes, like bones," Monsignor McColl said. There was a vague strain now in his voice. "The relics are usually moved to a place of distinction below an altar at a church bearing the saint's name. It is my fervent wish that someday his relics would be moved to a new church named after Saint D'Angelo of Lawton."

The church bell bonged the half hour. The priest said brusquely, "I'll have to go now. I have midday mass to say."

"No problem," Gallagher replied. "How can I get in touch with the witnesses to the miracles?"

The priest's face clouded. "You can't," he said. "My father was the last. He died two years ago."

"But you must have written accounts of what they saw and pictures of them I might be able to use."

Monsignor McColl's expression hardened further. "I have notes, but I have not yet composed the narratives. Those won't be ready for a year at least. I told you, sainthood is a long, long process."

"Can I look at your notes and the interview transcripts?"

"No!" he fumed. "Absolutely not, not without the permission of the bishop."

"I thought we had a deal you'd help me as long as I was assisting the cause."

"I didn't realize what you were interested in looking at," the priest replied icily. "I'm still gathering the preliminary materials that have to be sent to Rome. What I have is unorganized. You going through the documents . . . would be premature."

"But I could ask the bishop for his permission?"

Monsignor McColl seemed to fight for control of his voice. "You could, but I'll recommend he not grant it. My opinion on the subject carries a lot of weight."

"I'll ask anyway, then get back to you," Gallagher said blithely before reaching out to shake the priest's hand. A moment of unmasked anger flashed through McColl. He turned and stomped away through the garden.

Chapter Twelve

The afternoon and evening after Gallagher's strange interview with Monsignor McColl passed uneventfully. The bishop's office had said they would side with the Lawton priest about access to the files on Father D'Angelo.

Frustrated, Gallagher fished the evening rise downstream of the cabin because he could not imagine again entering the pool where he'd pulled Hank Potter to the surface. The cold air hanging over the central Green Mountains was preventing the insects from hatching and he had to be content to use nymph patterns rather than dry fly.

After dark Gallagher had stumbled to bed without dinner and dreamed of Emily Beckworth.

They became lovers on the fourteenth day of their journey through the jungles of India. They had traveled by boat, bus and train far into the interior and were heading north of Dinàjpur, looking for an ancient Hindu Tantric temple ruin Emily had heard rumors of but had not been able to find while researching her book.

There were eight in the film crew, including Emily and Gallagher. And after six days of fruitless searching they were ready to give up and head back toward the Ganges. Jerry had already left to search for new locations. The remaining crew slept in thatched-roofed huts at the edge of the jungle. One hot, muggy night Gallagher suffered insomnia and rose an hour before dawn to walk toward the forest. There was a small stream exiting the jungle and he had sat on its banks listening to monkeys bark in the distance.

"Praying it somehow holds trout?"

Gallagher jumped about three feet in the air. "You must be some kind of predator."

"Me?" Emily asked, taking a step closer. She adjusted the thin purple batik cloth she had wrapped as a nightgown around her full, remarkable body. "Why?"

"Because you have the uncanny ability to get close to me before I know it's happening," he said.

"Soft soles," she said, smiling and holding out a tapered calf and bare foot. Her toenails had been dyed with henna. "Yesterday I found a nice hole upriver that probably holds fish. Come on. I'll show you."

They walked along the river in the gathering light, talking about the project. Emily was convinced that if they stayed in the area another day or two they might find the temple. But Gallagher argued for moving on and filling in that section of the film with another ruin two hundred kilometers to the east.

The riverbank soil was black and fetid. Pungent flowered vines hung in twists over the trail like a rastaman's braid. Gallagher had to help Emily over the tangled roots of silver-barked trees and through dense stands of bamboo.

"Where's the fishing hole?" he asked after they'd walked nearly half an hour.

She gestured ahead through a swath of green bathed in

dawn light. He eased through the curtain and froze. The pool was still and beautiful. Insects hatched and rose in the thick air. Fish slapped the water, feeding. But on the bank on the far side of the river a tiger crouched. He panted. His Asiatic eyes were yellow half-moons, rolled up halfway into the head. He watched a young wild pig watering at the hole.

Emily came up behind Gallagher, blind to the hunter. He reached back and placed his hand flat on her lower tummy to stop her. She pressed into his hand. The tiger sprang.

Gallagher spun and hissed, "Tiger! Run!"

There was a splash, then the pig squealed and shrieked as they sprinted back down the trail. Emily tripped, staggered and fell. He got her up under the armpit and they tore ahead into the maze of paths that jutted off the riverbank. They made a wrong turn almost immediately. Five hundred yards later they stood in the jungle silence before the vague outline of a small stone building strangled in yellow jungle flowers. The air was saturated with their perfume. Monkeys chattered in the trees.

"We found it!" Emily cried. "The temple!"

She grabbed Gallagher and tugged him toward the entrance. The stairs were built of pitted, igneous rock. They had to tear away the vines, then duck to get inside. A monkey scrambled between their legs, scaring the hell out of them. Gallagher shone a flashlight. On the walls were carvings and chipped paintings of men and women joined in intercourse.

"The Tantrists believe that it is possible to discover the divine within ourselves through sexual union," Emily whispered.

Perhaps it was the fear of the tiger replaced so suddenly by the excitement of discovering the temple with its explicit art, but Gallagher was suddenly more aware of her than he had ever been with a woman. Emily was staring at him. A wave of pressurized, buzzing warmth enveloped his head. The soft glow of day came through the temple entrance and bathed Emily's damp skin in a copper light. They moved toward each other. The blue cloth around her fell away.

Somewhere far off in the jungle, Gallagher heard the tiger roar at the beat of distant drums.

Chapter Thirteen

The drums grew louder, closer and more insistent, and Gallagher awoke and realized it was midmorning and someone was pounding on the door to the cabin. He got up bleary-eyed and stumbled down the stairs, peeked out the curtains, and found it was pouring again. His Explorer was the only vehicle parked under the birch trees.

Gallagher opened the door and found Andie Nightingale sopping wet, wiping tears from her eyes. "My truck's broke again," she sobbed. "I need a ride. Now."

The pelting rain and the patchy fog on the River Road switchbacking up the south flank of Lawton Mountain created the claustrophobic illusion of a slick pearl tunnel corkscrewing into the blind sky. The truck fishtailed wildly in the two inches of mud the storm had whipped onto the surface of the road.

"Can't you go any faster?" Nightingale demanded.

"Not without killing us," Gallagher yelled back, clawing at the wheel for control.

His head pounded with the speed and severity of the morning's events. There had been a fire. Olga Dawson was dead.

Nightingale yelled at herself as if she could not believe it. "When I left yesterday, she was alive and fine, but not thinking straight. I should have stayed. I should have stayed with her!"

Then she fell silent again and searched the fog for familiar shapes. She hiccuped. Gallagher wanted desperately to soothe her, but the words would not come. At his mother's grave and the day Emily left were the two times Gallagher had endured what he could see enveloping the detective.

Gallagher's mother's fifty-seven-month Bloody Mary binge began the day after they buried Seamus. He had lost himself in books to avoid watching her destruction. The only way Gallagher could tolerate Agnes' presence was to erect mental glass walls that encased him, made him like an audience watching a tragedy unfold in a film.

Agnes received fewer and fewer acceptance checks for her writing. For a brief time she worked at night fund-raising for the ACLU, then lost that position for drunkenness on the job. Her friends and Gallagher begged her to seek help. She refused. "Vodka is my only love now," she yelled. "You can't take that away from me."

The summer Gallagher left for Cornell, his mother went on welfare and barely held onto the apartment. He rarely went home during vacations, preferring the life he was inventing for himself outside the horrors of 2120 Clinton Street.

One Easter break, in the spring of his junior year, Gallagher was in a sporting goods store in downtown Ithaca when he spotted Isabel Martin buying a reel for a fly rod. He had attended a lecture Isabel had given on her research into the forced settlement of the Tuareg, a previously nomadic tribe of the western Sahara.

Gallagher went up to Isabel and told her he had enjoyed the talk. She was eleven years older, darkly beautiful, funny

and possessing a remarkably lusty laugh. She was legally separated from her husband, and was working on a year's teaching
contract at Cornell while seeking a more permanent position.
Isabel's favorite pastime was fly-fishing, a skill taught to her by
her father. She and Gallagher talked anthropology and fishing
for a long time. Gallagher had never fished in his life, but her
excitement about it was contagious. She invited him to come
with her to a nearby limestone stream to learn.

In a whirlwind three months Isabel Martin taught Gallagher
the meditative benefits of the rod and the river as well as the
physical profits of a healthy sexual appetite. She returned to
her husband in June, somehow leaving him both wiser and
more confused than ever.

The day after Isabel's departure, a social worker contacted
Gallagher to say that his mother had been hospitalized. She
was failing fast. He went to New York to say his good-byes.

Agnes' skin was the yellow of a scuffed and bruised lemon
when he walked into the room. Racked by deliriums, she barely
understood that her son was present, mumbling only one coherent sentence for him to hold onto: "Pat, be a good boy and
get your mum some tomato juice."

During the night, she gradually blackened as her liver
failed. She died at six in the morning, leaving Gallagher
scorched inside. He walked the streets for hours, ending up at
his father's grave site in Queens. He stared down at grass wet
with dew below Seamus' stone. He tried to erect the glass walls,
but they would not go up. Gallagher had collapsed on the
ground in front of his father's headstone and cried for hours.

Driving up the River Road, Gallagher could see Nightingale
fighting the same sense of hopeless loss, of being cast adrift
without oar or anchor. She slammed her fist into her thigh. "I
left Olga helpless. I should have taken her with me."

"Don't go second-guessing yourself," he warned her. "It does no good."

Before she could reply, they crested a rise to see the familiar blue and red flaring lights of police cars, fire engines and ambulances. Beyond, the charred skeleton of a farmhouse smoldered in the rain. Smoke lifted off the beamwork that had survived the fire, lofted and melted with the mist to become a silica-colored veil that billowed and curled like gnarled fingers above the dairy barn and the fields beyond.

Nightingale was out and moving toward the burned house before Gallagher had halted the truck. Deputy Phil Gavrilis, clad in a blue, ankle-length raincoat, stepped in her way. The rain poured off his hat brow. "It's rough. You sure you want to go up there, Andie?"

"Yes, Phil, I do," she said, struggling to keep her jaw from trembling. "When did it happen?"

"Sometime between midnight and dawn, before the real rain started; otherwise I don't think the place would have burned that hard," Gavrilis replied.

"Where's Chief Kerris?" she asked.

"Not here yet," the deputy said puzzled. "We've got calls out for him, but he's not responding. Tony Fulton, the arson investigator, is already up there."

Nightingale turned to go up the hill. Gavrilis walked away toward a knot of volunteer firemen. Seeing Gallagher get out of the same vehicle as Nightingale, the three state troopers and the dozen firefighters arrayed on the knoll must have figured he belonged on the scene, because no one moved to prevent him from following her toward the smoking house. Nightingale got to the charred ruins, took one look into what used to be Olga Dawson's kitchen, spun around and put her hand to her mouth. She staggered toward the blackened trunk of a red oak and held on, taking huge gulps of air.

Gallagher moved up to look for himself.

Olga Dawson rested on her right side in a jumble of black, fallen timbers about fifteen feet from the scorched brick chimney. One of the beams had burned through and the halves made a V near what was left of Olga's skull. The flames had engulfed her in such intense heat that it had pinched her body so she seemed like a praying figure in an igneous sculpture. Dozens of fissures vented the blackened skin around her spine.

Gallagher wheeled, took about six strides past Nightingale and got the dry heaves. When he was able to stand again, she said weakly, "You shouldn't have seen that."

"It's a little too late," he gasped.

Just then a squat, swarthy man walked up. Nightingale stood, wiping at her nose and choking. "Tony, I told her every day not to smoke in bed."

Fulton, the arson investigator, shook his head. "Wasn't cigarettes. The way she's lying and the scorching on the outer fire wall point to her being overcome by smoke from a creosote fire and then being enveloped in a hot flash. See the way her skin's broken in those three-inch gashes?"

Nightingale nodded.

"Skin pops like that when it's exposed to intense heat in a brief time," Fulton said. "I figure it for a chimney fire."

"She had it cleaned six months ago."

Fulton shrugged. "Maybe she forgot to shut the stove door, an ember popped and hit the rug."

Nightingale pursed her lips, thinking. You could tell she did not believe this theory. Then she saw Gallagher still standing there.

"Go back to your cabin now, Pat," she said. "I'll be here a while. I appreciate the ride."

It was the first time she had called him Pat, which he seized on as a positive amid horrible circumstances. "If you need anything, Andie—"

"I'll be fine," she said before he could finish.

Gallagher nodded absently, then wandered back through the crowd milling about in the midmorning rain. He felt too fucked-up to drive, so he sat on the hood of the truck, watching raindrops strike a puddle. In each alternating ripple Gallagher saw Olga Dawson's blackened body and water draining from Hank Potter's mouth. And then he saw himself.

Which triggered the sudden and desperate need to walk. As if outward motion could calm the churning within. Gallagher walked a hundred yards beyond the police cars to where the muddy road met a spur path that angled down through an open wooden gate. Forty yards downslope, the path forked. One arm led to the barn. The other curved across an overgrown meadow toward the southern tree line.

Ribbons of fog spiraled through the trees. He stopped, almost hypnotized as dozens of thoughts collided and caromed in his head. Olga Dawson. A chimney not cleaned. Or a woodstove left open. She blips off into the void. Unlike Gallagher's parents, Olga had done nothing to precipitate her own death. But the parallel cruelty was that, like them, she was alive one moment and gone the next. She was no more than memory and artifacts for someone like Gallagher to sift through, record and analyze. There was no evidence Olga Dawson continued to exist in any sense.

Plato, Descartes and Kant had all argued in favor of the immortality of the soul, of death as a mutation of one form of living for another. Gallagher shook his head, thinking about their theories and how he had rejected each in turn. Then he thought of all the places he had been in the world: Jerusalem, equatorial Africa, Jidda, Tokyo, the Himalayas, Peru, India. In every location he had heard holy men utter wonderful suppositions about the constancy of the spirit and God. But not once had Gallagher found evidence strong enough to make him abandon his father's gospel of disbelief. It came down to this: where was the experience? Where in all he had learned was the tingling, emotional, ecstatic sensing of the immortal and the omniscient?

Standing there in the wind- and rain-swept field behind Olga Dawson's barn, Gallagher had to admit that the closest he had come to believing in anything or anybody was Emily Beckworth.

A squall burst across the open field below Olga Dawson's barn and pelted his face. He drew up his hood, unwilling to think any more about Emily that day.

Gallagher turned his back to the squall and noticed a white, long-haired cat stained with soot and meowing in the grass next to the double door to the bottom of the barn.

"C'mon, cat," he called, walking toward it. The cat darted into the barn. He followed. It was gloomy inside. He waited for his eyes to adjust. Box stalls ran the length of the barn on both sides. The odor of cow lingered. The cat was nowhere in sight. He came to an abrupt stop halfway down the aisle. Mud clots dried on the cement floor, clots that had been stamped into a Z shape by a boot tread. They led toward the last stall.

Inside the stall was an open trap door. A staircase descended into a dark tunnel. On the opposite side of the staircase, knee-high rubber boots had been positioned carefully under a rough-hewn pine bench. A peach-colored rain slicker, with a few beads of water still clinging to it, hung on a peg next to a sweater woven of gray Icelandic wool. The cat sat on the bench, meowing and watching Gallagher.

"C'mere, cat," he said again. The cat hesitated, then trotted toward him and he picked her up. She purred and rolled over in his arms. Playfully she batted at his cheeks with her paws.

"Aren't you a sweetie?" Gallagher said, scratching her under the chin. She purred.

He took a step into the stall and happened to look away from the cat toward the staircase into the tunnel.

A piece of sketch paper had been stuck on a nail below

the trap door. The figure of Charun had been drawn different from the first one. His head was cocked now in the direction of the viewer. A fingernail of white shone at the bottom of the black cavities of his eye sockets. One of the stitches that held his mouth shut hung loose. Surging up from between his legs was an enormous phallus painted rust-red. One taloned claw held it.

The monster was leering at Gallagher.

Chapter Fourteen

The cat sprang from Gallagher's arms. He bolted after it toward the barn door and was just about to exit when he saw Andie Nightingale coming down the two-track. The rain fell in sheets now. Her hood was up and angled toward the woods. He hesitated to go out because she had all but ordered him to leave the property. First Gallagher finds Potter's body in the river. Then he finds another of the killer's warped artifacts. Too much coincidence, he thought. Suspicion will logically fall on me.

So he watched Andie through the cracked door, hoping she'd wander away so he could sneak back to the car and wait for someone else to find the drawing. At the Y, Andie turned to briefly consider the barn. His stomach fluttered. She took the path toward the forest.

"Keep going," he whispered.

She stopped after twenty yards. Another squall swept across the meadow and Andie dropped her head into it. She took another step. Her carriage stiffened. She moved quickly to her right, squatted, reached into the mire at the path's edge and picked up an object Gallagher couldn't make out.

Andie held it in her palm, studying it as if she couldn't believe it. She chewed at her bottom lip and looked into her palm again, the incredulity in her expression changing clearly to dismay and then to fear.

She jammed whatever it was into the right pocket of her slicker, then stood there in the squall for several moments as if she could not decide what to do. At last she picked her head up. The cat scampered from under a bush back through the barn door and sat purring contentedly at Gallagher's feet. Andie came toward the barn, clucking and calling, "Come here, Tess."

Knowing he was caught, Gallagher simply stepped out.

Andie jerked to a halt. "What are you doing here?"

"I . . . I didn't feel well after seeing . . . Mrs. Dawson," he faltered. "And I just went for a walk to get some air—"

"I told you to leave."

"There's mud on the floor inside," he blurted. "Fresh mud. It leads to a stall . . . there's another one of Charun's pictures. Those wounds on Olga's body weren't from heat!"

"Olga?" Andie said. Her face took on a dazed expression, as if she'd been wind-robbed by a punch to the solar plexus. Then her knees buckled and she collapsed into the mud. Two inches of gold chain now hung outside her raincoat pocket. She looked up at Gallagher, then down at the chain, and that alone seemed to bring her back from the brink. She reached into her other pocket and got out her gun shakily. "Get back," she ordered.

"Hey, put that thing away!" he cried.

"Move!"

Gallagher took five steps backward. Andie came to her feet like a newborn colt and stuffed the rest of the chain into her pocket, watching him as a cornered animal might.

"I know what you're thinking," he said.

"And what's that?"

"That I went in there to plant the picture."

"A mind reader, an anthropologist and a killer," she said. "You are talented."

"I didn't kill anyone!" Gallagher said. "If I was the killer, wouldn't I have left the drawing last night? How was I supposed to know that your truck would die and I would be allowed on the scene?"

Andie didn't answer. Her attention was jumping from Gallagher to the barn and back again. And with each jump her expression gravitated toward that brink again. She blinked and rubbed at her eyes as if blinded by an invisible light.

Gallagher pleaded his case again. "Why would I wait until Mrs. Dawson's farm is crawling with police officers to leave a calling card? I'd have to be an idiot."

Andie hesitated, then dropped the gun to hip level, muzzle down. "Show me. You go first."

When they reached the mud on the floor, Andie ordered Gallagher to take off his boots and stand against the wall. She picked up one mud clot and studied the design. His boots were chain-style, rubber-bottom boots. The clots on the floor had that Z design. She kicked off her own boots, then motioned Gallagher forward, warning him to be careful not to step on any of the remaining mud clumps. "Where's the drawing?"

"Last stall," he said. "It's tacked to the frame under the trap door."

"How did you know there was a trap door in that stall?" she demanded.

"I didn't," he protested. "It was open when I got there."

Gallagher led her to the stall, but remained outside on her orders. She put on latex gloves, went over to the boots under the pine bench, turned them over and inspected the tread. They and the Z clods were obviously the same.

"She wasn't in any condition to take a walk, especially at

night," Andie mused, talking more to herself than to Gallagher.
She crossed to the trap door.

"Where does that staircase go?" he asked.

But Andie only half heard. She was already transfixed by
the drawing. She mumbled, "To a tunnel that runs under the
yard to the house. Olga's father-in-law built it back in the
twenties so he could come out and tend to the cows in the
winter."

"So could she have gone out?"

"No, I . . . I don't know," she said. She glanced over at
Gallagher. "The drawing . . . the creature has a . . ."

He nodded.

"He raped Olga before he killed her," Andie said. She
snatched the drawing as if it were the vilest thing on earth.
She seemed poised to shred it.

"Don't!" Gallagher yelled.

There was a moment of absolute silence in the barn. "Don't
do it!" he whispered.

"Sergeant Nightingale?" Lieutenant Brigid Bowman's voice
called from outside the barn door. "Are you in there?"

At the sound of the lieutenant's voice, Andie let the drawing
slip from her fingers, then staggered toward the bench and
slumped onto it. Her sopping hair hung like tentacles over her
face. "I don't know what to do," she moaned softly to herself.

By then Bowman and Chief Mike Kerris had entered the
far end of the barn.

"Take off your boots!" Gallagher called to them, nervously
casting his attention from them to Andie and back. "Pull yourself together!" he hissed. "The lieutenant's coming. You can't
let her see you like this."

Andie shook her head like a donkey Gallagher had once
seen in the Sahara that had been whipped so hard it refused
to move. He walked toward the law enforcement officials,

pointing to the mud. "Sergeant Nightingale wants everyone to take their boots off. Charun was in here."

"Charun?" Lieutenant Bowman's forehead knotted.

Kerris groaned. He had changed his clothes since yesterday, but he looked worse. His posture was stooped. His "Chief" baseball cap was on backward. And the bags under his stainless-steel eyes were larger than Gallagher's.

"Where is Sergeant Nightingale?!" Bowman demanded.

"In that last stall," Gallagher said, trying to figure out ways to delay them. "There's another drawing."

Kerris' eyes darted about. He fumbled in his pocket for a lollipop. "I'm going to have to call my uncle about this."

"No one's calling anyone until I say so," Bowman countered. She kicked off her rubber boots, watching Gallagher suspiciously. "Why are you in here, Mr. Gallagher?"

"I found the drawing, then went and showed it to Sergeant Nightingale."

"You found the . . . Chief, please make sure Mr. Gallagher does not leave," Bowman ordered, then she moved past.

Gallagher tried to hurry after her, but Kerris grabbed him by the collar. Despite the obvious strain he was under, he was three inches taller and fifteen pounds of muscle heavier than Gallagher. Kerris spun Gallagher around neatly. His breath smelled of grape. The stick of the lollipop stuck out of his mouth. "Where do you think you're going, bright boy?" he asked.

"Disney World," Gallagher said. "What's it to you?"

Kerris' upper lip arched. "Lawton doesn't need your kind. Why don't you just go back to New York or wherever it is you're from?"

"Look, Chief," Gallagher said. "I don't know what your problem is, but I helped Sergeant Nightingale interpret the last letter. I thought I might be able to help with this one, too."

"I'll bet you did."

"And what's that supposed to mean?"

Kerris gave him a malevolent grin. "Andie Nightingale's a damn fine-looking woman. But I wouldn't get too close. She's so cold she could be dangerous to your . . . mental health."

Before Gallagher could reply, Lieutenant Bowman called out in an agitated voice, "Chief Kerris, would you escort Mr. Gallagher up here, please?"

Gallagher feared finding Andie sprawled on the floor. But she was back on her feet. Her pallid, damp complexion, her sunken eyes and the visible tremor in her hand made it seem as if she had just gotten over a virus.

Lieutenant Bowman's jaw was set hard. "Mr. Gallagher, I'm going to want to search your cabin. Will I require a warrant?"

"No, go ahead. I've got nothing to hide," he said.

"Chief Kerris will arrange it."

"If he's involved, I'd like to be there, if you don't mind."

"That's your right," Bowman said. "In the meantime, I'd like you to look at this letter."

"You're going to let a suspect look at the letter?" Kerris barked incredulously.

The lieutenant shot the police chief a patronizing smile. "If Mr. Gallagher is the killer, then he's already seen it, hasn't he? If not, he might be of help."

Gallagher winked at Kerris, then went to the bench where Andie had laid out the piece of paper with the drawing and the note. Andie stepped to one side. Her breathing was asthmatic.

Angel was my Persephone, the letter began. *I could not see. But like the old man and father, she said she knew the way. She said the little death would steer our boat.*

I will have what Angel knows now for sure. And if more be rowed across the river until I have it, so be it. You condemned me, Lawton. Now I condemn you!

Angel said we all will die. We all will die. Will we see the other side?

The eerie madness of the letter worked its way up the back of Gallagher's spine and centered, pounding, in his head. He recalled the drawing of the leering fiend on the other side of the note, shuddered, then forced himself to reread the words.

"Well?" Bowman asked.

"We're dealing with an intelligent but very sick mind."

"Takes one to know one," Kerris said.

"That's enough, Chief," Bowman said. "What else?"

"He's got a beef with Lawton, so he's probably local, or was, and feels wronged by the community. Which counts me out, by the way."

"Not in my book," Kerris said.

"Who's Persephone? Who's Angel?" the lieutenant asked.

"Both mythological figures, but they're from different cultures," Gallagher said, ignoring Kerris' glare. "Persephone's from Greek mythology. Angels are Judeo-Christian figures.

"Persephone was a daughter of the harvest goddess, Demeter," he went on. "She was raped and abducted by Hades, king of the underworld. While there, she ate three pomegranate seeds and was doomed to stay forever as Hades' bride beneath the earth. Her mother, Demeter, sought her daughter everywhere, sorrowing and completely neglecting the crops. When the crops of the earth withered, winter appeared for the first time.

"Humans beseeched the gods to intervene in the dispute and a compromise was reached. Persephone would spend half a year in Hades and the other half with her mother on earth," he added.

Andie's voice was gravelly and high. "How did Persephone get back and forth between the underworld and earth?"

Gallagher thought about it and nodded soberly. "Charun would have been her boatman."

"And Persephone was raped by the king of the underworld?" Andie asked the question as if a sharp bone had caught in her throat.

"Yes."

Kerris looked away, his face flushed. "If you ask me, it's a bunch of nutso mumbo jumbo. Where's the real evidence?"

"That's what I want to know, too," Bowman griped. "Mr. Gallagher, did Charun have sexual relations with Persephone in the myths? The penis—it's exaggerated."

Gallagher shook his head. "Charun didn't have any romantic relationships that I can remember. He's a minor figure in the more major myths."

"What about this Angel?" Bowman asked. "How does she fit in?"

Gallagher shrugged. "He's jumbling these references. It doesn't make sense. Unless . . . the meaning is his own."

"What the hell are you talking about?" Kerris asked warily.

"Since the dawn of time, myths have been the way people explain the unexplainable to themselves," Gallagher replied. "To the early Greeks, the Persephone legend was a way to explain the cycle of winter and summer. But your killer is altering the telling, changing the meaning."

"To what?" Bowman asked.

"To suit his own experience," Gallagher said. "To make sense of the evil he's done."

"Or is going to do," Andie mumbled.

She had been sitting on the bench during the last part of the conversation, looking vacantly at the trap door that led to the staircase. Now she cradled her stomach and rocked back and forth as a mad person might in a padded room.

"What's that, Sergeant?" Bowman asked.

"He raped Olga, didn't he?" Andie groaned. "He raped her,

then hacked her to death! And before he burned her, he used her blood to draw that—"

She rocked faster. "He's going to rape us and kill us all and we won't even know why."

Kerris and Bowman exchanged glances. Bowman went over and sat on the bench next to her. "Andie, are you all right?"

The detective stared at them as if they were strangers. She held her head in her hands and moaned, "I don't know! I just don't know!"

They had a trooper drive Andie and the cat down the River Road to her house under orders from Bowman to take two weeks off to rest. An evidence team accompanied Kerris and Gallagher to the cabin. The search lasted for four hours, but as Gallagher had predicted, they found nothing. The cabin was empty again around six.

Gallagher felt wasted by the day's events. Starving, he cooked himself a steak, then for the second night in a row stumbled upstairs and flopped on the bed fully clothed. His sleep was deep and dreamless for several hours; then the horrible images of the day surfaced and whirled in that intuitive state on the edge of consciousness. He saw the charred body of Olga Dawson, the monster taunting him with his bloody phallus and Andie Nightingale's sudden and puzzling collapse.

Then Gallagher's mind zipped backward and he sat up alert, speaking to the darkness: "Andie never told Lieutenant Bowman about that gold chain."

Chapter Fifteen

The wind outside blew hard. Gallagher's flashlight played on the wet, swirling leaves along the two-track that led from the cabin out to the River Road and to Andie's house. Through the hedgerow he could see a light burning downstairs. And he hurried, pondering this question: why had a veteran homicide detective kept secret a gold chain found near a murder scene?

Gallagher rapped at the back door, waited and then knocked sharply again. He heard a melodious, haunting noise in the wind behind him, frowned, turned and peered into the darkness. It sounded like a flute trilling against the shake of a gourd rattle, the same one he had heard when waking up a few mornings before. But almost immediately the sounds were swallowed by the wind. Gallagher opened the door and stepped inside, calling softly, "Hello? Anybody home?"

There was no noise but the snap and rush of the fire in the undampened woodstove. No smell in the kitchen but of her, and when he drew closer, another scent, horribly familiar. The odor of Gallagher's mother's breath.

Andie had given in to it with her forehead nestled in the crook of the forest-green chamois shirt she wore with a pair of jeans. At her elbow, the lip of a tipped-over juice glass met the barrel of a fifth of vodka. Nearly a third empty. She was barefoot. Her right arm was stretched out across the table. A frail gold chain wove among her curled fingers. Attached to the chain and resting in her palm was a delicate crucifix. Above the intersection of the spar and standard was the chip of a tiny red jewel.

Next to Andie's arm lay twin strips of forest-green cloth attached to a liver-dyed oilskin pouch, six inches long, ten inches wide, cracked with time. An exact replica of the gold chain and the cross with the tiny red jewel spilled from the jaws of the pouch, as did a bundle of yellowed parchment, ragged at the left edge and so brittle and translucent that Gallagher could make out the faint scrawl of handwriting even though the pages were folded inward.

The ancient pages stirred in his gut an inexplicable, shallow nausea. Gallagher's attention traveled to the vodka bottle next to the outstretched arm, which aggravated the nausea until a flame crept up the back of his throat. He saw himself as a little boy wandering into a kitchen, finding his father the same way, trying to wake Seamus and crying because he was frightened he would not. Gallagher wanted to go right then, to leave Andie to wrestle with her demons as she saw fit.

But there was something about the yellowed papers that called to him, would not let him leave. Gallagher picked them up, sat in the overstuffed chair next to the woodstove and began to read:

NOVEMBER 3, 1893
They shall kill me tonight. I am sure of it.

But I am not scared because I have only to face it now. Then I shall dance with Ten Trees and Painted Horses; and the pale red dust shall rise under our feet into the warm air and the singing shall be like a tornado out on the plains.

I've got to close my eyes to hear it true, the stamp of feet joining a thousand, then ten thousand of my brothers and sisters, and our feet shall become like the thunder hooves of the buffalo come back. All of us dancing in a great circle around and around and around. Until Wakan Tanka hears the pounding of our moccasins against the land and the sky cuts open and we walk the earth again.

Grandfather, I am sending a voice. To the heavens of the universe, I am sending a voice.

I've been hiding here in the root cellar below the basement for hours. There are carrots, potatoes and gourds here, enough to feed me right for a week. And a bottle of oil for the lantern. And water running in the seep. I have Ten Trees' pipe, the sacred stones and enough tobacco to finish the ceremonies.

Then they shall come. As they always have. Out of greed. Out of spite.

They shall try one last time to make me teach them the sacred ways I learned from Ten Trees and Kicking Bear. But I shall be true to my word and not speak. And then the killing shall be done. Because I am a squaw. And they are white. Because they believe what I am is rightly theirs to take or toss away like a bone on a heap.

I am not fearful of them or death. Ten Trees always said to face death when it comes. He said you've got to go into death with open eyes to pass clean into what is yonder.

Ten Trees, Crazy Horse, Sitting Bull, Big Foot, Painted Horses and now me, Many Horses. Sure enough, winter is the Lakota's time for death. The first storm of winter came in last night, cold and mean like a wolf pack on a hunt. They are out in it, looking for me. I will kill some of them before I die.

*   *   *

When I think of my mother, Painted Horses, I think all of us shall come to be like the blizzard wind—icy, sharp-toothed and chasing after the fury of our lives.

I cut off a hunk of my hair and bathed it in the smoke of sweet grass I picked down by the Bluekill in August. I showed it to Heaven, to Earth and to the four corners of the universe. I wrapped it in buckskin like I was taught. This hair can free my soul.

But who shall guard my soul and my hair until I can be set free? Who shall kill the young cow buffalo for her robe? What woman shall care for my bundle? What woman shall hang my soul on a tripod looking south and cover it with a buffalo hide and the feathers of a spotted eagle?

I am not scared to die. I am done now and ready for them. But I won't go easy, like some scared deer caught in a pit trap. I shall run through the night in the snow to my secret place and dance there one last time. After the dance, let them come if they dare.

Grandfather, I am sending a voice. To the heavens of the universe, I am sending a voice.

A moist pressure built in Gallagher's lungs as he read those final words. It was a piece of an old journal or a diary, though he had never read anything like it in all his years of research and travel—shattered, almost hallucinatory thoughts scribbled down under the threat of death more than a hundred years ago. Who was the writer? What had happened to her? Gallagher's heart raced with the chance that this was a major anthropological find! He had to call Jerry.

The pouch shifted in his lap. A lock of jet-black hair about five inches long, sealed between two pieces of wax paper, spilled out onto his thigh. Several strands of the hair jutted free of the paper. Gallagher ran the tips of his fingers lightly over them, then jerked back at a mild stinging similar to the sensation he'd endured when fire ants crossed his hand in Africa years before.

"That's not possible," he whispered.

There was a chunking sound as the pistol action drove a cartridge into the chamber. Gallagher looked up from the hair. The muzzle of Andie Nightingale's service pistol pointed dead at his chest.

Chapter Sixteen

Andie elbowed herself forward on the kitchen table with both hands wrapped tight around the butt of the gun—only six feet away now and cobra-dancing in the air. One bloodshot eye peered above the tritium sights. "Put it back or I'll kill you," she slurred.

"What—"

"Do it!"

Jittery, Gallagher took up the wax paper so as not to brush the hairs again and placed it in the pouch. Then he folded the parchment pages and put them away.

"Slide it across the table," she ordered. "Slow."

All he could see was the black hole of the pistol barrel when he pushed the pouch toward her. She grabbed it, clutched it to her chest, then came around the table with the gun still trained on him. "Who are you?" Andie demanded in a thick-tongued voice. "What are you after?"

"I'm not after anything," Gallagher stammered. "I saw you find that gold chain in the meadow behind Olga Dawson's barn and wondered why you didn't tell anyone about it. Then here you are—passed out with that journal and the hair and two gold chains and two crosses."

She regarded him as a squirrel might a hawk, but did not respond.

Gallagher said, "The writer, she's an Indian, isn't she?"

In one motion, Andie flung the pouch on the table and dropped into a combat-shooting position. "How do you know about her?" she rasped. "Tell me, or so help me God, I'll shoot."

"Who do you think I am?!" Gallagher cried.

"The sick bastard that mutilated my mom's best friend and, before that, Hank Potter. Now you're here for me and my pouch." She angled toward Gallagher's chair in a predatory crouch, then ordered, "On the floor. Spread-eagle, belly down."

Gallagher eased himself out of the chair onto all fours. Andie took a semi-drunken step toward him as if to push him down. Before she could, he swept his right leg through her ankles, then drove his left hand up to control her right elbow and get the gun out of his face. The middle knuckle of Gallagher's right hand smacked her just below the rib cage at the kidneys. She made an *oomph* sound as she crashed backward through a stand of potted seedlings. Her gun spun crazily across the wide-planked floor. He dove on top of her and pinned her by the wrists.

"Get off me!" Andie shouted, squirming underneath him. "I won't let you! I won't let any of you—"

"If I was Charun, you'd be dead by now!" Gallagher roared. "Think about it!"

They stared at each other, gasping. Then Andie looked left and right at Gallagher's hands against her wrists. She looked at his thighs pinned against hers and in a voice that wavered with effort, said, "Please get off me, then. Please? Now?"

Gallagher stood up and backed away quickly. "Your gun's under the desk."

Andie blinked as if returning from a terrible memory, then got up onto her elbows. "Where . . . did you learn to fight like that?"

"Tokyo," he said. "My ex-wife and I spent eighteen months there, studying and filming in an aikido dojo. The film shows up on cable now and then."

Andie's attention never left Gallagher as she sidled to the desk and retrieved her gun. "I want to know how you knew the hair and the writing are an Indian's."

"Because she says she's Lakota. But so what? There are New Age white guys from Westchester County who live out in Sedona, Arizona, and say they're Lakota. What's important is that phrase that's repeated in the journal, 'Grandfather, I am sending a voice.' I've heard it before."

"Where?" Andie asked skeptically.

"My first three years at graduate school, I had a job researching for a professor making a film about Sitting Bull—that's how I got interested in documentaries in the first place. That line about the 'Grandfather' was in songs the Sioux sang around that time. Wakan Tanka, the Great Spirit, is also called Grandfather. She is Sioux, isn't she?"

Andie nodded. Her hair was sweated and hung in her face. She pushed it back.

"Now I want some answers," he said. "If that journal and those crosses are related to the killings, why didn't you tell Lieutenant Bowman? Why are you withholding evidence?"

Andie glared at Gallagher, hating him, then brought up the gun and aimed it at his face. For a second there was craziness in her eyes and he thought he was going to soil his pants. Talk her down, he thought. Talk her down like you used to talk Seamus down from one of his tirades.

"Forget about that for a second, Andie," he said in a soft, even tone. "I'm sure you had your reasons. But what you're really upset about is that you picked up the bottle again. Am I right?"

Her grip tightened. Her finger closed around the trigger.

Gallagher swallowed, but went on. "You're feeling guilty and angry and you're afraid you're heading back into the bottle full-time, aren't you?"

There was a long moment; then her finger softened. "Yes," Andie whispered in resignation.

"It's just a slip, just one day. You don't have to go down there again if you don't want to."

She let one hand come off the gun. "I've been trying so hard."

"The best way not to go back in the hole is by talking, right?"

She nodded.

"Why didn't you tell the lieutenant about the chain?"

Slowly the pistol faded to her side. She slumped into a kitchen chair, that bird with the broken wing, and said: "Because I promised my mother I'd keep it secret. And when I saw the crucifix lying there in the mud, I thought: Olga had a piece of the journal, too. And then you found the letter from Charun . . . and . . ."

Andie let her attention sweep to the vodka bottle, then held her head in her hands and sobbed. Gallagher stood, scooped the bottle off the table and walked toward the sink, where he emptied it with a sadly familiar motion.

"Start at the beginning," he said, filling the water kettle and setting it on the stove.

She snuffled, then nodded and gazed up at the ceiling as if seeing a movie in the swirls of ivory plaster. Nearly three years ago, Andie's mother fell off a ladder and broke her femur. Grace Nightingale lay nine hours on the kitchen floor until her daughter came home from work and found her. The death certificate reads that Grace died of pneumonia brought on by an infection she developed after the operation to fuse her leg bone. Grace was in glaring pain the last night of her life. Restless. Moaning. In and out of consciousness.

At 2 A.M., she bolted upright and grabbed Andie's arm with terrifying strength. Grace told her daughter to go home right then and find a loose fieldstone in the chimney in their basement and bring back what she found behind it. Andie tried to hush her mother, but that only made the old woman more frantic.

" 'Go right now, Andie,' " she had pleaded, Andie said. " 'I never wanted you to have it, but there's no one else. You got to go now!' "

Alone, in the middle of night, Andie found the pouch in the chimney. She held the lock of hair. She read what Gallagher had read.

"I'd always thought of my mom as this simple, honest person who'd suffered more than her share of tragedies," Andie said. "When I found the bundle in the chimney, it was like she'd led this secret life and I didn't know her anymore."

Gallagher scooped coffee into a French-press maker. The kettle whistled and he poured the steaming water into the glass vessel. He filled two mugs and handed her one. Her hands shook from the booze and sparked images of his parents nursing their hangovers before breakfast. Gallagher swallowed, then asked: "When you took the pouch back to the hospital and showed her, what did your mother say?"

Andie's lower lip trembled. Relief at speaking at last. "She said her father gave it to her and my great-grandfather had given it to her father. It's part of a diary kept by a Sioux woman who supposedly lived here in Lawton a long time ago."

Anticipating his next question, Andie said she did not know how a Sioux had come to be in Lawton. Her mother said it was all about something awful that happened in Lawton more than a century ago, something "unholy."

Gallagher leaned forward. "What do you mean, unholy?"

Andie took an unsteady sip of the black coffee. "My mom was a strict Catholic. She saw everything in terms of her religion. She called what was in this pouch 'evidence of an abomination.' "

"That's all she said?"

"No, that's not all she said," Andie responded testily. "But with the drugs in her, most of it didn't make sense, except that a long time ago, some people in Lawton wanted the Sioux woman's story to be preserved, but they didn't trust just one person to preserve it. So they divided the journal."

"Who has the other pieces?"

"My mother said there were six others, maybe more, but she didn't know who. Neither did her father or her grandfather. It was almost like it was planned that way."

"By who?"

She shrugged. "I wish I knew. Maybe then I could save the others."

"You think Charun is killing the people who hold the journal?"

"Yes, but I can't prove it. I called Paula Potter and asked her if she'd ever seen anything like the pouch. She didn't know what I was talking about."

Gallagher squinted at her. "Why didn't you tell the lieutenant about all this back there in the barn? Why don't you call her up and tell her now?"

"You don't know anything about me, do you?" she stated wistfully.

He did not reply. Andie pressed her fist to her lips. The cat came strolling across the kitchen floor and leaped into Gallagher's lap. It purred and rubbed its head under his chin. Andie noticed and her eyes widened, then softened.

"Tess doesn't like anyone," she said, puzzled.

"Nobody, huh?" he asked, scratching the cat behind the ears.

"Well, she likes me, too," Andie said.

"You know, I can't say that's a surprise."

Andie reddened and lowered her head at his teasing, but she allowed herself a smile.

She admitted that there was a history of alcohol abuse in her family. Her father farmed and logged in the winters. When Andie was seven, he was alone in the woods when a tree fell and pinned him by the leg. He dug his way out from under the tree and crawled out of the woods. He lost his leg below the knee but was back at work in six months.

But when her older brother, Billy, died in Vietnam, her father's legendary toughness cracked. He drank himself to death in seven years.

"My mother was able to do it in five," Gallagher said.

"I'm sorry."

"For you, too."

They were silent for a long time.

Andie went on to say that she had had a drinking problem as a teenager, but had been sober for nearly ten years when her mother died. Two months after Grace's burial, Andie decided a screwdriver at lunch was a good way to dull the pain of loss. Soon there were screwdrivers at breakfast.

A year after the drinking began, she was called in on a double murder in Newport, along the Quebec border. She caught the Canadian dope dealer who had pulled the trigger, but mishandled the evidence. The defense attorney forced her to admit she'd been drinking at the crime scene. The doper walked. Andie was put on suspension, went through a rehab program and hadn't had a drink in nearly two years, until last night. She hadn't worked a real homicide case in that long either. Bowman kept her away from murder, assigned to cases where little old ladies fell down the stairs and died with no witnesses.

"That still doesn't explain why you didn't tell her about the pouches—"

"Because I lost it, okay!" she shouted. "Have you ever just lost it? I found that cross on the ground and realized Olga must have had a piece of the journal. Then you found that second drawing and it was like all these voices started chattering in my head, telling me to do this, don't do that, say this, don't say that. It got so I couldn't hear what I was saying. Then Brigid told me to go home. Did you know that the worst thing you can tell an alcoholic on the verge of a pickup is to go be alone?"

"Call her right now," Gallagher said. "Get it off your chest."

She shook her head violently. "I didn't tell her right off about the drawing left at Hank Potter's because I was trying to show her I could be a good homicide detective. That almost got me thrown off the case. If I come forward and tell her I did it a second time and was drinking, too . . . well, I can kiss this job good-bye. This job is my life."

Her predicament hung between them, like a shroud.

"There's only one thing you can do," Gallagher said, mustering bravado. "Figure out who Charun is, then haul him in just like they do in the movies."

"Easier said than done," she said, but she smiled again and almost laughed. She got out a Kleenex and blew her nose.

"I'll help you," Gallagher blurted out, surprised at the offer.

Instantly there was a wariness about her. "Why would you do that?"

Gallagher felt himself immediately wanting to back away from the offer. What was he thinking? Part of him wanted to get up and leave. He'd had enough of the convoluted lies drunks conjure up to last a lifetime. But there was the mysterious allure of the drawings and now this journal of the Sioux woman. And one thing more.

"Because I get the sense you and I are very much alike," he said. "And you need help."

"Have you been a drunk?" she asked.

"No," he replied levelly. "But I was raised by drunks. Both died of it. And I understand the urge to block out pain. My ex-wife liked to say I used the accumulation of information the way my parents used booze—as an insulator from the raw nerve endings of life."

She stared at him for the longest time and then actually laughed. "Did anyone ever tell you that you talk really strange?"

"You're not the first."

They grinned like idiots at each other for ten seconds, then Gallagher broke the spell by asking, "You must have some theory as to why Charun is killing for the journal of a Sioux squaw."

Andie nodded. "He said in both of those letters that he was after something that was stolen from him. He must believe the pieces of the journal belong to him."

"Then he could be Native American," he said, "a descendant of the Sioux woman."

"Possibly," Andie agreed.

"Is there a record of her death here in Lawton?" Gallagher asked.

"After my mother's funeral I looked at old newspaper clippings and county death certificates, but I never found any record of a Sioux," she replied. "Then again I didn't even have a name to go on."

"Did Olga ever tell you she had the journal?"

Andie shook her head. "Never. But I think she was trying to tell me the last time I saw her. She was talking about bears and secrets and I was too damn preoccupied to listen."

"So did Olga drop the cross in the meadow or did the killer?"

Andie chewed at the inside of her cheek. "There'd been so much rain, all the tracks were washed away. And the mud on the surface of the cross marred any chance at fingerprints."

"Let's say it was her, so where'd she go that night? Toward the woods?"

"She was weak. I can't see her doing that," Andie said. "Unless . . . unless she was really scared."

Gallagher tried to imagine it: the stricken old woman leaning on her cane, going through the tunnel to the barn to get her boots and her rain slicker; then, with the cat, struggling through the high grass of the meadow where the tangles—

He snapped his fingers. "Okay, she was scared. Let's say she gets to the field and she trips and falls. And when she does, she drops that cross. If she kept her pouch the way you did, then . . ."

Andie's jaw dropped. "When she fell she was carrying her piece of the journal! She was trying to hide it!"

"The question is, where?"

Andie pressed her fingers into the tabletop and gazed at the grain of the wood as a seer might a crystal ball. Then she jumped up from the table. She dodged into a closet and there was a great clatter and she emerged wearing knee-high rubber boots and holding a powerful hand-held spotlight. Her jaw was set and her eyes flashed with anticipation. "Get your stuff. We're going to see if the bears are still in their dens."

Chapter Seventeen

In the last blinded hours of night, the wind surged after a low pressure system fleeing toward the gulf of Maine. The moon came, left and came again among the swiftly moving clouds. Rain had heaved the soil and now the scent of moldering decay hung in the woods. Scraggly dead leaves beat themselves against beech whips crowding the abandoned logging road that climbed a steep, forbidding slope toward the peak of Lawton Mountain.

It was nearly four-thirty in the morning when Andie and Gallagher fought their way through the whips by flashlight. They crossed through an overgrown apple orchard before clawing up a series of benches where shagbark hickory grew in meadows of still, pale grass. An hour of steady climbing found them emerging from a pine break into a meadow choked by low junipers.

There was no talk as they climbed. And the sharp evergreen odor in the darkness reminded Gallagher of a group of children and their parents herding goats up a narrow mountain path in

Lebanon. As he climbed, he saw himself and Emily lolling in the late-afternoon sun on a ledge above a path in Lebanon, breathing the cedar air and staring out toward Beirut and the sea.

Emily's sandals were drawn up against the hem of her khaki shorts. She had her Red Sox baseball cap turned backward and looked very tired. They had been on the go for nearly two years, husband and wife, lovers and partners. Gallagher did the field research and partnered with Jerry on the writing. Emily had become their cinematographer. India, Tokyo, Tanzania and now Lebanon. Gallagher had been to Beirut before while researching the series on children of war that had won him the Pulitzer Prize. They were back ten years after that series to find the same children and put together a documentary on what had become of them.

"I want kids," Emily announced out of the blue.

The sun dropped behind the mountain and the ledge was cast in shadow. Gallagher looked down at the little boys and girls walking up the mountain path and was filled inexplicably with dread. "I like our life the way it is," he replied.

"I do, too," Emily said, tugging on her sweater. "But I can't help feeling a little empty sometimes. We're voyeurs, Pat. We watch people do life."

"I don't feel empty," he said. "I've got you."

Emily snuggled up next to him. Her tanned skin glowed against the white sweater. As the goat herders moved over the ridge, Emily said, "It's just a feeling I get now and then."

Andie snapped on a flashlight and shone it upward so Gallagher would avoid an overhanging branch. In the glow, her face was yellowed with hangover, and he could still smell the vodka in her sweat. She noticed that he noticed and turned away. Her light came to rest on an orderly pile of slate. The field had been a potato farm a century or more ago; all that was left was the slate foundation, a landmark that had once helped Olga Dawson show a bear's den to a little girl.

They skirted the foundation and angled to the field's north corner. Here the terrain turned into a series of steep-faced ledges and they traversed east until the footing became reasonable. Andie groped downhill along the seam of rock face and earth for one hundred and twenty-five feet. Gallagher slid along behind her, falling twice.

Their flashlight beams licked the trunks of the mountain ash, cherry and spruce trees, made their trunks glossy against the withered ferns that cowered on the flat below the ledge. An owl hooted at dawn. A grouse drummed. And from far down the slope, a turkey shock-gobbled.

They were standing on a rock shelf that jutted out from the cliff. Andie pushed her way into a maze of wild raspberry. The brown, thorny stalks that store at their rain jackets eased to reveal a wide, oval cave mouth. "This is where Joshua and Caleb Danby used to hold their seances in the summer," she said. "There's a tunnel in there that leads to another, smaller cave Olga called the bear's den."

Sure enough, at its entrance the cave was perhaps eight feet high and fifteen feet wide for the first ten feet, then it lowered and narrowed dramatically to a tube about twice the width of Gallagher's shoulders. Andie shone her flashlight around the interior of the outer cave. There was nothing but sticks and leaves and bird feathers quivering in the dank breeze that blew along the cave floor.

Andie got down on her hands and knelt before the tunnel. Her flashlight blinked twice and died. Gallagher got down next to her with his torch. The beam cut back into the gloom, revealing that after fifteen feet the tube doglegged to the left and widened into a grotto. Andie crawled in first. The roof of the grotto was tall enough to allow them to stand. She took his flashlight and cast it around the rough granite walls and along the ceiling and floor. There were rocks, twigs and leaves, but no pouch.

"We're chasing ghosts," Andie remarked at last, sighing. "Maybe it was just a coincidence that I found the cross in Olga's field. Maybe it doesn't have to do with Charun after all."

"Or maybe Olga hid the pouch somewhere else," Gallagher replied.

"I wouldn't know where to begin to look," Andie said in despair.

"Why don't we go back down and figure out what to do next after we've rested?"

"I don't think *we* will figure out anything," she retorted. "I was wrong to even let you tag along up here."

"Tag along? If it wasn't for me, you would have been—" He stopped in mid-sentence, not wanting to finish.

Her shoulders drooped. "Go ahead, say it."

Gallagher felt like he'd just kicked a sick dog. She handed him the flashlight with an expression of total defeat plastered across her face. "Shine it into the tunnel so I get home to my bottle," she said.

"Andie, I'm sorry—"

"Just shine the light, Gallagher. You've got no reason to believe in me."

He squatted, furious with himself. He pointed the beam into the tunnel and happened to tilt it toward the roof where it doglegged. Andie gasped. Just visible over the lip of a narrow ledge was a strip of faded green ribbon and the faint outline of a liver-covered leather pouch.

Andie fumbled with the ties and turned back the flap while Gallagher held the flashlight. She drew out a wad of folded papers and then two polished stones.

"There were stones mentioned in your piece of the journal," he said.

Andie nodded and handed them to Gallagher. He rolled them in his hands. They warmed quickly and he flashed on the uncomfortable sensation generated by the lock of hair in Andie's pouch. He dropped them back in the bottom of Olga's pouch, then pointed the light at the pages now unfolded on her knees.

"December 29, 1891?" Andie said. "This section was written almost two years earlier than my piece. And look, you can see the ragged edges where they were torn out of a book of some kind."

The light flickered. They moved closer so they could read together. During that awkward moment Gallagher thought of Emily dropping her sarong in the Tantric temple, but the faint scent of vodka on Andie's breath forced him to turn to the labored handwriting on the yellowed parchment.

DECEMBER 29, 1891

Miss Mary Parker taught me to read and write at the mission school at Standing Rock. She said, Sarah, writing shall set you free. Some folks at Standing Rock did not like me reading and writing the white language.

But Sitting Bull, Painted Horses' brother, said it was a good thing that I had the tongue for it even if I was a girl. Speaking the white language, I might help my people be free again, he said.

I don't rightly know what freedom is. Sitting Bull used to talk about the free life along the Grand River when he was young, about the buffalo and the deer and the eagle. He told us about the Thunder Beings who lived on the cliffs of the Black Hills and watched over us. But these days I get to thinking the only way a Sioux can be free is by dying or dancing the Ghost Dance.

Gallagher glanced up at Andie, "That's where I heard that line about the 'Grandfather' in your piece of the journal. It's from the Ghost Dance."

"Ghost Dance?" Her skin seemed to glow of the flashlight.

"After the War for the Black Hills, when Crazy Horse was killed and the last of the Indians were sent to the reservations, there was this Paiute shaman named Wovoka out in Nevada who had a vision in which the Great Spirit showed him a Ghost Dance that could drive all whites from America, revive the warrior dead and bring back the buffalo herds. The ritual was an odd mix of Native American tradition and Christianity—with its messiah imagery—and it spread like wildfire, especially among the Sioux. Sitting Bull was killed because of it."

"And she says she's Sitting Bull's niece."

"Amazing," Gallagher agreed.

More than thirty of us walked six days to Big Foot's camp at Cherry Creek after Sitting Bull was killed because of the dance. Then his band and ours lit out toward the agency at Pine Ridge for Red Cloud's protection.

Some of us went on foot, some on horses, a bunch of us in wagons. Big Foot kept us along the river so the soldiers would not see us. The sky turned ice-blue and held like that for three days. Day and night we moved south. Big Foot lay sick in a wagon. His cough sounded like a rusty saw biting a green tree.

Three mornings after Christmas, Miss Mary Parker's favorite day, our wagons stopped. Painted Horses whispered there was cavalry below on the creek called Wounded Knee near Red Cloud's camp, and to make ready to run. Four braves went down the side of the cliff in a morning light that made the earth glow like a copper penny. They carried a white flag and came back with a doctor who said Big Foot had the wet cough.

By sundown we was camped and soldiers watched from cliffs on three sides above us. I went with Painted Horses to the ravine to get wood for the fire. A soldier with black teeth and hair like hide strips dipped in buffalo fat asked if I wanted to go to the creek bottom with him. I ran hard.

*   *   *

Eight soldiers and six of Big Foot's men guarded the chief. Painted Horses and I were asked to help tend him because they knew that Ten Trees had taught us medicine. The soldiers kept poking the old men with their guns, asking them if they was at Little Bighorn. I heard Big Foot tell one of his men to be humble for the sake of us all.

A bugle woke me at dawn. Painted Horses said the menfolk had been ordered to the center of the camp for talks with the soldiers. She pointed up on the hillside and said the soldiers had brought guns on wheels.

They searched our wagons, took our axes, our knives, guns and awls. They pointed guns at us and pulled the triggers on empty barrels. Above us I could hear the click and slide of soldiers loading.

When Painted Horses and I reached the council circle, my father's cousin, a medicine man named Yellow Bird, was dancing the Ghost Dance toward the rising sun. Shakes Bird joined him, calling to our dead for help. I wanted to dance with them, but Painted Horses held me back.

The foot soldiers told Yellow Bird and Shakes Bird to stop, but they did not. Yellow Bird sang to the spotted eagles that he wanted to die instead of us. He picked up fresh ash from the council fire, threw it into the air and sang, "This is the way I want to go, Grandfather—back to the dust."

Some foot soldiers tried to get to Yellow Bird. Others had their hands on Black Coyote, who was old, sick and could not hear right. They wanted his rifle. In the struggle it went off. And the soldiers commenced to shooting.

Painted Horses spun and dropped at the first firing. Part of my mother's right arm hung by a strip of skin. She looked up at me stupid-like. "Save yourself, Many Horses."

The guns on wheels boomed liked thunder. The cold sunny day turned smoky and the only sound was guns and screaming.

I picked my mother up and dragged her from the smoke toward

the ravine where we'd picked firewood. We almost made it. But the cannon roared behind us and Painted Horses rose up like roosters at dawn. A river of blood poured from my mother's mouth and she fell down the ravine into the plum bushes where old men, women and children hid.

The horse soldiers rode the top of the ravine, firing. The guns on wheels rolled in above us and everyone hiding commenced to run down toward the river. But there were too many in front of me to make it to the bottom, so I dragged Painted Horses' body into a thicket of cedar and pulled it over me while thunder shook the day.

When it was dark, the shooting slowed to the sound of wood popping in the night fire and then, at last, the night was just the creak of wagon, the moan of the wounded and the shout of far-away soldiers. I crawled out from under my mother. Her eyes were open and I shut them. I cut off a lock of her hair so I might free her spirit as Ten Trees had taught me. And then I left her.

At dawn I walked alone to the south. The sun was hidden in clouds and a wet cold blew the yellow grass where our steaming bodies lay.

A horse kicked stone on the butte above me. The soldier with the black teeth and the hair like hide dipped in fat saw me, laughed and spurred his bay into a dogtrot gait. I did not run, but faced him. I prayed to Grandfather that the soldier might shoot me down.

The soldier kicked out his boot. It struck me in the jaw and all went to night.

I woke to the pain of him between my legs. Snow fell. I took his thrusting, and pretended to sleep still. When he fell on me, his eyes closed, mouth wide and slick like a summer dog's. I bit his nose off and spit it in the snow.

He howled and rolled off me, clawing at his face. I tugged

the pistol from his belt and shot him twice between the legs and left him to scream.

From the top of the butte I saw a blizzard hunting us from the west. The frozen bodies of us all were twisted far below me, like branches burned, then tossed in the snow.

I turned and walked east with the soldier's horse, singing songs of death as the storm came for me.

Chapter Eighteen

"That poor woman," Andie murmured for the twentieth time as they trudged back down the mountain. "That poor, poor woman."

They had been in the woods for hours. Splattered with mud, anesthetized by fatigue. Gallagher could barely put one foot in front of the other. The rain had ebbed, but the woods were soaking and soft underfoot. The wind had turned out of the northwest again, a sordid Canadian breeze, and Gallagher had to fight to keep his teeth from chattering, unable to dispel the grim pictures the journal had provoked and the questions it had raised. How had Sarah Many Horses, as they had taken to calling her, gotten from Wounded Knee Creek, South Dakota, to Lawton, Vermont? If Many Horses had been murdered, as they assumed from Andie's portion of the journal, who had done it? And how was that mystery related to the Charun killings?

Lurking about the edges was an idea Gallagher could not ignore—that he was using these puzzles as a way to avoid dealing with his own problems. Not that that was surprising. He'd been doing that for years. Only now he might destroy his partnership with Jerry Matthews, something he could ill afford to do. Gallagher's last look at his bank account had given him a rotgut feeling. He had to tell Jerry what was happening in Lawton.

They crossed a hickory bench just above Andie's cornfield. A hundred yards below them on the flat adjoining the field, a man who moved like a professional football linebacker leaped over a rotting log, then zigzagged into a softwood grove that ran due south. The man was dressed head to toe in a camouflage suit made of hundreds of loose strips of fabric. Each strip had been dyed dull green, black or dun. He carried a matte-black, pump-action shotgun.

Andie's face screwed up. "I've had the place posted for five years and the damned turkey hunters still sneak in here. C'mon, he's using a trail that loops the fields before cutting across the road to your cabin."

Using the thin beech trunks as handholds, she swooped down the embankment. Gallagher's heels went out from under him in the wet leaves and he had to scramble to catch up. Andie angled into the softwoods without looking back. Gallagher huffed and puffed after her on a trail carpeted with pine and hemlock needles. The running hunter had kicked up wafers of forest duff. At a fork in the trail, he had gone left.

Andie waved to Gallagher over her shoulder to take the right fork. Even at less than a hundred yards, the shaggy camouflage made the hunter difficult to pick out. Then Gallagher saw a flash in the thick hemlock understory. The hunter was jogging sixty yards in front of them where the trails rejoined.

"Stop where you are!" Andie yelled. "You're trespassing on posted property!"

The hunter twisted athletically at her shout. His face mask was a cowl that came down across his face and shoulders like a medieval executioner's hood. The strips of camouflage fabric were soaking wet. They threw off spray and slapped at his torso as he spun toward her, putting Gallagher in mind of a painting he'd once seen of a bog man, a monster in Celtic legend that comes up out of the mire caked in swamp vegetation to wreak havoc on the world.

The hunter slid to one knee and shouldered the gun in the same motion.

Even with the last dregs of the vodka fuzzing her perception, Andie caught his intent. Just before he pulled the trigger, she lunged toward a moss-covered log, not knowing that as she dove, Olga Dawson's leather pouch came free of the pocket of her rain jacket and spun in the air.

Gallagher halted flat-footed, watching the pouch fly across the trail and land in a pile of dripping brush. The leafy cowl followed its trajectory, too. Gallagher took a step toward it. The hunter's gun swung in his direction. There was flame and deafening noise and Gallagher's legs kicked back from under him and he sprawled on his belly in the middle of the trail.

"I'm hit," Gallagher said dumbly.

The hunter pumped another round into his shotgun, rose and aimed down on Gallagher, who looked up and across the narrow clearing into that cowl. The unblinking eyes inside were like polished black marble. They held Gallagher transfixed the way a cobra's stare freezes prey—by reflecting an infinite, timeless vacuum that defies understanding.

Andie rose from behind the log with her pistol cupped in two trembling hands. "Police officer!" she shouted.

The hunter stared as if recognizing her. He whispered, "Angel!"

"Drop your weapon!" Andie commanded.

The hunter tugged the gun to the left and pulled the trigger. A branch next to Andie blew to the ground. Andie's pistol went off and the bullet ricocheted off an exposed rock to the gunman's left. He pumped the gun. She dove again and he shot once more, the pellets ripping the air high over her head. Then the hunter was up and sprinting away. He wove through the trees, looped west, and with that leafy camouflage on his shadows became the shadows of the forest. He was gone.

Andie made as if to give chase, but her legs would not support her and she had to hold onto a tree. Time slowed to the trickling of blood through Gallagher's jeans.

"He—he tried to kill me," Gallagher stammered. "Oh, man, I'm bleeding. I'm bleeding!"

Andie scrambled to his side. And then she had her arms around him, telling him that he was going to be all right. Gallagher closed his eyes and believed her.

She got him back up against a pine stump and took out a knife to cut a long slit up his jeans so she could inspect the wounds. Gallagher felt far away, almost watching himself. The nine pellets under his skin looked like peppercorns in Tabasco sauce.

"You're going to be sore and bruised, but you'll live," Andie announced. "We'll get you a doctor. I'll call Kerris and the game warden to see if they can find that asshole."

She was all business now. And it occurred to Gallagher that if Andie Nightingale was a bird with a broken wing, she was an eagle with a broken wing.

She helped him to his feet. Gallagher wobbled as adrenaline gave way to the weakness of shock, and that faraway feeling deepened. Andie wrapped his arm around her shoulder. She was a deceptively strong woman and they managed a reasonable pace until reaching the cut cornfield that lay between the pine forest and her farmhouse. The hard, relentless rain of the past few days had turned the field soil gooey and sucking.

Halfway across the field, Andie halted. A series of ten-inch puddles, alternating left and right, cratered the mud straight across to where the stubble corn met her lawn.

"Oh, God, no!" she cried, wrestling herself out from under Gallagher's weight. She sprinted through the muck toward the house, leaving him to hobble after her.

When Gallagher limped into the kitchen, Andie was hunched over the table, hysterical. "He got both crosses, the pouch, the hair, all of it!" Her mouth gaped in disbelief and her hands slapped at the pockets of her rain jacket. "Olga's pouch! Where's Olga's pouch?!"

Gallagher's thighs felt as if cigarettes had been stubbed out on them. "It's out there," he mumbled woozily. "When you dove, it landed in that brush pile where the trails met—"

Andie was already sprinting out the door and Gallagher realized he had just survived a face-to-face encounter with the madman behind the Charun drawings. He lurched toward the kitchen sink, gagged, then released his mortal awareness.

When Andie crashed back into the house, Gallagher was sprawled in the easy chair by the woodstove with towels draped across his thighs. The despair plastered across her face said it all: the killer had circled back and stolen Olga Dawson's pouch, too.

Andie went straight to the cabinets, tugging the doors open, slamming them shut. Furious, she spun and pointed at Gallagher. "Where's that bottle?"

He flashed on an image of himself at fourteen with his mother screaming the same way, for the same reason. Deflecting these scenes was like riding a bike, an easy, instinctive act once you learned how, he thought. You just imagined thick, bulletproof windows that roll up around you. With the windows come distance, separation, refuge.

"I poured it out," he said.

Andie turned and dug back through the spices until her fingers closed around the cooking sherry.

"It answers nothing," Gallagher said.

"You're wrong." She held the bottle before her as if it were a baby. Tears boiled and ran down her face. "Sometimes it answers everything."

She twisted the cap and gazed down the open bottle's throat. Her tongue wetted her lips. For an instant Gallagher himself fantasized tearing the bottle from her hands. Instead he got up and staggered to the door.

Outside, the raw wind slapped him alert, made him believe he could get back to the cabin and to his truck and to the hospital alone. Thirty yards up the driveway, his legs went to rubber. Gallagher toppled and lay stupefied in the wet gravel, wondering what the hell he was going to do.

"Gallagher!"

He got up on all fours and looked over his shoulder at the porch. Andie took a step toward him and poured the sherry into the bushes.

Chapter Nineteen

Getting involved with a drunk, even one in recovery, means an inevitable snaring in a web of lies. But because she chose sobriety in a crisis, Gallagher went against his instinct to flee and agreed to Andie's request not to report to the police the loss of the journals or the encounter in the forest.

"I've been thrown off this case," Andie explained as she raced him to the hospital. "To get the department to believe, we need hard evidence. Those pouches were our evidence. Now we have nothing to prove they even existed. We have to find something tying together the murders, the killer and the journal, or my lieutenant won't believe."

In his hazy state, it sounded logical. Especially because he needed the evidence, too. Gallagher needed something concrete to convince Jerry Matthews that this story took precedence over that of Father D'Angelo.

As they turned in to the Lamont Powell Memorial Clinic, which looked more like a sprawling Cape Cod cottage than a hospital, Gallagher agreed, but with two reservations: one, if she drank he would leave; and two, the second they found proof linking the journals to the killings, they would tell Bowman everything.

Andie pursed her lips, but nodded.

Bill Wilson, the emergency room physician, was an intense little man with curly brown hair and a bow tie. He gave Gallagher injections of antibiotics, Novocain and a general painkiller, then dug the shots from his legs.

"We'll need to report it," Wilson said.

"I already have, Bill," Andie reassured him. "I've taken Mr. Gallagher's statement myself."

Her concocted story had Gallagher wandering through the early-morning woods with his fishing pole in search of a remote riffle on the Bluekill River, only to wander into the shooting lane of a turkey hunter lined up on a spring gobbler. The hunter saw Gallagher hit the ground, panicked and ran.

"Any idea who this joker was?" Dr. Wilson asked. He plucked a bit of shot from under Gallagher's skin with scalpel and forceps. It made a clanking noise dropping into the tray.

Andie was very cool. "Only that he was trespassing on my land."

The painkillers made everything soft and warm for Gallagher. He thought of the bronze bust of the hospital's namesake he'd just passed in the hospital lobby.

"Lamont Powell, is he related to the mayor?" he asked the doctor.

"The better question is, who isn't?" Andie replied.

"Lamont was the current mayor's grandfather," Wilson said. He dug out another bit of shot. "Small town like this, most people are related one way or another."

"Like who?" Gallagher asked dreamily.

Wilson cocked his head in thought. "Chief Kerris, for one. He's the mayor's nephew. I think that's right, isn't it, Andie?"

Andie tightened and looked away, but nodded.

"Are you related?" Gallagher asked Andie.

"Absolutely not!"

Wilson said Gallagher had a choice to remain overnight in the hospital or go back to the cabin under Andie's supervision and rest. He chose the latter; Gallagher never liked hospitals. Wilson said he'd likely run a fever. But if it lasted longer than twenty-four hours, Gallagher was to return. The doctor prescribed a course of painkillers and powerful antibiotics and told him to stay off his feet at least for the next few days.

But it wasn't until Gallagher had struggled on crutches from his truck back to the cabin, crawled into bed and swallowed the pills Andie handed him that he relived the horror in the woods. Gallagher had directly confronted the black wall he had always anticipated at the end and seen zero, not even a short rehash of his own life. Have I meant nothing? he asked himself. Would my death matter to someone? Has life meant nothing to me? Gallagher understood the melodramatic tone to his questions and did not care. Shivers tore through him. He curled into a ball and pulled the thick blankets around his chin.

Andie came up the narrow staircase with a butterfly quilt under one arm. She wore a green-and-yellow University of Vermont sweatshirt, pants and wool socks. Her hair now rioted about her shoulders like river rapids. She sank exhausted into the chair in the corner with the quilt across her legs. Tess the cat padded up the stairs and curled on the floor between them.

"Go to sleep now," Andie whispered. "I'll be right here if you need me."

Gallagher tried to sleep, but his shivers would not stop. Andie got out of her chair and climbed on the bed to lie tight behind him on top of the blankets, the butterfly quilt over the both of them.

No words were spoken. Her body heat and woman's odor worked with the slow drift of the painkillers, massaging his spine, comforting his head with a muggy embrace, and Gallagher slept.

Gallagher's fever peaked and broke three times during the night. Each time Andie changed the sheets, then bathed his face and chest with a hot washcloth before feeding him more pills and crawling back under the butterfly quilt.

An hour before dawn, he wrestled with the fever as it surged a final time. The steady, warm headache where his neck met his skull crept forward until it was like a cowl, provoking dreams of Emily. . . .

They sat in a cafe just off Boulevard St. Germaine des Près in Paris. Gallagher ordered a bottle of wine.

"I'm not drinking," Emily said. She'd been distracted for days.

"It's our anniversary," Gallagher protested. "Four years ago today, we found the temple."

She played with the cuff of a leather jacket she'd bought earlier in the day. "I'm pregnant, Pat," she said.

His head began to thrum. His vision swayed. He held onto the table, understanding he could not have stood had he wanted to. "How?" he asked. "When?"

"You know how and when!"

Other patrons in the cafe were watching. "What are we going to do?"

"I don't know, Pat," she said. "What are we going to do?"

In Gallagher's dream it was suddenly night and the Boulevard St. Germaine became a river of oil. The bodies of Hank Potter and Olga Dawson drifted on the surface, spun round and round in an eddy. The eddy picked up speed, turned into a whirlpool and sucked the bodies down.

He went with them, drowning in the river of oil. Somewhere in the pure liquid night around him he heard the shake, shake of a gourd rattle against a wooden flute's delicate whistle and a woman's clear and proud singing in a language he did not understand.

Which startled Gallagher awake. Or at least halfway awake. He was no longer dreaming now, but adrift in that strange realm of knowing between sleep and alertness. He sensed fuzzily that he was still upstairs in the cabin, that Andie dozed behind him and that he'd been asleep for many hours. There was a vague awareness of the blankets around his shoulders, of the rug's mildew odor and the rain beating on the roof.

Then, out of the darkness, came a hot ball of light, a prismatic beacon discharging spasmodic hues of violet, rose and daffodil. The shake, shake of the rattle sounded more constant, like radio static. The ball of light widened. The beams of color broke up into pixels. Each pixel became a new source of charged radiance. Within the electric swirl of colors, Gallagher beheld the kaleidoscopic, barely discernible image of a woman. Her body was at an oblique angle. Her face pointed away.

It was like one of those pointillist paintings that, under scrutiny, seems a mishmash of dots, but from a distance suggests a dynamic figure in motion. Only her image was in his head as if on a screen, and each pixel seemed to spark with a random energy that leaped from hot point to hot point, obscuring the exact nature of her features.

Now the swirl of colors slowed to suggest a flowing blue skirt, plain black boots and a robe of thick brown buffalo fur around her shoulders. Her blouse was handwoven cloth, blood-red and embroidered with indigo symbols of the moon and stars. The pixels swirled and lost color, until they dazzled like a blizzard. The woman held the reins of a saddled horse in her hand. She trudged head-down into the whiteout. The horse crabbed sideways against the gale, then rose on hind legs, fighting against the reins.

The woman held on, turning her face to look right at Gallagher. Her voice echoed as if from across a desert canyon. "Help me," she pleaded. "Help me to go on!"

Gallagher bolted upright in the bed, drenched in cold sweat, flailing his head from side to side, searching in the gloomy room for he knew not what. Andie stirred at his thrashing and got up beside him. "Lie down," she soothed. "It's the fever again."

"No!" he gasped. Then stopped for a moment with his mouth agape. "I had a dream. But not like any I've ever—"

The cabin seemed suddenly charged with hidden meaning. "She lived here, didn't she? Sarah? Right here in this room. That's her in the etching downstairs next to the medium, isn't it?"

"It could be, but I don't know," Andie said in the sort of voice one uses with a three-year-old. "Those pictures have been in the cabin forever. Lie down now."

"You said Caleb haunted this place," Gallagher fretted.

She smiled ironically as she pressed him back into the pillow. "Why? Did you see the ghost?"

Wings fluttered in his stomach. A ghost? Impossible. He didn't believe in ghosts, or in any sort of afterlife, for that matter.

"No," he said at last. "It must have just made sense to me that she lived here once."

Dawn had come and with it an orange sky that filtered through the window and spoke of yet another spring storm's approach. Andie went down to the kitchen and soon there came the thump and bang of the woodstove being lit, and then, on the warming air, the smell of eggs frying. Gallagher stared out the window at the pine trees and the river, unable to shake the dream. He tried to explain it as his subconscious digesting the events of the previous five days. To be expected.

But the texture of the experience—that was inexplicable. Sarah Many Horses had appeared not as a body in any recognizable sense, but more as a gathering of excited electrons that had somehow touched down inside his mind. He wondered whether he was going crazy.

Andie came to the doorway with breakfast. She put pillows behind his back. In order to lay the tray across his lap, she had to lean close. She no longer smelled of booze, but of an intoxicating mix of sleepy woman and greenwood smoke. The wings in Gallagher's stomach fluttered faster still and for an instant he imagined that her skin had broken up into shimmering pixels.

"I think you'll feel better today," she said.

"I already do," he said, gazing at her.

Andie flushed and turned away with the back of her hand against her cheek. She took up a coffee mug from the pine bureau and sat in the overstuffed chair in the corner with her legs drawn up under her. She would not look at him.

As Gallagher wolfed down the eggs, toast and coffee, the bird wings faded to the flit of August butterflies. By the time he finished, he could believe that the dream and even the moment that had just passed between him and Andie had been some physiological crosscurrent of chemical imbalance, fatigue and hunger pangs.

Andie looked out the window toward the Bluekill. She bit at the quick of her fingernail. "Charun didn't come just to get my piece of Sarah Many Horses' journal," she said quietly. "And I can't help thinking he'll come back and there'll be one of those sick drawings tacked to my door."

The juice Gallagher was drinking caught in his throat. He looked at her and felt a deep hollow in the pit of his stomach. "You're safe," he said. "We're safe."

———

"For now."

A bluejay landed on the windowsill and bobbed his head before flying on. Downstairs in the woodstove, a burning log popped. At last she said, "Somehow Charun knew I had a piece of the journal. He must have figured out who has the other pieces."

"How?"

"I don't know, but if he can do it, we can, too," Andie replied.

"So where do we start?"

"I have no idea!" Andie cried. She threw up her arms. "My mother never said who the other journal holders were, and it's not the kind of thing you can put an advertisement in the paper about: 'Beware, Vermonters. You might be the next victim of a serial killer if you happen to have a piece of the journal of a Sioux woman who exists only in the mind of a disgraced, drunk police detective.'"

"Don't beat up on yourself," Gallagher chided. "That only goes one place."

"What do you know?" she demanded in a knife-edge tone. "Have you ever had these thoughts and they repeat and repeat and get bigger each time? Have you ever felt that the only way to silence them is with a drink?"

Gallagher was suddenly very angry at her. "No," he yelled. "But I've seen what happens when you try to stop the voices with the bottle . . . and so have you."

She visibly shuddered at that. Her shoulders rounded and she hung her head. "It must be painful to be here with me."

His anger faded as quickly as it had come. "Sometimes. But you're different than them."

"I'm a drunk, too."

Gallagher struggled to attach words to the conflicting feelings buffeting him and seized on one that surprised him. "You know about the woman you were named after, don't you? Andromeda?"

She waved a hand in the air. "I don't know. My mom said it was her grandfather's mother's name. They were from Greece."

"It's from myth," he said. "Andromeda was a great princess, raised to be a warrior. You helped Perseus become a hero, slay Medusa and thwart an evil king."

She smiled. "I did all that, huh?"

"Yes."

They were quiet again for a long time, acutely aware of each other in the tiny bedroom. At last Andie cleared her throat. "Okay, we keep going. We need to make a list of what we don't know and figure out a plan."

Over the next thirty minutes they came up with more than a dozen questions, including these: how was Many Horses' journal connected to these killings? And how could they find the other journal holders before more were killed?

"I think the answer's in the journal itself," Andie said at last. "And we've lost two parts of it."

Gallagher thought about that, then seized on another possibility. "We may have lost two parts, but we've read them. We know what's in them. What we don't understand is the significance. If we can figure out what makes Many Horses' story so important, we might figure out who wants it enough to kill for it."

Andie nodded. "We need to talk to an expert on the Sioux."

Chapter Twenty

"Ridiculous!" snapped Roger Barrett. He wagged his hand so frantically that the silver bracelets on his left wrist clanged. The professor was in his early fifties, with a sharp face, brush-cut black hair, a turquoise earring and a gaunt body. Barrett was an archival specialist from the University of Nebraska who was spending two years attached to Dartmouth's School of Native American Studies. His cluttered office was just off the school's library.

"It's real," Gallagher insisted.

"No. If such a journal existed, I would know of it," Barrett declared snippily.

"We've seen it," Andie insisted.

"A hoax, most likely. But bring it if you must and I'll take a look."

"The two pieces we had were stolen," Andie said.

"Then we're all wasting our time," Barrett sniffed, and with a flamboyant wave of dismissal, he swiveled his desk chair and began rummaging through a stack of printed material on the floor.

Andie yanked out her badge, leaned across the desk and shoved it under the professor's nose. "I didn't want to use my official status," she said in a soft yet commanding voice that caused Barrett to turn. "But the journal may be related to murders in Vermont."

"Murders!" Barrett shot upright. He toyed with a heavy turquoise ring. "I haven't heard anything about any murders involving a Sioux journal."

Gallagher glanced at the cover of the *Rutland Herald* in his lap and wondered how long the silence might last. Lieutenant Bowman had somehow kept the ramifications of Olga Dawson's death from leaking to the press. The story on today's regional page said simply that the fire remained under investigation. There was no mention of Charun, the drawings or the connection to Hank Potter.

"We're keeping that part of the investigation quiet," Andie said. "Professor, would such a journal be valuable enough to kill for?"

Barrett rubbed a bony finger along his lower lip. "From an anthropological as well as a historical perspective, I imagine a nineteenth-century journal written in English by a Lakota woman would be extremely valuable, especially if she survived Wounded Knee and told us how she danced the Ghost Dance."

"Why's that?" Gallagher asked.

"Because the details of the actual Ghost Dance from that time were closely guarded," Barrett explained. "We have descriptions of it by whites watching from afar. But we have no personal blow-by-blow, this-is-how-you-do-it from the peak of the movement."

Gallagher frowned. "But aren't there Native Americans who still practice the ritual on reservations out West?"

Barrett nodded. "Yes, but that Ghost Dance is a modern

interpretation of the rite. It could be argued that the ceremony as it was practiced in the 1890s largely died at Wounded Knee. So I guess what I'm saying is that such a journal's value—either intellectual or monetary—would depend on the writer and what she was writing about."

"We can tell you what we've read," Andie offered.

Barrett sat forward, elbows on his desk, chin cradled in his hands, as they told him everything they remembered about the two pieces of the journal.

"If this is a hoax, it's a sophisticated one," the professor said when they had finished. "Some of the things you are describing—the lock of hair and stones, for example—are unrelated to the Ghost Dance, but deeply rooted in other Sioux religious practices. The stones are sacred talismans used by shamans during many of the various ceremonies that make up Lakota spiritual life to this day. The hair relates specifically to a ceremony known as The Releasing of the Soul.

"When Many Horses says the hair can set her free, she's probably referring to that rite, which was actually outlawed around the same time the Ghost Dance was banned," Barrett continued. "In Lakota society, after death, a lock of hair was snipped from the deceased and purified in sweet-grass smoke, then wrapped in buckskin and stored in a special place in a relative's home. It was believed that the soul lived in the hair and had to be kept for at least a year before it could be released. During that time the family would gather what was necessary for the ritual—a buffalo cow robe, among others—and then there would be a great celebration in which the soul would be released to go on toward the life beyond."

"And all Sioux believe this?" Andie asked.

"Not dogmatically as a Catholic or a Jew might," Barrett admitted. "The Sioux religion is a charismatic one, passed on from one generation to the next, interpreted anew by each generation. That's why we don't know what the Ghost Dance was really like. Each successive Sioux, in a sense, invents his or her own religion, based on the spiritual ways of those who have gone before. Which is a verbose way of saying that a given Sioux may or may not believe in a ceremony like setting free the soul. But if she believes, she believes fervently."

Gallagher asked, "Why did the government outlaw the soul-releasing ceremony and the Ghost Dance?"

"You'd have to understand the way people thought a hundred years ago to—"

Barrett halted in mid-sentence, turned to his computer and began typing. Now came the screech of a modem and then a beep as the computer connected. He typed in a series of codes, followed by the words "Mooney/Tinmouth," then hit Enter.

Immediately there popped up on the screen a heading that read:

Tinmouth Correspondence Relating to the Army Investigation of the Battle of Wounded Knee and to the Sioux Campaign of 1890-1891. James Mooney et al; Report of the Secretary of War, Volume Nine, Appendix 3, pages 8004—8009. U.S. National Archives.

Barrett highlighted the entry and hit Enter. The transcript of a letter popped up on the screen and he turned it so Andie and Gallagher could read.

Major John Appleby
Chaplain, U.S. 7th Cavalry
Camped near Cheyenne River Agency, Dakota Territory

22 October 1890

Major General Horace Tinmouth
Chief of Chaplains

GHOST DANCE

U.S. War Department
Office of the Secretary
Washington, D.C.

Dear General Tinmouth,

At your request, I have passed seven weeks among the Sioux on the agencies at Standing Rock, Cheyenne Creek and Pine Ridge in Dakota Territory. Your concern about the growing influence of the Ghost Dance here is more than justified.

The situation grows more volatile every day.

The most dangerous Sioux, including Sitting Bull and Hump, have embraced the rite. Big Foot is jubilant ''about the coming of a messiah.'' All braves under Big Foot have Winchester repeating rifles, General.

Beyond that, however, the stated policy of the United States is for the Indian to be assimilated into our Christian culture. This ceremony represents a giant step backward in our efforts to eradicate savage custom.

Two weeks ago I got into position above No Water's camp at Pine Ridge at first light. Below me, a throng of eight hundred gathered around a twenty-foot aspen festooned with offerings.

Through the monocular I observed braves and squaws form a circle some four hundred yards in diameter. The squaws wore loose white robes with wide, flowing sleeves. The robes were painted blue at the neck, which is cut in a deep V and decorated with figures of birds, the moon and stars. The braves' Ghost Dance shirts were adorned with painted eagles and feathers attached by quills to the wrist and left to fly in the breeze. Many of the dancers painted their faces red with black half-moons on their cheeks and foreheads.

As the sun rose, the savages held hands and began a stamping pattern to their left. Their feet raised a fine red dust on the plain. And their detestable singing made what little hair I have left stand on end.

This went on from dawn toward midday. Shortly after twelve hundred hours, a fast-moving storm, the first after a tiresome, parched spell out here, advanced from the west. The sky turned purple. The wind hastened; and so did the dance and the song, until the whole pack of heathens whirled and howled.

I have a strong faith in Jesus Christ, General, and as the Chaplain of the 7th Cavalry since the massacre at Little Bighorn, you know my faith has been tested many times. But I do not rightly know how to explain what happened next. The motion of the storm cloud turned circular, but opposite in direction to the dancers below. A misty, swirling funnel emerged from the belly of the clouds. Rain fell on the dancers. Lightning flashed. Thunder clapped. At least fifty of the dancers pitched forward into the mud.

They convulsed and twitched, then lay stone-still. Some of the stricken lay in the mud for an hour or more while the storm raged and the frenzied dance went on around them.

Around thirteen hundred hours, the cloud retreated to the east. One by one, those who had fallen rose again. A section of the multitude broke from the circle and closed around each of those who had risen. And every time that happened, the one who had fallen would speak and gesture wildly and the whole lot of them became even more frenzied.

I left the bluff as frightened as I have been in my lifetime.

I still cannot explain what occurred that day. But you have known me nearly fifteen years, General, and at the risk of you thinking me mad, during that ceremony I felt the presence of something, something that must be stopped for the good of all.

Please relay my concerns to the Secretary of War.

Yours in Christ,

Major John Appleby

Barrett said, "That gives you an idea of the world your journal writer was living in shortly before the massacre."

Andie gestured toward the computer. "How extensive is your archive?"

"The most comprehensive repository of its kind," Barrett said proudly.

"Is Sarah in there?" Andie asked.

Barrett's eyebrows shot up and his nervous foppish energy

returned. "I've never heard the name, but possibly, possibly. Most of the documents have been scanned in by my graduate students."

The professor turned the computer screen back in his direction. Gallagher got up on his crutches, grimaced at the fire in his thighs, but came around the desk. Andie followed. A white bar appeared on the flat blue screen. Barrett typed: "Lakota/Many Horses." The computer came back: "No matches found."

Barrett looked up. "Does she mention any relatives?"

Andie said, "A mother. Painted Horses."

Barrett thought, shrugged, sniffed and typed the name. The computer came back: "No matches found."

"She mentioned a man named Ten Trees," Gallagher said.

The professor's mouth curled up in a sly grin. "I know Ten Trees." He tapped out the name on the computer, hit Enter, and immediately a text file filled the screen. The brief biography identified Ten Trees as a prominent Sioux shaman who fought alongside Crazy Horse during the War for the Black Hills. After Crazy Horse's death, Ten Trees joined Sitting Bull in exile in Canada, only to die of pneumonia. No mention was made of Many Horses, but at the end of the article there was a cross-referencing code of letters and numbers separated by semicolons.

"Photo-One," Gallagher read out loud. "You have pictures of Ten Trees?"

Barrett got an odd look on his face. "I've never seen one, but that's what it means," he said. He highlighted the code and hit Enter.

There was a beep and then there flashed on the computer a sepia-toned photograph of a powerfully built man, a woman and a young child in front of a tepee. The man stared into the camera with defiant, almond-shaped eyes. He had a broad, flaring nose and his hair was long and loose, except for a plait gathered in rawhide and decorated with a single feather that hung at the breast of a collarless, flowing denim shirt.

The woman was hauntingly beautiful, almost as tall as the man, with her hair in two dark braids and her neck surrounded by a high choker crafted of quills. A plaid shawl around her shoulder matched the skirt she wore. But it was the girl at the woman's side who almost caused Gallagher's knees to buckle.

No more than five, she had her mother's soft, round cheeks and her father's deeply set, almost Asian eyes, which looked shyly up at the camera and out through more than a hundred years in a way that made his head spin.

"Where did that picture come from?" Gallagher demanded shakily.

Barrett scrolled down to the bottom of the picture. "Ten Trees and family; Mary Parker family genealogy and photographic collection, Rapid City Historical Society, Rapid City, South Dakota."

"She said Mary Parker was her teacher at the mission school at Standing Rock!" Andie crowed. "That girl has to be Many Horses!"

Gallagher's head spun faster and he thought he might faint. It was impossible but true: the little girl had the young face of the woman in his dream.

"Are you all right, Pat?" Andie asked.

"I'm feeling faint," he said. "My legs."

They got Gallagher to a chair where he sat in numb shock. Barrett did several more searches, all of which confirmed that Mary Parker had been a Catholic missionary teacher on the reservation for ten years, beginning in 1880. Then he downloaded the photograph and printed it out. "I'm sorry I couldn't be of more help," he said, handing Andie the picture.

"You've been more help than you know," she replied. "Pat, I think I know how we can track down the rest of Many Horses' journal!"

Chapter Twenty-one

"Why the church?" Gallagher asked, hobbling out of the truck two hours later. They were parked in the lot across the street from St. Edward's Catholic Church in Lawton. Pigeons flushed from the belfry on a chill, damp wind that blew hard out of the northeast. A ragged vent of powder-blue sky opened, then shut in the storm canopy.

"The crucifixes," Andie said. "If the bundles all contained a crucifix, then I've got to believe that the people who hold them are like my mother and Olga, descended from Catholics who lived here in Lawton at the turn of the century. If Professor Barrett can find Miss Mary Parker in old documents, maybe we can find the other holders in the church records."

Gallagher nodded. But his mind was lurching about, which it had done repeatedly since they left Barrett's office. How was it possible that the girl in the photo archive matched the one in his dream? Gallagher's skin itched as if he had been invaded somehow.

Lost in these troubling thoughts, Gallagher crutched his

way out into the street. A cherry-red, jacked-up Ford F-350 with mud tires and a rack of overhead spotlights sped toward him. Andie jerked Gallagher back. The truck fender brushed the crease in his pants. Gallagher caught a glimpse of the driver. Bernie Chittenden, the dour owner of Lawton's general store, threw him a hatchet stare as he passed. He speeded up, then squealed tires around the corner and was gone.

"Hey!" Andie cried.

Almost immediately, a blue Chevy Suburban turned onto Whelton Lane. Chief Mike Kerris slowed to a stop and rolled down his window. He was alone. There were two bait-casting rods in the back seat. He popped a grape lollipop from his mouth and flashed a shark's grin.

"Your cousin just tried to run us over!" Andie shouted.

"Which cousin?" Kerris replied laconically. "I got a lot of them."

"Bernie Chittenden."

"Bernie?" Kerris laughed and pushed back the baseball cap on his head. "No way. Bernie's weird, but he wouldn't hurt a fly. Christ, he doesn't even hunt."

"I'm telling you, he almost hit Pat."

"Pat?" Kerris smirked knowingly. "Did Bernie hit you, Pat?"

"Just missed."

"Well, then," Kerris said dismissively. "But if it makes you feel any better, I'll go have a talk with the Bernster. By the way, how goes the mental-health vacation, Andie?"

Andie's body went rigid. Her fingernails dug into her palms. "Keeping busy."

The chief's grin disappeared. "Not in my town, I hope. Not while you're on leave."

"I'm a citizen, too, Mike," she said evenly. "By law I should be able to walk the streets without fear of someone running me over. By law I should be able to talk to whomever I want to."

Kerris' eyes went half lidded. A candied, purple tongue

flickered at his lips. "You go sticking your nose into official business when you've got no official business and I'll arrest you, Andie, obstruction of justice."

"Justice!" Andie scoffed. "You don't even understand the concept."

The chief stared at her with a sudden hatred that surprised Gallagher in its depth. "I spent seven years paying. What more do you want, Andie? My skin?"

"Isn't that what I lost?" she seethed.

Kerris threw the Suburban in gear, but held his foot on the brake pedal. "That is over, Andie," he said. "Forgotten around here by everyone but you!"

With that he released the pedal and burned rubber speeding away.

Gallagher shook his head, bewildered. "You want to tell me what that was all about?"

"No," Andie said icily.

She marched across the street and up the stairs to the rectory. By the time Gallagher got up on the porch, the door was opening and Libby Curtin had poked her head out. Her wooden cross dangled over a simple white fleece pullover. Libby saw Gallagher first. Her granny glasses slipped off her nose and she caught them. "Mr. Gallagher, the monsignor said to say if you came again that we can't help you."

"It's not about Father D'Angelo," Andie said. "We'd like to review some parish records from the Eighteen-nineties."

Curtin's hand flew to her mouth. "Eighteen-nineties?"

"That's right."

"Oh, Lord," she said.

With that the parish secretary scurried down the hallway, her cork-bed sandals scuffing on the blue Oriental rug. Andie and Gallagher followed her straight into McColl's office, where the giant priest was already rising behind his desk.

"Andie Nightingale!" he boomed. "Haven't seen you on Sundays in quite a while."

Andie shifted awkwardly. "I'm sorry, Monsignor, I've been busy."

He rubbed his massive hands together. Then he saw Gallagher and his exuberance cooled. "The bishop already gave you his response. You don't think bringing the police in on your side's going to change things, do you?"

Gallagher repositioned the crutches under his arms. "No, Monsignor. I get the feeling you're not easily swayed by secular authorities of any kind."

McColl's jaw set hard at that crack, but he gestured to them to sit, asking, "Is your request to see the records from the Eighteen-nineties official or unofficial, Andie? And what might your role be in this, Mr. Gallagher?"

"Something wrong, Monsignor?" Andie replied.

"Answer my question, I'll answer yours."

"Right now it's unofficial," Andie said. "Pat has taken an interest in my project. We're sort of working together."

"On?"

"I'd rather not say. Why the concern?"

The priest drummed his fingers on the desktop. "Because many of the original records from that decade, and indeed from the forty years prior, were stolen."

A few minutes later a very worried Libby Curtin played with the wooden crucifix around her neck and in a stammering cadence said that back in mid-March, she'd received a phone call from a man who told her he was doing genealogical research. He thought his maternal great-great-grandmother was from out Lawton way and he wanted to know about the condition of the parish's baptismal and death records for the years 1865 to 1895.

Libby said the records were in excellent condition and offered to look through them herself, but the man said he liked examining the documents firsthand and would be out sometime soon to have a look. In the meantime, Libby went on her honeymoon.

At that point, McColl chimed in to say that during her absence he had traveled to a conference in Boston. When he returned, someone had jimmied the lock to the back porch and taken five hundred dollars, a silver Eucharist plate and the records.

"And damaged the painting of Father D'Angelo?" Gallagher asked.

"Yes, that, too," Monsignor McColl replied. His face flushed. He pulled out a handkerchief and mopped at his sweated brow. Then he reached for a bottle of antacid pills and swallowed two. "I'm sorry. This stomach thing won't quit. And I've been under a lot of stress lately."

In the outer office, a phone rang. Libby Curtin quietly opened the door and slipped out.

"Monsignor," Andie said, "in your research into Father D'Angelo, did you ever come across mention of an Indian woman, a Sioux?"

"No," he said immediately. His face flushed again, redder this time.

"Her name, we believe, was Sarah," Gallagher said, watching McColl closely. "Sarah Many Horses."

"No, no," the priest said, shaking his head vigorously. He made as if to get up and then thought better of it. "I would remember that name. A Sioux, you say? How in God's name did a Sioux get to Vermont?"

"That's what we're trying to figure out," Andie said.

The monsignor hesitated. "So that's why you wanted to review the baptismal certificates?"

"Yes."

The priest forced a chuckle. "Well, I can tell you there are no Sioux in our records here."

"We weren't expecting to find her in the records," Andie replied. "Just people who might have known her."

He crossed his beefy arms. "What's this all about?"

"Let's say I suspect this Sarah, the Sioux woman, was murdered in Lawton a hundred years ago."

"A hundred years ago?!" Monsignor McColl cried. "No offense, Andie, but is this the best spending of the taxpayers' money?"

"It is if it's connected to the two murders here, as I believe it is."

"The two murders?"

"Hank Potter," Gallagher said. "And Olga Dawson."

"Olga Dawson?" he repeated slowly, rolling the words meekly in his mouth. He was staring out at the birdbath in the garden. "No one told me she was murdered. I'm to say her memorial service tomorrow."

"Maybe you can help us," Andie said.

He patted his forehead with the handkerchief again and turned away from the window. "Yes, yes, of course, anything, Andie."

Libby Curtin quietly reentered the room and shut the door behind her.

Gallagher said, "We want to put together a list of parishioners who would have been active at St. Edward's in 1894."

The priest sat silent for a moment, his jaw moving as if he were chewing or talking to himself. Then he leaned back in his chair. "I'm afraid those certificates were your best bet."

"Dead end?" Andie asked.

"I'm sorry."

"Monsignor?" the secretary said.

"Yes, yes, what is it, Libby?"

"I'm sorry, Monsignor, but if it's old lists of parishioners they're after, I know where to find them."

Chapter Twenty-two

A fine mist fell when Gallagher and Andie drove past the village of Cartersburg in south-central Vermont three days later.

"McColl's hiding something," Gallagher said.

"That's at least the twenty-fifth time you've said that since we left his office," Andie replied sourly. "I say he looked like a man who can't kick a stomach flu."

"I'm just telling you what I saw."

"I heard you the first time. We decided to focus on finding the journal holders, remember?"

There had been a significant cooling between them in the past few days. After leaving the rectory, Gallagher had made the mistake of bringing up Chief Kerris again. Ever since then, their interaction had been strained. A voice inside Gallagher told him to withdraw his help and focus on Father D'Angelo. But then the memory of his dream of Many Horses would reappear, and instantly the thought of quitting would be discarded.

"That must be Nyren's driveway up there on the right,"

Gallagher said, looking at the manila folder and the map on his lap.

According to the records, the driveway belonged to David Nyren, the head librarian in Cartersburg. Nyren was the sole living descendant of Martha and Paul Nyren, who in turn were descended by matrilineal lines from Arthur Webb, a St. Edward's parishioner and former first constable of the town of Lawton in the 1890s.

Libby Curtin had described a file at the Lawton Historical Society that included rosters of the Knights of Columbus and the St. Edward's parish going back one hundred and twenty-five years. Those lists yielded thirty-two names. It had taken them two days to track forward eighteen of the thirty-two, using state and local birth and death records as well as the Internet and CD-ROM telephone directories to identify a possible hundred and seventy-six descendants, sixty-seven of whom were living in Vermont. Before spending another two days tracking forward the remaining fourteen names, Andie and Gallagher had decided to take a look at as many of the known descendants as possible.

They had feared a cold telephone call might provoke a false response, so they had gone to the homes or businesses of sixteen of the possible journal holders in the past twenty-four hours, all of whom lived in the southern half of the state, and all of whom had greeted their questions about a journal and a crucifix with blank stares and, in several instances, incredulous laughter. Four didn't even know they had relatives who hailed from Lawton.

Nyren was possibility number seventeen.

His dirt driveway was almost a quarter of a mile long. They drove through a dense spruce forest and Gallagher's mind drifted back, as it had so often in the past few days, to Monsignor McColl and his work for Father D'Angelo. His nervousness when questioned about the soon-to-be-venerable priest nagged at Gallagher.

They broke through the forest. Nyren's house, yellow with a gambrel roof, was set on a manicured lawn. The lime sprouts of tulips showed along a brick walkway. A late-model white Honda Accord was parked in a turnoff under a white pine.

When they got out, Gallagher grunted at the stiffness in his thighs, but knew the crutches were no longer necessary. He left them in the truck.

The storm door to the front porch flapped open against the shake-shingle siding. Rain puddled on the warped, wide-planked porch floor. Spirals of violet and blue twisted on the dappled water surface and ran downhill toward the interior door, which was also ajar. The air reeked.

"Gas?" Gallagher said.

Andie nodded. She pushed the interior door open another couple of inches. The fumes became even stronger. "Mr. Nyren?" she called.

At the far end of the short hallway, a grandfather clock struck the quarter hour. From upstairs came a squeaking noise, as if a piece of furniture, possibly a chair, had been pushed across the wood floor. Andie took several steps inside, with Gallagher right behind her taking inventory of the decor. Sprays of baby's breath highlighted the light blue wallpaper in the hallway. A maple drop-leaf table covered with a white doily rested against the wall below a gilt overmantel mirror. Queen Anne chairs in faded chintz braced the table.

"Welcome to Grandma's house," Gallagher murmured.

"Quiet, he might hear you!" Andie hissed. Then she called out, louder this time, "Mr. Nyren? I'm Sergeant Andie Nightingale with the Vermont Bureau of Criminal Investigations. Hello?"

The clock ticked. The steam register knock-knocked. Light rain splatted against the windows.

Andie's lips pursed. She drew her pistol. She went up the staircase with a powerful grace. Gallagher trailed three feet behind, listening to the amplified roar of blood at his temples. When he stepped on the fourth stair, it whined. Andie twisted, nostrils flared, and motioned with her toe that he should come up the inside of the riser.

Above them, the floor broke around to the right and she craned her neck to see up over the landing. Gallagher wondered what he'd do if there was gunfire. Running like hell seemed the obvious choice, but to his surprise, he knew he wouldn't. Not while Andie was there.

On the landing, the drawers of two legal-size filing cabinets had been tugged open, the files and papers within thrust up in disarray. One cabinet sprawled on its side. Thousands of pieces of paper were strewn across the green carpet.

Andie came to the landing in a crouch. The door on the left opened into an office. The burled walnut desk had been turned over. The computer screen still radiated blue despite its cracked housing. Files and papers from three more cabinets were tossed about the room. The bookcase was toppled. Nyren's framed diploma in library science from St. Michael's College and two honorary plaques from the Vermont Historical Society hung askew on the white wall beyond the desk. A floorboard was propped against one of the standing files. A hole gaped in the floor below.

Andie brushed by Gallagher and, over the gas scent, he smelled the good, clean autumn odor of her that had surrounded him the morning after he was shot. A pleasant feeling came over him, only to be washed away in the next instant by a surge of dread, for him and for her; and he wanted to tell her they should leave the librarian's house before they looked in that other bedroom.

But Andie was already sideslipping across the blizzard of paper on the landing. She pressed against the jamb, reached out and turned the mock crystal doorknob. It turned easily. She motioned to Gallagher to stay back. In one movement, Andie used her left hand to push open the door while looping around and into the room with the gun leading.

Her breath came in a snap and a whoosh. Gallagher stepped in behind her and the first flares of disbelief and revulsion mutated to vertigo. The floor seemed to float away underneath him.

The linen on the sleigh bed lay a-tangle. Green drapery billowed free in the dank breeze coming through the open window. Nyren was on his knees, his white terry-cloth robe hoisted up over his fat, naked back. Two leather belts strapped his legs around the chair legs. Sash from the drapery bound his wrists to the arms of the chair. A second sash was wound around his neck and tied to one of the chair slats. An orange washcloth jutted from his mouth. The index finger on his left hand was gone at the second joint. Blood from a series of brutal oblong wounds to his upper torso drenched the terry-cloth robe. A similar blow cleaved triangularly into the side of his head above the right ear. Dried snot and tears streaked those portions of his cheeks not bloodstained.

Pinned on the left arm of the mutilated corpse was a third drawing.

Andie waved her left hand at Gallagher, but did not take her eyes off the librarian. "Go . . . go back downstairs to the hallway," she said. "I saw a phone. Call nine-one-one."

Gallagher moved as if in a trance. Over the years he had witnessed many disturbing things—an exorcism in western Africa, a circumcision puberty rite in Papua New Guinea—but never a ritualistic killing like this. By the time the brutality of it broke through the protective shock that had cradled him in the librarian's bedroom he had reached the head of the landing and began to choke.

Suddenly, the air in the hallway below gusted unnaturally and a six-foot incendiary wave of reddish blue heaved up, hungry, hot and explosive, across the saturated rug, gorging on the gasoline fumes. The flame stumbled at the bottom of the stairs, then gathered hellish strength and came on.

The entire house breathed asthmatically as the blaze sought vapor and the oxygen pouring through the open window in the librarian's bedroom.

"Fire!" Gallagher bellowed. "Fire, Andie! Get out!"

He sprinted back across the sea of paper, tripped and went headlong into Andie as she appeared at the door. They crashed together at the dead librarian's feet, then scrambled up as the incandescent cloud sniffed the gas-soaked paper behind them and the fire's breathing became the labored rumbling of freight cars at night.

Gallagher had Andie by the upper arm, dragging her toward the window. A metal climbing piton jutted from the sill. A blue rope fell away into space. "Go down the rope!" he yelled.

But she jerked away just as the flame pillowed in the doorway, went back and fumbled at the corpse. She got the note, then looked around.

"What are you doing?!" Gallagher screamed.

"Looking for the journal!" she yelled. "The crucifix! Anything!"

"They're not here," he bellowed, grabbing her tighter this time. He hauled her to the window and forced her through even as the flames sawed furiously across the royal blue carpet, enveloped Nyren and set the drapes and his gas-dampened pant cuffs afire. Gallagher dove out onto the steep roof, clawed for the rope, missed, tumbled twice and then, still burning, twisted into space.

Chapter Twenty-three

"If I don't get a straight answer on how you two came to be in a burning house with a dead librarian strapped to a chair, I'll arrest you both, trooper or no trooper, big-time filmmaker or no big-time filmmaker," Lieutenant Brigid Bowman fumed.

Andie and Gallagher huddled with blankets around their shoulders on a gurney in the back of an emergency response van. The EMT said two of Andie's ribs were bruised. Gallagher had minor burns on his calves. Outside, a crew of volunteer firemen soaked down what little remained of the antique Cape. The rest of the yard was already taped off. Troopers were scouring for evidence.

"I'd like to hear this, too," Chief Kerris said, appearing from behind the ambulance door. He looked like he hadn't slept in days. He had scratches on the backs of his hands and one large scratch across his cheek. His fourteen-inch rubber boots were coated in mud.

Bowman's focus wavered. "How did you get here so soon, Chief? Lawton's an hour away."

Kerris reached up to adjust the brim of his baseball cap. "The family has a camp on a lake about ten miles from here. I was clearing some brush, getting it ready for summer, when I heard the call on my scanner. Is it him again? Charun?"

Bowman nodded, then said to Andie, "I'm still waiting, Sergeant."

Andie examined the stitching of the blanket around her shoulders with the sort of lost facial cast Gallagher used to see on his father when Seamus was preparing to pick up the bottle again after one of his intermittent layoffs. She took a deep breath as if to prepare herself for the long fall into the abyss.

"It's my fault," Gallagher blurted. "I found a crucifix on a gold chain in the meadow down by the barn at Olga Dawson's and I should have shown it to you right away, but after seeing the drawing, I forgot."

Bowman glared at Gallagher and then at Andie. "Crucifix? Olga Dawson? Out with it. I want it all and I want it now."

Gallagher lied straight-faced, saying he'd brought the gold chain to Andie the night after the search of his cabin. Andie hesitated, glanced at Gallagher, then haltingly spoke of her shock at seeing the cross, of the story of her mother and the pouch and the journal and something horrible that had happened in Lawton one hundred years ago; and how she and Gallagher had gone looking for Olga Dawson's piece of the journal and found it in a cave on Lawton Mountain. Gallagher broke in with another bald fabrication, saying that both sections of the journal were stolen from Andie's house while they were at Hank Potter's trying to determine whether he'd had a portion of it or not.

Together they explained the logic of going to see Monsignor McColl and how eventually that had led them to the librarian's house. The killer had been upstairs when they knocked at the front door. He bailed out the window on a climbing rope, then torched the place just as they were finding the librarian's corpse.

Even through the sacklike jacket Chief Kerris wore, Gallagher could see his rib cage rising and falling quicker and quicker as he and Andie wove their web of truths and falsehoods.

"This is bullshit," he said when they finished. "I don't believe a word of it."

Andie held up the killer's latest drawing and missive. "This was pinned to the librarian's chest when we found him. What don't you believe?"

Kerris gaped at the drawing as if he were hypnotized. Charun's head was fully turned now. The sliver of white in his eyes had become a quarter moon. A third of the stitches along the lips had been sliced open to reveal a single sharp tooth; the left corner of the mouth was arched in a sneer. The phallus was bigger and bloodier than on the drawing he'd left at Olga Dawson's house. There was a noose tied around the tip of the penis.

Andie flipped the paper over so Kerris and Bowman could read the note:

Angel said there were many ways to go and return. My Persephone said we could get closest through the shaman's mixture and the rope. She swelled deliciously tight around me. She bucked and gasped, "Vida!"

The mushroom took my head and I came up, arms spread wide, hard and strong with the rope. Persephone has left me behind. Blind and deaf and mute.

But now my mouth opens to taste the mystery. And the light reaches my eyes.

"Satisfied, Chief?" Andie asked.

Kerris cranked his head around. Beads of sweat dripped off his nose, but his jaw set tense and determined.

"I still don't believe these killings are linked to something that happened in Lawton a hundred years ago," he said. "My family goes back a hundred and fifty years in this town. I've never heard of anything about an 'abomination' or whatever your mother called it, Andie. Until last week, there've only been two recorded murders in Lawton and those were close to thirty years ago."

Andie gripped the edge of the wool blanket. "C'mon, Mike, you know better than most that it's not hard to bury things if you know how."

For an instant pure hatred crossed Kerris' face, but he kept control. "I still don't buy it."

"What's going on with you two?" Bowman demanded.

"It's personal, Lieutenant," Andie said, never letting her eyes leave Kerris. "But Mike knows what I'm talking about. Lawton's always kept secrets. It's part of the code among certain families in town."

"I don't know what she's talking about," Kerris said evenly.

"Old habits die the hardest, don't they?" Andie responded.

Bowman pointed at the two of them. "Whatever it is between you two, I won't have it cloud this investigation. I—"

An older trooper in a black rain slicker came across the lawn. "Sorry to interrupt, Lieutenant, but we've got a few things you should know. We found the Explorer about two miles from here, pulled off into the ditch. We ran the dog on the scent, but he lost it not far from the truck. Killer must have gone to water and then out into a swamp. We've got troopers working all the roads, but it's wilderness up in there for twenty miles in every direction."

The mist had lifted. And for the first time they all felt the forbidding presence of the mountains and the vast hardwood forests that soared above Nyren's property. A man could hide from himself in there for weeks, Gallagher thought. And then he had the creepy-crawly sensation that they were being watched. He scanned the forest, but saw nothing.

"Anything in the truck, Harry?" Bowman asked the trooper. "Files? Maybe an old leather pouch or something?"

"No files or pouches that I saw," Harry said. "Fresh bloodstains, though."

"Damn it," Andie groaned. "He got our list of names and we don't have a copy."

"Have the whole vehicle dusted for prints, though I get the feeling we're not going to find any," Bowman ordered. "Get samples of that blood, too, and see if it matches records of the librarian's blood type. With the fire, I don't think we'll be doing any DNA matches, but just the same . . . And start a door-to-door a mile to either side of where that Explorer was found. Anything else I should know about?"

The trooper nodded. He held up two plastic evidence bags. In one was a swatch of green camouflage about four inches by two inches long. In the other was a scarlet wooden bead, thin, about the length of a fingernail.

"He left big footprints going out of here, too," the trooper said. "And a muddy glove print on a birch tree. From the height of it, he's a huge son of a bitch. We're taking casts of the footprints."

"Good, good," Bowman said, allowing herself a smile. "He's finally leaving traces of himself behind, besides what he wants us to see. Now we'll get him."

As suddenly as that rare smile had passed her lips, Bowman turned steely again. "Sergeant, this is the second time you've kept vital information back in this case, and I want to know why."

"Would you have believed me, Brigid?" Andie retorted. "Or would you have chalked it up as the ravings of a drunk female cop, especially after the pieces of the journal and the two crosses were stolen and I had no evidence to back me up?

Even if you did believe me, would you have let me work on the case?"

The lieutenant held herself stiffly. She looked away toward the woods for a moment, then said, "So we don't have any of this journal?"

"No," Andie said. "Right now, we do not."

Bowman rolled her tongue around the inside of her cheek. "I've got to ask this, Andie. How long are you from your last drink?"

Andie flinched and swallowed at the question. There was the slightest upturn at the corners of Kerris' lips and Gallagher wanted to punch him in the face.

"I was twenty-one months and twelve days sober until I found my mom's best friend hacked, burned and possibly sexually assaulted," Andie said. "I am now four days sober."

Bowman fiddled with the buttons of her raincoat. Droplets stood out on the moussed spikes of her white hairdo.

"You've got to believe me, Brigid," Andie pleaded.

"I don't believe what I don't see," Bowman snapped. "We don't have the journal, but we do have this third note from the killer. We do have a piece of his clothing. We do have a bead. We do have his semen from Hank Potter. We may have more evidence from Gallagher's Explorer. Those pieces of concrete evidence are where I'm going to focus this investigation."

"You're not going to pursue the journal?" Andie cried. "There are other people out there who are at risk!"

Bowman held up her hand to end further protest. "Look at it from my perspective. My team has a current caseload of twenty-two active investigations and half that many investigators. Where do I put my manpower? On a trail that's an hour old—maybe someone saw someone leaving the librarian's house after the fire was set or after abandoning Mr. Gallagher's truck or running through the woods. Or maybe someone saw him drawing this picture at a local McDonald's. You know as well as I do that I've got to proceed where the evidence is the freshest. If that runs out of steam, we'll push the journal."

"Now you're talking," Kerris said.

The lieutenant shot the chief a quick glance of disapproval, then returned to Andie. "Because of your . . . recent actions, I'm forced to put you on an additional fourteen-day leave on top of the original fourteen, which will mean you'll be thirty days dry when you return. Which gives me three investigators to work on this case."

"Brigid, you can't!"

"Sergeant, I can. And you're lucky not to be suspended indefinitely."

Chapter Twenty-four

"I won't stop," Andie vowed. She paced back and forth across her kitchen. "She's wrong and I'm right!"

"She's letting her bureaucratic side get in the way of the investigation," Gallagher agreed.

"I admit it: I drank and didn't tell her about the journal! But that's no reason to . . . I'm not stopping!"

"Then I'm not, either," Gallagher said.

Andie shook her head. "I can't let you get more involved in this."

He pointed at his legs. "I've been wounded twice by this bastard. It's gotten personal."

"But—"

"No buts. I'm not backing off, either."

Her finger wormed into the weave of the Irish wool sweater she wore. She shuffled to the bay window and looked out. It was nearly four o'clock in the afternoon. Despite the prolonged chilly spell, the grass on her lawn was inches taller than it had been when Gallagher arrived in Lawton. Red-winged blackbirds sang in the rushes of the lily pond. The rusty hulls of the maple-tree buds littered the rich dark loam of her overturned garden. On the trees themselves were the faint brush strokes of the year's first leaves. But winter still embraced the upper two-thirds of Lawton Mountain.

"It will be time to plant my garden soon," she remarked.

Gallagher walked over and looked out the window. "Why do you like to work with plants so much?"

"I suppose it's my way of getting in touch with my higher power," she said. "My way of attaching so I can get through the bad times."

"So you believe in God?"

Andie turned and gazed at him with a slightly furrowed brow. "Believing in a higher power is the only way to recover."

"I don't believe," he said.

"I know," she replied with a trace of sadness in her voice, and it occurred to Gallagher that he enjoyed watching the broad range of emotions she displayed. Andie was the most alive being he'd ever known.

Before he could tell her that, she said, "I owe you a thanks."

"For what?"

"Well, for starters, you got me out of a burning house," she replied. "And then you stood up for me with Bowman and Kerris. No one's done anything like that for me in a long time. No one's cared to."

She stood on tiptoes, then pecked Gallagher on the lips. He froze. Disappointment flickered across her face; then her expression tightened and she turned away from him. "It's because of my drinking, isn't it?"

Gallagher's throat constricted. "No, I . . ."

"Do you want to hear about my drinking, the whole thing? I've never told anyone the whole thing."

"Why would you tell me?"

"Like you said, we're alike. I figure you might understand."

Gallagher wanted to go out into the night and walk and not hear. But the wounded expression on her face would not let him leave. "I'll listen."

Andie said that during the downward spiral of her father after the death of her brother, the farm, once one of the best-run in Lawton, fell into disrepair. Her parents fought. Andie herself was a lonely little girl whose best friends were her mother and Olga Dawson.

But the summer between her fifteenth and sixteenth year, nature transformed Andie Nightingale from a gawky, shy girl into a tall, well-proportioned, beautiful young woman. For the first time in her life, boys paid attention to her.

Just before the end of her junior year in high school, she met Mike Kerris, a freshman at the University of Vermont. He was handsome and related through his mother to the Powells, the richest and most powerful family in Lawton. Kerris was also the rising star of the UVM football and ski teams.

She met him at a party in early June, around graduation time. Kerris gave her her first drink: vodka and orange juice. The drink made everything shimmery and warm and he kissed her before dropping her off at home. Kerris went away for part of the summer, then came back and they ran into each other a second time at a party. She got very drunk and he told her he loved her. Her life at home was dreary, and here was a glamorous new beginning. She told Kerris she loved him, too.

"I woke up the next morning to discover I'd lost my virginity," Andie said, smiling weakly at Gallagher. "Not exactly how I'd planned it. And I didn't hear from him for a long time after that."

Andie took a big breath and unraveled the rest of her tale the way a woman struck with vertigo might approach the edge of the Grand Canyon. Kerris called out of the blue in late August to invite her to a third party after the Shrine game between Vermont's and New Hampshire's football all-stars.

Andie told her parents she was going to spend the night at a friend's house.

Kerris gave her a drink the moment she walked into the condominium some older kids had rented at the base of the Lawton ski area. Every time her glass emptied, Kerris gave her a drink.

"I remember dancing, everything so shimmery and funny," Andie said. "Then the shimmers blurred until it was dark. Mike was with me on a bed in a back room."

She stopped. Her chin did a slow dance in the air and her eyes watered.

"You don't have to tell me this if you don't want to," Gallagher said.

"There were other boys in the room with us—they—" Andie choked. "Olga found me wandering in the streets downtown. I didn't have many clothes on. To this day I have no idea how I got there."

The hatred that had sparked between her and Kerris at the librarian's house was there on her face again.

"Did you press charges?" Gallagher asked.

"I went to the police, but—" Andie stopped. "You don't understand Lawton. The Powells have been around forever. They're like the Kennedys. When one of them gets in trouble, they close ranks."

Kerris' uncle Bruce, once the local state's attorney and now the esteemed and entrepreneurial mayor of Lawton, went to Andie's father and convinced him to convince Andie that a public trial would only serve to damage a lot of young people with their whole lives ahead of them. In exchange for dropping the charges, they cut a deal. The Powells would completely pay for Andie's education. Kerris would leave Vermont and go to Chile to be a ski instructor at a resort owned by a family friend.

"He was gone six or seven years down there," Andie said.

"But what he'd done haunted me every day. I tried to channel my anger by becoming a cop. But sometimes it would get the better of me and I'd remember how shimmery the world was that night; and, sick as it sounds, I'd sneak drinks by myself so I'd feel what it was like before the rape."

Andie sat in the easy chair next to the woodstove, drew her heels up to her buttocks and cleared her throat. And cleared it again.

"How the hell did Kerris get to be police chief?" Gallagher demanded.

"The Powell way," she said, shrugging. "The family decided seven years in exile was long enough and they arranged a slot for him at the state academy over in Pittsford. He spent two years as deputy on the Lawton force; then the mayor eased the old chief out. Now the mastermind of my rape is the law in town."

Her eyes ran bloodshot. She put her head in her hands and her shoulders shook. Gallagher flashed on an image of his ex-wife in the same defeated posture. "Andie?"

"What?" she mumbled.

"I'm sorry I pulled away from you."

He walked over to her. His hands shook before they came to rest on her shoulders. She smelled of freshly fallen leaves. A vein pulsed gently at the nape of her neck. He kissed her on that vein, then felt panic at the sense of a gaping hole that opened up in front of him. She must have seen the same yawning chasm, too, because the muscles between her neck and shoulders tightened and her hand shook when she reached out to stroke his cheek.

"I haven't . . ." Andie said, so soft and so vulnerable. "I haven't since then."

Chapter Twenty-five

Through the rain-streaked panes of Andie's bedroom window, Gallagher watched a band of blackbirds land in a stand of staghorn sumac and peck at the crimson seedpods. The blood-red shells fell from their beaks like scabs picked off a fresh wound. Pewter clouds broke up behind the birds. The sun rose, flooding the sky with pink light.

Andie's breasts swelled against his back. She made gentle noises in her sleep that struck him as the most soothing sounds he had listened to in a long time. Her hand came across his chest.

They had taken it ever so slowly. Each time Andie tensed at his kiss or his touch, Gallagher had backed off and waited for her to get through whatever barrier she had to cross. Somewhere in the middle of the night they were at last joined, and they both cried out in a release stunning in its intensity.

Gallagher knew he should have been content lying there. But instead he felt threatened. Andie was capable of opening the glass boxes in his head, of making him feel in a way he had not thought was possible. And he realized that, for some reason, the swelling of that strange emotion inside him scared him as much as the thought of facing Charun again. He tried to move out from under her arm, but couldn't; and he lay there for the longest time staring blankly at the sunrise, trying to think about the murders and Many Horses' journal as a way to avoid thinking about Andie Nightingale.

That last message from Charun stayed with him.

Angel said there were many ways to go and return. My Persephone said we could get closest through the shaman's mixture and the rope. She swelled deliciously tight around me. She bucked and gasped, "Vida!"

The mushroom took my head and I came up, arms spread wide, hard and strong with the rope. Persephone has left me behind. Blind and deaf and mute.

But now my mouth opens to taste the mystery. And the light reaches my eyes.

Who was the old man? Gallagher asked himself. Was it Charun's father? He didn't remember any paternal figure mentioned in the Charun myths. Where did Charun and Angel want to go and return? The smoke and the rope? The imagery of swelling suggested sex. But why did Angel gasp "life" in Spanish? Where did she go when she left Charun? Why was light reaching Charun's eyes because of the homicides? How was all this related to the killings and the journal? And why had Charun whispered "Angel" before he shot at Andie in the forest?

Playing against the back wall of Gallagher's questions was a larger, perhaps even more disturbing query: how had Gallagher become so involved, when he had come to Vermont hoping to escape?

Fatigue crashed over him like a wave. His eyelids drooped,

blinked open, then shut finally, and despite his every effort, he drowsed into the intoxicating rhythm of Andie's breath.

In Gallagher's dream, fog snaked along a river bottom choked with silver-barked trees. Cedar scented the air. The fog swirled and his mother staggered toward him singing, only to change into Emily shuffling out of a hospital in Paris. It was a warm, sunny July day. She hugged her stomach as if overcome by a sudden illness. Gallagher ran through the traffic to her.

"You okay?"

"I'll survive," Emily answered stonily. The sharpness of her emerald eyes had become blunted in the two hours she'd been inside the hospital.

"Here, take my arm. We'll go back to the hotel, take it easy the rest of the day."

"Why did we do it, Pat?"

"C'mon, we agreed last night. No second thoughts, Em," he pleaded.

"I didn't understand what I was agreeing to."

"Yes, you did," he said.

"I didn't agree to feel like this!" she shouted. Her fists balled up and she pounded at his chest.

"Calm down!" he soothed. "It's just the hormones going haywire, like they said."

"No, it's not."

Gallagher shook his head, not believing how wrong it had gone. "Think of it this way," he urged quietly. "It's in a better place now."

Emily slapped him across the face. "You hypocritical bastard!"

Andie suddenly appeared at Emily's side. She cradled a whiskey bottle as if it were a newborn. Then the fog came again and Gallagher was on a river. There were tall, wet granite boulders standing on the far shore.

From out of the boulders walked an electric, pointillist version of the girl in the photograph of Ten Trees. Many Horses lifted her arms toward Gallagher and when she did, contrails of many-colored lights arced in the air. The light was blinding and he called out in frustration, "What do you want from me?"

"I want you to set me free," she said.

"But I'm not keeping you here."

"Of course you are," Many Horses said. "I was eaten not by fire, nor water nor earth, but by man."

She gazed at Gallagher as if he were an unknowing child, then walked back among the boulders.

Chapter Twenty-six

The Cartersburg Library was an imposing brick-and-white-trim edifice with a central rotunda under the peak of which was a circulation desk manned by a pair of twin women in their late twenties with iron-straight hair parted in the middle, pale skin and rheumy oval eyes.

The twins snuffled in near-perfect syncopation. Their mascara unwound down bleached cheeks like the support lines of a spiderweb. The one in a green Henley shirt was Danielle Carbone. She hiccuped every time Nyren's name was mentioned. Rachel, her sister, who wore a black sweater, wheezed.

"Can you tell us what Mr. Nyren's state of mind was?" Andie asked.

"State of mind?" Danielle snuffled.

"You know, was he happy, sad, agitated?"

"Jeesum, I don't know," Rachel wheezed. "He—David, I mean—he was very professional."

"But sweet," Danielle said, before hiccuping and blowing

her nose. "One of those guys more comfortable with books than people. I mean, a librarian, right?"

"Right," Gallagher said. "You said he was in here copying late. Was that unusual?"

"Copying?" Danielle repeated.

"Or late?" Rachel echoed.

"Both. Either," Andie said, gritting her teeth; it was infuriating to talk with them. But it had been her idea to come to the library. She wanted to get to Nyren's staff, the people who supposedly knew him best, before Bowman's detectives did.

"He was always copying something," Rachel said. "And work late? Sometimes, like everyone."

"Where would he work?" Andie asked.

The twins led them across the reading room and down a dark hallway into his office. It was a well-organized warren of tall, whitewashed shelves neatly jammed with books and stacks of papers and magazines. There was an expensive copy machine in one corner.

"What was he copying Saturday night?" Gallagher asked.

Danielle shrugged. "Jessum, I don't know. We went home at six. Sometimes he stayed all night Saturdays working."

Andie tried the desk. The center drawer was filled with rulers, pens, paper clips and yellow Post-it notepads. The single side drawer slid back heavily, filled from back to front with bulging files. Andie fingered her way over the carefully labeled tabs, noting a file on the recent discovery of the wreck of Benedict Arnold's missing gunship from the battle of Valcour Island on the bottom of Lake Champlain; and another file on the history of the Abenaki tribal settlements along the Clyde River in the Northeast Kingdom. Danielle began to blubber and Andie glanced up long enough to make a motion that Gallagher should get the twins outside.

As he passed through the reading room, he saw the headline across the front page of that morning's *Rutland Herald:*

MADMAN STALKS CENTRAL VERMONT

Under fire from the press, Lieutenant Bowman had come out and admitted that the three killings—Potter and Dawson in Lawton and Nyren in Cartersburg—appeared to be linked. She refused to describe exactly how the slayings were tied together, but "a source close to the investigation" had leaked a copy of the last Charun drawing, which had set off a media feeding frenzy. *The Boston Globe* and *The New York Times* had stringers following the story. And CNN had made mention of the case on the morning newscast.

Bowman's investigation now centered on a green van a neighbor of Nyren's had seen racing from the area. She also mentioned that they had gathered important DNA material from a vehicle the killer used to escape the scene of Nyren's murder. The article ended with an assurance from Bowman that the FBI's profiling team was now giving the case full priority, but a response was still ten days away.

Under the headline A RESORT TOWN IN GRIP OF FEAR, a sidebar chronicled the reactions of Vermonters and especially Lawtonites to the news of a vicious killer in their midst. People admitted sleeping with loaded deer rifles next to their beds. Local security and alarm companies were being deluged with calls. Elementary schools had brought in counselors to talk with hysterical students.

Chief Kerris was promising extra patrols with help from the county sheriff's department. The New Jersey ski-hotel-and-condominium developer was now waffling on a deadline for closing the megadeal that would transform Lawton into a resort town with the stature of Stowe. Mayor Powell was pleading for calm.

When Gallagher returned to Nyren's office, Andie was on the floor, going through stacks of books and paper.

"Anything?"

She shook her head, then turned around to sit with her back against the wall. "Maybe we're wrong about the journal. Maybe Nyren never had it and it was just sheer coincidence that he became Charun's third victim."

"I don't believe in coincidences like that," Gallagher said, crossing to Nyren's desk. There was a long, awkward silence. At least the tenth long, awkward silence of the day. Each of them remained unsure of what the evening before had meant.

To make matters worse, Gallagher was still reeling from the second dream of Many Horses. Over the years he had talked with dozens of mystics who'd claimed to have had visions, and he'd always been able to explain them away as some altered chemical state brought on by a hallucinogen or an overdose of oxygen. Now Gallagher's mind whirled and leaped backward and forward in search of some rational explanation for the vivid quality of his dream. But try as he might, he could not come up with one; and that realization was like a lava flow, bubbling hot, capable of melting everything in its path.

Gallagher felt claustrophobic and stalked around the back of Nyren's desk to open the window. Warming air rushed in. He turned and happened to look down at the open drawer to Nyren's file cabinet. "What's the Vermont Asylum?"

Andie looked up from a stack of files in her lap. "Probably something about the history of the Brattleboro Retreat. It used to be called the Vermont Asylum for the Insane. Why?"

"Because the other files in here are maintained with a neatness that borders on the anal," he replied. "That one looks like I might have filed it."

Andie got up, came over and tugged at the thick file. It took several tries before it came free and she could flip it open on the desk. She skimmed the first page, then rapidly pawed her way through the file before looking up at Gallagher, beaming. "Don't you just love obsessive-compulsives!"

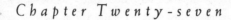

Chapter Twenty-seven

A half hour later, Gallagher looked up from the file. "You never heard of any of this before?"

"Not a word," Andie replied in awe. "I can't believe it was kept quiet all these years."

The file contained a synopsis of the slain librarian's research on mortality and insanity rates in Lawton shortly after the turn of the century. There were also several pages of notes in which Nyren described how he had received a leather pouch from his father and speculated on whether it was related to those mortality and insanity rates; and, to Andie and Gallagher's utter astonishment and delight, a photocopy of the librarian's section of Sarah Many Horses' journal.

Nyren's father, who suffered from diabetes, had told his son the week before he died that Sarah Many Horses had indeed been murdered in Lawton and that the circumstances of the slaying were heinous. His father also said that the relatives of those who now held the journal had helped avenge the murder of Sarah Many Horses, though in what manner he did not say.

Like Andie, Nyren had tried to track down more information about the journal, but had been unsuccessful and abandoned the effort years ago.

Six months prior to his death, however, while researching an unrelated subject in Montpelier, the librarian had come across a scantily documented report from the Vermont Department of Health, dated 1910, that noted an unexplained cluster of suicides and killings in the town of Lawton in a nine-year period around the turn of the century.

Nyren's subsequent inquiry had not only supported the report of the abnormal incidence of self-slaughter and murder, but also revealed that during the same nine-year period, an inordinate number of Lawton citizens were committed to both the Vermont Asylum for the Insane in Brattleboro and the Vermont State Mental Hospital in Waterbury.

The last page of Nyren's notes included a list of names. After each name was information, in parentheses, that noted whether the person had gone insane or committed suicide or was involved in a violent killing. Andie pointed at the twelfth name down the list and whistled: "That's Lamont Powell, the guy the hospital was named for. He's the mayor's great-grandfather! Mike Kerris' great-great-grandfather."

"Are you sure?"

"Positive!" Her eyes danced, pitched and manic. "Lamont Powell was mayor of Lawton around nineteen hundred. They made a big deal of the relationship when Bruce Powell was elected mayor fifteen years ago. He was the fourth generation of his family to hold the office stretching back to Lamont."

Gallagher remembered the Lawton police chief looking at Charun's note in Nyren's yard. "Kerris sure didn't want you pursuing that journal, did he? And he sure got to the Nyren homicide awful quick."

Andie nodded, but her hands worked nervously.

"You're scared of them, the Powells, I mean." Gallagher said.

"You're damn right I'm scared of them!" she snapped. "I know what they're capable of."

"So what do we do?"

"First thing we're going to do is read Nyren's piece of Many Horses' journal," she said.

"Looking for Lamont Powell?"

"Among others."

SEPTEMBER 1891

By June the horse was dead, but I'd made it to Iowa. The hot air on the dusty road looked like sun on water. The fields were leaf green with young corn. It was late afternoon and I had a powerful hankering for food. The last three days I had only eaten four eggs I stole from chicken coops, cracking the tops off with my knife and sipping the yokes like liquid gold.

As the sun got low, I hunted for a place to sleep and a chicken coop to rob. Then eight wagons, two with white canvas, the others more like shacks on wheels, bucked down the road, tugged by horses whiter than bones. There were flies at the pink noses of the horses. The side of the first shack on wheels was painted the color of birds' eggs with a big eye in the middle. Fire shot out of that eye. And above that burning eye was gold lettering in the shape of an upside-down horseshoe. It said:

DANBY BROTHERS MYSTICAL SPECTACULAR
AND RARE ODDITY EXTRAVAGANZA

The lead wagon whoaed and a man called to me, asking me if I was Injun. Joshua Danby perched up on that wagon bench like he was a hawk, nose up, taking me in sideways. He had greased hair and a twirly mustache and a beard like a little spear tip under his lip. He wore a white shirt with one of them high collars, a string bow tie, a black bowler and a waistcoat. Mostly, I was studying the meat sandwich in his hand.

Another man sitting next to him on the driving bench grinned at me in a way that made me think he was addled. Caleb Danby was older brother to Joshua. His pink eyes and skin put me in mind of the horses' noses. His hair was like the last white feathers that stick to the skin of a duck after you pluck it.

Joshua asked me what kind of squaw I was.

I picked up my head, proud, and told him I was Hunkpapa Lakota. He got this right odd smile on his face and asked me where was I going, a Sioux squaw alone in Iowa, when by law I was supposed to be on an agency near a thousand miles away.

I lit out down the road. Joshua smacked the horses' rumps. His wagon jolted beside me, the white horses snorting and chomping on their bits. Then Joshua jumped down, stopped me and told me not to be scared, that he had a proposition for me. He said he could make me money if I'd let him. He said until the month before, an Ojibwa woman had traveled with the Danby Brothers Spectacular, but she went back to her people after a show outside of St. Paul. He asked me if I wanted her place in the show. Ten dollars a month, my own wagon to sleep in, food every day.

Sitting Bull once went all the way to London, England, with Buffalo Bill's show. I asked what I had to do.

He said I had to dance.

There was something about Joshua that I did not take to and still do not. He talks like he's trying on the way he talks the way some folks try on clothes. And he's got a way of looking at you, right slow and gentle, that makes you believe you are powerful important to him even though you hear a voice inside that says you are not. I think it's his eyes make you feel like that. They ride so far up in his head the bottoms look like the last week of the moon.

I asked him what direction he was heading in and he said east for the summer, south for the winter. I told him long as he did not head west, I'd dance.

*   *   *

Joshua's dancing is not hard after you do it three times.

But the first and second times, when you take off your shirt
for the men, you feel smaller and weaker and meaner than before.
I did not want to do it. But Joshua said the men would pay
good for the show. On the posters Joshua nails up, I am Sitting
Bull's Dangerous Daughter. He says men will come to see Sitting
Bull's Daughter take off her shirt, but not his sister's daughter.

I fretted awful that first time. I went on after the Great Dimitri,
who is from a place called Macedonia. Dimitri and his wife,
Maura, walk across a rope hung between two high fence posts. It
is something to see.

The way it works, the Spectacular has two tents. There's a
show every half hour, one tent, then the other, back and forth.
After Dimitri and Maura finish, all the womenfolk and children
head on over to the other tent to see Mr. and Mrs. Small, the
dwarfs who do a right nice fight with the longest snake ever.

Mr. Cosotino's from Italy. He lets ten men stand on his
stomach. He lifts triangles of iron over his head. His wife, Isabella,
makes the white horses that pull the wagons line up and walk on
their hind legs. Isabella made the buckskin dress and vest I wear
to dance.

Between the two tents Joshua has a booth where he sells his
Magic Elixir. Caleb says it is corn liquor and a liquid that comes
from cocoa plants down in a place called Colombia. Joshua's got
the formulation down in a way that two spoonfuls set the mind
to flying like an eagle above the Grand River.

The men that first night crowded onto the benches. And I was
right scared enough to drink some of that elixir before I went on
stage. When the piano commenced to playing, all them men hooted
and hollered. I got dizzy and then all the men had the face of
the soldier with the black teeth. They yelled at me to take my
shirt off, so I did straightaway, then lit off the stage like a
spooked deer.

Joshua was right mad at me. Caleb tried to get between me and him, to tell me it would be okay, but his brother slapped him in the face and told him to go get ready for his show.

Joshua said I had to torment the men, make them think they can't take no more tormenting before I take off my shirt. Joshua said that's the way things work. It's like telling a story. The listener thinks they want the ending right now. But they don't. They want the ending when they can't stand it no more.

He made me come and watch Caleb's show so I'd see how it was done.

Caleb sits in a box on the stage. Before the lights go out, Joshua tells the story about Caleb and him when they was boys back in a place called Vermont. He says his mother's great-great-grandmother was one of the witches in Salem down in Massachusetts who got burned at the stake.

Joshua tells the people in the tent that it was from his mother's great-great-grandmother that he and Caleb got their powers. When they were babies, people used to see ghosts near their cradles. When they were in school, pencils flew near them and windows opened by themselves. Joshua rolls up his sleeves and Caleb's sleeves and shows the audience the scars on their arms. Joshua's father burned him and Caleb with a fire iron to try to drive the spirits from their bodies.

Then Joshua says Caleb's gonna call up some spirits.

The lights go down. Joshua stuffs Caleb into a wooden box. He closes his eyes and puts his hands on the box. He says he's helping Caleb into his spirit trance. Pretty soon, a nice-dressed man with a white cloth wound up like a hornet's nest on his head comes popping out on top of the box and people get right fidgety then. He says he is a spirit from India named Mamood. He plays a flute.

It took me about ten times watching the show up close to figure out Mamood is Dimitri. But most people are scared and have never seen Dimitri before, so they don't look close. Later on,

Dimitri's wife, Maura, comes out of the box. She's dressed as a woman who died tending to the wounded during the Civil War battle at Gettysburg. Everyone likes her. Some nights five spirits come out of Caleb's box.

It's a funny thing. But most everyone wants to believe what they see in Joshua's show. He's got a way of making people believe what he wants them to believe.

My job, Joshua says, is to make the men believe I am Sitting Bull's Dangerous Daughter. I drank more of that elixir, then went out on stage like I hated the men, which was not hard. I looked at them like I wanted to kill them. That made them crazy. Then I looked at them like I wanted to kill them real slow. And it was like Joshua said: in their lips and their eyes they could not take it no more and I stripped off my shirt and they got to shouting loud and coming toward the stage. Caleb and Joshua and Dimitri had to make sure I got off safe.

Joshua picked me up and kissed me, said I was a natural.

That was the worst of it. I've been dancing in the tent four months now. When I go out onstage it is like I am someone else, Sitting Bull's Dangerous Daughter, and not Many Horses. If I think of myself dancing the Ghost Dance with Painted Horses in the cottonwoods near the Grand, I can't hear the men calling at me no more.

Except the night before last.

I was commencing to take my shirt off when a man holding a Bible like the one Miss Mary Parker used to read from came through the tent flaps and yelled at all the men, asking them did their wives know they were in here looking at a naked savage. Them men stopped their hooting and acted like they was whipped dogs.

Cosotino told Joshua we'd better pack up our tents and skedaddle before things got powerful ugly. But Joshua was in an awful spell. He got a letter that morning and him and Caleb had been in their wagon jabbering all afternoon. Joshua doesn't like to be told what to do. He said people paid to see him and Caleb summon the spirits and he didn't want to give that money back. He said he needed that money now.

So he and Caleb started the show. About the time Joshua laid his hands on the spirit box, the minister charged into the tent with half the men that an hour before were hooting to see me naked. He called Joshua a blasphemer. Joshua commenced to yelling back, and the next thing you know, the minister and his men were coming at the stage. Joshua bolted like a horse that's been snake-bit. Dimitri, too. Caleb was tied up in the box.

I hid in the trees and watched the mob drag Caleb outside and tear his clothes off. They painted his body with tar, then tore up pillows and shook feathers over him. They tied his wrists and ankles to a post and carried him into town the way menfolk used to tote dead antelope back at Standing Rock. They rode Caleb around for near an hour, calling him names and kicking him and having a good old time. Then they dumped him in a pile of cow dung beside a barn on the road to Rosedale. I waited until their voices had gone to nothing before I went for him.

Caleb was blubbering. I told him not to fret none, that it would be okay once I got the ropes off him. I stole some kerosene and some rags from the cow barn to clean the tar and feathers off his body best I could. Caleb never said nothing while I cleaned him. He just stared at me in the moonlight with them pink eyes. It wasn't like the soldier with the black teeth neither. I don't think Caleb thinks like that. But it made me feel windy inside anyway and I told him to stop it.

You're right kind for an Injun, he said, and his cheeks went in and out like a horse the flies are after. He asked me if he could tell me a secret and I said okay. Caleb said his scars were for real. His pa used to hurt his ma and his kids. The day Joshua turned sixteen, he shot Caleb's pa in the back of his head while he slept. Some ways, Caleb's ma was happy, but she was afraid someone would figure out what happened and it got so she could not stand to see Caleb and Joshua around. She sent them away with a traveling show that come through Lawton.

We been out here ever since, Caleb said. Fifteen years. Imagine that.

Caleb looked up at the moon and commenced to sniveling a third time. He said Joshua had gotten a letter in the morning telling the brothers their mother died.

I went and stole a horse blanket I seen in the barn and we set back up the road toward Gilead.

On the way, Caleb said Joshua had done the right thing keeping the show open because I needed the money, too. I told him I didn't need it so much he had to get rode on a fence post.

But Caleb said I did. Joshua was figuring to shut the Spectacular down. Their ma had left them the farm and a passel of money. They were going home to Vermont, after fifteen years. Imagine that. And if'n Caleb had his way, I was gonna go, too.

Chapter Twenty-eight

It was late Monday afternoon by the time Gallagher and Andie got back to Lawton.

But Andie did not take the turnoff to her house or the cabin. She kept on straight through town until the two-lane curved west. They went up a road that looped up Gorm Ridge, an imposing edifice of ledge and timber holdings that composed the vast north flank of Lawton Mountain.

The road's first mile passed through hayfields that ringed the base of the ridge. Along the edge of the fields, tractors churned up swathed grass and mud as farmers tried to turn over the saturated soil in the hope that the weak sun would dry their fields and allow them to plant crops.

All too quickly, however, the well-maintained asphalt near the bottomland farms and the tony vacation homes turned to heaved and potholed macadam; and the broad and fenced level ground gave way to steeps pocked with ramshackle, mountain-hollow farms. Junk cars rusted in dirt front yards along the upper reaches of the Bluekill. Bracken and thorn overgrew what had once passed for pasture. Water shoots throttled the apple trees.

Finally there were no more farms at all and the road became a muddy, almost washed-out track that serpentined toward a desolate gulf of hemlock, hardhack and ash. Amid the gnarled, winter-bruised trees stood ponderous granite boulders coughed up by ancient glaciers. Gallagher recalled the boulders in his last dream of Many Horses and shivered as if that bleak landscape had the power to resonate within observers of a similar character.

"When I rented the cabin, you said the Danbys were all dead."

"What I said was that they were all gone from Lawton," Andie replied, her attention on the deeply rutted road. "And they have been since I was ten."

They bounced across a water bar and then another. Gallagher's head smacked the roof. Andie strained against the shoulder strap of the seat belt, studying the woods on her left. They approached the crest of the eastern shoulder of Gorm Ridge, where they passed through a gap. A quarter mile down a grade, Andie's head jerked in recognition. She slammed on the brakes. "That's it, I think."

She wrenched the truck into reverse and it bucked in protest back up the steep, slick incline. She maneuvered it to a flat spot off the road, turned the key in the ignition and pointed to the faintest hint of a path winding into the forest.

"My father showed me the trail to it one time, but I've never been down it," she said. "After reading that piece of the journal and seeing that Many Horses knew Joshua and Caleb Danby, I thought we should take a look."

Gallagher got out and zipped up his oilskin jacket. Back in the village of Lawton, the temperature had flirted with sixty. Here, high on the north-facing slope, it was in the low fifties with a raw wind that gusted through crooked tree trunks. Briar, saw grass and stunted saplings consumed much of the trail, but faded ax hash marks on the bigger trees defined the way. After nearly a half mile of fighting brush, they came to a gushing mountain stream, the origin of the Bluekill. Water from a seep feeding the stream had devoured the soil around the footings of a rotting bridge of rude logs spiked to four-by-eight braces. They took turns crawling across.

Beyond, the ill-defined trail continued and bisected the hummocks of an old-growth hardwood forest where moss smothered fallen logs. Another five hundred yards and the hummocks gave way to a joyless opening in a dark spruce grove at the far end of which leaned a weathered and swaybacked, tar-papered cabin with a stepless porch.

The shack's roof had buckled at its center. Shards of glass clung to the window sashes; tentacles of thorny vines crawled out from inside. A hole had been kicked in the front door's lower panel. Running up the closest wall was the skeleton of a stovepipe chimney.

In front of the shack a rusted bedspring lay in the withered curls of last year's stinging nettles. To the right an outhouse sprawled on its side. The rim of a moldy toilet seat lay nearby. In the woods beyond were the ruins of at least a half-dozen more shacks. And the foundations of a half dozen more. Ravens croaked from their rookery.

"On the map it's called Gormtown," Andie said. "But when I was a kid, everyone in Lawton called it Danbyville. This is where the last of them eked out a living."

Andie started around the other side of the cabin, toeing aside shattered brown glass and tin cans. "Unless you've had your tetanus shots, I'd be careful where you step," she called.

Gallagher stepped gingerly through the debris and went up to look in the window.

The shack was a one-room affair with a sleeping loft. Wide-planked floors of rough-cut timber. Two-by-four ribwork and plywood walls. A blackened potbellied stove. The door to the firebox was unhinged. Next to it was a larger, wood-burning cookstove, the flue of which had been torn from the side wall to leave a gaping wound. Next to the cookstove stood a crudely fashioned shelf on which were visible a grimy coffee cup and a rusted box of cocoa.

Squirrels had robbed the couch of stuffing. Twin kerosene lanterns drooped off nails in the corners. Rusted metal folding chairs tilted against a three-legged table; its yellowed Formica top was blistered and curled. A filthy enamel washbasin and a metal bucket. A twin-sized bed crafted of the same two-by-fours and plywood as the cabin walls. No mattress. A yellowed calendar from 1968 was turned to the month of November.

Gallagher tugged at the door, trying to get it open.

An owl dodged out of the shadows, leading with talons like curved black knives. Gallagher threw himself backward, arms up and across his face. The talons caught in his coat, tearing and then freeing. He felt the bird's wings slap at his face and hands. His feet got tangled and he stumbled to the right off the porch and crash-landed in the tin cans of an old dump pile. A porcupine startled and rushed off through the cans.

Andie raced around the corner, her pistol drawn. She saw Gallagher and his pitiful expression. She saw the porcupine but not the owl, which had disappeared into the trees. She began to laugh. The laugh seized her entire body and as she rocked back and forth, the laugh enlarged her somehow. For a moment the demons that lurked about her were banished and Andie became luminescent, serene and extra human in a way that shockingly reminded Gallagher of the vision he'd had of Many Horses the night before.

She came over to help him up, still giggling. "Oh, look," she said before he could take her hand. At the edge of the dump pile there was a ten-foot square of pine needles. Growing from the needles were tender green stalks from which hung delicate rose-and-white flowers shaped like dancing shoes.

"Lady's slippers," Andie said, kneeling to cup one. "I haven't seen one in years. They're very rare."

"They're beautiful," he said.

Andie gazed radiantly at the flower. "Lady slippers remind me that nature can allow loveliness and goodness to occur even in the most desolate time and place."

At that moment Gallagher realized he loved her. He leaned across the flower and kissed her. "I've been wanting to do that all day and I couldn't bring myself to before now."

She smiled, then gave him a puzzled expression. "You've been hurt as deeply as I have, haven't you, Pat?"

Gallagher averted his eyes. "It's more that I hurt someone else."

"Do you want to talk about it?"

"No," he said, shaking his head. "Not now. I just want to enjoy this feeling."

They kissed again, then stood there grinning until the porcupine bustled through the cans once more and ended the moment.

"So tell me the myth of the Danbys," Gallagher said.

Andie sat on the front porch and wove a story of a family in an ever-downward trajectory. The old Danby homestead used to stand on the flat at the base of Gorm Ridge along the Bluekill River. It was there Joshua and Caleb and their siblings held their fabled seances. But after Joshua disappeared and Caleb killed himself, the surviving Danbys had been unable to keep up the farm. The house burned down, the land changed hands and the money was squandered. The Danbys were forced into exile on the back side of the ridge, the most isolated spot in Lawton.

The Danbys became what Andie's father used to call hedgehogs. The men logged for a living when they worked, collected dole payments when they didn't. One Danby or another was

forever under arrest for jacklighting a deer or chucking dyna-
mite in the Bluekill to float trout or burgling some flatlander's
vacation home. Over three generations the Danbys died, one
by one, by all manner of calamity: crushed by stones, poisoned
by rancid food, stabbed, drowned in the river, suicide.

By the time Andie was a little girl, the Danby clan had
dwindled to the last remaining family. The father's name was
Franklin. People called him Franco. He was six feet six inches
tall, two hundred and sixty-five pounds, a logger with a history
of violence. The mother was Lulu Belle, Franco's first cousin, a
buxom slut forever cheating on Franco. Lulu Belle and Franco
had one son, Terrance, who attended grammar school with Andie.

"He was older than me, but I remember he used to come
to school smelling of woodsmoke, with dirt on his face and
overalls that had patches over the patches," Andie recalled. "For
lunch he ate stale white bread with that Velveeta cheese they
give out at food banks. I don't think he had a friend in the
world."

She looked at the ground and shook her head, then looked
at Gallagher with a pained expression. "Kids made fun of him."

"Did you?"

Andie nodded sadly. "One time when I was about six or
seven I was playing on the floor of my father's pickup when I
heard my dad say something about Lulu Belle. I sat up quick
to see her by the side of the road, hitchhiking by raising her
skirt to passing male motorists. Terrance was trying to hide in
the bushes. I told all the kids in school."

"Kids can be cruel," Gallagher said, reaching up to touch
the knots behind his ear where the rocks had hit him as a child
on the playground.

When Terrance turned ten, Franco caught Lulu Belle busy
with a French-Canadian logger in the front seat of a pickup
outside a bar. Franco broke a beer bottle over the Canuck's
head, then stabbed his wife in her calf with the busted glass

while her lover lay passed out on top of her. The Frenchman revived and he came up to Danbyville after Franco. Both men were drunk on rotgut. It was the first hot, humid night of the year, mid-May, early for the kind of stultifying summer weather that for a brief time every year turns Vermont into a tropical rain forest. The biting black flies and the mosquitoes tore at the men's exposed flesh. They fought with hatchets.

Terrance was the only witness. Franco and the Canuck circled each other, testing each other with little flicks of their primitive weapons. A nick across the forearm for Franco. A shallow slice along the Frenchman's jaw. Then Franco got it in the thigh. He raised up and struck the Frenchman at the shoulder. When the Canadian screamed and tried to run, Terrance's father went after him and swung at the same time that the logger turned and swung, too. Franco's hatchet cleaved the Frenchman's left arm at the elbow. The Canadian's hatchet split Franco's chest wide open.

Gallagher flashed on his father swinging from a rope. "Terrance saw it all?"

"The whole thing."

"The logger die, too?"

Andie shivered and looked off through treetops that clawed the approaching dusk.

"Andie?"

"Terrance claimed his father managed to hit the logger one more time before he died, and then the logger died, too," she replied. "But most people in Lawton didn't believe it. They thought that when Franco died and dropped his hatchet, Terrance picked it up and chopped at the logger, avenging his daddy's death. They found the little ax buried in the side of the Frenchman's head, just above the ear."

"You're thinking about the way Charun has killed them all."

"Yes."

Cold raindrops splattered the broken glass at their feet.

"We'd better get back to the truck before we catch pneumonia or get lost in the dark," she said.

Gallagher took one last look around the shadowed ruin of Danbyville, then hustled after Andie, who was already moving back down the trail. He asked himself what must it have been like for a ten-year-old boy to walk out in the steamy darkness after killing the man who killed his father? That question triggered a memory of himself as a ten-year-old, standing alongside his parents' bed in the early morning. Gallagher had an empty vodka bottle in his hand and he wanted to strike them both in the head. He was dumbfounded by the recollection, because in the next moment it was replaced by a longing to talk with his parents, to explain to them how it was that he'd become the man he was. How was it possible for one person to embrace both emotions? he asked himself.

"So what happened to Terrance after the fight?"

Andie opened the door to the pickup. "He lived up here with Lulu Belle another five or six months. Then one day, right around Thanksgiving, she brought him into town and dropped him off at school. She never came back."

Gallagher climbed in the other side and they sat in the darkness.

"They sent Terrance to Hennessy House, the Catholic orphanage up in Burlington," she went on. "For most people I knew, including my mom and dad, that was a good thing— the Danbys, as far as Lawton was concerned, were done and gone. And I hadn't done much thinking about them until I saw that Many Horses worked for Joshua and Caleb."

"That's it?" Gallagher asked. "You don't know what happened to Terrance after that?"

Andie's voice became strained. "About a year after he'd been gone, someone from town ran into a couple of the house parents at the orphanage and asked after Terrance. They said he had read the orphanage's entire library in one year. Turned out he had the IQ of a genius. The way I always thought about it was that after living for so long in such harsh conditions, Terrance found that knowledge was free and he decided to steal all of it to show us we were wrong about him."

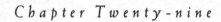

Chapter Twenty-nine

The switchback road down Gorm Ridge turned slick and granular in the cold rain. Andie crept down at low speed. Her scent surrounded Gallagher again. That and the story of Terrance Danby made him want to open up and tell Andie what had happened to him.

"Andie, I need to—" he began.

The crash was deafening. A blasting screech of metal on metal. The whir of tires against wet gravel. The rear of her pickup wrenched left and the back left tire hung spinning off the edge of a narrow and deep gorge at the bottom of which the Bluekill boiled. Andie screamed.

Now came the crunch-clank of gears shifting, the revving of a turbo-charged engine and a violent shudder as the vehicle that had struck them disengaged and spun backward into the darkness. There was a moment of shocked silence; then they were blinded by hot white light. Truck headlights, fog lamps, a rack of overhead spots. A high-beam grid of blazing electricity, faceted and primordial like a giant insect's eye. The engine under the eye revved again.

Gallagher threw his hands up to block the glare. "He's going to push us off the edge!" he shouted. "Get us out of here!"

Andie downshifted again and jammed on the gas. The pickup's frame vibrated and lurched but did not get free. Gears chunked. From fifty yards back, the bug's eye bore down.

"Shit!" Andie screamed. She dove for a small yellow lever beyond the shifter, tugged at it and the truck settled. A garish, metallic light surrounded them. Gallagher scrunched down, waiting for the impact, waiting for the long tumble into the gorge. Andie smashed down on the accelerator.

A split second of hesitation and then the other three wheels caught low gear and they fishtailed out into the road. There was a tremendous catlike wail as fenders caught then slipped off.

"Hold on!" Andie yelled.

They went careening down Gorm Ridge like a bobsled amuck, slashing through turns, caroming off red-clay banks. The giant insect behind them was swallowed in darkness and for several moments Gallagher thought they'd lost it.

All four of the truck's wheels left the ground when they lurched out onto the stretch of busted macadam. Chickens pecking along the road flushed in terror. A mongrel dog tore out of the darkness trying to run alongside the pickup, then yelped in fear and dove into the ditch when that startling, iridescent grid growled in behind them again, bathing them in a white dazzle.

Gallagher's head snapped forward and back before he heard or felt the impact against the rear bumper. Andie's forehead cracked off the steering wheel. The pickup veered and for a single, gut-wrenching instant seemed incapable of righting again. But it did, only to drift into a full three-hundred-and-sixty-degree spin across the ditch and up a grade.

An opening in a rock wall. Saplings growing in the opening. They smacked the saplings. Headlights shattered. The waist of a hundred-year-old maple trunk flashed by within inches. A volcano of mud and grass erupted. The pickup tipped up on its side, threatened to roll, then thudded back in the soft pasture soil.

At that same instant, all the lights on the attacking vehicle turned off. Gallagher caught the shadow of a jacked up four-by-four pass. Then the last remaining headlight on Andie's truck sputtered and died, leaving nothing but quiet rain and tree frogs peeping. A man's voice called out in the darkness. "Leave it alone, or next time you'll be in the river!"

Then there was weird laughter and the sound of the truck grinding away.

"The chief's up there on Gorm taking a look," Deputy Phil Gavrilis said. He tapped his pencil on a notebook while Andie held an ice compress to her forehead. It had taken five stitches for the emergency room doctor to close the gash at her hairline. She and Gallagher stood at the ambulance entrance, giving Gavrilis their story.

"Oh, he'll be a big help," Gallagher said.

Gavrilis reddened, but did not respond to the jab. "You've got no description of the truck that did it?"

"Jacked-up pickup," she said. "A lot of lights."

"There's ten thousand rigs like that in Vermont," Gavrilis said.

"That guy Bernie Chittenden's got one," Gallagher said. "That asshole's already tried to run me over once."

A figure approached from the far end of the parking lot. Chief Kerris sauntered up with that baseball cap jauntily pushed to one side.

"I just stopped at Bernie's store coming down off Gorm Ridge Road," he said. "I can tell you his truck's spotless, no mud anywhere. And there's nothing up on Gorm to speak of other than your tire tracks gouging up Ron Boucher's cornfield."

Kerris wormed his mouth around. "You sure some truck ran you off, Andie? Or is it possible you and your Hollywood pal here went up to Gorm to have a snort or two at sundown and your rig got away from you."

"Kiss my ass, Mike," Andie shot back coldly.

He smiled and held open his palms. "Hey, no offense. I had to ask."

"Let's go," Andie said to Gallagher. "We won't get any help here. You're driving."

Kerris pulled himself up to his full height and stepped in their way. He put his hand on Gallagher's shoulder. "Not so fast. I want to know what you two were doing up there."

Gallagher said, "Looking for lady slippers. Hand off, please."

"Yeah, lovely day to look for flowers," Kerris said, not moving his hand an inch. "I want to know what you were doing up there."

Andie got between them. She glared at Kerris. "We were looking at Lawton's past, Mike. Does that scare you? Your uncle? Or does it scare your whole family?"

There was a twitch at the corner of Kerris' mouth; then he got control, leaned right down in her face and smirked. "I don't have the first idea what you're talking about. And anyway, no one's going to listen to you, Andie. Everyone who counts in this town knows you've gone off the deep end again. Crazy, drunken Andie Nightingale."

She did not flinch, merely returned the same smirk. "You don't get it, Mike, do you? I don't care what people think anymore!"

That night Gallagher watched Andie as if she were an exotic member of some long-forgotten tribe. She was susceptible and sensitive yet had the capacity to be remarkably tough. In that way she reminded him of Emily. He had wanted to talk to Andie about his ex-wife before someone tried to run them off the road, but now that seemed more dangerous than any possible auto accident, and he asked himself if he'd ever be content to just be in a room with a woman who comforted him.

Andie was chopping up last year's garden vegetables put up in Mason jars.

"What are you thinking about?" she asked.

Gallagher flushed and said, "Who we go after now: Kerris or Danby or Lamont Powell or the rest of the journal."

She dropped the vegetables into a hot wok. They seared. The room smelled suddenly of ginger. "I think it's all one story. We go after all of it."

"Too much ground to cover," he said.

"Not if we split up," Andie said.

Chapter Thirty

The Vermont State Mental Hospital in Waterbury is a Kremlin-like gathering of large red-brick buildings with ornate leaded-glass windows and turrets. Long green lawns flank the main entrance. Towering over the complex is a dormant brick smoke-stack perhaps eighty feet high.

In the bowels of one of the outlying buildings, Eunice Mar-cous, the hospital's archival clerk, took a sip from a diet Pepsi can before belching softly and complaining: "This took me the better part of two hours to dig up."

"You don't know how much I appreciate it," Andie said, looking at the cracked brown folder cradled in the emaciated arms of the woman on the other side of the counter. The blue shadow under Marcous' penciled eyebrows matched the color of her blue muumuu dress.

Andie held out her hand for the file, but the clerk stepped back, clutching it to her bosom. "I saw you on the local news the other night. This part of them Lawton killings?"

"No," Andie lied. "Now, I really need to go through those documents, Ms. Marcous, and it's getting late."

Seeing finally that Andie was not going to let her in on the reason behind the unusual request for records dating back to 1899, Marcous reluctantly handed over the half-inch sheaf. Andie turned her back on the clerk, went over to a green metal table under a naked bulb and flipped open the file on Lamont Powell, former mayor of Lawton, great-grandfather to the current mayor, Bruce Powell, and great-great-grandfather to Chief of Police Mike Kerris.

At some point in the past nine decades, the documents had been water-damaged and many of the notes written by various case workers in dark black ink had been smudged.

But according to a cover sheet that included data on his birth, nearest kin and the like, Lamont Powell had been committed to the hospital in March 1899 after a diagnosis of "violent dementia" and had remained within the asylum walls until his death. The preponderance of the record was arranged in reverse chronological order.

In the year before Powell's suicide, the doctors in charge of his case had been encouraged by "vast improvements in his general mental condition" and had been allowing him increased freedom of movement around the hospital. During this time Powell had "displayed none of the tendencies toward self-mutilation exhibited upon committal," the narrative noted. Indeed, in the last two months of his life Powell had been granted orderly status, which, in effect, had given him access to the entire facility, including the outer grounds.

Andie read the next paragraph and recoiled. On June 28, 1906, Powell had used torn sheets to hang himself from a tree in the woods behind the smokestack. Before killing himself, he'd cut his tongue out with scissors stolen from the hospital's barbershop.

She pressed her knuckles to her lips at the gruesomeness of the suicide. She took two deep breaths and read deeper into the file. Sparse notes described a twenty-four-month period Powell had spent in a near-catatonic state broken only by fits of hysteria in which he claimed to have conversations with the dead. She flipped a page to an annual evaluation dated May 12, 1902. Here was a section describing the patient's physical status, including a digression regarding the results of a recent dental examination:

"Three years into treatment, patient Powell still suffers from vivid hallucinations. These hallucinations continue to directly precede efforts to slash at his gums with any object available in order to rend his teeth from his mouth."

Andie stared at the paragraph in horror, then looked up to find Eunice Marcous studying her from the wire-caged window. "Five-thirty, time for me to close shop," the clerk announced.

"Just fifteen more minutes," Andie pleaded. "And I'm going to need a copy of this when I'm finished."

"Records that old you got to run through an archival copier, and the only one available to us is over to Montpelier," Marcous sniffed. "Take at least a week."

"That would be fine," Andie said. "I'll take notes for now."

Marcous arched one of her penciled eyebrows. "Fifteen minutes and that's it. I got grandkids'll be tearing the house down for their supper if I give you much longer."

Andie returned to the file, scanning the subsequent pages for further mention of Powell's hallucinations. In the eighteen months that preceded the 1902 evaluation, she found two minor asides that vaguely mentioned delusions. Both of those notations followed incidents in which the former mayor had managed to dig teeth out of his gums, once with a fork, the second time with his own fingernails.

She did not find another reference to hallucinations until

she came to a long diagnostic narrative written in the months directly after Lamont Powell's committal to the insane asylum.

When she finished, she almost doubled over with nausea and fear. "Oh, my God!" Andie whispered.

Chapter Thirty-one

At the same time, nearly halfway across the state, a clear tube ran from a pale yellow oxygen tank into a splitter, where it became two hoses threaded into Oscar Stubbins' nostrils. Stubbins' mottled hands shook with anticipation as his wife, Cornelia, lit the cigarette, then held it to his lips. Stubbins placed his fingers over a hollow nub of plastic that jutted from a stoma at his trachea. The cigarette tip sparked and ran. Blue smoke trickled out of the plastic nub.

"Another puff," Stubbins croaked on the exhale.

"No more," Cornelia snapped. "Doctor'd have my head if he knew."

"Won't ya love me when I'm gone?" he asked in a froggy voice.

Cornelia would not meet his gaze. Then she nodded and snuffled, "That won't never die, Oscar."

"Then give us another puff, bunny girl."

She held the cigarette to his lips again. The cigarette glowed hot. His eyes closed in the pleasure of it and then he chortled into a hacking liquid cough. He twisted and groaned in the wheelchair. Cornelia jumped up in alarm. She fitted a thin hose into the stoma. There was a whooshing noise and a slug of bile came sucking up the hose.

Stubbins hacked again, then breathed easier. He looked at Gallagher and croaked, "I got a month, maybe two. Gunk's all through me."

"I'm sorry," Gallagher said, trying to fight the desire to race outside and gulp fresh air.

"What the fuggh?" Stubbins said. "Death comes for everyone sooner or later. What do ya want, Mr. Gallagher?"

"I'm here about Terrance Danby."

Stubbins accepted the name as if he'd been expecting it somehow. "He in trouble?"

"I don't know."

"You're bullshitting me."

"It's possible he's in trouble."

"What kind?"

"His name has come up in connection with homicides. Three of them."

"Not those killings down in Lawton we been reading about?" Cornelia asked.

Gallagher nodded.

"That spider," she said in disgust. She was at least a hundred pounds overweight and had stuffed her folds into a stained pink sweatsuit. But what made her almost impossible to look at was that two of her upper incisors had grown in wrong; they came horizontally out of her gums like little yellow tusks, and peeked through her lips even when her mouth was closed.

Despite the freak-show quality of their home, Gallagher realized how lucky he had been to find the Stubbinses. The couple had worked at the orphanage where Terrance Danby had been placed after he poleaxed the man who killed his father. Oscar had been night house manager at Hennessy House. Cornelia had been the cook.

Founded in 1867 as the Catholic Home for Abandoned and Wayward Children, Hennessy House provided shelter to generations of Green Mountain orphans for the next one hundred and eight years, until the state of Vermont and the Archdiocese of Burlington decided that such institutions were not in the children's best interest and closed the house in favor of a foster-home system.

Gallagher had stopped at the state social services office in Burlington to pick up some background literature on Hennessy House and casually asked how he might track down people who had worked there the last few years it was open. One of the older social workers had remembered the Stubbinses. Gallagher found them living in a forest-green ranch house on a bluff above Lake Champlain, just south of Ferrisburg.

Their family room had been set up like a hospital ward: a white adjustable bed, a wheelchair, an oxygen tank, an old metal television table stocked with medicines, folded sheets on the couch where Cornelia slept. Overpowering everything was the harsh scent of antiseptic cleanser.

"Smartest fella I ever saw at the house," Stubbins said. "Read everything. But my sweetie's right: Terrance was a spider."

Cornelia slid the tip of her tongue around her right tusk and clucked her approval. "Just waiting for you to get snarled in his web, that one."

"Why did you think he was a spider?"

Stubbins glanced furtively at his wife. She got up out of her chair on two wooden canes. "Go on!" she cried, shaking one cane at him. "You always said we should tell someone, make people know. Now you're about done for. Here's your chance."

The dying man hesitated.

"Go on!" Cornelia cried again.

"Give us a puff first," he croaked.

In hoarse starts, through puffs and choking fits over the course of an hour, the whole shameful story came out. Terrance Danby arrived at Hennessy House in late 1968. Ten years old, with the frozen look a deer gets in headlights and kids get when they've gone through a shocking loss. But behind the look lay a deep and abiding craftiness.

"Spider eyes," Cornelia said.

"That's enough spider talk!" Stubbins choked.

"Just the same," she retorted smugly, "that's what they were."

Terrance found the library and started to read. Two, sometimes three books a day. Science, novels, biographies, newspapers, magazines. Anything that was printed. By the time he was twelve, he had read all of Shakespeare and the Bible, and was studying Latin and Greek. He had also developed a fearsome reputation in the house. One of the boys, a bully named Alan Haig, picked on Terrance because he was reading all the time. Terrance took it and took it—"waiting in his web for the fly," as Cornelia put it.

Then one night as he was making his rounds, Stubbins found Haig strapped to a chair in an empty office. Haig was gagged with duct tape. The foreskin of the boy's uncircumcised penis had been stapled to the chair seat. Haig refused to tell anyone what had happened.

"But ya could see after that that he was terrified of Terrance, this kid half Haig's size," Stubbins said. He stopped to consider his hands. There were dark blotches of purple on his skin.

"You ain't done by a long shot," Cornelia said. "Tell him."

Stubbins took a deep, garbled breath. "We don't know what happened for sure, sweetie. Maybe it's best to let the story die."

"That ain't right, Oscar, and you know it," his wife protested. "You don't tell, it's all a lie."

"What's a lie?" Gallagher asked, confused.

Stubbins waved one of his skeletal fingers at him and

croaked, "We had nothing to do with it. We tried to tell people back then . . . but no one would listen till it was too late."

Stubbins said that the year Danby turned thirteen, the diocese appointed a young priest as headmaster in an effort to turn around an institution in chaos; six of the boys at Hennessy House had been expelled from school for one infraction or another in the prior semester. The priest was an authoritarian, bigger, stronger, faster and meaner than any boy in the orphanage.

"If a kid got out of line, he'd haul the little shit off into his office," Stubbins said, then started coughing. He gestured wildly at his wife to continue.

"He'd spank on 'em, even the biggest boys," Cornelia said. "Not that I'm against a good spanking when it's done right, but—" She paused and tongued her tusk again. "I don't know how to say this, but after a while you got the feeling he liked it. Hitting 'em, I mean."

"And God only knows what else he liked," Stubbins gasped, then went on to say that the priest played favorites. And the biggest favorite was Terrance Danby. By the time Danby was fifteen, he was often overheard talking about books and languages with the priest, who was a Jesuit, a learned priest.

That same year, while Stubbins was making his nightly rounds, he found the beds of Danby and another boy empty. He rushed down to tell the priest, only to find Danby leading the crying boy back to the sleeping dormitory. Danby said the boy had been bad and the priest wanted to see him.

Over the course of the following two years, Stubbins had many nocturnal encounters with Danby and other boys who had been bad. While Hennessy House boys no longer got expelled from school, the orphanage became, in Cornelia Stubbins' words, "dark and nasty. A loveless place."

One day in the summer of 1975, Cornelia overheard Danby's old nemesis, Alan Haig, telling another boy that he "was tired of it all. I'm going to the bishop or the police or something unless it stops."

A week later Haig's body was found in the woods north of Burlington. His throat had been slit. Danby was an immediate suspect, but the priest gave the teen an ironclad alibi. They had been hiking all day on the back side of Mount Mansfield.

During the course of the murder investigation, detectives got several of the boys to talk about life at Hennessy. Within months, the diocese decided to close the orphanage. Terrance Danby was seventeen and forced into the Army. The priest was quietly sent off to Central America to work as a missionary.

"A missionary?" Gallagher said, flashing on a memory of a photograph. "What was his name?"

"McColl," Stubbins croaked. "Timothy McColl."

Chapter Thirty-two

"Lawton's become this festering wound," Andie fretted. "I don't know who to trust anymore, Pat."

It was nine o'clock on Wednesday night. She and Gallagher had lowered the blinds on all the kitchen windows. They sat at the kitchen table with her notes from the Lamont Powell file at the Waterbury hospital between them. She wore faded denim overalls, a white jersey embroidered with purple flowers and makeup—the first he'd ever seen her use—to cover the bruising from the stitches.

"You can trust me," Gallagher said.

"Can I?" she asked.

"I've stuck by you, haven't I?"

Andie nodded, reached over and squeezed his hand. "I'm sorry. I'm scared."

Gallagher squeezed back. "Apology accepted. What else happened to Powell?"

She turned the page in her notebook. "Listen to this: 'Patient Powell was admitted after being found in his office tearing his upper canine teeth from his head with a pair of pliers.

" 'Patient has spent the last three months alternately in a straitjacket and in a four-point restraint system in C Ward for the violently insane,' " she continued. " 'Patient Powell suffers prolonged periods of severe dementia where he claims to be visited by a Sioux squaw that he says haunts him because he helped murder her.

" 'Powell claims the squaw hovers in front of him and tells him he is damned because'—and this is evidently a quote from Powell himself—'she was eaten not by fire, nor water nor earth, but by man.' "

Gallagher spilled his coffee across the table. He stood up, stunned. "Say that last part again."

" 'She was eaten not by fire, nor water nor earth, but by man,' " she repeated.

Gallagher heard in his mind the echoes of the second dream he'd had of Many Horses. His head felt close to splitting. How could his subconscious have bubbled up those exact same words prior to hearing them read from a report written nearly ninety-five years ago?

"Are you sure you wrote that down correctly?"

"The handwriting was blurry, but I'm pretty sure," Andie said. "Why?"

Gallagher felt like he was going nuts and he had to tell someone. "I heard that in a dream the other night."

Andie stared at him. "A dream?"

"That's right," Gallagher said, flushing at the idea. "I keep having these dreams of Many Horses and she talks to me."

Andie allowed herself a smile. "Here I thought you were an atheist who didn't believe in ghosts."

"I am an atheist who doesn't believe in ghosts!" he snapped. "And besides, it wasn't like Casper came to call. It was just a dream, a coincidence, or maybe my mind's trying to convince me that that's what I heard in my dream. Déjà vu. I . . . I don't know."

Her amusement turned to concern. "I hate it when people ask me, but are you feeling all right?"

"Yes," Gallagher insisted. "I'm . . . just keep reading."

Andie watched him for several moments, then returned to her notes. "Here's another quote: 'Subsequent interviews with Patient Powell's son, Lamont Jr., and two daughters—June of Glens Falls, New York, and Lenore of Poultney, Vermont—indicate he has been in a continually weakened mental condition since the passing of his wife, Katherine, in 1891. June and Lenore said Patient Powell dabbled in spiritualism and other tangents of the occult, as have many in recent years. But they assert that Patient Powell has never been west of Albany, much less to Indian territory.

" 'Discussions with Lawton Police, while cursory, indicate no recent slayings of Indians. And indeed, no record of any Indian having lived in the town since the last Abenaki family left in 1874—' "

"We know that's not true," Gallagher interrupted.

"The police must have been lying," Andie agreed. "Do you think Powell helped kill Many Horses?"

"If he did, he didn't do it alone," he replied. "If he was a single loony, they would not have covered up the killing. So there had to be several people involved. And the killing had to have been brutal. I mean, the guy digs out his teeth, cuts off his tongue and then hangs himself because of it, right?"

Andie picked up her pistol off the table and checked the safety. "And because of it, someone tries to run us off the road. I think Kerris, the mayor, Bernie Chittenden and God only knows how many others know some of this. At least about the fact that Lamont Powell went insane claiming he'd helped kill an Indian woman."

"Fits the cover-up theory," Gallagher agreed. "But is it

enough motivation to hunt down and kill three people? I mean, I wouldn't want to be known as the descendant of a murderer, but would I care enough to kill people who might reveal that knowledge to the world?"

"I don't know," Andie said. "But I'll tell you one thing: no one in Kerris' family has a cabin on a lake down near Cartersburg. Remember? That's what he told Lieutenant Bowman outside Nyren's house—that he'd gotten to the scene because a relative had a camp nearby and he heard the dispatch calls."

"Yeah, so?"

"So I ran into Gavrilis, Kerris' deputy, this afternoon on the way back from Waterbury. Phil doesn't know anything about a cabin down south. The story Kerris gave Gavrilis is that he went fishing. Gavrilis also let me know that the chief's marriage is on the rocks. His wife's got a restraining order on him and he's been away fishing, out of radio contact, two or three times the past few weeks, including the morning Olga's house burned."

"And Kerris has a history of sexual violence," Gallagher said softly.

Andie tightened, but nodded. "I don't think we're close to having the whole story on this."

"You got a good chunk of it today, but not all," he said, then pondered something bothering him. "The Waterbury records say Mayor Powell dabbled in spiritualism and the occult. The Danbys?"

"In Lawton, who else?" Andie replied. "So we still can't rule out Terrance."

"Or Monsignor McColl," he said.

"Monsignor McColl!" Andie cried. "What are you talking about?!"

Gallagher related the details of his conversation with the Stubbinses, including the fact that the priest had run the orphanage while Terrance Danby was a resident and had been suspected of brutality and possibly of accessory to homicide.

"He's been our parish priest for nearly ten years," Andie said, stunned. "He said my mother's funeral mass. She thought he was some kind of saint."

"Some kind of saint," Gallagher repeated, thinking about Father D'Angelo for the first time in many days. There was something about his earlier meetings with the monsignor that was still nagging at him, but he couldn't figure out what it was.

"I'm going to have a talk with Monsignor McColl tomorrow morning," Andie promised.

"I can't tell you how much I'd love to be there for that little chat," Gallagher said. "But I think I'm better off going to Washington."

The second Gallagher left the Stubbins' house, he'd used his cellular phone to call Jerry Matthews, his partner. It had been nearly two weeks since they talked, two weeks since he'd turned forty and Emily had remarried. The second Jerry answered, the image of Gallagher's ex-wife lying on some beach with her new husband played in his head, but he forced himself not to ask about her or the wedding. Those kind of answers threatened almost as much as the killer stalking Vermont.

Instead, he gave Jerry a rough outline of what had happened since their last conversation, including the bodies, the journal, the drawings of Charun and the story of Danby. Jerry had covered the military for the old *Washington Star* before joining *Time* in a similar position. Like Gallagher, he had an undergraduate degree in anthropology and had tried to cover the arcane world of the Defense Department as a culture to be deciphered. That had led to the writing of books, and, eventually, film scripts, which was how they had met.

Jerry was furious at first that Gallagher had done so little work on the D'Angelo story, but the more he heard about the Lawton killings, the more intrigued he became.

"The hell with a documentary!" he advised. "You write the story as a book, make a million, then sell the film rights."

"The American way," Gallagher cracked.

"C'mon, be cynical," Jerry replied blithely. "But be rich cynical. If you let this one get away, you're more far gone than I thought."

"I'm not letting it get away," Gallagher assured him. "Right now, I need everything you can find out about Terrance Danby's military history."

"It might take a couple of days,"

"Fast as you can," he said. "People are dying up here."

"Okay. Pat?"

"Yeah."

"It's good to have you back. Working, I mean."

An hour and a half later, just as Gallagher passed through the covered bridge that led into Lawton, his cell phone rang. Jerry sounded shell-shocked.

"Partner, you set off some big alarms with that name. I dropped Terrance Danby in the hopper with a couple of my old sources in the Defense Intelligence Agency, figuring they could track the guy quicker than anyone else. I just got a call back—out of the blue, fifteen years since I've last seen him— from one of the spookiest guys I've ever met."

Gallagher gripped the phone tighter. "Tell me."

"Uh-uh, no way. Not on a cell phone," Jerry said. "You get yourself down to D.C. pronto. Harold wants to talk to you in person tomorrow afternoon."

"Who's Harold?" Andie demanded after Gallagher had related the story.

"Jerry refused to say anything more," he replied. "But I know my partner. He's got a lot of faults, but being scared isn't one of them. He's covered four wars and been through three divorces, and this was as shaken as I've ever heard him. I'm flying out of West Lebanon first thing in the morning."

Andie was silent for almost half a minute, then she blurted out, "All the way back from Waterbury I wanted to stop and have a drink, Pat. I don't know if I can see this through. It's like we're chasing bits of something so terrible that I—"

"You're going to be okay." He leaned across the table to rub her forearm. "Remember who you're doing this for: for Olga and your mother and Nyren and Hank Potter. And Sarah. Right?"

"I know, but it's like we're spinning in the middle of this nightmare that no one else sees. Or wants to see."

Andie looked at Gallagher with her pained green eyes. He wanted to go inside them and hide for just a while from all the killing and the dirty, violent history they were uncovering. And, very much, wanted her to hide inside him.

Gallagher took Andie's hand and they went upstairs. It was their second time together and it was like waking up all over again, each of them showing the other how to give and receive pleasure without restriction.

Afterward they lay in the darkness clinging to each other. "Will you leave when it's all over?" Andie asked.

Gallagher could hear the yearning in her voice, but then he had an image of Emily and he was paralyzed. "I don't know, Andie."

There was a silence before she said, "Even though we haven't known each other a long time, I feel good with you, Pat."

Gallagher closed his eyes, trying to fight off the cornered feeling. "I do, too. I just need a little time to figure out exactly what that 'good' means, Andie."

"Oh," she said, and she rolled over with her back to him.

The bed, which had been a warm refuge, became exposed and windswept. Another man might have reached over to embrace her, to reassure her. But Gallagher could not.

He stared into the darkness, seeing a swift-running stream in upstate New York. It was October, nineteen months before. The maple leaves were brilliant red. The brown trout were breeding and rising to his dry flies. Emily and Gallagher had finished the documentary on Lebanon's war children, and another on the supernatural life of the Australian Aboriginal tribes. They had been on vacation for nearly two months, trying to figure out what project to take on next. It was a year after the abortion in Paris, and Gallagher believed they had moved on.

Emily sat on a rock behind him. She flipped a smooth, round stone in her hand. She had not said a word in almost an hour, and neither had he.

Suddenly, she announced, "I'm tired of films, Pat. I've decided I'm going to do that book in Mexico. I'll be gone six months."

Gallagher's stomach dropped. They had not discussed that project with any seriousness. He managed to rally with a cutting barb. "An intimate look at the culture of a tortilla factory?"

Emily whipped the stone into the pool he was fishing. "Always hiding behind the joke, the fly rod and the quick, snide comment, aren't you, Pat?"

"They've always gotten me through the hard times before," Gallagher replied. "But how's this: you're going to Mexico just to hurt me."

"It's always about you, isn't it?" Emily cried. "This time it's about me. What *I* want."

He stared at her. "You said you were okay with our decision in Paris. You agreed."

Tears streamed down her cheeks. "I'm thirty-four, Pat. This is not an abstraction anymore."

"You trying to say it was an abstraction to me?" Gallagher demanded.

"Life is an abstraction to you!" Emily shouted. "You've spent all this time studying and filming cultures and religions, but you don't believe a word of it. You haven't found meaning in any of it, or in anything, for that matter—life, God, death, souls . . . me!—we're all abstractions to you!"

"That's not fair!" he shouted back.

"No, it's not, but it's true," Emily said, standing. She snuffled, wiped her nose on the sleeve of her cotton sweater and fought for composure. "I'm due on a plane day after tomorrow. I'm taking my car and going down to the city to get packed."

"Am I allowed to visit at least?"

Emily hesitated, then choked out, "No." She turned and ran up the path. Gallagher watched her go the way he used to watch his parents as a child—as if through smoked glass.

Lying there in the darkness beside Andie, Gallagher was aware that his thoughts looped. Images crisscrossed and bounced. Emily. Andie. Then Many Horses and now Terrance Danby led boys through dim hallways to Monsignor McColl. Mike Kerris motioned his cronies toward a young drunken innocent in a darkened condo bedroom. Mayor Lamont Powell dug at his gums with sharpened fingernails. The bodies of Hank Potter, Olga Dawson and David Nyren floated on a river in Gallagher's daydream.

Behind him, Gallagher heard a gentle heave of breath that told him Andie was crying. His thoughts accelerated, flashing through the same circular pattern over and over, faster and faster. He held tight to the edge of the mattress, asking himself if this was what his father had felt like in the last days of his crack-up.

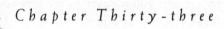

Chapter Thirty-three

THURSDAY, MAY 21, 1998

Andie slammed her police bubble on top of her battered truck and accelerated toward Lawton in the pouring rain.

It was less than an hour after Gallagher had left for the airport at West Lebanon, less than ten minutes since she'd received the phone call from Lieutenant Bowman. Her lips burned. So did her fingertips. And the back of her throat.

"Get down to Lawton Center," the lieutenant had barked into the phone. "The parish secretary at St. Edward's has been murdered. The husband said she had a piece of an Indian woman's journal. Charun left evidence. A lot of it. Get down there *now.*"

Andie spun off the River Road by the Otterslide General Store onto Main Street. She hunched over the steering wheel, her knuckles bone-white. "God grant me the serenity to accept the things I cannot change," she whispered. "The courage to change the things I can and the wisdom to know the difference."

Andie repeated the prayer over and over again, then told

herself to take ten deep breaths. With each inhale and exhale, she talked herself down.

Libby Curtin had lived in a double-decker, red Victorian house at the dead end of Front Street. There was a black wrought-iron fence separating the yard from the street and the children's playground next door. Halfway to the house was a blooming perennial garden in the middle of which stood a painted ceramic statue of the Virgin Mary.

The street outside was already a sea of umbrellas and raincoats. A television truck from a Burlington station already in town to do a story on the killings had just pulled in and parked. A CNN van came in behind it. The lights went on.

Up on the porch, almost a ghost through the gray, driving rain, Brigid Bowman gestured at two troopers weaving yellow tape through the balustrade of the wrought-iron fence. In the camera glare Bowman appeared older, harsh, almost grainy.

The second she saw Andie, she broke away from the troopers and stepped behind a dense tangle of morning-glory vines that walled in the east side of the porch.

"You were right. I was wrong," Bowman began in a no-nonsense voice. "Eddy, the husband, says Libby had a piece of a Sioux woman's diary and a little crucifix passed on to her by her grandmother."

"You just wouldn't believe me, would you?" Andie asked.

Bowman clenched the top of her trench coat. "Everyone makes mistakes, Andie."

"I've learned that," Andie allowed. "Have you?"

Bowman clicked her thumbnail with the nail of her ring finger. "You aren't going to make this easy for me."

"Have you made it easy for me?"

"I'm sorry. I was doing my job."

"I want my job back," Andie said. "The lead on this case."

After a long moment, Bowman nodded.

"Good," Andie said. "Let me see her."

Together they went into the house. Plants had been tipped over on wooden floors recently varnished. Drawers had been tugged from a refinished chest in the corner. The white upholstery of the butcher-block living room furniture was slashed. Bright blue fish from an overturned saltwater aquarium lay still and cold on sopping-wet newspaper.

Bowman said, "With this amount of damage, a neighbor must have heard something. I've got teams fanning out."

They went up a narrow staircase to a bedroom. An evidence technician dusted the jewelry box on the highboy dresser. A second worked at the window over the porch roof where a climbing piton had been driven into the frame. A third technician snapped photographs. Clothes were strewn across the floor. A television tuned to a religious cable channel lay on its back. A nun in her habit was hosting a talk show.

What had been a snowy-white comforter was now a tapestry of rose and rust. Libby Curtin's body lay in the middle of it, curled into a fetal position facing the door, as if trying to hide from the blows.

Libby's white cotton nightgown was soaked in blood and indistinguishable from her flesh in places. She was gagged. Her eyes were stretched open. She appeared to be staring at the crucifix on the opposite wall. Four of her fingers had been clipped off as if with garden shears.

Shakily, Andie put on latex gloves. She picked up the half-full wineglass next to the bed and sniffed the stale Chablis, then put it down abruptly at the sight of the fourth drawing pinned to the bedstead above the body.

Charun's penis was being throttled by a rope cinched tight, causing the tip of it to mushroom above the shaft. The monster's eyes were half-moons now. The pupils were rolled back in his head. The irises had been painted crimson. Every stitch in the creature's lips except one was severed. The mouth grinned and gaped, revealing razorlike canine teeth and swollen gums.

Andie glanced at the wineglass, then unpinned the drawing and turned it over.

I fucked Angel blindfolded and ear-plugged right to the far shore. Fucked until she stepped into the muddy water and climbed beyond.

I stayed in my Persephone warm and alive. Warm and dead. Cold and dead, but even with the cord lashed tight around us, I never saw. I left her on the bank and she walked on while I rowed back alone.

You think you know me now, Lawton, but you don't. I am the boatman. I am the lover. I am the shaman and I am the mutator.

Summer comes. And Hades has returned Persephone to Earth. I have seen her. I will have her again, for one more boat ride.

"He's not human," Bowman said, looking over Andie's shoulder.

"Yes, he is," Andie said. "That's the problem. Humans are capable of creating beauty or carnage."

She called out to the three technicians working in the room. "Anything?"

"Lots of clear prints here," said the one working on the jewelry box. "But there are several smudges with no partials around them; I think our boy was wearing gloves again."

"Damn it!" Andie said.

Mel Allen, the state's assistant medical examiner, crouched beside a white braided rug on the far side of the bed. "Andie?" he called. "You better come take a look."

She and Bowman came around the bed and Allen smoothed a bushy eyebrow before pointing at soil from a boot at one end of a six-foot throw rug. Thirty inches from the dirt was a bloodstain and three pubic hairs. The rug had been slashed.

There was a charred hole in the rug and a two-inch mound of what looked like burned tobacco mixed with little chunks of a mushroomlike substance lying beside the hole.

"What's your explanation, Mel?" Andie asked.

"He lay here after the killing," Allen said with a look of distaste. "His boots were where the dirt is. His penis was at the pubic hairs. And those slashes—he hacked at the floor. It's like he can't stop the frenzy."

Andie crouched next to the examiner, looking at the rug, then back at the note.

"How is it possible that someone smart enough to write that note, then draw these drawings in a sequence, goes so maniacal during the killing?" she asked.

Allen shrugged. "They've got psychiatrists to explain that kind of thing. I'm just telling you what I think he did."

The medical examiner leaned over and with a forceps took up two of the charred fungal pieces. One had a bluish tint at the stem. The other looked like a chunk of wet leather.

"We'll have to run tests," Allen said, "but this one looks like a psyllocibin mushroom. The other one's peyote. He's smoking it, probably mixing it with marijuana and God only knows what else, from the smell of it."

"No wonder the guy's out of his mind," Bowman said.

"Bag the rug and everything and get it to the Waterbury lab," Andie told the technician standing behind Allen. "I want every inch of this room in the Waterbury lab."

Then Andie turned to the lieutenant. "Where's Libby's husband?"

Eddy Curtin slouched in a hammock chair in a corner of the ruin of his kitchen. The young snowboard entrepreneur stared into an empty cup of espresso with the look of the damned. His lank, dirty-blond hair hung down around his face. The sleeves and collar of his khaki canvas work shirt were

unbuttoned, revealing a powerful upper body and sinewy arms.
A uniformed female trooper sat mute in a chair opposite Curtin.
Andie motioned for her to leave and she took the trooper's
seat. Lieutenant Bowman stood in the doorway, listening.

Curtin glanced up. "Hi, Andie."

"Hello, Eddy," she said softly. "It's been a long time."

Curtin nodded. "You don't expect to run into your old
baby-sitter this way. Can I call the funeral home for them to
come and get Libby now?"

"She'll be going somewhere else first, Eddy," Andie said.
"We have to gather evidence."

Curtin ran the knuckle of his index finger along the under-
side of his wispy goatee. "We were going to take off for Montana the end of the summer, move the business out West. It
was our secret."

"I'm sorry, Eddy."

His chin trembled. "You want to ask me questions, I
suppose."

"It will help catch the son of a bitch that did this," Andie
said.

Curtin had left the house at ten o'clock. He liked to work
on his snowboard designs at night when no one was at the
factory. He'd been absorbed in his work until nearly six-thirty.
He'd last talked with Libby at 11 P.M. She'd been watching
television.

Andie said, "You told the lieutenant that Libby had a piece
of a journal from a Sioux woman."

Curtin nodded. "In a pouch with a crucifix in it. Her grand-
dad gave it to her when she was sixteen and told her to keep
it because it was an important piece of Lawton history. At least
the history nobody in Lawton wanted to talk about. It's all
about the seances they used to have up there at the old Danby
place. Libby kept her promise to her grandpa, but she didn't
like having the pouch."

"Why?" asked Bowman from the doorway.

" 'Cause it gave her the creeps," Curtin replied. "I've read it all and it's like you were reading something that was never meant to be kept, but couldn't ever get rid of. I don't know, like it was testimony, you know?"

Curtin turned the cup of coffee over on its saucer. "You think someone slaughtered my Libby because of some shit that went down here a hundred years ago?"

"Yes, Eddy, I do," Andie said.

Tears welled in Curtin's eyes. He slammed his fist off the table. The cup jumped and crashed on the tile floor. "If I'd have known this was going to happen, I would have burned that damn pouch the first time she showed it to me!"

Andie thought of her mother. "I feel the same way, Eddy."

Now the young man began to sob: "What could be in that thing that someone would do that to my sweet Libby? How could God let that happen to someone so devoted?"

"That's what I'm trying to find out," Andie murmured soothingly. "Where did she keep it?"

Curtin got hold of himself and wiped his forearm across his face. He reached around behind him on the floor and picked up a framed piece of needlepoint—daffodils and pink tulips and a monogram of their names, Libby and Eddy, separated by a heart.

He turned it over, then fiddled with hasps that held the back to the frame. Andie's breath caught in her throat when she realized the killer had not found Libby Curtin's section of Many Horses' journal.

Eddy eased out the red leather pouch and gave it to Andie, who took it in both hands. Bowman stepped forward to see that which she had not believed existed.

"I promise you, Eddy, I will find out who did this to Libby," Andie said.

"That it? That her pouch? What's it say?" came two male voices from the hallway beyond Lieutenant Bowman.

Chief Kerris and, right behind him, Mayor Powell. Kerris had a reddish patina to his skin. His eyes glistened with nervous excitement. Mayor Powell was standing on tiptoe, trying to see into the kitchen.

Andie stood and held the pouch behind her back. "Lieutenant, I would prefer these two men be escorted out of here."

"What?" Kerris shouted. "This is our town. You can't order us out of here."

"The woman's way out of line," the mayor grumbled in agreement.

"I've got my reasons," Andie told Bowman. "You said I was lead."

The lieutenant dug her fingers into a knotted muscle at the back of her neck.

"Lead?" Kerris cried. "You've got to be kidding!"

"She's not kidding," Bowman said at last. "And I'm sorry, Chief and Mr. Mayor, but you'll have to go. Sergeant Nightingale is in charge here."

"I'm not moving," Powell stated flatly.

Kerris nodded. "Not until I know why we're being kept out."

"How about because, around the turn of the century, your great-great-grandfather went nuts," Andie said. "He dug his teeth out of his head because he believed he'd helped kill an Indian girl."

She shook the pouch at them. "The Indian girl who wrote this journal. I think you're trying to cover that up. I think that for some reason, you'd like this whole investigation to go away."

Kerris and Powell both blanched.

"I don't know what you're talking about," the mayor puffed at last. "And I won't have my family's reputation impugned in this way. Lieutenant, I protest this slanderous, unfounded accusation!"

Bowman's fingers dug deeper into the knotted muscle. Andie brought the journal around in front of her and held it where the lieutenant could see it.

"You're sure," Bowman said at last.

"Sure?" Andie replied. "No. But convinced? Yes."

Bowman called out into the hall to troopers standing on the porch. "Please escort these gentlemen outside the yellow tape."

Kerris glared back over his shoulder as he was led out. "You'll pay for this," he snarled. "The both of you will pay for this."

Andie followed them out onto the porch and watched the troopers walk them into the pouring rain, down the slate side-walk to the wrought-iron gate. There were bouquets of flowers placed against the fence. The crowd had swelled and stretched fifty yards down Front Street. A half-dozen television vans were there now with cameras already set up under plastic tarps.

"The press is crawling all over this," Bowman remarked gloomily. "And there are only going to be more of the vultures."

"Let them circle," Andie said. "We're going to use them."

"How?"

Before Andie could reply, one of the troopers who had escorted Kerris and Powell jogged back through the rain and up the porch stairs. "There's a priest down there, says he wants to come in to console the husband," the trooper said. "He says the victim worked for him."

Andie put her hand to her brow to search the crowd pressed in against the fence. The massive upper torso of Monsignor McColl thrust up and over an ornamental yew. He wore a black raincoat and was hatless in the driving rain. The priest had lost weight in his face and neck during the past week. Skin hung loose and gray like a turkey's waddle under his chin.

"In the letter Charun left at Nyren's house, he said Angel cried out, *Vida*."

"So?" Bowman replied.

"So *vida* is the Spanish word for 'life'," Andie said. "Mike Kerris lived in Chile six years. Monsignor McColl lived in Guatemala for nearly ten."

Bowman stared at her in total confusion. "What are you—?"

"Monsignor McColl stays outside, too."

"But the man's a priest."

"He's a suspect," Andie declared. "I'll explain it all later. Right now, we're going to go down in front of those cameras and tell the world about the journal and the pouch. At the very least, we prevent another killing. At best, we lay a trap to catch a psychopath."

Chapter Thirty-four

It was in the hot, humid twilight that Gallagher first caught sight of Harold. He strolled along a path through parallel beds of flowering shrubs from the direction of the Lincoln Memorial. He wore a crisp blue seersucker suit and a starched Egyptian cotton shirt with a blue polka-dot bow tie, all draped on a hanger-thin physique. He jauntily sported a slim black cane with a silver tip and an ivory handle carved into the face of a wolf.

The slight limp only served to amplify his confident, almost aristocratic bearing. Without invitation, he sat between Jerry Matthews and Gallagher on a park bench in the trees near the Vietnam Memorial.

Harold placed both palms over the wolf's head and crooned in a velvety Southern drawl: "Viburnum. Isn't the scent intoxicating? I have often thought that viburnum is the perfume of reincarnation, of spring awakening from winter."

Up close Gallagher could not tell whether Harold was sixty or ninety. His steel-colored hair was still full and had been slicked back on his head, preppy-style. His skin was taut and pale to the point of translucence. His lips were bloodless, almost blue. He took a deep sniff and beamed with pleasure. "Ahhh, viburnum!"

"Cut the shit, Harold," Jerry barked. Jerry sported a black beard, stood five-six in his dress shoes and, with his jowls and ample beer belly, resembled a bulldog in a suit. "Why are we here?"

Harold batted his lashes at Jerry. "I see your impertinence and your preference for the scatological has not ebbed with the years, Mr. Matthews."

"I actually hoped never to see you again, you sick bastard."

"The feeling was mutual, you insolent, nosy pup," Harold replied in that modulated drawl. "But call it kismet that we meet again."

Jerry had grabbed Gallagher at National Airport when he stepped off the eleven o'clock shuttle from Boston. They had seven hours to kill before the meeting. In that time Gallagher heard the whole story of Harold, which is how he had introduced himself to Jerry on that very park bench early in the Bush Administration. Jerry had been working on a story for *Time* about the so-called "black budget" that funded the various intelligence agencies. During the course of researching that story he heard rumors of a clandestine organization funded out of unaudited intelligence slush funds. Jerry had only the barest of details about the group, but his early research led him to believe that one of its functions was political assassination, something the U.S. Congress had outlawed nearly two decades before.

Jerry worked that angle off and on for nearly a year and a half. His sources had pointed to specific incidents—the strangling of a banker in Peru, the disappearance of a Lebanese diplomat in Paris, the shooting of a Hong Kong trade representative in Jakarta—yet he had been unable to pull the pieces together into any pattern coherent enough to publish.

Then in mid-1990, someone sent Jerry an unsigned letter telling him to look into the activities of an import-export business based in Miami. That corporation had ties to a Louisiana bank that had undergone exponential growth during the Reagan years. Jerry began making inquiries about Pluto Ltd. Two weeks later as he left his office, a limousine driver approached him to announce that a representative of Pluto requested the immediate pleasure of his company.

Jerry was driven to the Lincoln Memorial and told to walk to a bench near the Vietnam Memorial. Harold waited for him with a thick folder in his lap. Inside were photographs of Jerry naked on a Jamaican beach with his boss' wife. There was also a dossier detailing his younger brother's involvement in a cocaine deal. Jerry's stomach had hollowed at the blackmail, but he'd figured that his boss was a prig who never treated his wife well. Lauren would be better off divorced. As for his brother, Jerry had written him off long ago. He could survive those hits and told Harold as much.

Harold had merely smiled, then taken out two more pictures, these of young girls playing in a park near Fort Collins, Colorado. There were tapered black lines joining over the head of each girl. The photographs had been taken through a telescopic rifle sight. The girls were Jerry's nieces.

Jerry's will for the story dissolved on the spot. Indeed, hunger for any journalistic scoop ebbed shortly thereafter, and so he had come to write books and scripts, and so he had come to work with Gallagher.

Now Harold turned. His waxy fingers fluttered, then settled on the cane. "You are a policeman, Mr. Gallagher?"

"No, but I'm working with the Vermont State Police on these murders."

Harold batted those long, feminine eyelashes at him. "In what capacity?"

"Researcher. I'm a cultural anthropologist and filmmaker."

"Odd skills for a homicide consultant. And you bring what to the table?"

"Insight."

"Hmmmm," Harold said, his eyes burning like embers blown by the wind. "Mr. Gallagher, I sense you are a disturbed man, hiding something. To whom do you offer insight—the police or yourself?"

The question unnerved Gallagher and he was at a loss for an answer. Emily, Many Horses and then Andie flitted through his mind. He had the sudden urge to call Andie, to apologize for his rebuff the evening before, to tell her that he cared, that he wanted whatever they had to go on after all of this was over. Harold seemed to smell his conflict.

"Mr. Gallagher?" he said softly.

"Both," Gallagher finally sputtered.

Harold allowed himself the barest hint of a grin. "Honesty is the beginning of self-understanding."

"Who are you?" Gallagher demanded indignantly. "What are you?"

His lips bowed into broad amusement. He cast one hand lazily off in the direction of Capitol Hill. "I am retired now. But in the local bureaucracy I was known as a facilitator. You can think of me as a baseball scout or a literary agent, a recruiter of emerging talent."

"Is that how you know Terrance Danby?" Gallagher persisted.

"Why, yes," Harold said.

Jerry sat forward, ten years of painful wonder echoing in his voice. "What kind of talent did you recruit, Harold?"

Chapter Thirty-five

"Go check it out," Andie ordered. She thrust the pink phone-message slip at a waiting detective. "If it's real, if they've got a piece of the journal, call me immediately."

The detective nodded and rushed out of the crowded room.

"We've got another one," cried the dispatcher, a flamboyant man in his early fifties. Chris Shaddock was chubby and he had overdyed his curly red hair. "This guy's in Bellows Falls."

"Shaddock, take the information, then fax it through to the Rockingham Barracks," Andie said. "And—"

"I know, I know," Shaddock whined. "If it's real, call immediately."

"Right," Andie said.

The Bethel Barracks of the Vermont State Troopers, where she and Lieutenant Bowman had decided to set up the headquarters of the manhunt, was approaching pandemonium. Phones rang. Detectives shouted. Fax machines whirred. The barrack's blinds had been drawn to cut the glare of the klieg lights of the television cameras hungering in the parking lot outside.

Someone had leaked the fact that Andie's team was calling the killer Charun. The glib, blow-dried reporters were eating it up. WBZ-TV in Boston had led with a story about the "Myth Killer of Vermont."

Andie had gone before the cameras at noon to warn that anyone else holding the journal of a Sioux woman accompanied by a tiny gold crucifix was in terrible danger. Since then, the Bethel command center had received more than three hundred calls and tips from people who said they knew where a piece of the journal could be found.

So far, detectives following up the leads had uncovered three Civil War-era diaries, the letters of two spinster sisters in Richmond, Vermont, the journal of a missionary who'd worked among the Apache, four Hopi kachina dolls, several black-and-white photographs of the Sioux medicine man Black Elk, three arrowhead collections and an offer by a Burlington medium to track down the last two pieces of the journal for a small fee and the rights to the story.

Andie was spending fifteen minutes of every hour performing criminal triage, deciding which tips had to be run down immediately and which ones could wait. One team of detectives had been sent to discreetly follow Chief Mike Kerris. A second team would report on the activities of Monsignor Timothy McColl.

She glanced at her watch. Seven-fifteen P.M. In forty-five minutes she was scheduled for another live stand-up before the cameras. She grabbed a cup of coffee, then told the dispatcher: "I'll be in interview room A. Don't disturb me unless it's urgent."

"I know," Shaddock moaned. "If they get a piece of the—"

"Not just the journal," Andie interrupted. "If a man named Patrick Gallagher calls, put him through immediately."

Shaddock's head popped up like a periscope. "We don't have a Pat Gallagher in Vermont BCI," he said slyly. "FBI? State's attorney?"

Like most compulsive gossips, the plump redhead had a
honed instinct for novel information. Indeed, Andie had long
suspected the dispatcher might be the source of media leaks
on high-profile cases handled out of the Bethel Barracks.

"It's personal."

"Ohhh!" Shaddock replied. He grinned at her wickedly.
"Andie Nightingale, I've taken your calls for nine years now. I
don't recall any personal messages . . . from a man. And there
were some who thought you strolled on my side of the street."

Andie reddened and covered a smile with her fingertips.
"Just put him through, Shaddock, okay?" she said.

"So it's official?" he asked. "I mean, you and this Patrick?"

Nightingale's face fell slightly. "No, it's not official."

"Have hope," the dispatcher said conspiratorially. "That's
what life is—hope!"

Andie nodded uncertainly, then turned and plucked Libby
Curtin's pouch off her desk before heading down the hallway.
In the interrogation room—a Spartanly furnished affair with a
mirror on the wall—she located the phone and moved it onto
a metal-topped table next to her.

From the pouch she got out the pages of Many Horses'
journal. She positioned a yellow, legal-sized pad next to the
phone and wrote, "Does the journal hold the answers to Many
Horses' fate? Does it hold the answer to why a man thinks he's
the incarnation of a mythological creature and is willing to kill
for it?"

AUGUST 1893

*Two years now since we rode the wagons into Lawton. And in
two years I have seen Joshua Danby become like McGloughlin,
the Indian agent at Standing Rock. McGloughlin believed he was
God above us, that he could order us to stop singing to our Great
Mystery, that he could order us to stop dancing, that he could
tell his men to kill my uncle and we would not fight or run neither.*

There are people living here with us now who believe Joshua has the power to raise the dead, like he's Wovoka.

Joshua's heard the talk enough times that I think he believes that's what he is. A prophet. And I am right fearful because when folks commence to believing that they are more than what they are, the spirits beyond always strike back.

I better put it down the way it has all come to be.

Joshua and Caleb got more than the farm when their ma passed on. She left them and their three sisters, Alice, Karen and Edna, and their little brother, Bobby, a passel of dollars. They gave the cows and the crops a go, but you could see right off neither man had the gumption to take on the farm as their life. Six months after we came to Lawton, Joshua called all of us left from the Spectacular show—me and Caleb, the Dimitris, Mr. and Mrs. Small, Mr. Cosotino and his wife, Isabella—into the front parlor room.

Joshua said he'd had a vision, which made me sit up and listen. A vision is not something you ignore, even if it comes from someone like Joshua Danby.

Joshua said a voice in a cloud told him to take the money his ma left and rebuild the farmhouse as a temple. Joshua said the cloud told him that people would come to listen to him and Caleb summon spirits like they did at the Spectacular.

Joshua's sister Alice is yellow-haired and pinch-faced. She did not like the idea, seeing as how she and her sisters had been the ones who'd stayed with her ma all those years, but Joshua stared at her with those eyes like the last week of the moon and he told her to join up or scat. Alice is twenty and mean as a badger, but she's got no place to go like the rest of us. She and her sisters and little Bobby stayed.

We commenced to building the next week. It took two hundred dollars and all of April and May to finish. Joshua had how it should look figured out on paper. First they built a stairs around the chimney going up from the kitchen. Then they put a wall around the stairs. On the second floor they added what Joshua called the "seance room." It's got low ceilings, a stage and a black wooden box smack against the chimney. On the box we painted an eye with lightning bolts. We cut a door between the box and the chimney stairs that you could not find and open from the inside even if you tried. Someone's got to work the latch from the chimney side.

The box is for Caleb to sit in and be sent into a spirit trance by Joshua. It does not appear so, but that box is big enough even Cosotino can get by Caleb and out to the stage.

When every lick of the scrap wood left over was burned and raked away, we had our first seance. Joshua let the word go out that since he and Caleb came back to Lawton, the spirits talked to them again just like when they were boys. He told people there was nothing wrong with talking with the spirits, that it was a good thing and he and Caleb would show people they could do it, too.

Ten people came the first night, all of them town folk, including the mayor, a right sad man named Powell. He lost his wife in a carriage accident last year.

Andie lifted her head, excited. "She knew him," she said out loud. "She knew Mike's great-great-grandfather."

Before reading on, she picked up the pen again and jotted these notes: "Death of Lamont Powell's wife=his insanity? Where Kerris now? Mayor Powell?"

Joshua figured out just where to put the seats for the people to watch the seance and where to put the one kerosene lamp in the room so they see just what he wants them to see. And he had them all drink from his elixir, which he told them would relax them enough to witness the spirit world. Ten Trees and Painted

Horses used to call potions and spells that called on the dark side "spider medicine." And that's what I started calling the elixir.

Joshua came on stage in a red robe Isabella made for him. He didn't say a word, but crooked his finger at Caleb, tied him up, stuck him in the box, drew the curtains and raised his arms toward the heavens. It got quiet. We commenced to whispering through holes drilled in the walls. I pounded a drum. Isabella blew a flute. Cosotino stuck his hands through a black curtain at the left side of the stage and played a tambourine. Dimitri and Maura were next to Cosotino, waving with gloves that had been dipped in phosphorus.

In the low light it musta looked like ghost hands because people commenced to bellering and carrying on even before Mr. Small popped out of the top of Caleb's box wearing raggy clothes and a wig that Alice sewed from horse-tail. Mr. Small jumped around like a rabbit with a busted back leg. He conjured all sorts of noises of no sense.

The town folk that weren't screaming were straining forward in their seats like drivers when a team of galloping wagon horses sees a snake in the road and quits hard.

I came out next, dressed in my Sitting Bull's Dangerous Daughter outfit, got up on the box and spoke in Lakota. Darn if one woman didn't faint dead away! The nicest thing about the seances is I don't have to take my shirt off no more.

Afterward, Joshua turned up the lights and told them all how life did not end with death, that we was everlasting, Joshua invited the mayor and another man from town to open the curtain and look at Caleb. He was laid up against the wall, sweating and drooling spittle. He's right good at that.

The next night twenty people came. And the next forty and the night after that Joshua turned ten folks away. Pretty soon there was people up to the Danby farm from far away as California and Europe to drink the spider medicine and see the spirits.

Lots of folks, mostly the rich ones who've been here a long time, think Joshua's got the power to talk to the dead and make the spirits what he calls "materialize." Miss Mary Parker would call that a fool's dream. The only way you can talk to the dead is by following the ceremonies to let your spirit break free, walk and cry for visions. Not Crazy Horse, not Sitting Bull, not even Wovoka could make the dead walk, far as I know.

But like I said, there are people who believe Joshua can do it. And they treat him like he's the Great Mystery itself. Mayor Powell comes almost every night, expecting his wife to appear from the box. Mrs. Effington's a hook-nose rich lady from New York City that done lost her husband and son to pneumonia ten years back. She wears a different hat to the seance every night and, like the mayor, has gotten right fond of the spider medicine. Mrs. Effington comes every night with a fat, gray-bearded man named General Talbott, who says he served under General Custer in the Civil War.

General Talbott wrote a story for a newspaper in New York City saying he surveyed every inch of the Danby temple and found no explanation for the Lawton occurrences. He also wrote that the elixir was a "mystical quaff that promoted a harmonious spirit" and that the recipe had been passed directly to Joshua by the people from the other world. Way I figure it, General Talbott knows that Mrs. Effington wants to believe in Joshua and he don't want to disappoint her.

Same with all the other folks worshipping Joshua Danby. It's like they want to believe so bad, they don't want to look too close. There are fifteen or twenty people just from Lawton who stopped going to the church. They follow everything Joshua says, especially that there's another way to think about the life after this one other than what them priests say. He says they should not be scared to pass on.

Which is true. But Joshua don't know a thing about it. He's just feeding off what other people want to see in him. But I'm

*alive and safe and got a roof over my head and food to eat, so
I don't say a whole lot.*

There was a sharp knock at the interrogation room door.
Andie lifted her head. The door opened and Peter Frawley, a
stocky, bald-headed detective, peered in. "Can't find Kerris,
Andie."

"What do you mean you can't find him?" she demanded.
"Doesn't his office know? Phil Gavrilis? His wife?"

"His wife and his deputy say he was seriously pissed off
when you booted him and the mayor off the Curtin crime
scene," Frawley replied. "He told them if Lawton was going
down the tubes, he wasn't going to hang around and watch.
Said he was taking a few days off, going fishing."

"Fishing where?"

Frawley shrugged. "They didn't know. They said he's real
secretive about his fishing, that he takes off at all sorts of odd
hours. Sleeps in his truck."

Andie bit at her knuckle, then said, "Get his Suburban's
license plate number from Gavrilis and send it out over the
wires with a request not to approach if spotted. In the meantime, one of you watch his house. The other wait near the
Lawton police station."

Frawley nodded and shut the door. Andie picked up the
pen for the third time, flipped to a fresh page, then wrote:
"Kerris—six years Chile. Enough time to become a killer?"

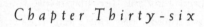

Chapter Thirty-six

Five hundred miles away, Jerry asked Harold a second time: "What kind of talent did you recruit?"

The old man pursed his lips gracefully. "I am retired now, insolent pup. Everything about Pluto has been carefully expunged from the record. What I was, at least as far as the public is concerned, will remain nothing more than the rambling fantasies of a senile old man."

"I don't care if I ever prove and publish it," Jerry insisted. "I'm over that now. What kind of talent, Harold?"

Harold batted his lashes again. "Why, violent talent, of course."

They never got the entire story. Harold avoided particulars whenever he could. But this much Jerry and Gallagher learned: Harold first discovered Danby when the boy was nineteen and newly graduated from boot camp. Terrance had achieved exceptional scores on the U.S. Army's physical and intelligence tests, but failed to graduate at the top of his class because of several fighting incidents. Always on the training field, always cruelly accomplished. He snapped one man's wrist with his bare hands and broke another man's jaw with his foot.

Subsequent psychological testing by the Army revealed Danby as a fierce, cunning loner, which is how his file came across Harold's desk. He went to talk to Danby at Fort Benning.

"A brilliant autodidact," Harold recalled, relishing the memory. "You knew it within moments of speaking with him. His thinking patterns did not fit the Western norms—extremely creative, wide-ranging, thought-provoking. And gifted physically. He could take tremendous punishment. A sociopathic mind in a gladiator's body. A rare, rare talent."

Harold arranged for Danby to attend all of the prestigious Army training programs: Jump School at Fort Bragg, Ranger School at Fort Merrill, sniper training in San Antonio, the language program in Carmel. Danby excelled in every instance, especially sniper school, hand-to-hand combat courses and the language school, where he studied Arabic, Spanish and Russian.

But there were blemishes on Danby's record—persistent reports of unwarranted savagery. These allegations came to a head during the Panama invasion when Master Sergeant Danby found his unit pinned down in the streets of Colón. Two of his troops were badly wounded. One was dead.

Danby single-handedly killed four Noriega loyalists and saved his unit. But what should have been grounds for the Congressional Medal of Honor turned gruesome. One of his men reported that near the end of the firefight, Danby chased a fifth loyalist into an abandoned restaurant. The loyalist turned, dropped his gun, then raised his hands in surrender. Danby kicked the man in the groin, then slashed his throat with a combat knife, nearly severing the soldier's head from his body.

The court-martial board gave Danby the benefit of the doubt and accepted his claim that he had acted in self-defense, that the loyalist was going for a pistol in his waistband and he had reacted with the knife. But part of the plea agreement was that Danby would accept a straight discharge.

Harold could not have planned it any better. He had stayed in close touch with Danby over the years, offering him advice, acting as the man's mentor. Then he became his agent.

"I offered him a job with a consulting firm I ran for nearly twenty years," he said, smiling condescendingly at Jerry. "You had it all wrong back then, you know. We were private contractors. The government bought our services piecemeal, as did many other countries, though I must add that we were highly selective in our client base and always pro-NATO—"

"I'm only interested in Danby," Gallagher cut in. "Where is he?"

"Isn't it obvious that's why I'm here, too?"

"You don't know?" Jerry cried.

"You don't know how much I wish I did," Harold said with a tinge of desperation in his voice.

Within three years of joining Pluto, Danby had become one of the top professionals in the world. He specialized in combat-oriented missions, often parachuting in under cover of darkness, then using his Ranger skills to navigate toward his target. He made millions for himself and for Pluto. What set Danby apart in Harold's mind, however, was the fact that death became a fascination for the assassin.

"He wasn't the ordinary killer who tries to divorce himself, compartmentalize and justify what he did," Harold explained. "He became a student of his craft, studying the history of assassins and the lore of death across cultures. Over dinner one night in San Salvador, he even claimed that some long-lost relatives of his could actually talk with the dead."

Harold chuckled at the idea. He rolled the index finger of his left hand toward Gallagher. "You especially, would find Danby fascinating to talk to." His expression turned puzzled and he moved his head closer, studying Gallagher in the gloom. "You look like him, you know?"

Gallagher's gut soured at the thought. "Lucky me."

"Get on with it, Harold," Jerry groused. "Tell us what they might be dealing with up there in Vermont."

Harold said that six years ago he began receiving reports that Danby was spending his downtime with primitive tribes in the far reaches of the Amazon. He hunted with them in the jungles. He participated in ceremonies where hallucinogens were blown up his nostrils. On assignments he was seen snorting a raw cocaine paste and drinking heavily.

Twice during missions, Danby inflicted ancillary casualties on civilians, which were inexcusable and marred Pluto's surgical reputation. Harold warned Danby several times that the abuses could lead to termination of his contract. Four years ago Danby abruptly notified Harold that he was going into business for himself.

"He used the skills we taught him well and disappeared before we could freeze his accounts and prevent him from stealing clients." Harold sighed. "The rumors were that he had decided to focus his business in Central and South America, and there were several operations over the following eighteen months that tasted to me like Terrance; then nothing."

"Nothing?" Gallagher repeated. Moths darted around a streetlight down the path from them, touching the bulb and falling to the ground.

"Not a single word for three years until your inquiries reached me last night."

Gallagher absorbed it all and played with it, then asked the old man, "Did he ever mention a fascination with the mythological character named Charun?"

"Charun?" Harold was bewildered. "No."

"How about a woman named Angel? He mentions her in several of the notes."

"Terrance was a whoremonger," Harold sniffed. "If he had a steady relationship, I was never ever aware of it."

"Was he an artist? Could he draw?" Gallagher asked, thinking of the intricacies of the sketches.

Harold shrugged. "It would not surprise me. Terrance may be mad, but he's capable of anything he puts his mind to."

"Was he interested in the Sioux?"

"As in Indians?" Harold frowned. "I'm sure he read about them at one time or another. He had vast interests."

Jerry scratched at his beard and then his belly. "Where was Danby last seen?"

"Southern Mexico near the border of Guatemala, April, two years ago."

Monsignor McColl had been a missionary in Guatemala ten years ago. Gallagher asked Harold if Danby had ever mentioned the priest.

The old man hesitated, thinking. It was nearly full dark now. The lights around the Lincoln Memorial cast a soft sodium glow through the humidity.

"Not by name," he said slowly. "But prior to his being offered a contract at Pluto, we required a further series of psychological examinations. Terrance told one of the analysts that he was abused by a priest in his teenage years, but he laughed it off, told us he'd fixed the priest but good."

Gallagher gave Harold a brief overview of the killings, including the savagery of the murders, the Charun illustrations and the notes. He asked Harold if he thought Danby could be the killer.

"If he is, he's more far gone than I thought," the old man said, shaking his head. "He was once so controlled. So beautiful in thought and deed."

For the first time that evening, Jerry smiled. "This isn't damage control, is it, Harold? You're not out here trying to keep Pluto buried. This is personal. You care about this fucking nutcase."

There was a long silence.

"I'm growing old, Matthews," Harold said at last. "I always thought of Terrance as a son. I would like to talk to him before the end."

Chapter Thirty-seven

The phone in the interrogation room rang and Andie's attention snapped away from Many Horses' journal. She picked up the receiver. "Nightingale."

"This is Sand," a male voice replied. "We can't find the priest."

"What?" Andie cried. "What are you guys, incompetent? You lose Kerris and now McColl?"

"Hey, we missed him, what can I say?" Sand retorted angrily. "There's a sign out front of St. Edward's that says, 'Masses are canceled due to the recent tragedy.' The rectory's dark, no answer. You want us to jump the back wall, take a look around?"

"Are you nuts?" Andie barked. "Without a warrant? Without probable cause? We'd be defiling the sanctity of a church. Do not go in. I repeat: do not go in. Get a make and license on his vehicle from DMV and send it over the wires with orders to stop and detain."

She slammed the phone down and stared at the legal notepad. She circled Kerris' and McColl's names and put a line between them with a big, bold question mark on top. Then she sighed and went back to Many Horses' journal.

Summertimes we seance outdoors at a cave up on the mountain behind the Danby farm. When all the folks who believe in Joshua and Caleb sit around the cave under the moonlight, I climb up the back way and come out on a ledge above the mouth of the cave and give a speech Joshua wrote. They look up at me the way the young men used to look at Ten Trees when I was a girl, like I can give them something they have a terrible hankering for.

Last week right there at the end, the priest in Lawton, the one they call Father D'Angelo, came charging through the forest with a passel of men and women who go to his church. In the lantern light D'Angelo looks like a tree that's lived in cold wind its whole life. He's got a head looks like a goose nest with one egg in it. He pointed his finger up at me, called me a heathen and sent some of his men to climb the rocks after me. I went off the back side and out into the woods, with Caleb behind me lickety-split.

Caleb and me ran so hard our sides were set to bust. We lost Father D'Angelo's men and Caleb wanted to circle on back to help his brother, but I asked him if he had forgotten the way Joshua let him be tarred and feathered and ridden on a fence rail the last time a preacher broke up one of the seances.

I took Caleb to my secret place—the rock cliff on top of Lawton Mountain that looks west. Below the cliff, all the trees are cleared for miles. In the sunshine far as you can see, there's nothing but rock and green. It's near to the Dakotas in springtime, only rolling. It was full moon when we got up there. Owls hooted and the crickets played fiddle and what Caleb said were cicada bugs, coming out of the ground after seventeen years in the earth, whined like babies missing their mothers.

Caleb said he missed his ma something awful and wished all the time he could talk to her because he did not get the chance before she died. I felt right sorry for him and told him it was a sad thing, because I could talk to my dead mother.

Caleb looked at me with them pink eyes in the moonlight. You know that ain't true, he said. Ain't no one can talk to the dead for real.

I can, I said. And I told him a little about the ceremonies Ten Trees, Painted Horses and Sitting Bull had taught me as a girl. I told him about our pipe and our stones. I told him how young men and some girls get taken to mountains where they cry for visions. I told him I had seen the spotted eagle in my vision. Eagle takes our prayers to Wakan Tanka, Great Spirit, Great Mystery. Then I told him about Wovoka and the Ghost Dance and how during the dance I walked and spoke with my dead a whole lot of times.

Caleb blinked and told me to show him.

In the moonlight on the cliff I showed Caleb my stones and Ten Trees' pipe, and I had him smoke from it. Then I danced the Ghost Dance and sang the Ghost Songs. I danced and sang for hours until the August sun come up over the moon and Caleb became a lump of white on the cliff. It was like the cicada bugs cried inside me. Then the sunlight turned to a green rain and out of it walked Painted Horses in her favorite buffalo robe. She opened the robe and I pressed myself to her and felt strong arms come around me. Then I smelled Ten Trees behind me and felt him put his arms around me, too.

Fear not, he whispered to me.

When I woke up, Caleb crouched over me, sniveling and blubbering. The sun was near straight up in the sky. My tongue ran dry over my lips and tasted salt. I raised my hand and put it on Caleb's arm. He jumped back, scared at first, then he laughed and laughed and said he thought I was dying on him. One minute he said I was dancing and singing so pretty he thought he saw another world in me. And then I started to terrible choking. My

eyes climbed in my head. Caleb said I pitched forward in the dirt
and wasn't breathing no more. My tongue went backward down
my throat and he couldn't hear my heart at all.

I don't remember. Same as when we danced at Standing Rock.
Folks always had something to tell us about what our bodies had
done once our spirits crossed to the other side.

Caleb tried to say something, but couldn't. Then his eyes got
right wide and his skin turned pinker than trout meat. He held
his hands out and looked at them like they was new hands. And
he said while I laid in the dust the air around me was not hot
and sticky, but cold and smelled peppery like it was October and
the leaves were changing. He asked me if that is what it is like—
cold and peppery but good—when you die.

I shook my head and told Caleb dying ain't like in the poetry
we read with Miss Mary Parker. Dying is a right awful thing
about skin and bones and blood. Dying is cruel and hard, like a
blizzard you get swallowed in. But then it is over and your spirit
has passed through to a place from where it can still see and
watch the living. Like an island in a river. The spirit goes beyond
there, too. But that island is where both the living and the dead
can see and hold each other. I told Caleb that maybe that was
what he had smelled and touched—that island in the river between
two worlds.

Caleb gape-jawed at me for the longest time. His skin was
commencing to burn in the sun. He put his hand on my shoulder
and I did not like it. Ever since the soldier with the black teeth,
I don't take kindly to men putting their hands on me. He asked
if I would teach him to talk with the dead and I said no. Caleb's
fingers dug into my skin. He asked why not. He said we was
friends and he asked why a friend would keep a friend from talking
to his ma.

I did not rightly know what to say to that. But Ten Trees,
Painted Horses and Sitting Bull always told me that the pipe and
the stones and the ceremonies were ours alone, and that they must

be passed on with care to those with a pure heart. And every pure heart that uses the pipe and the stones and the ceremonies finds its way to talk to the Great Spirit. That's why everyone I knew who'd crossed had a different way of telling it. I might tell Caleb everything to do and say to go to that island, but he might not find his way there.

Ten Trees said some folk have the sense of it from the day they are born. Some lose the sense. And some never find the way. It can't be passed on from one to another like a pipe or a stone. It's something the Great Mystery gives to you, a gift like the animals that come and speak to us in visions.

But I saw that Caleb, the whitest white man I have ever known, would not understand. I told him if he was my friend, he would not tell anyone what I'd shown him.

Caleb was not happy, but he promised.

This morning, that pinch-faced Alice came to the kitchen after breakfast and told me Joshua wanted to talk. I went to his office. Joshua wore the red robe he uses during seances. Caleb sat on the sofa. He would not look at me.

Joshua started talking in the voice I call his wanting voice, the one he uses when he's fixing to get something for himself. He stroked that pointy beard of his and slicked back the long black hair he'd grown. His nose was all runny and his eyes were big and black and shiny like a marble. That's the way they get when he's been sampling the spider medicine too much. Joshua said Caleb had told him an interesting story and that I had something to show him.

I shook my head and said there's some folk supposed to understand and some folk that aren't. Joshua got right angry then and said he wanted the ceremonies and dances and songs that give you the power to talk with the dead. I told him it was not like that. And anyway, he'd only use it wrong to get money out of people.

Caleb curled up like a wet cat on the sofa, sad and scared.

Joshua's face got bunched up and redder than the faces of McGloughlin's men just before they killed my uncle. I figured to run.

But Joshua come around the desk faster than I could move and grabbed me by the hair and shook me like I was no better than a dog. He said he took me in when I was a starving squaw sleeping in haystacks, a fugitive from the U.S. Army. I owed him.

Caleb jumped up from the couch and made to grab Joshua. Joshua's black eyes with them whites like the last week of the moon never left me. He just crooked out with his left hand and cracked his brother across the mouth. Caleb pitched on the floor, bleeding from his lips and blubbering again.

Joshua got his face close. He said, you really think you're more powerful than me?

I heard the pounding of hundreds of moccasins and I heard us singing to our grandfather. I heard the guns on wheels drown out the pounding of our moccasins and I saw my mother rise up and pass blood from her mouth. I felt the bite of the snowstorm when I walked away into this life, such as it is. Then the snow became Joshua's hand twisting my hair up so tight, I felt my scalp was likely to tear. I saw in Joshua the face of the soldier with the black teeth riding down on me, hungry and hateful at the same time.

Caleb told me to tell Joshua or I'd end up like his daddy, dead in his sleep with a bullet in his head. Joshua smiled in a way as to make me sick. And for the first time I saw that he was not right in the head. He'd been using the spider medicine almost every day, sunup to midnight. That and all the worship during the seances had pushed him outside his normal course, like a river that's done jumped its bank.

I was powerful scared and wanted to run all the way back to Standing Rock. But Ten Trees and Painted Horses taught me to be clear-eyed. I was months walking from Standing Rock. If

I were to go home, I needed time and a plan to gather what I'd need.

I told Joshua I was obliged to think on how best to teach him our ways because it can't be done in one pull. Joshua trained them last-week-of-the-moon eyes on me and I looked into them until I felt I was commencing to tumble. He leaned forward and kissed me hard on the lips before I could step back. He tasted like water when an animal has fallen in the well.

It is night now, more than a week since he kissed me, and Joshua's breath still hangs around me like the smell of black teeth. I have thought on it and thought on it and I cannot do this alone. I need help, but I cannot count on Caleb or the rest of them. They are all trapped by Joshua's spider medicine.

Tomorrow I'm gonna go see Father D'Angelo.

Chapter Thirty-eight

The dispatcher burst through the door to the interrogation room, waving another one of those pink slips in the air. "I just took this call myself!" Shaddock said breathlessly.

His furtive eyes came immediately to the pouch and the yellowed papers on the metal tabletop in front of Andie. Before continuing, the gossip licked his lips, fascinated yet nervous in their presence. "Orin Loomis, a clockmaker down south of Windsor. He told me he had a red leather pouch with an excerpt of a journal and an old pipe bowl inside."

"A pipe bowl?" Andie cried. "I never mentioned a pipe bowl on television! Who's left out there?"

"Just Lieutenant Bowman and little old you, but I suppose you'll be wanting to stay around, waiting for Patrick's call?"

"Knock it off, Shaddock," she said. "I'm going to pay Mr. Loomis a visit."

"Do you want me to hold onto that?" Shaddock asked, nodding toward the journal.

"Why, so you can leak it to *Hard Copy* or something?"

"I'd never!" Shaddock said indignantly. "But what's it say anyway?"

"None of your business," she said, gathering up the journal papers and sliding them back into their pouch.

That evening there was a break in the line of storms buffeting Vermont. The setting sun refracted through fast-moving clouds of the departing front, bruising the sky ruby and purple as Andie crested a rise about a mile from the turnoff onto the dirt lane that led to Orin Loomis' home. The late-day riot of color and light played out over fields where cows grazed. The bottoms of the mountains showed first leaf now. A thousand vertical feet higher, the maples were just in bud. But at the highest reaches winter still gripped the forest.

The thinly settled lane passed a general store and two farms, then climbed through tamaracks toward a plateau of sorts. She passed a brick ranch house, three trailer homes and then a white Colonial with a heart-shaped pond. Around the next bend was a sign, GREEN MOUNTAIN CLOCKWORKS.

Andie parked, tugged on a green sweater, then got out and mounted the steps to the clock-shop porch and knocked. No lights shone inside. No answer. She knocked again, waited and was turning to leave when the entire house began to clang, vibrate and bong. Startled, Andie jumped off the porch, her heart pounding. Then she heard laughter, spun and saw a young freckle-faced boy in a blue tank top, straddling a mountain bike.

"Ain't it great?" He grinned. "Eight o'clock, that's a good one, but an hour from now, nine o'clock, that's a racket. Orin says 'cause it's the only hour all the grandfather clocks seem to work right."

Andie laughed at herself even as the din petered out to the tinkling of some smaller timepiece. "Where is Orin?"

The boy pointed toward a two-track overgrown with grass

that disappeared into the woods behind the clock shop. "He and Missy and the girls live just up the hill. Not far."

The detective glanced at her pickup, then decided to walk. The boy stood there watching. It was a balmy evening, the first blessed warmth from the relentless cold rain of the past two weeks. The still-damp grass in the middle of the two-track sopped the ankles of Andie's gray slacks. The road curved alongside a streambed, climbed a hill, then gave way abruptly to a clearing in the middle of which sat a larger version of the clock shop, flanked by two apple trees blooming in the gathering dusk.

A mare and a colt grazed in a paddock beyond the house. In the lighted kitchen window, a gangly man about thirty was stirring a stove pot. Beyond him at a kitchen table, two girls colored.

A dark shadow slipped along the side of the barn. It halted as Andie strolled into the light cast from the kitchen window, then circled quickly behind a broad-waisted rhododendron bush, hesitated, then rushed out and bore down. Out of her peripheral vision Andie caught the flash, spun and crouched, clawing for her pistol.

The chocolate Labrador retriever skidded to a halt inches in front of her, shaking its butt like a hula dancer, then dropped a tennis ball from its mouth and barked happily.

"You little stinker," Andie whispered. The dog fetched the tennis ball, flipped it toward her feet and barked again, behind wagging faster than tail.

"Missy, you stop now," the gangly man called from the doorway. Then he saw the gun in her hand and took a step backward.

Andie holstered the pistol, then walked toward the porch. "I'm Sergeant Nightingale. Vermont State Police. Are you Orin Loomis?"

"Yes," he said, relieved. "I'm sorry. I haven't known what to do since that report on television. That was you, wasn't it?"

Loomis had pale skin, a ski-jump nose and a kind face. Barefoot, he wore a blue apron over a tan short-sleeved shirt and jeans. The Labrador scampered up to him, circled his legs and sat panting beside him.

"Yes," Andie said.

A pretty little brown-eyed girl about seven years old appeared on the other side of the French doors. "Daddy?"

Loomis looked at his daughter, then at Andie, and he gave her a quick shake of his head to tell her the girl did not know that he'd called. The clockmaker said, "Tina, do me a favor, honey; help Jenny get washed up for supper, 'kay? I've got to talk with Ms. Nightingale about a clock."

The girl nodded uncertainly and went back inside, and Loomis turned to Andie.

"Is it true?" she asked. "Do you have a piece of Many Horses' journal?"

Chapter Thirty-nine

Jerry Matthews dodged his rental car through bridge traffic toward Ronald Reagan National Airport. "You're gonna just make it!"

Although Gallagher had less than twenty minutes to catch the last shuttle to Boston, his attention was not on the road, but on the photograph in his lap.

Before he melted off into the viburnum-scented night, Harold—or whatever his real name was—had given them a photograph of Terrance Danby. It was a ten-year-old shot of Danby on the day he had made sergeant major: a lean, close-shaven giant with a bull's neck and stone-colored eyes. He wore a black beret. Ribbons and medals festooned his jacket.

Jerry rubbed his nose on his sleeve and glanced at the picture before wrenching the car right to speed up the exit ramp. "Harold wasn't shitting you. The guy's close enough to be your brother."

"Kind of makes me queasy to know that I look like an assassin."

"Better than being one," Jerry grunted. He slammed his fist on the steering wheel. "Fucking Harold! I should have buried that bastard when I had the chance."

"He might have had your nieces killed," Gallagher replied. "Nothing you could do about it. You made the right call."

Jerry stewed for a moment, then nodded toward the cell phone. The Flight Departures area was just ahead. "Don't you think you'd better tell the detective you're working with what Harold said?"

"I'll wait until I get off the ground."

"What's her name again?"

"Nightingale, Andie Nightingale."

There must have been something in the way Gallagher said it that made Jerry take his eyes off the road. They bounced up on the curb and a skycap yelled in protest.

"Don't tell me—" Jerry began.

"Okay, I won't," Gallagher said, already halfway out the car.

Jerry grinned. "Hey, man, good for you. See? Midlife crisis ain't so bad."

Gallagher ignored him. "How long until you and the camera crew can get to Lawton?"

"Two days. Three, tops."

"See you then."

Gallagher waited until the plane had been airborne twenty minutes before placing the call to Andie's cell phone. The line rang several times, then forwarded, and a man with a whining nasal voice answered: "Bethel Barracks. Vermont State Troopers."

"I'm looking for Sergeant Andie Nightingale."

"You and everyone else in the state," the man said. Then his voice dropped an octave or two. "You with CNN?"

"My name's Patrick Gallagher."

"Not *the* Patrick Gallagher?" the man gloated. "You mean her personal Pat Gallagher?"

"What?" Gallagher asked, puzzled. "Is she there or isn't she?"

"No, but I'll patch you through to her cell phone," he replied.

"I just tried that. I was forwarded to you."

"She's away from her vehicle, then," the dispatcher replied. His voice dropped conspiratorially. "She's going to tell you there's been another killing. Libby Curtin, the parish secretary. They found her portion of the Indian's journal and now Andie's out after another piece of it. I took that call. A clockmaker down in Windsor's got it."

Gallagher clenched the phone tighter, his heart racing. "I need to talk to her."

"Can I tell her where she might reach you?"

"I'm on a plane between D.C. and Boston," he said. "If she calls in, tell her I'll try again around five past nine. Tell her it's about Danby."

"Danby," the dispatcher said thoughtfully. "The plot thickens. How about a first name and a spelling?"

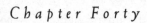

Chapter Forty

Orin Loomis hesitated, grim-faced, at Andie's question about Many Horses' journal.

"My girls don't know anything about it," he said at last. "Neither does my wife. She's out on the West Coast for the year, completing her master's. I don't want any of them to know I kept it from them."

"I understand," Andie said. "I had a piece myself."

Loomis looked at her now with great curiosity. "I always wondered who else had it," he said. "Don't think I'm weird, but part of me believes it's cursed. Whenever I held it, it made my skin crawl and I couldn't explain it, because all it is is a pipe and some old pieces of papers. I know I must sound goofy, but it always seemed like there was a bad energy around them. I almost burned the pouch once, but it was like I couldn't, you know?"

Andie nodded. "You and your girls will be safe now. Can you get the journal for me?"

"It's hidden in the shop," Loomis said. "Hold on, I'll take you down."

Loomis went inside. Behind Andie came the chorus of tree peepers and then from an unseen pond the first *bruumphs* of the bullfrogs' mating ritual. A light breeze stirred the scent of lilac. One of the horses neighed in the near dark.

When the clockmaker emerged from the house, he had on a purple fleece top and white running sneakers. Tina wore a blue windbreaker and held the hand of a petite and pretty two-year-old in a pink bunny jumper sucking her other thumb. Loomis introduced her as Jenny.

They climbed into Loomis' rusting jeep Wagoneer. Missy, the Labrador, tried to jump in, too, but Loomis shooed her out. It was dark now. The moon, nearly full, was rising and casting shadows. The dog ran ahead and raced in a circle when they parked in the little gravel turnout next to Andie's truck.

On the porch, the clockmaker held Jenny in one hand and with the other punched in an elaborate code on an alarm pad. He opened the door. Missy wriggled between their legs and darted off into the dark interior. Loomis switched on the lights to reveal two large, connected rooms filled with every imaginable sort of timepiece hanging from or leaning against a wall. Heavy, ornate grandfather clocks, nineteenth-century banjo clocks, French table clocks. And among the timepieces, strewn over a half-dozen wooden tables, were old music boxes in various stages of assembly and repair.

Tina and Jenny immediately went to the music boxes and began turning them on. Tinny music filled the air and the two little girls started to dance.

Loomis led Andie into a back room that smelled of light oil and was filled to overflowing with the delicate tools of his trade. The clockmaker carefully moved an old music box off the top of a set of oak drawers. These he tugged back from the wall, then groped at the floor for several moments before coming up with a zippered black rubber bag. He handed it to Andie as if it were a distasteful thing.

Without speaking, she unzipped the bag and retrieved the red leather pouch. It bulged at the bottom. She untied the green ribbons and peeled back the flap. Tucked in beside the folded yellow sheets of Many Horses' journal was a pipestone. She gently drew the stone out and studied the black bowl on which a silver buffalo and two red triangles had been painted. Andie ran her thumb into the bowl and found it rough to the touch, then nearly jumped when the bowl grew warm, almost hot in her hand.

"She talks about the pipe in the journal," Loomis said, pointing to the yellow papers jutting out of the pouch. "It's all about old shamanic ceremonies taught to her by her mother and father. Most of it I don't get."

"Who gave the pouch to you?"

"My dad," Loomis said. "Week before he died. He said his grandmother had passed it on to him and that she'd gotten it from a priest she used to work for."

"What priest? You mean D'Angelo?"

Loomis shrugged. "Yes, I think that was the name."

"It makes sense that D'Angelo would be the one to disburse the journal," she said excitedly. "But McColl said he'd never come across anything about a Sioux."

"You've lost me." Loomis shook his head, puzzled. "Who's McColl?"

"Forget you heard that. I'll bring in troopers to guard you and the girls for tonight. Do you have anywhere you can go first thing in the morning?"

"Karen's sister has a summerhouse in Maine."

"Fine," Andie said. "What I'd like to do is have a trooper who looks like you stay here in the house after you're gone."

"You mean, like bait?" Loomis asked, worried.

"Something like that." Andie returned the warm pipestone and the journal to the pouch. "I need a phone."

The clockmaker directed her to a portable on the wall, told

her to turn off the lights and shut the front door behind her. The electronic lock would set automatically. He took one last glance at the pouch in Andie's hands, then gathered up his girls, whistled to the dog and went back out into the night.

Andie called the Bethel Barracks.

"You just missed your ardent admirer," the dispatcher said. "He's been calling here every twenty minutes. He's stuck in Boston overnight. They canceled the last flight to West Lebanon. He'll try you again in another fifteen minutes. Says it's important. Very important. Now, who's this guy Danby, Sergeant? How does he fit in?"

"Stay out of it, Shaddock," Andie ordered. "And if that name gets out, I'll have you fired."

"I've got twenty-three years in state civil service," Shaddock sniffed. "You can't have me fired."

"Watch me," Andie promised. "Now get me four troopers in plain clothes to the Loomis home immediately."

"Loomis had a piece, didn't he? I knew it! I took that call!"

"Shaddock!"

"All right. All right."

Andie hung up. She flipped off the lights and shut the door behind her, hearing a whirring and clicking noise in the wall.

The peepers and bullfrogs had gone silent. Her shoes crunched gravel. The moon was luminous and pale stars shone amid the swiftly moving clouds. Andie opened the truck window so she'd hear if the cell phone rang and leaned against the bumper, waiting.

From behind and to her left, from the bushes along the two-track that led up the hill to Loomis' house, a tennis ball shot out and bounced past her. There was a soft padding on the gravel.

Andie turned from the ball to shoo the dog. "Go home, Missy. Go on home," she said. The car phone buzzed behind her. The hundred clocks in the shop struck the nine o'clock hour with a resounding clangor.

With her attention diverted and divided, the realization that the form was not canine but creature came to Andie in a slow motion unfolding. Crepe-soled black boots spit out gravel. Strips of leafy camouflage flapped moistly at the swift, hulking body that bore down on her. A machete in one hand. A tomahawk in the other.

Andie screamed and went for the pistol in her pocket.

"Angel! Alive!" came a raspy voice from under the cowl as the monster closed the final yards.

Andie's fingers gripped the pistol butt and she thumbed the safety off before attempting to turn the barrel up at the charging figure and shoot him point-blank.

But the creature must have sensed her intent. He dropped his back foot away from the barrel's line of fire and slashed the square end of the tomahawk in a quick, horizontal action. The blow deflected her wrist outward just at the moment of discharge, just as the hundred clocks in the shop struck the last stroke of nine and all but swallowed the gun's sharp report.

Andie's gun skittered across the gravel in the echoing silence. Somewhere up the hill in the woods, a little girl screamed.

"Alive!" the creature bellowed.

Her hand went numb and she felt the cold snap of the wet strips of camouflage as he slipped in behind her and what felt like an iron bar closed across her windpipe. She cocked her elbows and hammered backward into the creature's solar plexus. He grunted, not with pain but with pleasure.

"We're going to the other side, Angel!" he whispered. "But this time we're going together."

He closed the choke hold at her neck and ground his pelvis tight against her buttocks. She tried to scream, but couldn't. Unconsciousness came for Andie in dots that danced against the full moon and the pale stars like fireflies on a sultry August night.

Just before blackout, she fought one last time to sip air through her nostrils. In that trickle she smelled something saline and primal and thought, this is what it must be like to drown tangled in a bed of seaweed.

Chapter Forty-one

"She's dead, isn't she?" Gallagher demanded frantically. "You're going to find her in a ditch somewhere with one of those goddamned drawings stuck to her, aren't you?"

"Mr. Gallagher, calm down . . ." Lieutenant Brigid Bowman said.

His attention jumped off her to dart around the crowded squad room of detectives hushed at his outburst. "Why are you all just sitting here?!

"Or don't you care?" he asked, softer, more bewildered now than angry. "That's been it from the beginning, isn't it? You've all written her off the way everyone writes off the drunks in their lives."

The entire room whirled. Andie had been missing for nearly fourteen hours. The plainclothes troopers had arrived at the clock shop only to find signs of a struggle in the soft soil, Andie's footprints, a size-thirteen footprint, her service pistol, an empty 9mm shell casing and a tennis ball. Loomis and his daughters were sure they'd heard a shot before her truck started and drove off. Her Toyota was discovered a mile away on a logging road in the woods. Gallagher landed in West Lebanon at nine A.M., almost a half-day after Andie went missing.

Bowman took him by the elbow and ushered him out of the squad room and down the hall into her office. An eight-by-ten glossy of a younger Andie Nightingale in dress trooper uniform lay on the desk. He gazed at it with a tubular and rancorous anxiety, trying desperately to avoid the idea she might be gone from his life forever.

The lieutenant's normally stiff bearing had melted and her voice quivered with emotion. "I haven't handled much of this case the way I should have because I didn't believe in Andie Nightingale the way I should have," she confessed. "Maybe it's because, as the only other woman in BCI, I expected more out of her. That's something I may have to live with for a long time. But every person in this department cares. Every man and woman out there in that room is into their second or third shift since she went missing.

"Copies of her picture are in every police car from Virginia to Quebec," Bowman went on. "Her face will be on the news all over New England tonight. And we've got all-points bulletins out for Chief Kerris and Monsignor McColl."

"Why don't you just search their houses?" Gallagher demanded.

"Because we have something called the Fourth Amendment to the Constitution," she replied. "If we search without probable cause, we violate their rights. Based on the evidence we have, I don't think a judge would grant me a search warrant on either of them. We need more."

Gallagher sat in a chair with his head in his hands, then remembered Danby. From his briefcase he remembered the picture Harold had given him. It turned out that Andie had briefed Bowman on Danby's early history and his relationship with

McColl before leaving for Loomis' farm. Gallagher filled her in on the rest.

Bowman sucked in her cheeks. "I'll make sure this picture goes out over the wires immediately. Now go home, Mr. Gallagher—you've done enough already."

A ball worked its way up the back of his throat at the thought of being alone in the cabin; then he blurted out: "All I've been able to think is that I'm going to lose her."

A throat was cleared behind him. Gallagher turned to find a plump, redheaded man waving his fingers into the open doorway.

"Yes, what is it, Shaddock?" Bowman asked.

"Sorry, Lieutenant," he said. "I couldn't help overhearing and . . . could I say something to Patrick Gallagher?"

"Do I know you?" Gallagher asked.

"The dispatcher," Shaddock said, taking a step into the room. "I just wanted to tell you that when she talked about you—well, I've known Andie a long time, poor girl. And when she talked about you, Patrick, I never saw her so happy. I hope she told you."

Out Bowman's window, Gallagher could see the stultifying air mass that had gripped Washington, D.C., now hovering over Vermont, choking the hillsides in a muggy embrace.

Gallagher's entire body felt shot with painkiller during the hour drive back from Bethel to Lawton. Andie's disappearance was the lead story on an all-news radio station out of Burlington. In one of the reports, Mayor Bruce Powell did everything but execute a backflip to distance the town from the murders. No mention was made of Chief Mike Kerris, Monsignor Timothy McColl or Terrance Danby.

Gallagher drove aimlessly around the town, hating the brilliant light and the heat. Here on the river bottom, winter was vanquished, yet he found no joy in the first crab apple blossoms, the maple leaves tearing through their bud walls or the flocks of bluebirds, orioles and barn swallows flitting in the sky. A cow moose with her calf crossed the road in front of him. His mind centered on Emily, and he opened the door and threw up.

A half-dozen television transmission trucks were parked at City Hall. Cruising down Main Street past the trucks, he had a straightaway view up the flank of Lawton Mountain toward Gorm Ridge. There, at the very top, the trees remained dead and gray.

Midafternoon, Gallagher finally drove up the River Road, intending to head toward the solitude of the cabin. But as he passed the farm, he was overcome by the need to be close to things that were Andie's.

He parked in her yard, climbed out and was immediately attacked by a cloud of black, biting flies hatching in the sudden warmth. Their scissors teeth drew blood at his neck and forehead and ears and he ran inside to escape them. The house was silent. The fallen-leaf scent of her hung thick in the air.

Tess meowed and strolled out from the front room. Gallagher poured some dry food in her bowl and stroked her back while she ate. The cat curled in his lap as he sat in Andie's chair and read the copies Lieutenant Bowman had made for him of Libby Curtin's section of Many Horses' journal as well as Charun's last note.

I fucked Angel blindfolded and ear-plugged right to the far shore. Fucked until she stepped into the muddy water and climbed beyond.

I stayed in my Persephone warm and alive. Warm and dead. Cold and dead, but even with the cord lashed tight around us, I never saw. I left her on the bank and she walked on while I rowed back alone.

You think you know me now, Lawton, but you don't. I

am the boatman. I am the lover. I am the shaman and I am the mutator.

Summer comes. And Hades has returned Persephone to Earth. I have seen her. I will have her again for one more boat ride.

Gallagher's blood ran cold at the images of necrophilia he wove. He turned over the note and studied the drawing. The monster seemed to taunt him with the knowledge that he had his life in his hands. He threw the drawing down, got up and wandered aimlessly through the darkened house, searching for those places where Andie's scent was pooled.

Her fragrance was strongest at the mouth of the closet in her bedroom and Gallagher stood there hyperventilating until he collapsed in a heap on the rug. The cat watched impassively from the doorway.

Gallagher closed his eyes and tried to sleep. In his mind all memories were tinged in scarlet. Andie walked by, gloriously naked, and he reached out toward her stomach, only to have it turn into Emily's stomach.

Gallagher groaned and wrapped his arms around his head as if to ward off sharp blows. But there was no stopping the pain now.

Six months after Emily had left him to go to Mexico, she strolled unannounced into an editing facility Jerry and he had rented in Manhattan for postproduction work. Emily had gained a few pounds, which became her. She was tan and wore a very loose black cotton shift. The instant Gallagher looked up from the video screen and saw her, he had fantasized about a reconciliation.

A hundred times a day for the entire six months Emily had been in Mexico, he'd fantasized about a reconciliation. At least ten times a day he'd thought about flying south to find her. But a part of him had held back. A part of him knew she had to return on her own. Only then could their life go on, a partnership that looked perfect on paper and had functioned well except for one brief, rocky period.

Emily told Jerry to take lunch, then shut the door behind her.

"Mexico looks good on you," Gallagher said, more than a little nervous. "Cripes, Em, you're glowing!"

He came around the editing console to hug her. She did not rush to embrace him, but did allow his arms to come around her. He pulled her to him and his stomach pressed against a large round ball.

Gallagher stepped back flooded with relief, fear and, from deep, deep within, a trickle of something warm and hopeful that he didn't understand. "You're pregnant," he croaked.

"Five months," she said brightly. She put her hands on her stomach. "The kicking just started a week ago. It's incredible."

"Here," Gallagher said, pulling up a chair. "You should sit down."

He stared at her belly, feeling that trickle of hope grow to a stream and then to a river. Emily reminded him of the fertility goddesses carved on the temple walls in Athens. He wanted to touch her stomach again.

Emily caught his fingers in midair. "It's not your child, Pat."

The river evaporated and between them there opened a great arid divide. "No, of course it isn't."

Somehow he got back to his chair behind the editing console without falling. Through what sounded like the buzzing of a bee swarm, Emily told him what had happened. The first week in Mexico she met and befriended an attorney and his barren wife. After knowing them less than a month, she offered to carry a baby for them. She made love to the attorney several times while his wife watched. She left Mexico City for the interior with promises to call them the moment she missed her period.

"But once I knew, I couldn't call," Emily said.

"You didn't tell them? You stole their baby?"

"It's my baby," she snapped. "It's growing inside of me. Who the father is doesn't matter."

An invisible hand crushed Gallagher down. "It could have been ours," he mumbled. "It would have mattered then."

Emily's eyes went flat and hard. She fished around in a tan leather pocketbook.

"No, it wouldn't, Pat," she said, handing him a set of divorce papers. "When I first went to Mexico, I used to think that we'd get back together. But the more I thought about you, the more I realized that was not possible."

"But why?"

"Because you don't believe in the afterlife," Emily said.

"What does that have to do with anything?" he cried.

"It's a circle, Pat," Emily replied calmly. "To believe in an afterlife, you first have to believe in this life, which takes a belief that love is more powerful than death. At some level you could not get yourself to totally commit and believe in our love, so you destroyed the truest expression of it. Our child."

She waited for her words to sink in. She rubbed her hands over her belly. "This, Pat, could have been your afterlife."

For the ensuing year Gallagher had stood in a near coma on rivers all over the country, fly casting like some idiot savant, telling himself that Emily was the one who was wrong, that she was the one who bailed out on the marriage and stole some stranger's sperm for a monstrous exercise in self-gratification.

Now, lying on the rug outside Andie's closet, he heard Emily's words echo around him. *This, Pat, could have been your afterlife.* And for the first time, he admitted Emily might have been right. He didn't believe in life. He didn't believe in love, either. How could he? He'd never been taught to love, only to survive by retreating, by keeping life at arm's length. Gallagher had watched life as if it were an ironic drama unfolding in a fishbowl.

When it counted, when he could have committed himself totally to Emily through their child, he'd pressured her into aborting it and killed the relationship. When it counted, when he could have made some response of love toward Andie on their last night together, he'd retreated inside one of his glass boxes.

"I had a second chance and I blew it," he moaned in disbelief. And then he began to cry. For himself. For Andie. And, yes, for Emily.

"I'm sorry," Gallagher whispered. "I'm so, so sorry."

He lay there, helpless and hopeless, for the longest time, wanting the impenetrable black wall to come for him and end the misery.

Then he found himself doing something he'd never done before. He got up on his knees. His hands came together of their own accord to beg the invisible for some sign of hope, some sign of forgiveness. He prayed to something beyond himself that he could change and that Andie might be spared.

Hours later Gallagher stopped, exhausted, convinced that it had been a wasted effort. Seamus had been right all along. There was no God. There was no afterlife. We blip into a cruel existence. We blip out of a cruel existence.

Andie Nightingale would die senselessly at the hands of a madman and there was nothing he could do to stop it. Gallagher punched his hand against the door to the closet until it splintered; then he staggered to her bed in the late-afternoon heat and passed out on top of the quilt.

His sleep was a deep and dreamless suspension in an unwavering blackness. But around midnight, Gallagher stirred up from the abyss into that state between conscious and unconscious. A warm prism of light appeared in that hollow space between his eyes. It rotated, gaseous and ignited, soothing his head as the stroke of a woman might a troubled man. Gallagher was at once awestruck and mother-comforted by its beauty and heard pulsing, like the thump of a stick against a leather drumhead, a thump he recognized as the beat of his own heart. The light slowed and took shape, vague at first, then more certainly into a woman in a buffalo robe with a single eagle's feather hanging from her hair.

"Help me, Sarah," Gallagher begged.

"All I wanted was to go home," she replied. "All anybody wants is to go home. You can take me there. You can find her there. Only you can set us free."

Many Horses turned and stepped back into the whitest part of the light. It swallowed her the way a snowstorm might a lone traveler on an empty plain, and the light ebbed from brilliance toward the gentle radiance of sunset on a distant horizon.

Chapter Forty-two

The wind clacking tree limbs returned Andie to the edge of consciousness. Her throat burned from the choking. Her lips ached from the gag he'd forced into her mouth, then covered with duct tape. Her feet were swollen from the parachute cord and the tape that bound her ankles. Her wrist throbbed where he'd hit her with the tomahawk.

She heard crows caw in the distance and forced open her eyes. Her vision doubled, fuzzed, then cleared.

Andie lay on her side on a filthy mattress in a cramped, low-ceilinged loft. A shuttered window creaked in the stiff, humid breeze. An old horseshoe was nailed to the wall alongside a faded metal sign advertising Winchester rifle cartridges. At her feet, the top of a wooden ladder jutted over the edge of the loft and she had an ill-formed memory of being carried up it. Clouds of mosquitoes hovered and whined around her in the dusky light. There were blackflies, too; they clustered around her eyes and crawled up her nose and bit. She groaned, snuffed and rolled over onto her back, trying to get away from them.

The crown of the mossy-boarded roof was busted through in several places. Thunderclouds rolled overhead.

Andie struggled to sit up against a pole supporting the roof. She arched forward, trying to see over the edge of the loft into the room below. Sheets of indigo cloth had been hung on the windows. Candles burned in the middle of the floor. A narcotic smoke, fungal and acid, wafted in the shadows.

"It's summer and you're back among the living, Persephone," a deep voice purred directly over her shoulder.

Andie screamed into the gag. He came crawling around into her line of sight and she screamed again.

His torso was naked, darkly tanned and shaved. There were rings pierced into his nipples. Smears of blood from insect bites dribbled over his sweated skin and rippling muscles. He wore baggy green camouflage pants and that cloth hood that covered his shoulders like an executioner's cowl. Through the slits in the hood his eyes glistened like mussel shells in a crimson sea. His lips were blue-toned and cruel.

"So alive," he said in a hoarse and indistinguishable voice. "But soon I will be reborn, too. I can join you, Angel. I have the squaw's ceremonies now! The old man never lied to me. Father never lied to me. We'll finish it now and walk the far bank together, sweet Persephone!"

His hand traveled to his groin. His lips curled into a smile of lust and delight. "Remember? You and I, Angel? Just like before? Only this time I'll dance with ghosts, too. There is another way! I told you it was true."

Andie shuddered and swallowed. She mustered up a gaze of sympathy and understanding and directed it at the creature. His eyes flared and held hers transfixed. He pressed his hand tightly against his crotch.

With a fragile motion of her chin, she made it known she wanted him to remove the gag. He hesitated, then slid over next to her and she saw the tomahawk up close. He danced it before her, a chipped obsidian blade that had been shoved down into the split leg bone of an animal, then anchored with sinew. A primitive hatchet. An Indian weapon.

"No one will hear you if you scream," he said raspily. "Do you understand?"

Andie nodded and tried to appear grateful. His free hand struck like a snake, tearing the duct tape and the gag from her mouth in one vicious motion. He slid back several feet, then sat Japanese-style on the backs of his lower legs. Andie worked her aching jaw, then croaked, "Water."

He did not move for the longest time. "Please, Charun," she croaked. "Your Angel wants water."

He cocked his head, studying her. Then he reached around to draw a drab green water bottle from the shadows. He slid toward her a second time, his hand snatching her hair and wrenching her head backward. The water poured into her throat. She gulped, sputtered and swallowed again.

When Andie had had her fill, he let the spout drift an inch below her lower lip. He moved the stream back and forth across her chin. The water poured down her neck, pooled and soaked the yellow blouse about her breasts. His eyes devoured her.

She took a deep breath, as if preparing to step off a high precipice, then shoved her chest out at him. "Do you like Angel's breasts?" Andie whispered.

The dead eyes flitted from her face to her chest and back. He put down the water bottle and his hand came up and cupped the weight of her left breast. His breath issued forth raspy and excited. His hips thrust forward, prodding against her arm. Her eyes spun in their sockets as if seeing fragmented, herky-jerky images of a long-ago night, but she did not scream.

"Do you like Persephone's breasts?" she managed to whisper again.

He grunted with satisfaction, pinched her nipple, then ran his hand down across her stomach to press his open palm between her legs. She squirmed and cried out: "No!"

The monster's other hand dropped the hatchet and immediately his fingers were like a knotted cord around her throat. "Why not?!" he seethed. "You used to say fucking was the closest we'd ever get to the power, Angel. Every time closer to the other side, you said. I was your boatman, you said. I was your rower!"

Andie did not struggle, but adopted that look of sympathy again.

"You were my boatman, Charun," she whispered. "Tell me about our rope. Tell me how I got to the other side."

Inside the hood, the eyes became unscrewed and glazed. His hand turned viselike at her windpipe. "You wanted it tight around our necks, tight while we fucked, Angel," he said.

"Make me remember," Andie implored. "You left me there on the other bank, but I can't remember. Make me remember."

"We smoked until our heads fired," he replied. "You said the drugs would take us farther, quicker. Then you made me cinch the rope tighter and tighter. You said orgasm was the first instant of life. You said if we could get to the edge of death at the first instant of life, it all might balance for a moment and we would see . . ."

"Into eternity?" Andie asked.

"Yes!" he gasped.

"But I passed over and left you behind, didn't I?"

His hand fell away from her throat. "Yes," he gasped again.

"You have the squaw's ceremonies," she reminded him. "You can cross."

"We'll smoke and perform them," he said huskily. "We'll smoke and dance her Ghost Dance. The old man said we will see the other side! Father said so, too. Lawton said it was theirs. They took the secret from us."

He leaped to his feet, his fists shaking against the sky. "Lawton gave me the power of death. Now I will take back the power over death!"

Chapter Forty-three

After midnight still more heat flooded north out of the mid-Atlantic, a stifling and creeping air mass that squatted over central Vermont. There was a halo of red around the setting moon. Far to the west Gallagher heard thunder. Three different turkeys shock-gobbled off the roost down by the Bluekill. An owl hooted in return. The interplay of the sky's rumbling and the cries of the territorial birds opened up hollow, ominous places in his stomach that he did not know existed.

"Omens," Gallagher murmured, and in that he understood. After so many years a willful voyeur gadding about the world to record the legends and mores of various cultures, he was at last being forced to live his own myth. Many Horses was his Goddess. The Lawton killings, Gallagher's epic journey. He was haunted Perseus searching for his Andromeda, held captive by the forces of madness.

Gallagher gripped the pump-action shotgun he'd found in one of Andie's closets and got in the truck he rented at the Lebanon airport. Ground fog wafted through the birches that lined the lower River Road. A squad of troopers manned a blockade set up at the covered bridge. One of them was the rawboned trooper who'd waded out to help him pull Potter from the Bluekill a lifetime ago. He told the trooper he couldn't sleep. The trooper asked if the shotgun was loaded and Gallagher lied, and said no.

Except for several prowling state police cruisers, the streets of Lawton were almost deserted. Here and there, lone figures hustled through the predawn toward jobs as maids or breakfast chefs. One of them, a younger woman, watched Gallagher pass. When he slowed, her hand flew to her mouth and she sprinted in the other direction. Both clerks working the all-night shift at the Lawton minimart where he stopped for coffee had pistols shoved in their waistbands. It was as if a fiend had cast a spell of fear and distrust over the country town.

Over on Whelton Lane, yellow spotlights illuminated the facade and steeple of St. Edward's Catholic Church. Gallagher parked around the corner from the rectory, then slipped behind the church and scaled the garden wall. The scent of freshly turned earth permeated the air as he sneaked toward Monsignor McColl's residence. The birdbath with the small horse statues lay on its side next to a gaping hole in the ground.

Gallagher's heart came high in his throat as he knelt next to the hole. He flipped on the headlamp he ordinarily used when night casting for big brown trout. It had a red lens that did not disturb the feeding fish. The pit was more than five feet long by two feet wide by six feet deep. A grave.

There was a basement door under the porch. One tap on a cracked windowpane and Gallagher's hand was through and on the knob. Cobwebs feathered and broke across his cheeks past the furnace toward eight standing file cabinets. Ten of the legal-sized drawers were dedicated to Father D'Angelo. All locked.

He thought about breaking in, but decided against it; he

didn't have the time to look for clues to Many Horses' death. Sarah had obviously come in contact with D'Angelo shortly before she died and told him of Joshua Danby's threat to kill her unless she taught the bogus spiritualist to commune with the dead. The Charun killings were related to Sarah's murder a century ago. Gallagher was sure of it. But digging through drawers of material looking for the link could take days.

Andie didn't have days. She had hours. Maybe less.

Besides, Gallagher had other, more quickly verifiable suspicions to confirm. He slipped upstairs into the hallway. His lamp shone on the damaged painting of Father D'Angelo. With a little effort he was able to lift the portrait down off the wall. The tear in the canvas at the priest's left hip had been bothering him ever since he learned that Father D'Angelo must have known Sarah Many Horses. Perhaps the hole in the painting was neither an accident nor a random act of vandalism. Perhaps it had been done deliberately.

What do priests wear at their hips? Gallagher asked himself, as the backing peeled off the painting. He shone the lamp at the hole from the back side.

"I knew it!" he whispered. The canvas had not been sliced with a knife as Monsignor McColl had suggested, but was punctured with a narrow, blunt object, like a cane tip or a broom handle. Shards of canvas bent inward, away from the hole. He gently pushed the torn canvas back into place, then flipped the painting around again, leaned it up against the wall and bent down to get a better look. A set of rosary beads hung from a sash around the priest's waist. At the end of the rosary was a tiny gold crucifix encrusted with a red jewel.

"Father D'Angelo was one of the journal holders," Gallagher whispered. "Which means Monsignor McColl is one of the journal holders."

Now Gallagher crept down the hall toward the priest's office. The door creaked open. His headlamp played over the pictures on the wall behind his desk, stopping at the photograph of the priest mountain climbing in the Andes. He carried the sort of blue rope and pitons they'd seen outside David Nyren's window.

He moved the beam over another picture of the priest, this one with the orphans of Hennessy House. Row after row of boyish faces. For the second time Gallagher's attention tripped over one youth in the third row. He had Gallagher's eyes, cheekbones and hairline. But his lower front teeth overbit his upper lip and his shoulders bunched like the back blades of a mongrel dog that has decided to attack the man who whips him. Was he Danby?

The third photograph showed Monsignor McColl in front of his church in the jungles of Guatemala. Gallagher peered at an older girl standing right next to the priest. She was maybe fourteen, possibly fifteen, beautiful and sad in a way that reminded him of Andie. Was this girl Angel?

Gallagher trailed the headlamp beam off the pictures, over carved bowls, and brought it to rest on two empty brackets where a machete had been displayed the first two times he'd been in the priest's office.

It was four-fifteen in the morning by the time Gallagher got back to the truck. The empty grave, the tear on the painting, the climbing experience and the missing machete. McColl was the killer. He was Charun. The evidence was too strong to be a coincidence. Gallagher stopped at a pay telephone at the convenience store and dialed.

"Hello?" a sleepy voice answered.

"It's Pat Gallagher. But I'd prefer if you consider me an anonymous tipster."

Lieutenant Bowman groaned into the phone. "What are you talking about? It's four-thirty in the morning!"

He told her what he had found outside and inside the rectory.

"You're admitting to breaking and entering here, Mr. Gallagher," Bowman snapped, now fully awake. "That's a felony."

"I don't care," he said. "This sick son of a bitch has got the woman I—"

"What do you want me to do?" Bowman interrupted.

"Put out an all-points bulletin on him. Tear that rectory apart. Have every cop in the state looking for him!"

"Slow down now! What's his motive?"

Gallagher shifted the phone receiver to his other ear. "He's covering up Father D'Angelo's involvement in the death of Sarah Many Horses because the real story would mean the end of his chances at sainthood. He's presenting himself as a psychotic serial killer to throw you off the track of what he really is—a cold-blooded, rational killer. He's using the Charun stuff as a cover."

"A cover-up?" Bowman said skeptically. "Is that enough of a motive?"

"I think it is for a zealot whose own aunt was saved by D'Angelo."

In the end, Bowman agreed. But only halfheartedly. She would put more men on McColl and she'd get a judge to issue a search warrant for the rectory. Then she warned Gallagher to stay out of any more rectories and hung up.

Dawn was coming. In the sky, towering thunderhead clouds boiled east toward Lawton Mountain. Just as they reached the peak, the rising sun hit them and the sky turned a rich and troubling magenta.

Gallagher drove at a snail's pace north through the waking town, trying to see in the faces of Lawton's citizens an explanation for the feeling that circled his neck like a noose. In that lurid dawn, the chrome glowed weirdly on the rack of headlights mounted on the roof of the jacked-up red Ford that

Bernie Chittenden spun into the narrow lot behind the Otterslide General Store.

Andie's shotgun came to his hands as if of its own accord, and before Gallagher had time to think, he was out of the truck and slipping up behind Chittenden as he fumbled with a padlock to the store's back door. The muzzle touched behind the storekeeper's left ear and he jerked and looked down the barrel.

"What the—"

"Why did you try to run me and Andie Nightingale off the Gorm Ridge Road?" Gallagher demanded.

"You're freaking crazy!"

"That's right, I am," he said, grinning maniacally. He pressed the shotgun muzzle to the end of Chittenden's nose and clicked off the safety. "Now tell me why."

Sweat gushed off the man's forehead and slurried down in his scraggly beard. His breath came out thick and forced. " 'Cause Mikey told me to."

"Mike Kerris?" Gallagher said. "Chief Mike Kerris?"

"Eh-yuh. He told me to scare ya."

"Why?"

"Can ya take the gun off my nose, man? I feel like I'm gonna sneeze and you're gonna blow my fucking head off."

"That's the idea," Gallagher said. "Now why?"

"He said it was old family business you and Andie were looking into, stuff some people didn't want to come out."

"Family people, as in the Powell family?"

Chittenden nodded. "My mom's a Powell."

"What are the Powells hiding?"

Chittenden shrugged. "Don't know."

"You blindly follow Kerris' orders without even knowing why?"

"Don't want to know," Chittenden said. "My business done good, this whole town done good the past fifteen years 'cause a the Powells. Anyway, I made sure ya didn't get hurt. Just scared."

"Where's Kerris now?"

"Don't know," the shopkeeper said. But for a second his attention shifted off the barrel.

"You're lying," Gallagher said, pressing the muzzle so tight against his nose it flattened and his nostrils made little whistling sounds.

"Jesus, take it easy, man!" Chittenden whimpered.

"Talk!"

"Last I seen Mike was day before yesterday," the storekeeper said. "One of my headlights busted free of the rack when I was chasing after you. I told Mike and he said he'd head up Gorm to find it before you or Andie Nightingale did."

Chapter Forty-four

Halfway up Gorm Ridge, Gallagher heard and felt the first thunderstorm hit. Bolts of lightning slashed the sky. The truck shook from the explosions. The wind accelerated. Hail pummeled the deserted rutted road all the way to the gap on the ridge.

There was no sign of Kerris' truck or the black Thunderbird Lieutenant Bowman said Monsignor McColl drove, for that matter. It had occurred to Gallagher during the drive that the priest was a mountain climber. He could survive the elements. But the question that nagged at him was whether Andie Nightingale could. Or whether Charun had already left her body behind a mossy log or tossed it to the bottom of a ravine.

Gallagher pulled the truck over at the gap in the ridge. Hemlock branches provided slick handholds that let him lean out over the edge of the ravine, close to the source of the Bluekill, searching the early-morning gloom for his greatest fear.

Lightning flashed to the west over the Lawton valley floor.

Each crack granted him monochromatic still flashes of the Bluekill's endless frenzied wrestle with the rocky gorge. Wet, mossy walls. Frothed white water. A piece of driftwood wedged between two boulders. But no body.

Gallagher did not know what to do. Andie had been in Charun's clutches nearly thirty-six hours now. Or she had been dead nearly thirty-six hours. He fought back a dry heave, re-membering the brutal imagery of necrophilia in the killer's last note and the terrible humiliation in Andie's voice when she'd described what Kerris had done to her at the condominium party so many years ago.

He crawled back up the bank and stood defeated with his palms raised toward the sky. The rain splattered his face and he sank to his knees in the muddy road, sure now that he had lost his second chance forever.

The woods before Gallagher were spruce fir pocked with stunted hickory trees that quivered in the breeze and shifted outline in the cloud cover. A faint game trail led out through the trees toward a pair of towering glacial-cast boulders. There was a far-off trilling sound in the rain, like a cedar flute blowing on a mesa. Pale movement flickered to life, then disappeared beyond the boulders the way a form will surface and vanish in wind-driven clouds. Gallagher imagined a running woman with a waist-length black braid. She wore an indigo skirt and a vest adorned with red moons and white stars.

He got the shotgun from the front seat and went into the woods down the game trail. The forest was thick and electric with ozone. Two ravens lifted off the bones of a dead deer that lay in front of the stone pillars. He stood before the rocks, understanding that for him they were a gate into the underworld.

Gallagher stepped through the stone gate. A black cloud of insects immediately surrounded him. Biting blackflies and the season's first mosquitoes. The soil underfoot turned soft and oozing. Serpentine tangles of grapevine growing off the trees, the lower trunks of which were smothered in green and purple moss. Water dripped off every branch.

It took him nearly a half hour of sloshing to escape the swale and emerge into a vast grove of white pines, spruce and hemlock. The understory branches clawed at his face and hands. There was a flash of lightning to the west and he caught a silvery reflection on a bench above him.

The shotgun became an uncertain ally as Gallagher climbed the forty yards up the steep bank. Tire tracks rutted a logging road that ran along the bench. The tracks rounded a curve and stopped at a pile of fresh fir and pine branches. The pile ran twenty feet long and stood eight feet high and fifteen feet wide.

Slash pile, he thought. Probably a logger working in the area. He looked down the bank, trying to figure out where he'd been standing when the metal had reflected. There was a flash of heat lightning and there was that glitter again: ten feet ahead under the pile of branches.

The two trucks had been parked bumper to bumper on the logging trail, then covered with the debris. The front vehicle was a green 1983 Volkswagen camper. It was the same color as the van seen leaving the woods near Nyren's. The second was a midnight-blue Suburban with the Lawton police seal emblazoned on the door. Gallagher tried the door to Kerris' truck. Locked. He peered through the window. The wires to the radio hung torn and askew.

He tugged open the front door to the Volkswagen camper and froze. Hanging off the rearview mirror was a rosary at the end of which dangled a tiny gold crucifix encrusted with a red jewel. Beside it, attached to a length of black string, was a close-up black-and-white photograph of a woman holding the bridle of a horse. Her cheeks were more severely concave and her oval eyes were harsher than Andie's, but she had a similar facial construction and that same generous mane of hair, only duskier. She wore a black gaucho-style hat, a starched high-collar white shirt, black riding britches, and black jodhpur boots. She held the bridle of a stallion in one hand and a riding crop in the other.

"Hello, Persephone," Gallagher said. "Or should I call you Angel?"

Was it possible she was the same girl who stood next to McColl in the picture of the Guatemalan orphanage? And then Gallagher had the sudden thought that he had it all wrong. Maybe Kerris had met Angel when he lived in South America. Maybe Kerris was Charun and he used the Volkswagen truck not for fishing, but for a sick form of hunting.

By now it was two hours past dawn. The second violent wave of warm rain burst over the mountain peak. Gallagher bowed into it and followed the logging road for almost a mile. From the disturbances in the leaves, someone else had walked the trail recently, and he sneaked along with the gun cradled and ready. Every twig snap, every gust of wind, every clap of thunder seemed to contain more than it should.

The road looped a knoll and dropped off the other side of the ridge, angling back to the east. Three hundred yards later he crested a rise.

Below lay a decrepit squatter's shack overgrown with thorns. In the murky light Gallagher could see another wrecked hovel and then at least four other ruins in the woods. And then a clearing with charred stumps and a cabin with a sagging roof and porch. He had somehow come in on the opposite end of that squalor people from Lawton called Danbyville. Looking at it, he had a vague sense of déjà vu. And then he felt a tingling sensation where his spine met his head, as if a woman were dancing her fingers there. Andie was in that cabin. Gallagher was sure of it.

Gallagher considered turning around, racing the miles back

through the woods to the truck, finding a phone and calling Lieutenant Bowman. But he wanted to be sure before he sounded the alarm. He stood motionless and listened. There was nothing but the stilling breeze and the rain dripping off the trees, so he inched his way down the slope next to the first shack and found a tangled path leading off through the bracken toward the cabin.

The path forked twice. Side trails led off toward the various shacks and outbuildings that had once made up the Danby enclave in exile. On the steep bank behind the shacks Gallagher could see other paths leading up onto the mountain top. His path was only one of three main trails that crossed the overgrown plateau.

At the second intersection he noticed a length of taut green cord attached to a bent sapling perhaps four inches in diameter. He used a stick to clear out the leaves, revealing a snare setup like one he'd seen Aborigines use in Australia to catch rabbits. Only this one was big enough to catch a man.

Gallagher sidled around the booby trap. Off to his right, four ravens flapped up out of the brush surrounding the second ruin. Their wings panted the air in long, lazy strokes. They landed in a wind-stunted pine and cawed loudly, and he hunkered down until they stopped.

The shack closest to the main cabin was the one he'd seen from the clearing the day he and Andie had visited. An entire wall still stood. Gallagher crawled behind it, wiped the rain off his face, then peeked around the right corner.

Lime-green ferns fluttered. The forest's dripping muffled all sound. The cabin appeared unchanged. Except for the windows and the door. They had all been blocked off with dark fabric. If a helicopter hovered over that malignant clearing at night, the pilot would see no light burning inside. Andie was here. So was Charun.

Gallagher wanted to take one more look from another angle

before he ran to get Bowman and the troopers. As he crawled to the opposite end of the shack, thorns tore at his forearms and his face. So he wasn't looking down at the path as he made the corner. There was a flash of red in his eye and then a shrill beeping noise sounded over the dripping.

His legs and arms went rubbery and his head ducked and there was that flash of red in his eyes again. Strapped low on a pine tree trunk was a camouflaged housing from which cut the thin red laser beam that Gallagher had broken.

He sprang to his feet and went barreling back down the main path even as he heard the thud and scuff of feet sprinting across the wet porch.

At the second fork, Gallagher's right heel struck the trigger on the snare. The sapling sprang upright. The loop of green rope caught the very back edge of his boot heel and flung him out and forward on the feeder trail toward the second shack. He landed with a thud that knocked half the wind out of him.

Just beyond the second ruin, a tan trail climbed the bank toward safety. If he could make it there, Gallagher might get a shot at his pursuer as he came down the trails in the brush. Gallagher got up into a crouch, put the butt of the gun to his shoulder and duckwalked forward as fast as he could toward the second shack.

A green blowfly buzzed by his head. The wind puffed a sickening stench back at him. A tornado of the green flies spun up out of a pit that had been dug in the trail next to the ruin. There were hardwood limbs and pine bows caved into the pit. Wrapped around one of the saplings was a hand. Strips of flesh had been torn away, revealing bones, and for a second Gallagher thought with horror that the gold ring on a finger was one he remembered Andie wearing.

He looked down into the pit as he went by it and had to do everything in his power not to scream. Six sharpened sticks stuck through what was left of the body. The clothes hung in shreds. The ravens had been at the body so as to make it indistinguishable as man or woman.

There was crackling in the thorns at the other side of the pit. Gallagher leveled the gun, shot, then sprinted ahead. There was a crackling sound in the brush on the other side of the trail and he spun and shot at that, too, only to see a rock bounce out into the trail.

The pursuer was playing with Gallagher, throwing stones as a diversion. Gallagher had to make the top of the bank, where he could see down and get a clear shot. He clawed his way toward the top, slipping and sliding in the slick clay soil. It was so steep at the top that he had to reach up for a hand-hold he might use to haul himself to safety. His fingers curled around a knotty exposed pine root. He heard a crash in the thorns behind him and grinned. Gallagher thought he had his pursuer now.

Sudden, screwlike pain drilled through his hand. A black boot pinned Gallagher's fingers to the root. Polished obsidian eyes glared at him from inside the camouflaged hood. Charun sniggered at some private joke. Gallagher swung the gun up at his chest and jerked at the trigger even as the killer kicked at the shotgun barrel.

The gun went off, then jumped from Gallagher's hand and went end over end down the embankment. But the blast upset Charun's balance for a second and Gallagher got hold of his heel and upended him. As Charun fell, he lashed his boot sideways, bashing Gallagher in the chin, and all went to black.

Chapter Forty-five

A weighted metal object dragged across a rough wooden floor. Gallagher's tongue lolled, swollen and useless, against teeth that moved freely in his gums. He was propped up in a corner, hands and feet bound. The air was tainted with the fetid odor of marijuana mixed with much more powerful ingredients.

Gallagher opened his eyes, saw Andie in the shadows opposite him, thought it was a dream and smiled. She returned his smile. Her face was smudged and bits of straw hung in her tangled hair, but Gallagher thought she was still lovely. A lovely dream. Then, without moving another muscle, she rolled her eyes left and the dream turned black.

Charun had flipped the Formica-topped kitchen table against the door. Busted chairs, trash and boxes had been stacked atop the woodstove, leaving an open, orderly area in the middle of the cabin perhaps thirty feet in diameter. There was a radio-scanning device with eight little green lights glowing in the corner. Arranged on the floor in a semicircle, a dozen candles burned.

The hooded giant sat with his legs crossed under him, rocking before the candles as if in a trance. An executioner contemplating harsh work. Charun had the pieces of the journal laid out in front of him in separate piles. The lock of hair from Andie's pouch rested between the index finger and thumb of his left hand. He rolled the stones from Olga Dawson's pouch among the fingers of his right. He had drilled and fitted a length of river ash as a new stem for Ten Trees' pipestone. It lay across his ankles. A thin contrail of smoke sinewed up from the bowl like a cobra rising to the flute.

Gallagher came alert and glanced about the room, looking for the shotgun, but it was nowhere in sight. There was no weapon at all in sight except the tomahawk and the machete, each in a beaded sheath at the madman's either hip.

Andie looked at Gallagher, smiled again at him lovingly, then mouthed, "Trust me."

He nodded, but understood he had never been so frightened in his life.

"Terrance?" Andie said suddenly. She spoke softly, compassionately.

The body stopped rocking and seemed to swell in girth. The hood jerked swiftly toward her. He watched her for a moment. He tore the hatchet from its scabbard.

"Terrence Danby is dead, dead as the Lawton vermin that spawned him," he snarled. "Only Charun lives now!"

Gallagher pressed back into the corner, preparing for the onslaught. But in that next instant, the monster's physical attitude melded toward self-pity.

"They hated Terrence," he said. "They made fun of him! Persephone, do you think after all these years Lawton respects him?"

"You're all they talk about," Andie assured him. "Persephone knows how you've suffered, Charun. You were the one who took me to the other shore. You can take me again. Untie me. I can help you."

The hood drooped toward his left shoulder as if swooning from the smoky elixir coursing through his bloodstream. "Help me?"

"Yes." Andie spoke in the understanding tones of a therapist. "You know our myth, Charun: every summer I come back from Hades, from the land of the dead. I can help take you there, let you see what I see."

"I've smelled it," he said, talking to himself. "I've heard the silence of it."

"But you've never seen the other side," Andie observed. "Untie me. We'll dance the Ghost Dance."

The fiend stared at her for the longest time. Andie never blinked.

He put the hair, the bowl and the stones carefully on the floor before him. He stood, then came toward her gripping the tomahawk loosely. Andie held her bound wrists out toward him.

But halfway across the room he halted as if remembering something. He looked intently over his shoulder at Gallagher, who tried his best to hold Charun's gaze, to be like Andie facing death and not let him see fear. But when Gallagher looked into those eyes he saw the unexpected and instinctively kicked back toward the wall.

Charun came and stood before Gallagher. "What's your name, brother?"

"Patrick Gallagher," he croaked.

He drew the machete from the beaded sheath that looked almost exactly like the one on the wall in Monsignor McColl's office. "You know what has to happen, don't you, Patrick?" he stated as if they were old and bitter siblings.

He shuffled closer and slashed with the machete, stopping the blade a fraction of an inch from Gallagher's pulsing temple.

"Are ya scared, brother Patrick?" he demanded in a mock Irish accent that shockingly reminded Gallagher of his father's coarse brogue. "When ya see me, do ya smell the river?"

He tugged off the hood. Danby had aged hard since the sergeant-major picture; his face was harshly drawn down of flesh, his eyes had sunk back in their sockets and his hair and beard were sparse, flecked with gray and cut tight to the skin. His gums had pulled away from his teeth, which were yellowed. He leaned close and Gallagher caught the smoky, backwater stench of his breath. The derangement of it all became a pressurized thing, crushing Gallagher's will, making him want to curl up like a child alone in the night.

"Do you smell the river, brother?" Danby demanded.

Gallagher heard himself whimper, "Yes."

He caressed Gallagher's temple with the blade of the tomahawk. "Do you want to cross it now?"

"Charun!" Andie yelled. "Don't. You'll need him."

"Why?" he said, dropping the Irish accent. His gaze never left Gallagher, but it had shifted somehow, become more focused.

"The more dancers, the more powerful the ceremony," she coaxed. "When the Sioux performed the Ghost Dance, they had thousands—"

"Would you kill your love to believe?" Danby asked Gallagher before she could finish.

Gallagher looked into Danby's tombstone face and his jaw would not move. Gallagher knew that his life depended on how he answered. For a split second he tried to figure out what Danby wanted him to say. Against the dim back wall of his mind Gallagher saw Emily and the vague form that was their aborted child.

"Yes," he said truthfully. "I would kill my love to believe."

Danby let loose a humming noise from down in his chest. The machete hovered in the air and then found the beaded sheath. He shoved the hatchet handle between the duct tape and the parachute rope that bound Gallagher's wrists, then dragged his two hundred and twenty pounds across the floor like a small sack of potatoes.

Danby dumped Gallagher in front of the candles, then dragged Andie over and placed her at a forty-five-degree angle to him. Danby knelt between them with the piles of the journal, the lock of hair, the stones and the empty leather pouches before him. His free hand rummaged in a green knapsack and came out with a small Mason jar. He twisted it open and thumbed a wad of what looked like dried spinach and mushrooms into Ten Trees' pipe bowl. He leaned forward so the flame of the candle flickered at the bowl's edge, then sucked on it. The pipe glowed, flamed and smoked.

He held the pipestem out to Andie. She shook her head. "I want to dance, Charun."

Danby gave her a curious look. "You always said the smoke would get us to the other side faster, Angel."

Andie's attention darted to Gallagher, who nodded. She took the stem between her lips. He placed his mouth over the bowl and blew. She gasped and choked at the cloud that belched forth.

"Again," Danby ordered and she took a second and third inhalation. All tension fled her shoulders. He sliced the tape and rope around her ankles, then came toward Gallagher with the bowl. Gallagher anticipated that Andie would strike out at Danby then. His back was turned and her feet free. But the detective's mouth hung agape and she stared, stupefied, off into space.

"This is my religion, brother," he said, extending the pipe toward Gallagher. "This and the dance will take us across the river."

Gallagher bit down on the stem, trying to limit the quantity of smoke that would enter, hoping he might be able to attack

Danby should he free his ankles as well. But Danby blew on the pipe bowl again and caustic smoke flooded Gallagher's lungs.

On the first inhalation, a ringing started in Gallagher's head. On the second, the ringing was accompanied by an amplification and fine-tuning of all the background noise about the cabin: the whine of blackflies, the distant cawing of ravens, the snapping of shagbark in the wind. On the third breath, it all turned to the deafening roar of white water beating against submerged boulders.

Gallagher's body felt paralyzed and he panicked that he would not be able to breathe. Then he noticed his chest rising and falling. A sparkling emerald liquid spilled from his mouth with every breath. The sweat on Danby's body turned a metallic, iridescent fire. When he moved, tracers of flame spit out behind him.

Danby bent down and cut the binds from Gallagher's ankles. Gallagher screamed inside, fight! But every joint in his body had jellied. Danby placed the pipe on the ground in the lid of the Mason jar, picked up Many Horses' stones and her lock of hair, then gazed raptly at the pages of the journal, his lips silently wrapping themselves around words and phrases the world had last heard more than a hundred years ago.

The candle flames became huge, exploding balls of fire that licked the sky and threatened to melt Gallagher. And then the fireball ebbed and Gallagher was aware of a man's voice singing deep and hoarsely. Danby was on his feet, singing, with the pages of the journal held tightly between his thumbs and index fingers as if he were grasping a prayer book at a church service.

Danby's abdomen rippled as he chanted out undulating worship to a life force that in Gallagher's altered state was instantly embraced as truth. It triggered in Gallagher's mind the sepia-toned image of a band of copper horses racing tongue-weary across a blistering and dusty plain toward a mesa engulfed in storm. Lightning broke apart the sky above the mesa, but the horses kept galloping toward it until they were specks in a vast and barren wilderness.

Danby put a rope noose around Gallagher's neck and hauled him to his feet. Danby shoved the pipe bowl in Gallagher's face and leered at him. Gallagher took a fourth inhalation of smoke, and the air around him turned bubbly with froth. Andie appeared in the ferment with a rope around her neck, too. She seemed to be surrounded by a yellow glow, an aurora, that bulged and extended toward Gallagher with her every breath.

Danby's venous hands wrapped themselves in the nooses around their throats. He gathered them tight to him. His singing became louder, deeper and more urgent. He shuffled left, lowering and raising his upper body and so theirs. The singing went on and on, the words all fusing into one another, until, reaching a chorus, he chanted at the end of each segment: "Grandfather! I am sending a voice. To the heavens of the universe, I am sending a voice."

Gallagher could not help it; he sang with Danby: "I am sending a voice. I am sending a voice."

For what seemed like hours to Gallagher there was only the chanting, the rough noose chafing skin raw and one foot shuffling left and then the other. Then, with great effort, Gallagher was able to concentrate enough to look at Andie, searching for some sign that she was holding onto reason.

But her expression was vacant. Her jaw hung loose. She was a shell of herself pressed tight to Danby's chest.

Gallagher's vision went telescopic again, and Andie was transformed into one of those copper horses galloping out on the plain toward the mesa, getting farther and farther away. She disappeared into a canyon in one side of the mesa and Gallagher raced after her, hearing Danby's drumbeat chanting fade in the wind.

The air at the mouth of the canyon was cold and strangely still. Gallagher called out for Andie, but heard no response. He crawled deep into the mesa canyon. The rocks became slick with slime. He scrambled through mud and over oily plants and boulders toward the rear of the gulch. The wall there was curved and nearly vertical. It disappeared into fog a hundred feet up. Rivulets of rust-colored water trickled down out of the fog over mosses, ferns and toxic flowers that grew in the scabrous black soil that clung to the cliffwork.

The last hundred feet of the canyon floor were shaped like a bowl descending perhaps fifty feet down into the earth. In the center of the bowl, in its very bottom, grew a ring of brilliant red whips, devoid of leaf or bud, but covered with thorn spikes. They pierced and seared his skin as Gallagher passed, and he cried out in terrible pain. But the idea that Andie had come this way kept him going. He parted the last of the whips and teetered on the edge of a pit that yawed into darkness. The rank odor of decay billowed up out of the hole.

Gallagher swayed there on the edge, then pitched into the abyss, tumbling over and over, screaming at the sick, rushing weightlessness that expanded through his stomach and burst out the back of his spine.

Chapter Forty-six

Gallagher awoke in sunlight-dappled, sweet-smelling grass that grew in a forest of the palest cottonwood trees brushed by a breeze of insistent, perfect warmth. The air was alive with the flute music of a river shallowed by summer's heat.

Sarah Many Horses appeared over Gallagher, then strode away through the cottonwoods in a direction opposite to the sound of the river. She wore a threadbare denim blouse, a calico skirt and high leather boots. Her hair was drawn back and held together by a stickpin embroidered with porcupine quills. Gallagher sat up in the sweet grass and called after her, but she did not turn. He got up and ran through the pale trees but could not close the gap that separated them no matter how hard he tried.

After a long time Gallagher slowed and just followed. Out of his peripheral vision he saw the vague forms of men, women and children slipping through the woods parallel to him. And now he made out the sound of a second river ahead. For an instant his attention wandered off Many Horses to others journeying in the glade.

Walking slightly in front and to the side of Gallagher were his mother and father. Agnes was wearing the blue dress he'd buried her in. She trailed Seamus, who wore his old gray tweed coat and cap.

Gallagher wanted to feel anger, to stop and tell them he hated them for who he'd become, but to his surprise he felt only pity and for the first time understood that they, too, had been lost and searching in their own way.

Many Horses stopped to wait for Gallagher. He glanced toward her and back to his parents. But they had disappeared into the flow of the others in the forest, replaced by a little girl, no more than three. She had Emily's mischievous smile, her blond hair and her pert nose. But her eyes and chin and lips were Gallagher's own. She walked up and took his hand and urged him on through the woods.

Gallagher and the girl reached a river bank strewn with sun-bleached stones. A blinding sun was setting over the western shore. Close in, the river appeared shallow and easily wadable, but quickly gave way to a swift, dark and ominous channel.

People were leaving the island forest and venturing into the river. Many hesitated at the edge of the shallows. A few plunged resolutely into the fast water, swam the current with little struggle and disappeared into the blazing radiance of the sunset on the opposite bank. Others thrashed in terror midriver and were cruelly swept downstream.

Gallagher's parents separated from the crowd, then waded toward mid-river. He could not watch them after the water reached their waists.

Many Horses stopped where the water made her calico skirt cling to her thighs. She looked at Gallagher in longing. He took two steps in her direction before a hand grabbed him by the wrist and yanked him back toward shore. He turned to release the little girl's grip and found Andie holding tight to him.

She kissed him and led him back into the streaky twilight of the island forest. She took off her clothes and lay down next to Gallagher and covered them head to toe in a blanket of sweet grass that filtered the last rays of the western sun.

The white heat still seared in Gallagher's head when he came to and rolled over on the cabin floor. His tongue tasted of smoke and his nose gushed forth mucus. By the ambient light shining through the cracks between the indigo cloth and the rotting windowsills, it was late afternoon. The candles had burned toward stubs. One had already gone out.

Andie lay still and barely breathing next to him on the floor of the cabin. The worry lines had disappeared from her face. She looked ten years younger and so radiantly beautiful Gallagher wanted to cry. Her eyes fluttered open. The white heat in his head gave way to an unalterable calm.

"You brought me back," he whispered.

"No," she said. "You brought me back."

"The light—it's around you."

"Around you, too," she whispered back. "It's everywhere around us."

A boot scraped over rough wood.

Danby sat slumped against the far wall, his Goliath arms laid across his knees. He clutched the tomahawk in one hand. His stone-colored eyes looped high in their sockets under hooded brows.

"The old man lied," Danby fumed to himself, the way Gallagher's father had on the subway a week before his suicide. "The squaw lied. Father lied. They're all liars!"

With each word he hacked at the cabin floor with the hatchet blade. "Lied!" he bellowed. "Lied! And lied! You can never see beyond!"

Chunks of wood spit into the air. He panted now. He picked up a filthy wall mirror and whipped it across the room. It smashed off a support post. Thick shards of glass caromed around Gallagher and Andie and then stilled.

"Are you afraid of me?" he asked. His glare seemed calculated to humiliate and degrade and to give him some perverse pleasure. "Are you, brother?"

Gallagher hesitated only long enough to look at Andie and that gentle yellow aura that surrounded them. "No," he said. "I'm not afraid of you."

Danby swept out of his sitting position and up on his knees and toes. Veins stood out like writhing snakes across his chest, up his neck and at his temples. The muscles of his abdomen cavitated like plastic sheeting buffeted by gale. He lashed the air with the hatchet.

Neither Andie nor Gallagher moved or showed fear. Danby blinked in confusion. Then his head craned forward and he studied them as if seeing them new for the first time. The fury drained out of him. His eyes widened and his jaw hung agape.

"You . . ." he whispered. "You crossed and returned."

His shoulders slumped and he mumbled self-pityingly: "Charun rowed you across, but the gods would not let him see the far shore. Charun will never see the other shore. Charun is the boatman. The cursed boatman of the dead."

Outside, the forest had gone totally and unnaturally silent. No wind blew. No squirrels barked. No ravens cawed. Then there was a single snap of branch somewhere around the house and one of the little green lights on the radio receiver in the corner flickered.

Danby seemed not to notice. He let the hatchet drop forward from his fingers. The blade struck, cut and wedged into the planking. He drew it out and let it fall forward again, but added a snapping of his fingers. He did it a third time and a fourth and a fifth and a sixth; and as if that action were a pump sucking wrath from deep in his gut, Danby's scarlet rage returned.

He clenched the hatchet in his teeth and raced forward on hands and knees. His attention flared between the two of them. His teeth ground one on the other.

"Not afraid, brother?" he bellowed. "I'll show you fear!"

He leaped to his feet, grabbed Andie by the hair and dragged her across the floor toward one of the windows. She slashed her feet out at him, but he sidestepped the blows and backhanded her across the face, dazing her.

"We're going to the other shore again, Angel!" he simpered. "Hurry up, please, it's time!"

Danby flipped her over and twisted her up onto all fours. He grabbed her belt with both hands and tore her slacks down around her thighs, binding her legs tightly at the knees. Andie struggled weakly to get away, but he held her tight by the length of rope connected to the noose around her neck. He pulled down the front of his black trousers. He was erect.

Andie choked out low sobs. "No, God! Don't!"

Danby wrenched the tomahawk from his teeth, raised it above her neck, then beamed murderously across the room at Gallagher. "Now are you afraid of me, brother?"

Chapter Forty-seven

The assault came before Gallagher could speak or act.

It arced through time and space and indigo fabric, striking a glancing blow off the occipital bone at the back of Danby's head. At impact he jerked like a marionette that has busted a string, and something dark and electric pulsed through the room. The monster collapsed inward, then toppled to the floor, barely breathing.

The tomahawk clattered toward Gallagher. He lunged after it even as a black pant leg thrust itself through the cloth covering the window. Gallagher was over on his back. His fingers reached toward the hatchet handle. A stiff hiking boot kicked the weapon into the shadows.

"Thank God you came!" Andie sobbed.

She was squirming on her back next to Danby, struggling with her bound hands to pull her slacks up around her hips.

Gallagher stared back over his shoulder at the black shirt and cleric's collar of Monsignor Timothy McColl. The priest carried a length of oak limb about the size of a baseball bat.

It was mottled with green lichen. His skin was flushed. His jaw chewed the air. His eyes darted from Gallagher to Andie to Danby and then to the journal and pouches in the pile next to the candles.

"Cut us free, Monsignor," Gallagher gasped.

McColl ignored him and went to the journal. He picked up the pieces of it with trembling hands. "At last," he murmured unbelievingly. "At long last!"

"Please," Andie pleaded. "You've got to help us, Father."

McColl's head turned toward her as a desert lizard's might—slow, knowing and reptilian. Suddenly, his eyes clenched shut. He ground his teeth and clasped his stomach.

"Father?" Gallagher repeated softly to himself; and in that word alone, he knew that the priest was not their savior, but another manifestation of their doom. In all of Charun's notes, Gallagher had taken the reference to "father" as Danby's father, Franco. But now he remembered that Danby had known McColl long before he had been elevated to a monsignor. The priest was Danby's "father."

McColl's eyes opened and he breathed heavily. He looked around wildly, like a man who has jumped a gold claim and is already plotting his defense of stolen treasure. Gallagher struggled to get to his feet, to go after the tomahawk. Andie had rolled over and was trying to get hold of the machete trapped in the sheath under Danby's comatose body.

McColl moved quick as a cat now. He booted Gallagher hard in the ribs. Gallagher grunted and writhed. The priest kicked him a second time and Gallagher curled up and rolled away from the blows into the shadows just beyond the dwindling candlelight.

McColl crossed to Andie. He used the butt of the oak limb to push her back away from Danby toward the cabin wall. "Don't move, Andie," he ordered icily. "I don't want you to suffer any more than is necessary."

He grabbed Danby by the ankles and dragged the inert beast into the corner. When at last Gallagher's breath returned, his fingers closed on a cold and sharply jagged object under him. The piece of shattered wooden frame held a dagger of sharp mirror glass. He turned it in his hands and got the keen edge against the duct tape and parachute cord that bound his wrists. McColl looked his way and Gallagher froze.

"You knew who was killing in Lawton the whole time," Andie said. "You told Danby about Sarah Many Horses' journal, didn't you?"

"I didn't have to." McColl chuckled. He took his attention off Gallagher and looked at the pages with obvious enchantment. "Terrance told me about the journal when he was thirteen years old, and I just figured it was the odd fantasy of a very disturbed little man. Imagine that juvenile nonsense: that the scribbling of a heathen contained the key to looking into heaven."

McColl held his palm up and swept it over the pages, the stones, the hair and the pipestone. "But here it is!"

"What made you change your mind and believe it existed?" Andie demanded.

His attention turned fully toward her now. Gallagher sawed at the duct tape and parachute cord and felt the glass bite.

McColl was enjoying himself. "You want the whole tale, I see," he said. "I suppose it's the least I can do before . . . well . . ."

"Before you kill us?" she said.

"I am a man of the cloth," McColl protested. "Because of the fire that will engulf this place, the story will be that my beloved boy Terrance killed you for some twisted reason the police might never fully understand. It will fit part of his pattern. Death followed by fire or water. They'll come up with a theory—something about a terrible upbringing and an equally rotten manhood. I will receive some scrutiny, of course, but eventually it will pass. It always does. I've always been very careful."

The priest began carefully shuffling the fragile pages of the journal.

Gallagher looked at Andie and mouthed the words "Keep him talking!"

Andie nodded. "When did you believe the journal really existed?"

McColl looked up at her. "I didn't think about it for nearly fifteen years, until I had returned to Lawton and begun to research Father D'Angelo's cause," he said. "Father D'Angelo was a saint. He did perform miracles. My own father saw one. I heard about it all the time I was growing up, and I used to lie awake at night wondering what made him a saint when I was such a sinner."

The priest rapped his hand across his chest three times. "That's right, a sinner. I know what I am and what I have done."

Gallagher felt the outer sheathing of tape give way and stopped cutting when McColl glanced over at him. "You found D'Angelo's piece of the journal, didn't you?" Gallagher said.

"Four months ago," McColl agreed. He rolled Many Horses' stones into one of the pouches. "Deep in the files of Father's vast correspondence I found a letter to the bishop that somehow never got mailed after Father D'Angelo's death. It talked about the journal and his own seven-volume diary, and directed the bishop to a box stored above the rafters of the rectory's attic. The letter said that what was in the box would explain the 'tainted nature of his miracles,' as he put it. I went and found the metal box.

"Father D'Angelo had two parts of the Sioux's journal, actually," the priest went on. "The first part, ten pages perhaps, is a bunch of pagan gibberish about various ceremonies taught to her by her mother and father. The second part is from a time much later in her life and concerns her meetings with Father D'Angelo."

"When?" Andie asked. McColl turned his head toward her and Gallagher began to cut again.

"September and October 1893," he said, speaking as an academic might on a favorite subject. "She tells Father D'Angelo how Joshua Danby was making spirits appear during the seances. A total sham. Father rightly considered it a sacrilegious act. He meant to expose the Danbys. You have to understand the times. People were leaving the church all across the country to follow such charlatans, and Father D'Angelo despised Joshua Danby because he had most of Lawton believing in his 'religion.'

"Every time the squaw came into Lawton to see Father, she was more and more upset. She said Joshua was using a narcotic elixir almost constantly and the drugs were making him deranged and violent."

The duct tape and then a strand of parachute cord gave way. Gallagher's fingers explored the knotting, to see how much further he'd have to cut. He almost hissed in frustration; Danby had braided the cording into a rope almost an inch thick.

"This is when Father D'Angelo became a sinner like me," McColl announced. "This is the moment that led him to murder."

Andie gasped. "Father D'Angelo killed Sarah Many Horses?"

"Don't be absurd," McColl grunted. "But, good Catholic that he was, he felt as if he had a hand in her death. The last time he saw her, she begged for his protection and he forced her to return to Joshua's house to gather more information he could use to expose the blasphemous fraud. It haunted him until the day he died."

"How did Many Horses die?" Andie asked softly.

McColl reached down and picked up the lock of hair in

the wax paper and examined it in the flickering candlelight. Dusk was coming outside.

"Caleb Danby, Joshua's brother, came pounding on Father D'Angelo's door late one November night in 1893," McColl said. "Caleb said that his brother had gone insane on the elixir and had convinced himself and several of his closest followers—also elixir addicts—that the Sioux had stolen from him the power to make spirits materialize. Joshua convinced his followers that Many Horses was an evil threat to a new religion he had envisioned called Guidance. But for Joshua's power to be restored and his vision to become reality, he and his followers would have to kill Sarah, and, like the Catholics, take communion of her."

Gallagher stopped cutting. His mind jumped from the journal to the mental-hospital records about Mayor Powell's great grandfather to what Many Horses had said in his second dream: *I was eaten not by fire, not water nor earth, but by man.*

"No!" he cried.

"Oh, yes," the priest said. "Caleb begged Father to go to the farm and save the squaw before it was too late. Father D'Angelo got six of his loyal parishioners, including the chief constable, who I would guess was the Cartersburg librarian's— Nyren's—great-grandfather.

"According to Father's diary, it was snowing hard by the time the horsemen reached the Danby temple," McColl continued. "A dwarf and a strongman were packing crates in a wagon. They said they were leaving before they were sucked down into Joshua's mad plan. They said Joshua and a score of his followers had gone off into the snowstorm after the squaw. Father D'Angelo, his men and Caleb Danby followed the tracks in the snow up Lawton Mountain to a cave where Joshua used to hold seances when it was warmer."

Another strand of the parachute cord gave way. Six cords

to freedom, Gallagher thought. A second candle snuffed and smoked. McColl stopped, squinting into the gloom.

"Monsignor?" Andie said. "What happened?"

"It must have been a grisly thing to behold," the priest said. "Father wrote in his diary that he already knew what Hell would be like from what he witnessed and did that night in the cave. By the time they got there, Many Horses was dead. Joshua had slit her throat because she would not give him the secrets. He was in a frenzy. He had already cut off several pieces of her skin the size of wafers. Joshua was exhorting his followers to eat and drink of the squaw so that they might know their immortality."

Andie shook her head in revulsion. "That's why Lamont Powell cut out his teeth and his tongue before he killed himself."

McColl acted as if he had not heard her. "Joshua's followers had entered some kind of ecstatic, violent state brought on by the elixir when Father D'Angelo and his men stormed the cave," he said. "During the melee, Father D'Angelo got Joshua's knife away from him and stabbed him in the heart. And the moment Joshua died, it was as if a fog lifted from the minds of his followers and they confronted what they had done.

"They realized that if what had happened in Lawton that night ever came out, the town, the church and all its people would become as cursed and reviled as the Donner party," McColl said.

He glanced at Gallagher just as another strand let go. Andie called him, "So they decided to cover it up?"

McColl nodded. "What choice did they have? The mayor, a famous Civil War veteran and a Manhattan socialite had become drug addicts, spiritual fanatics and ghouls as well as accessories to murder under the influence of a sideshow messiah. The constable and five other parishioners had turned vigilante.

The parish priest was a hot-blooded killer. Everyone present was fouled by the deaths of Joshua and the squaw.

"So they dragged Joshua's body back down the mountain and buried him in the root cellar under the temple," McColl continued. "Everyone swore themselves to secrecy for the common good. Several people, including your great-great-grand-father, Andie, were for burying the squaw with Joshua and burning the journal and the things they found in a leather bag she carried—a pipe, some stones, this lock of hair.

"But Father D'Angelo would not hear of it. He buried her himself in sacred ground. He told the others with him that night that they were all responsible for her death. And they had the duty to preserve the relics of her story so that if the truth ever had to be revealed, Joshua's followers could not disprove his guilt. No one trusted any one person to hold the journal. So it was divided."

"And passed down from one generation to the next," Andie said. "With each generation knowing less and less about what really happened."

McColl did not answer. He dropped the lock of hair into a pouch before picking up Ten Trees' pipe and studying it with great relish. Behind him, Danby's hand moved ever so slightly.

Four strands to go, Gallagher thought. Unless McColl kept talking, he could not saw toward freedom. He watched for any sign that Danby would move again. But the giant lay still.

Gallagher thought about McColl's admission that he was a sinner just like D'Angelo, probably a murderer just like D'Angelo. He played with that idea against why the priest would want the journal himself. And then it hit Gallagher. The priest was not interested in preserving a cover-up. It was about salvation.

"Father D'Angelo murdered and yet performed miracles," Gallagher said. "You have sinned and you want the same gift."

Andie saw where Gallagher was going and piped up. "You

think D'Angelo somehow got his powers from Many Horses, don't you?"

Night was falling. Nine of the twelve candles had snuffed out. McColl's face flattened in the waning light.

"That's what Father D'Angelo believed," he said. "It haunted him that after killing his fellow man, he was granted the healing touch. He wrote that the Sioux visited him in dreams. He often wrote, 'Who gave me the gift, the Christ or the savage?' "

Gallagher's mind flashed on an empty hole in the rectory garden. "You believe she did, don't you, Monsignor?" he demanded. "You're like Joshua Danby—you believe the power is contained in Many Horses' bones, her writing, her relics."

"I'm a dying man," McColl announced wearily. "Two different kinds of cancer. Less than twenty months, the doctors figure. And I lost my personal relationship with Jesus many years ago. But relics are a proven way to touch the stuff of immortality. Maybe even to becoming a saint. Maybe even for a sinner like me."

Two more strands of cord gave way and Gallagher's fingers itched and tingled as blood returned to them.

"That's what my poor, mad, beloved boy didn't understand," McColl said, throwing Danby's inert form a sympathetic look. "The last time I saw him was nearly eight years ago in Guatemala. I gave him that lovely knife and sheath he wears. Then, two months ago, he showed up out of the blue at my office. We played our little game. I made him confess to his naughtiness."

The second-to-last parachute-cord strand broke free. Gallagher's shoulders relaxed forward. McColl snapped his head suspiciously toward him. Gallagher did not move another muscle. He just held the priest's gaze steady and true, telling himself, one more strand, one more strand.

Andie called to McColl. "Confess to what naughtiness, Monsignor?"

McColl hesitated, then curled his lips with distaste. "To

engaging in a bizarre, heathen, drug-saturated ritual invented by some South American slut who believed that through it you could experience death and return. Terrance killed the slut during a sexual act in which they each throttled the other with the kind of noose you both have around your necks.

"Terrance was wild at her death," McColl went on. "He told me he had to see his Angel again. He told me he was going to reclaim what was stolen from his great-great-uncles. That's the story the surviving Danbys passed down from one generation to another: that an Indian's journal describing a method to consort with the dead was stolen from Joshua. And that Joshua had been murdered by Father D'Angelo for wanting it.

"Of course, I immediately showed my boy the piece of the journal I had found, on the agreement that he show me whatever he might recover."

"But you didn't show him D'Angelo's diary," Gallagher said. "You didn't explain to him what really happened a hundred years ago."

"It was just one man's interpretation of the events, Mr. Gallagher," the priest said blithely. "As a filmmaker, you can understand that. I offered Terrance what he wanted—advice on how he might track down the other pieces and form his own interpretation."

"But you had the list of journal holders from D'Angelo's diary, didn't you?" Andie cried. "That's how he found the people so quickly. You knew, and the stolen baptismal certificates were your way of keeping anyone else from finding the journal. You let those people be killed one by one. You let him slaughter your own secretary!"

McColl sniffed insistently. "I offered guidance. How was I to know his desire for revenge on the town was as strong as his desire for the journal?"

"You're as big a monster as he is!" she shouted. "You used

him on the town the same way you used him to kill that boy at Hennessy House twenty years ago. You set a maniac loose so you could get the journal for yourself when the killings were done. You planned to kill Terrance all along. *Your beloved boy!*"

The priest was expressionless for a long, long moment; then he turned stony and distant. He dropped the stuffed leather pouches and a few loose pages of the journal onto the floor. "And now," he said, "I will have to kill three."

"You're mad!" Gallagher yelled.

"No," McColl replied. "I am not."

The priest's left hand traveled inside his coat. He came out with an exact replica of the machete Danby carried. He took three quick steps toward Gallagher and trumpeted, "May God have mercy on your immortal soul!"

McColl raised the blade up over his head just as Gallagher felt the final cord binding his wrists give way.

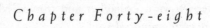

Chapter Forty-eight

Terrance Danby was a blur of doom in the twilight.

He sprang into a crouch and rushed the priest, kicking over a chair and one of the candles as he came.

"Time to die, Father!" he growled. "Time to take that boat ride across the river!"

McColl spun and slashed at the hurtling madman. Danby dropped and rolled. The priest's blade passed an inch over his back. Danby kept rolling, deep into the far shadows of the room. The priest stalked after him.

"You don't want to kill me, Terrance," the priest soothed. "My boy, my boy, I'm Father, the only one who ever understood. The only one who ever will."

Gallagher got up on all fours and saw the tomahawk lying underneath the overturned chair. He grabbed it and scrambled over to Andie. Neither man noticed. They were low, ready, ensnared in each other's movements.

"You're a liar, Father," Danby seethed. "You wanted it just

like all the others. You figured I was just a Danby and you could treat me like dogshit."

Danby's head glowed with death lust. But the blow to his skull had weakened the giant. He slurred and overbit his words. And every time he stepped to his left, there was a hesitation, a pause, as if he had to tell his body what to do next.

McColl must have seen the weakness, because just as Gallagher freed Andie, he stepped right and came at Danby with a vicious overhand strike. But the priest misjudged the depth of Danby's malady. The memory of thousands of hours of training bypassed the befuddled parts of the assassin's mind.

The madman lunged forward. His left forearm snapped out and cracked at the priest's wrist, loosening his grip. McColl's machete was flung through the air. Danby's blade trembled at the priest's throat.

"My boy, my beloved boy," McColl gasped. He stood on tiptoes. "Don't. I'm . . . Father!"

Danby hesitated for a long beat, then hissed these words slowly: "No, you're not!"

The cut was horizontal and deep. The priest's head lolled back at a sickening cant and there was a great gout of blood in the air and Monsignor McColl swayed and fell.

Danby tottered, transfixed by the quivering body below him. "You're not!"

Andie plucked up McColl's machete. She smiled at Gallagher in encouragement. "Now," she said. "Before he recovers."

She circled to Danby's left around the last burning candles while Gallagher went right, clutching the tomahawk. Danby became aware of them then, coming up from some deep abyss that he had explored and mapped too many times before.

His jaw jutted forward to expose the rank of his yellowed lower teeth. He was hunched so far forward that all Gallagher could see were the whites of his eyes. His bloody knife was poised in the air.

"Ever fought with a hatchet, brother?" Danby asked dreamily.

Gallagher said nothing, watching him, aware of Andie creeping closer. Danby went for his boot and came up with a short-bladed knife. He had two weapons now, both of them working the twilight.

"It should be darkest night," he said. "And the light should be from lanterns and the bugs should be at ya, biting. That's how ya have a hatchet fight. That's how ya die like this, brother. That's how everything dies like this."

Danby's voice had taken on the accent of the Vermont backwoods boy he once was. The muscles in his neck vibrated like piano wire. Gallagher brought up the tomahawk and pointed the blade directly at him. Danby grinned and sidled toward him while his eyes tracked Andie's progress. He made a sharp feint at Gallagher with the knife. Gallagher tried not to react, but he jerked. Danby laughed wickedly.

He made a second stab and then a third and Gallagher swung wildly again. Danby neatly dodged outside the attack, danced in and slashed his left arm. Gallagher leaped back even as Andie screamed at the sight of his blood flowing.

The pain was as if a welder's torch had stroked through his skin. Gallagher stumbled and fell to his knees, staring dumbly at the bleeding arm, the last two burning candles, the pile of leather pouches and the six loose pages of the journal on the cabin floor.

Danby grunted with pleasure and stepped in, readying himself to finish.

"Charun," Andie called, husky and soothing, with just the trace of a Spanish accent. "Come to me. Come to your Angel."

Danby's next step was off-balance. He weaved on his feet, confused. "Angel?"

"Your sweet Persephone, Charun," Andie said, thrusting her hips and holding her open arms toward him. "Come on. We'll try again to cross the river."

Danby took two steps toward her and ran his tongue halfway across his upper lip before halting. And a look of recognition crossed his face. "You're not Angel," he seethed. "You're one of the little Lawton cunts who used to tease me on the playground when I was a kid! You used to make fun of my mother!"

Andie froze in terror and he lumbered across the room at her, huge and looming; and Gallagher pictured Joshua Danby cornering Sarah Many Horses in the cave before he killed her.

Gallagher grabbed the loose pages of the journal. "Danby, don't, or I'll burn it all!"

The madman's great skulled head snapped in his direction.

Andie rushed Danby. She cut him hard and deep in the bulk of his upper back. Danby bellowed in agony, spun and stabbed. There was the low, hollow sound of a fist plumping a pillow; Andie coughed and looked over his shoulder at Gallagher with a surprised look of despair scrawled across her face.

Danby arched up as if in ecstasy and released his hand. Andie staggered backward into the wall and slithered down it. The hunting knife handle stuck out of her two inches below the right clavicle. She looked at the knife hilt, then up at Gallagher with a drunken expression. "Our love?" she asked.

A harsh and incomprehensible stillness descended over the cabin. The glowing around her ebbed and Gallagher saw the image of the total destruction of himself: a sunken-eyed man alone in the frigid waters of a winter river, desperately casting his line across sterile shallows toward the undercut bank of a foreign shore.

He thrust the free pieces of the journal into the candle flame. Dry and brittle, more than a century old, they burst afire.

Danby was grinning at Andie, enjoying her desperate struggle for life. "Are you afraid now?" he asked her wickedly.

Out of the corner of his eye, Danby caught sight of the burning journal pages and he bellowed in rage and raced toward Gallagher, the machete cutting the air. Gallagher slumped on his knees, showing defeat. His bloody left hand lay over his right, which covered the tomahawk between his thighs. The journal pages flamed out, turned to blackest ash, tumbled and fragmented in the still, rank air.

"Now Charun will row you across the river, brother!" Danby ranted.

Gallagher gazed up into his face and knew death, but was not afraid. "Do it, you sick fuck!"

Danby raised the machete with both hands as a farmer might a scythe before ripe wheat. As he reached the apex of his backswing high over his left shoulder, Gallagher spun on his knees, striking up and out with the tomahawk.

The stone blade shattered the low bones of Danby's rib cage and buried itself to the back block in his lungs. An inexplicable, electric force bolted down the hatchet handle, crashed through Gallagher's joints and exploded inside him. Gallagher's vision strobed in shades of ebony and pewter. He heard an owl hoot. He smelled the rot of a river's backwater.

Danby tried to scream, but all that issued forth was a series of long, moist rattles. The machete slipped from his hand. He buckled to his knees, and then forward on all fours, his body cringing, his head pitching from side to side.

Then he saw the red leather pouches Monsignor McColl had piled before the candle stubs and he reached for them in vain. The tips of his fingers brushed the ash of the burned journal pages and they crumbled to dust.

Danby collapsed onto his side, his soiled fingers splayed in fear and desire, his stone eyes staring through the expiring flame of the last candle before his lips moved one final time in knowing.

"Persephone!" he whispered.

Chapter Forty-nine

"I feel like I'm drowning," Andie choked.

There was surprisingly little blood around the knife handle, which seemed to be acting as a plug to the wound. But with each breath there was an audible bubbling and Gallagher knew her lung was pierced, filling and in danger of collapse.

"Am I going to die?" she asked.

"We never die," he replied, kneeling next to her. "Part of us goes on. You believe that, don't you? Our love will go on?"

"I want to think so," Andie said, smiling dreamily at the thought. She put her hand on his forearm and squeezed ever so softly. Then she closed her eyes and her head rolled to one side.

A blind panic tore through Gallagher. "No! No, not now!" he yelled into the darkness. "Don't let her go now! I'll give up forever if you let her live!"

Gallagher pulled off his belt and then his shirt and ripped it into strips with his teeth. One cloth strip stanched the deep gash across his bicep. With the second strip he tied tight the knife handle to Andie's flesh so it would not shift and do any more damage. Then he looped his belt around his neck as a sling to support his bad arm and lifted her.

The air outside the cabin was thick, humid and bug-saturated. The full moon was rising over Danbyville, sending tentacles of shadow through the hardwood forest. He ran east across the clearing, past the blackened stumps and the fire ring where Terrance Danby had first tasted and wondered about the mystery of death.

Gallagher found the path Andie and he had used during their first visit to the clearing, but halted before going forward. Danby had set out booby traps in the forest. That was Chief Mike Kerris back there in the spear pit, Gallagher was sure of it. Kerris must have stumbled onto Danby's green van when he was up trying to find his cousin's broken headlamp, recognized it from the description of the fleeing vehicle at Nyren's and come to investigate. And die.

Andie heaved as she fought for air in Gallagher's arms. Monsignor McColl had somehow figured a way in here safely. He would take the risk, too.

Gallagher veered off the path and plunged straight into the forest, navigating by the moon shadows through the thicket, down gullies, sliding in the mud. The wound in his arm bled again. He had not slept three hours in the past thirty-six. His head went foggy when he staggered into a clearing near the rivulet that was the Bluekill River's origin and laid Andie down so he might rest.

The moonlight shining on her through the forest canopy triggered in Gallagher the memory of Many Horses as she had appeared in his first dream—a fragmented, electric figure disappearing into a blizzard.

Gallagher picked Andie back up and began to run, aware of the forest before him, but inwardly focusing continuously on the perceptions of a terrified woman sprinting through a snowy forest under a full moon such as this a long, long time ago:

The powder snow blew on a cold gale, stinging exposed skin. Men yelled to each other in the woods behind Many Horses. Her lungs burned as she crossed a cliff and saw below her a lantern and, in the light, Joshua and Caleb Danby. Joshua was drinking from a brown cork-stoppered bottle and encouraging the others with the freshness of the track. Many Horses gripped the leather bundle that contained the mysteries of her people. She ran uphill.

Andie's breath was shallow, rapid and ragged when Gallagher broke free of the trees and out onto the dirt road that led back to Lawton. He sobbed as he stumbled up toward the gap on Gorm Ridge, which had became snow-drifted in his addled state.

He hallucinated a cave at the top of the rise and a light glowing at its mouth. With every step the cave glowed brighter.

Painted Horses and Ten Trees stood waiting at the cave mouth. Then they turned sideways to reveal a fire.

Gallagher settled Andie before the fire, which sparked and rolled into a blinding light. He tried to shield his eyes from it, but stopped when he became aware of shadowed forms dancing in and around the flames. He joined them, Ghost Dancing as Sarah Many Horses must have done a century ago when the voices of her pursuers closed around her.

Chapter Fifty

Early that morning, her coffin was towed through the streets of Lawton in an open-backed wagon harnessed to a single black horse. The June wind had held southeast for nearly a week, funneling heavy, hot air north over the central Green Mountain. Crickets whined. But the birds were oddly quiet.

The bells in the steeple atop St. Edward's Catholic Church tolled a slow, metallic dirge that echoed somberly across the rooftops of Lawton Mountain, now wholly clad in summer's green foliage.

Quietly, the people of Lawton filed out of their shops, homes and schools to pay their respects. As Gallagher heard the clopping of the caisson horse approach, he rested his forehead against the bark of an oak tree at the corner of Whelton Lane, unable to watch. His feet seemed as numb as his left arm, which despite several operations had not fully regained feeling. With hard work, the surgeon had said, he would eventually recover.

But of that Gallagher remained wholly uncertain. He knew

that in many ways he would never again be the person he was before Lawton.

The strike of the horse's hooves against the tar echoed in the thick air. A hand placed itself gently on his shoulder. "You look like you've seen a ghost."

"I have," he answered.

"Is the ghost beautiful or terrible to look at?"

"She's the most beautiful thing in the world to me."

Andie leaned in against the oak tree and kissed him. "The plane's ready for Sarah at West Lebanon," she said. "We should go."

The flight to North Dakota took four hours. Gallagher spent most of the time looking out the window at the vast terrain Sarah Many Horses had covered after the massacre at Wounded Knee. And he thought about the depth and range of her heart and understood he had been opened up by her story to an invisible world of hope and tragedy.

Andie slept for most of the flight. It had been more than a year since they had fought with death on Lawton Mountain, and the scars of her ordeal had not yet faded either. Her hair had silvered more at the temples. And she still insisted on wearing high-necked collars to hide the more dramatic wounds, including the tracheotomy the emergency rescue squad performed on her shortly after Deputy Phil Gavrilis' headlights caught Gallagher dancing in an incoherent frenzy around Andie's fallen body.

Gavrilis had gone up on the mountain looking for Chief Kerris and Gallagher after forcing the story from Bernie Chittenden. Within hours, television helicopters had circled over Danbyville, their searchlights probing the gloom for a glimpse at the shreds of the insanity that had reigned there.

The plane touched down in Bismarck around noon. The drive south to the Standing Rock Indian Reservation took two hours. There was a crowd of hundreds waiting. Six young Sioux men unloaded the coffin that held the bones of Many Horses. They carried it on their shoulders up onto the bluff above her beloved Grand River.

The Grand ran white and sparkling in two channels. In the middle was a narrow island where succulent sweet grass grew amid a stand of the palest cottonwoods. A warm wind gently blew through the trees and jostled the leaves as they laid her coffin down.

Lieutenant Bowman had found Many Horses' bones in a bag in the trunk of Monsignor McColl's car, hidden in the woods near the base of Gorm Ridge. The bones were coated with soil that matched dirt in the hole in the rectory garden. Father D'Angelo had buried her beneath the birdbath and watched over her relics for the last twenty years of his life.

Gallagher had decided that whether Father D'Angelo got his power to heal from those bones or from divine intervention was an unanswerable question. But he thought Monsignor McColl believed that Many Horses' bones were like the bones of saints, still imbued with the power of an infinitely generous soul and therefore capable of providing healing and forgiveness.

In the months immediately following the carnage on Lawton Mountain, people who had grown up in the various orphanages and parishes McColl had overseen came forward out of the shadows to testify about his abuse and the psychological terror he had used to control them.

The entire story of Mayor Powell's family's involvement in the killing of Many Horses came out, too. And that opened up a flood of stories about other crimes the family had covered up over the years, including Chief Kerris' assault on Andie twenty years before. In March, Mayor Powell was indicted on charges of accepting a kickback from the New Jersey developer who wanted to build the hotel-and-condominium complex at the ski area on Lawton Mountain.

But Gallagher's coming to some kind of closure as far as Terrance Danby was concerned proved a more difficult assignment. He spent a great deal of time in the prior year trying to learn more about Harold and his relationship to Danby. But he had little success tracking the man and had been officially discouraged from doing so on several occasions. Gallagher had come to think of Harold as one of those oracular creatures whom heroes are destined to encounter during their journey through hell.

Using his partner's other contacts, however, Gallagher had been able to put together the barest skeleton of Terrance Danby's life between the time he left Harold's employment and the killing of Hank Potter.

Danby worked as a freelance assassin all over Central and South America. During a party in Caracas four years before, he met Angel Abatido, the stunningly beautiful daughter of a right-wing colonel in the El Salvadoran army.

Three months before the killings in Lawton began, a cleaning lady entered Abatido's apartment in a swank section of San Salvador and discovered her body. Angel was naked on the bed, a noose lynched tight about her neck. Police found thirteen different, organic, mind-altering substances in the room with her. There was evidence her killer had lain with her long after death.

Gallagher had come to think of Angel's murder as the trigger that set Danby off. But he understood better than most that the tortured killing machine Danby became was forged long ago by heated events Danby probably never came close to understanding himself. In his own way, Danby was like Gallagher himself; he had been searching for proof that there was something beyond the ugly existence that had abused him mightily as a child. Despite the vicious amorality of his crimes, Gallagher could not help but see things in Danby to pity.

*   *   *

The shaman's name was Henry Long Lance. He was an intense, proud man with flowing black hair and the demeanor of a stoic old warrior. But this morning, as the coffin carrying Sarah Many Horses was lowered into the ground above the Grand River, not far from where her uncle Sitting Bull had been murdered and she had begun the long journey to Vermont, where she herself had been slain, Henry Long Lance's eyes welled with joy.

He carried a feathered eagle staff in one hand and in the other a sacred calf pipe purified and remade from the bowl that had belonged to Ten Trees in another life. He raised the pipe and the eagle staff toward the sky and began to pray.

The crowd had swelled and was perhaps a thousand people now, young and old who'd come out from the various Lakota reservations to see Many Horses buried.

Andie and Gallagher stood respectfully back from the crowd beside William Barrett, the professor from Dartmouth who had spent almost a year helping them arrange to bring Sarah home. In return, they had given him the first look at Many Horses' journal. Barrett called it a remarkable anthropological discovery, but could not hide his disappointment that Gallagher had inadvertently burned the pages that described her version of the Ghost Dance ceremony.

Long Lance raised the sacred calf pipe and sang in Lakota. Many in the crowd joined in and at every pause between verses they turned to a new direction: from the west, to the north, to the east and finally to the south.

Someone in the crowd blew through an eagle-bone whistle, and the shrill sound carried and bounced and returned from off a far butte. Gallagher could not help thinking about the discussions he'd had with Professor Barrett in the past few months. Most of their talk had centered on whether Sarah could actually talk with the dead; and whether he and Andie had actually crossed to the other side during Danby's crazed reenactment of the long-lost ritual; or whether they had merely been under the mechanical influence of the hallucinogenic mixture the killer had made them smoke.

Gallagher had looked at it in many ways and had come to believe that the rituals passed down by Ten Trees, Painted Horses, Sitting Bull and Wovoka were real and powerful because someone like Sarah Many Horses had proven faith in them over a lifetime. She believed she could talk with her dead, and Gallagher believed she did, too.

Now Long Lance launched into a prayer in Lakota. Andie wrapped her arms around Gallagher and rested her head against his chest, and he could not help thinking that Emily had been right in ways she could not have imagined the day she left him. She said that to believe in the afterlife, Gallagher had to first believe in this life. That takes a belief in love.

Gallagher hugged Andie close and added his own interpretation of what his ex-wife had been trying to teach him: if you allow another spirit like Sarah Many Horses or Andie Nightingale to come and live within you, they can never die. Nor can you, for acceptance means you have become the vessel of love, the immortal force that transcends life and death.

Gallagher had allowed Many Horses' story to live within him as it obviously had lived within Father D'Angelo for so many years; and because of it, he had been granted the ability to perform miracles. Gallagher had been given a vision of the afterlife that has allowed him not merely to survive but to finally embrace this existence for all its good and menace.

A group of men came forward and lowered Many Horses' coffin into the grave. They shoveled dirt into the hole as Long Lance began to sing again. As he sang, he scraped a circle on the ground next to the grave. He made a second circle with the dirt taken from the trough of the first, then crafted a cross that ran from west to east and then from north to south.

On the southern tip of the mounds in that second circle, he placed Ten Trees' pipe and a leather bundle in which he had placed Many Horses' lock of hair, her stones and a piece of paper on which she had written her journal.

Barrett leaned over and whispered, "He's beginning the rite of releasing the soul."

Andie and Gallagher held on tighter to each other. Gallagher prayed that she felt the same strength in him that he felt in her. Andie had not had a drink since the night he'd found her passed out with her mother's piece of the journal. And not once since had she ever expressed a desire for the bottle. She rotated around in his arms, so his belly was to her back. She placed her free hand on her stomach and smiled at him as the ceremony went on in the softly slanted light of a Dakota June afternoon.

Long Lance stopped singing. Then he smoked and passed the pipe among those gathered. A willow post had been set in the ground next to the circles and the grave, and on it was placed a buffalo-skin robe and a piece of buckskin on which a face had been painted. Professor Barrett whispered that the effigy represented Many Horses' soul. Women carrying bowls of food walked clockwise around the grave, the circles and the post. They hugged the effigy, then set the food before it.

Then four young girls came forward and Long Lance placed a small bit of food in their mouths and had them drink from a bowl that Barrett said held cherry juice.

When they were finished, Long Lance picked up the leather bundle and said, "You are about to leave on a great journey, Many Horses. Your father and mother and relatives and many strangers have loved you."

Then he walked the edge of the circle four times. The first three times he reached the southernmost point of the circle,

Long Lance held Many Horses' bundle up high and cried, "Always look back upon your people, that they may walk the sacred path with firm steps."

Far down on the river bottom, a gust of wind swirled and took pale leaves from the cottonwoods, and they shifted and spiraled upward in the late-afternoon light. Barrett leaned over again to say something, but Gallagher cut him off.

"I know," Gallagher choked. "Many Horses is crossing the river."

"Not all of her," Andie whispered. She pressed Gallagher's hand to her belly, already swollen for six months. "Part of Sarah is right here. Can't you feel her?"